an
amish
reunion

OTHER NOVELS BY THE AUTHORS

➤➤➤ *Amy Clipston* ⫷⫷⫷

THE AMISH HOMESTEAD SERIES

A Place at Our Table

Room on the Porch Swing

A Seat by the Hearth

A Welcome at Our Door (available May 2019)

THE AMISH HEIRLOOM SERIES

The Forgotten Recipe

The Courtship Basket

The Cherished Quilt

The Beloved Hope Chest

THE HEARTS OF THE LANCASTER
GRAND HOTEL SERIES

A Hopeful Heart

A Mother's Secret

A Dream of Home

A Simple Prayer

THE KAUFFMAN AMISH BAKERY SERIES

A Gift of Grace

A Promise of Hope

A Place of Peace

A Life of Joy

A Season of Love

→≫≫ *Beth Wiseman* ≪≪←

THE AMISH JOURNEY NOVELS
Hearts in Harmony
Listening to Love (available September 2019)

THE AMISH SECRETS NOVELS
Her Brother's Keeper
Love Bears All Things
Home All Along

THE DAUGHTERS OF THE PROMISE NOVELS
Plain Perfect
Plain Pursuit
Plain Promise
Plain Paradise
Plain Proposal
Plain Peace

THE LAND OF CANAAN NOVELS
Seek Me with All Your Heart
The Wonder of Your Love
His Love Endures Forever

OTHER NOVELS
Need You Now
The House that Love Built
The Promise

STORIES
A Choice to Forgive included in *An Amish Christmas*
A Change of Heart included in *An Amish Gathering*

Healing Hearts included in *An Amish Love*

A Perfect Plan included in *An Amish Wedding*

A Recipe for Hope included in *An Amish Kitchen*

Always Beautiful included in *An Amish Miracle*

Rooted in Love included in *An Amish Garden*

When Christmas Comes included in *An Amish Second Christmas*

In His Father's Arms included in *An Amish Cradle*

A Love for Irma Rose included in *An Amish Year*

Patchwork Perfect included in *An Amish Year*

A Cup Half Full included in *An Amish Home*

The Cedar Chest included in *An Amish Heirloom*

The Gift of Sisters included in *Amish Celebrations*

A New Beginning included in *Amish Celebrations*

A Christmas Miracle included in *Amish Celebrations*

When Love Returns included in *An Amish Homecoming*

->>>> *Kathleen Fuller* <<<<-

THE AMISH BRIDES OF BIRCH CREEK NOVELS
The Teacher's Bride

The Farmer's Bride (available June 2019)

THE AMISH LETTERS NOVELS
Written in Love

The Promise of a Letter

Words from the Heart

THE AMISH OF BIRCH CREEK NOVELS
A Reluctant Bride

An Unbroken Heart

A Love Made New

THE MIDDLEFIELD AMISH NOVELS
A Faith of Her Own

THE MIDDLEFIELD FAMILY NOVELS
Treasuring Emma
Faithful to Laura
Letters to Katie

THE HEARTS OF MIDDLEFIELD NOVELS
A Man of His Word
An Honest Love
A Hand to Hold

STORIES
A Miracle for Miriam included in *An Amish Christmas*
A Place of His Own included in *An Amish Gathering*
What the Heart Sees included in *An Amish Love*
A Perfect Match included in *An Amish Wedding*
Flowers for Rachael included in *An Amish Garden*
A Gift for Anne Marie included in *An Amish Second Christmas*
A Heart Full of Love included in *An Amish Cradle*
A Bid for Love included in *An Amish Market*
A Quiet Love included in *An Amish Harvest*
Building Faith included in *An Amish Home*
Lakeside Love included in *An Amish Summer*
Building Trust included in *An Amish Family*
Surprised by Love included in *An Amish Family*
What Love Built included in *An Amish Homecoming*

→»» *Kelly Irvin* «««-

AMISH OF BIG SKY COUNTRY NOVELS
Mountains of Grace (available August 2019)

EVERY AMISH SEASON NOVELS
Upon a Spring Breeze
Beneath the Summer Sun
Through the Autumn Air
With Winter's First Frost

THE AMISH OF BEE COUNTY NOVELS
The Beekeeper's Son
The Bishop's Son
The Saddle Maker's Son

STORIES
A Christmas Visitor in *An Amish Christmas Gift*
Sweeter than Honey in *An Amish Market*
One Sweet Kiss in *An Amish Summer*
Snow Angels in *An Amish Christmas Love*
The Midwife's Dream in *An Amish Heirloom*

ROMANTIC SUSPENSE
Tell Her No Lies
Over the Line (available June 2019)

an amish reunion

FOUR STORIES

Amy Clipston

Beth Wiseman

Kathleen Fuller

Kelly Irvin

 ZONDERVAN®

ZONDERVAN

An Amish Reunion

Their True Home Copyright © 2019 Amy Clipston
A Reunion of Hearts Copyright © 2019 Elizabeth Wiseman Mackey
A Chance to Remember Copyright © 2019 Kathleen Fuller
Mended Hearts Copyright © 2019 Kelly Irvin

This title is also available as a Zondervan e-book.

Requests for information should be addressed to:

Zondervan, 3900 Sparks Dr. SE, Grand Rapids, Michigan 49546

ISBN: 978-0-310-35271-6 (trade paper)
ISBN: 978-0-310-09870-6 (library edition)
ISBN: 978-0-310-35272-3 (e-book)

Library of Congress Cataloging-in-Publication Data

CIP data is available upon request.

Printed in the United States of America

19 20 21 22 23 / LSC / 5 4 3 2 1

CONTENTS

GLOSSARY *

ach: oh

aenti: aunt

appeditlich: delicious

bann: a temporary period of excommunication intended to cause a change of heart and end errant behavior in a church member

bedauerlich: sad

boppli/bopli/ boplin: baby, babies

brot: bread

bruder: brother

bruders: brothers

bruderskinner: nieces/nephews

bu: boy

buwe: boys

daadi: grandfather

daadi haus/dawdy haus: a small house built onto or near the main house for grandparents to live in

danki: thank you

dat/daed: dad, father

Deutsch/Deitsch: Dutch

dochder: daughter

dochdern: daughters

Dummle!: hurry!

Englisch/English/Englisher: English: non-Amish person

eck: married couple's corner table at their wedding reception

Fehla: sin

fraa: wife

freind: friend

freinden: friends

froh: happy

gegisch: silly

gern/gaern gschehne: you're welcome

Gmay: church district

Gott: God

groossdaadi/grossdaadi: grandpa

groossmammi/grossmammi: grandma

Gude/guder mariye: Good morning

gut: good

Gut nach/gut natcht: Good night

haus: house

hund: dog

Ich liebe dich: I love you

jah: yes

kaffi: coffee

kapp: prayer covering or cap

kichli/kuche/kichlin: cookie, cookies

kinner: children

kitzn: cat

krank: ill

kuche: cake

kuchen: cakes

kumm: come

leib/liewe: love, a term of endearment

maed: young women, girls

maedel: young woman

mamm/mudder: mom, mother

mammi: grandmother

mann: husband

mei: my

Meidung: avoidance, shunning

millich: milk

naerfich: nervous

narrisch: crazy

nee: no

onkel: uncle

Ordnung: written and unwritten rules in an Amish district

rumspringa/rumschpringe: period of running around when a young person turns sixteen

schee: pretty

schmaert: smart

schtupp: family room

schweschder: sister

schweschdere: sisters

sohn/suh: son

Was iss letz?: What's wrong?

Wie bischt?: How are you?

Wie geht's: How do you do? or Good day!

wunderbaar: wonderful

ya: yes

*The German dialect spoken by the Amish is not a written language and varies depending on the location and origin of the settlement. These spellings are approximations. Most Amish children learn English after they start school. They also learn high German, which is used in the Sunday services.

THEIR TRUE HOME

-«««-

Amy Clipston

With love and appreciation for Zac Weikal
and the members of my Bakery Bunch

FAMILY TREE

Featuring Characters from the Amish Homestead Series

Rosa Lynn (deceased) m. Elias Bawell

Marlene Bawell   Anna Bawell

Ada m. Jeptha Swarey

Rudy Swarey

Feenie m. Leonard Esch

Betsy Esch

Laura (Riehl) m. Allen Lambert

Mollie Faith   (mother—Savilla—deceased)

— CHAPTER 1 —

Marlene Bawell hugged her body as she stared down the side-walk at the stores that lined Highway 340 in Bird-in-Hand, Pennsylvania. Her heart seemed to turn over in her chest as the mid-morning June sun warmed her cheeks. Had it truly been ten years since she'd walked down this road?

She smiled as wonderful memories came rushing back to her. Whenever she and her mother visited this street years ago, shopping for groceries and supplies, their friends would call out to them to say hello. She missed those days so much that her chest ached. She squeezed her eyes shut, working to keep her emotions at bay.

Of course, that was before *Mamm* had died and before Marlene's father had moved her and her younger sister to Indiana in order to escape his own memories. While Marlene had cherished her life in Bird-in-Hand, *Dat* seemed to want to forget it all.

She shook the thought away and turned toward the front window of Lancaster Hardware and Supply. A Help Wanted sign caught her attention, and her stomach did a little flip. Although she'd headed to town this morning for groceries, she'd considered stopping by a few businesses to see if they were hiring.

This was what she'd prayed for: an opportunity to help her father. She'd hoped to earn enough money for her family to afford a house to rent in Bird-in-Hand so they could move out of her aunt and uncle's home. If she could help her father pay rent, maybe she could convince him to stay.

Marlene squared her shoulders and pulled the door handle, and the bell above the door announced her entrance. As she made her way toward the front counter, the aroma of wood stain filled her senses. She glanced at a colorful display of birdhouses and bags of birdseed, then took her place in line behind an Amish man purchasing a hammer and several boxes of nails. The young Amish man behind the counter made small talk about the weather as he looked down at the cash register and rang up the items. He looked vaguely familiar to Marlene, but she couldn't quite place him.

She fiddled with the strap of her purse and glanced around the store, taking in the aisles of tools and equipment. She'd have to learn how the items were organized, but doing so couldn't be too difficult. After all, she'd worked in a market in Shipshewana, so she knew she could handle working at a hardware store. Now if only she could convince the owners to hire her, then she could get her father's permission to work part-time—

"May I help you?"

Marlene's gaze snapped to the counter. As the young man addressed her, she took in his dark eyes. He was so familiar. Had they gone to school together? Or perhaps he was in her youth group years ago?

"Marlene?" His milk chocolate eyes flickered with recognition. "Marlene Bawell?"

"Ya?" She nodded and then snapped her fingers when she recognized him. "Rudy Swarey!"

"That's right." He leaned forward on the counter as a smile turned up his lips. "How long has it been?"

"Ten years." She hugged her arms over her chest as she studied his face. She was surprised to find it clean-shaven, indicating that he wasn't married. He had to be twenty-seven like she was since they had gone to school together and been baptized into the church at the same time. But just like her, here he was—unmarried. Her pulse quickened at the thought. When they were teenagers, she'd had a secret crush on Rudy, but he'd never seemed to notice her.

"You moved to Ohio, right?" he asked.

"Indiana," she said. "But *mei dat, schweschder,* and I are back now." She rocked back on her heels.

He stood up straight. "Well, welcome back to Bird-in-Hand. Are you back for *gut?*"

"I hope so. We're living with *mei aenti* and *onkel* right now." She pointed toward the front window. "I noticed the Help Wanted sign."

"*Ya.*" He pushed his hand through his thick, dark hair. "My two cousins work here part-time. One just got married and is taking over his father-in-law's farm. My other cousin only works on days that his *dat* doesn't need him at his furniture store."

"Oh." She touched one of the ribbons on her prayer covering. "So, you need someone part-time."

"Right." He quirked a brow at her. "You're looking for a job?"

"Yes, I am." She lifted her chin as a surge of confidence rushed through her. "I worked at a market in Shipshewana. I'm really good with a cash register, and I know how to stock shelves too."

He nodded but appeared unconvinced.

Marlene approached the counter, preparing to make a case for herself. "I'm a hard worker, and I will do a *gut* job." *And I really need to help* mei dat.

"Okay." Rudy stepped around the counter and gestured for her to follow him. "Let's go talk to *mei dat* about it. Ultimately he decides who we hire."

"*Danki.*" Marlene took in his tall, lean stature as she followed him through the store, silently marveling at how much he had changed since she'd last seen him. Though he had been slightly taller than her when they were teenagers, he seemed to have shot up during the past decade. His shoulders and back were wide and ended at a tapered waist. Any trace of the skinny teenage boy he'd once been was gone. And he was even more handsome than she'd remembered.

They stepped through a doorway and into a large room lined with shelves and boxes. She followed Rudy through the long room before stopping in another doorway that led to an office, where a middle-aged man sat at a desk peering at a ledger over reading glasses. The man's dark brown hair and beard were laced with gray, but his long face and nose resembled Rudy's.

"*Dat.*" Rudy tapped the doorframe and then leaned his forearm against it. "Do you remember Marlene Bawell?" He gestured between Marlene and his father. "Marlene, this is *mei dat*, Jeptha."

Jeptha looked up at Marlene as a smile crept over his lips. "Of course I remember you, Marlene. How are you these days?"

"I'm fine, *danki.*" Marlene smiled. "And you?"

"I'm well, thank you. It's been a long time. How's your *dat?*" Jeptha set his glasses on the desk as he turned toward her.

"He's doing *gut.*" She smiled at Jeptha.

"Are you here visiting family for the summer?" Jeptha asked.

Marlene shook her head. "*Mei dat* was laid off from the factory where he worked in Indiana. I'm hoping we're back for *gut* now."

Jeptha clicked his tongue and closed his ledger. "I'm sorry to hear that. What's your *dat* going to do?"

She shifted her weight on her feet and kept her eyes focused on Jeptha, though she was keenly aware of Rudy's curious stare. "*Mei onkel* gave *mei dat* a job working at his lawn ornament store."

"Oh, that's right. Your *onkel* is Leonard Esch," Jeptha said, and Marlene nodded. "His store stays very busy, especially this time of year. I'm sure your *dat* will enjoy working there. I'm glad you stopped by. We'll see you at church."

"Marlene is interested in the job," Rudy chimed in.

"Oh?" Jeptha divided a look between Rudy and Marlene.

"*Ya*, I am." She stood a little taller. "I thought if I got a job I could help out *mei dat*."

"It's part-time," Jeptha said.

"That's fine with me," she said.

Jeptha and Rudy shared a look.

"I've worked in retail before, and I'm a fast learner." Marlene folded her hands as if saying a prayer. "I'm reliable, and I'll work any hours you need me." *As long as Dat agrees . . .*

"We'll need help on the days that Neil can't work," Rudy said.

"*Ya*." Jeptha rubbed his beard. "So Monday, Wednesday, and Saturday for sure. Will that work with your schedule?"

Hope blossomed in Marlene's chest as she felt a smile curving up her lips. "*Ya*. Definitely."

"All right then," Jeptha said. "Can you start tomorrow?"

"Of course!" She nodded with such emphasis that the ties from her prayer covering bounced off her shoulders.

"Great." Rudy stood up straight as he turned toward his father once again. "I'll take the Help Wanted sign out of the window."

"*Gut*." Jeptha shook Marlene's hand. "I'll see you tomorrow."

"*Danki* for the opportunity to work here," she said.

Jeptha chuckled. "You might change your mind when you see how busy it gets on Saturdays. Tell your *dat* hello for me."

"I will." Marlene followed Rudy to the front of the store, grinning from ear to ear. "*Danki* for reintroducing me to your *dat*."

"*Gern gschehne.*" He swiped the Help Wanted sign from the front window and then turned toward her. "I guess I will see you tomorrow morning. How about eight o'clock?"

Marlene agreed, then gave him a little wave before stepping out through the store's front door.

As she walked toward the market, her pulse quickened. She couldn't wait to get home to tell her father and sister that she'd found a job. Hopefully her paycheck would help her family get back on their feet. If so, could they start building a new life in Bird-in-Hand?

-◀◀◀-

Later that evening, Marlene carried a platter of fried chicken to the table and set it in front of her father. The delicious aroma filled her senses, and her stomach gurgled in response. Anna, her younger sister, followed with a bowl of mashed potatoes. At twenty-three, Anna shared the same sunshine-colored hair and green eyes that Marlene had inherited from their mother.

Their cousin Betsy, also twenty-three, sidled up to Anna and set down a basket of homemade rolls before rubbing her hands together. "These rolls smell so *gut!*" Her light blue eyes sparkled in the sunlight streaming in through the windows as she pushed back a lock of blond hair that had escaped her prayer covering.

"I think that's everything." *Aenti* Feenie surveyed the table and smiled at *Onkel* Leonard. "Let's eat."

Marlene took her spot across from her father and between her sister and cousin. After a silent prayer, the large kitchen filled with the sounds of scraping utensils as they filled their plates with supper.

Marlene gazed over at *Dat*, who scooped a mountain of mashed potatoes onto his plate. She took in the streaks of gray highlighting his light brown hair and beard, the crow's-feet around his hazel eyes, and the wrinkles peppering his tanned face. He looked older and sadder lately. The thought sent a pang of melancholy through her.

"How was your day, *Dat*?" Anna's question brought Marlene back to the present.

Dat gave a halfhearted shrug as he lifted his glass and took a drink of water.

"I got a job today." The words burst from Marlene's lips as she smiled.

Dat's eyes widened as he set his glass on the table. "What?"

"I said I got a job." Marlene suddenly felt aware of her family's eyes focused on her. "I was in town earlier for groceries, and I saw a Help Wanted sign in the window at Lancaster Hardware and Supply. I went inside and applied for a job."

"That's Jeptha Swarey's store," *Onkel* Leonard chimed in.

"That's right." Marlene nodded at *Dat*. "He told me to tell you hello."

Dat studied her, his hazel eyes narrowing. "We never discussed your getting a job. The plan was for me to work and keep saving money until a job opened up in Shipshewana. We're only here until we can go back to Indiana."

Marlene's cheeks heated as embarrassment crept up her neck to her face. "I thought you would be *froh* that I want to help."

"You should have asked for my permission first." *Dat* pressed his lips together.

"I just wanted to help you." Marlene's voice was small, as if she were a little girl instead of a twenty-seven-year-old woman.

"It's not your job to support our family. That's my job." *Dat* pointed to his chest.

"We're a family," Marlene insisted, her voice growing slightly louder despite the churning in the pit of her stomach. "We take care of each other."

Dat picked up his spoon and waved it at her. "You had no right to go looking for a job without my permission." Then he pointed toward the counter. "You have obligations here at the *haus*. You're supposed to help Feenie, Betsy, and Anna with chores while Leonard and I work."

Marlene turned toward her aunt sitting at the head of the table. "I was only going to work Mondays, Wednesdays, and Saturdays, *Aenti* Feenie. I promise I'll do my chores on the other days."

Aenti Feenie's smile seemed hesitant. "I think it's your *dat's* choice if you can accept a part-time job or not."

Anna touched Marlene's arm. "I'll cover Marlene on the days she works. I can make sure all of her chores are done, *Dat*."

Marlene felt her body relax, and she smiled at her younger sister. *Praise God for you, Anna.*

Dat pursed his lips, dividing a look between Marlene and Anna. Then he turned to *Aenti* Feenie. "What do you think, Feenie?"

Marlene held her breath as her aunt sat silently for a moment.

"If you support it, Elias, then we do too," *Aenti* Feenie said. "Right, Leonard?" When *Onkel* Leonard nodded, she added, "I'm certain Betsy, Anna, and I can handle the chores."

Marlene blew out a puff of air as *Dat* nodded. "Fine," he muttered before looking down at his plate once again.

"So, Betsy." Anna turned to her cousin. "These rolls are fantastic. You need to make them again."

"*Danki*." Betsy's smile was as bright as Anna's. "You can help me make them next time."

Marlene felt some of the tension draining out of her as she took a bite of fried chicken. When she glanced over at *Dat*, he was still studying his plate. Was he angry with her? If only he'd look at her, then she could know for certain that she was forgiven. The thought lingered in the back of her mind, pestering her throughout the remainder of supper.

-‹‹‹‹-

Later that evening, the bed shifted beside Marlene when Anna crawled into the double bed they shared. Rolling to her side, Marlene faced the wall and glimpsed a sliver of light between the green shade and the window casing.

"Are you awake?" Anna whispered.

"Ya." Marlene pushed a lock of her thick, waist-length hair away from her face.

"Do you think we're going to be okay here?"

"Of course." Marlene nodded as if her sister could see her through the darkness that shrouded their small bedroom.

"It's just so strange to be back here in this *haus*. The last time we were here . . ."

"I know." Marlene reached over and touched her sister's arm. "She was with us."

Anna sighed, and a heaviness seemed to fill the air between them. "I miss home."

"I do too." Marlene's lip trembled as visions of the little house they had rented in Shipshewana filled her mind. Her thoughts moved to her friends and her job at the market. And yet, though she would miss her friends in Indiana, she wanted to be back here in Bird-in-Hand. This is where she was born. This was where she'd last seen her mother. This was where the memories of her mother had been made and where they lived in her heart and mind. This was her home— where she, Anna, and *Dat* belonged. If only *Dat* could see that

"I think it's great that you got a job."

Marlene shifted to face Anna in the dark. "You do?"

"*Ya.*"

"*Danki* for helping me convince *Dat* to let me keep it. I'm going to save all of the money I make and give it to him so we can find our own *haus* here in Bird-in-Hand to rent."

"I appreciate that."

Marlene thought she heard a trace of uncertainty in her younger sister's voice. It was Marlene's job to tell Anna that everything would be all right, even when she wasn't certain that it would be.

"I promise we'll be fine," Marlene said. "I'll make sure of it, okay?"

"If you say so." Anna rolled onto her side facing away from Marlene. "*Gut nacht.*"

"*Gut nacht.*" Marlene turned back toward the wall and sighed. She waited for sleep to find her, but her mind spun even as she heard Anna's breathing become steadier. Soon soft snores sounded from her side of the bed, and Marlene pressed her lips together. If only she could fall asleep as fast as her younger sister could.

A yawn escaped her, and she adjusted her head on her pillow. Her thoughts moved back to Indiana as she settled under the sheet. An image of Colin, her ex-boyfriend, filled her mind, and she stifled another yawn. She and Colin had dated for nearly four years, and he had proposed to her only a month ago.

Although she had enjoyed his company, she turned down his proposal. Regret filled her as she recalled the pained expression that had clouded his handsome face. But how could she marry him when she wasn't certain how she felt about him? Her feelings at the time were a jumbled mess since Colin had proposed just after *Dat* lost his job.

But now confusion settled over her as she lay in the darkness of her aunt's guest bedroom, her sister snoring softly beside her. Had she agreed to marry Colin, she would have been preparing to live with him on his father's dairy farm. They might've spoken about starting a family soon after the wedding. Had she said yes to him, she could have enjoyed a more certain future.

And she would not have been here in Bird-in-Hand to help her *dat* and sister.

Guilt nearly suffocated her. How could she even consider enjoying an easier life while her sister and father struggled? She had to stop thinking about the past. Instead, she had to dig deep inside of herself to find the strength to move forward.

But how could she when she felt so confused and lost?

CHAPTER 2

*G*ude mariye, Rudy!"

Rudy looked up from the counter and smiled as Marlene walked toward him. "*Gude mariye* to you." He glanced at the clock on the wall and then back at her. "You're early. It's only seven forty-five."

She shrugged as she approached the counter. "I wanted to make sure I was on time." Her lips turned up, but the smile didn't quite reach her eyes. "I'm ready to work."

Was something bothering her? He dismissed the thought. It was none of his business. She was here to work, not be his friend.

"Great." He clapped his hands together, then moved around to her side of the sales counter. "I'll give you a tour, and then I have some items you can price and put out on the displays. But first I have to explain how the store is organized." He motioned for her to follow him.

He led her down each aisle, pointing out how the items were arranged and drawing attention to their most popular sellers. She chewed her lower lip and nodded as he talked, appearing to concentrate on everything he said.

When they entered the last aisle of the store, he pointed toward a variety of ladders. "And this is where we keep the heavier equipment."

"Got it." She fingered her black apron and stared down the aisle.

A wisp of her light blond hair escaped from under her prayer covering, and he squelched the urge to push it back from her cheek.

What are you thinking, Rudy? He and Marlene were barely acquaintances. He'd hardly even spoken to her when they were in school and youth group together, so what would give him the right to even consider touching her?

"Do you have a place where I can put my lunch?" Her question broke through his contemplation.

"Of course. I should have shown you the break room first." Rudy had noticed the tote bag slung over her arm when she'd walked into the store, but it hadn't occurred to him it might have contained her lunch. "Follow me."

He steered her into the stockroom to show her where certain items were stored. Then he led her into the small break room that included a table with four chairs, a counter, a small refrigerator, and cabinets.

He gestured toward the refrigerator. "You can put your lunch in there."

"*Danki.*" She opened her tote, pulled out a purple lunch bag, and set it on the top shelf of the refrigerator.

"The bottles of water on the bottom shelf are for employees," he offered. "You can help yourself anytime."

"Thank you." When she looked up at him, he couldn't help but notice that her emerald-colored dress brought out the beautiful green hue of her eyes, reminding him of a lush pasture in springtime. Had her eyes always been that bright?

He shook away the thought and headed toward the doorway. "I was thinking that you could get started marking boxes of nails. We had a shipment come in late yesterday."

"Okay." She followed him over to the crate.

"I'll carry this out to the nail aisle for you," Rudy continued. "Let me get the pricing tool, then I can show you how to price items."

"I know how to use a pricer," she insisted.

"All right." He grabbed the tool and the price list, then got her started on the task.

Marlene was busy pricing a box of nails when *Dat* walked out of his office.

"*Gude mariye.*" *Dat* shook her hand. "It's *gut* to see you this morning."

"It's nice to see you too." She smiled, but unconvincingly.

"I see Rudy is already putting you to work." *Dat* pointed to the pricer and boxes of nails.

She lifted her chin. "*Ya.* I'm ready for the challenge."

"*Wunderbaar.*" *Dat* pointed to his office. "I'm going to finish some paperwork, but afterward I'll be out front to help with customers."

"Thanks." Rudy lifted a crate. "I'll carry this to the nail aisle for you, Marlene." He set the crate of nails in the aisle and then brought her a stool. He stood beside her as she continued pricing the boxes of nails and setting them on the shelves.

He took in her serious expression and determined eyes while she worked. Once again he wondered what was on her mind. If something troubled her, would she want to talk about it? He opened his mouth to ask her but then closed it again. It wasn't his place to intrude.

Then again, what if she needed a friend? It had to be difficult to move back to Bird-in-Hand after ten years.

After pricing several more boxes, she looked up at him, her brow furrowed. "Did you need something?"

"No." He shifted his weight on his feet and jammed his thumb toward the front of the store. "I'll be up front, okay?"

She watched him for a moment. "You can trust me. I've priced items and put them in the display before. In fact, I'm kind of an expert."

"Right." He chuckled and held up his hands. "Call me if you need me."

"I will."

Rudy shook his head as he made his way to the front of the store. Marlene seemed to have a handle on things, but he couldn't stop his curiosity from taunting him.

When the bell rang announcing the arrival of customers, he turned his attention to the Amish man entering the store.

"*Gude mariye*," Rudy called. "Welcome to Lancaster Hardware and Supply."

-<<<<-

The morning flew by at lightning speed. After Marlene finished pricing and shelving the boxes of nails, she tried to help some customers find other items. She was tidying the display of birdhouses at the front of the store when she felt that someone was watching her.

She turned and gasped as Rudy stood at the end of the aisle, his dark eyes focused on her.

"You startled me." She placed her hand on her chest and took a deep breath.

"I'm sorry." His lips twitched. "I was wondering if you wanted to take your lunch break."

"Is it noon already?" She craned her neck to read the clock on the wall and was surprised to find it was only a few minutes before twelve.

He pointed toward the back of the store. "*Ya*, it is. You can go now, if you like. I'll eat in a little bit."

"*Danki*." Marlene weaved through the aisles and found her way to the break room, where she washed her hands before carrying her lunch bag to the table. She sat down and, after a silent prayer, began to build a turkey and cheese sandwich. As she took bites of the sandwich, she flipped through a tool catalog she'd found on the table.

She was perusing different kinds of hammers when Rudy came through the door and moved toward the refrigerator.

She glanced at the clock and found it was only ten minutes after twelve. Was her lunch break already over? "Is it time for me to go back out on the floor?"

"Not at all." He retrieved a blue lunch bag and two bottles of water before sitting down across from her. "I was wondering if I could join you." He handed her one of the bottles.

She blinked at him. *"Danki."* Why would Rudy want to have lunch with her? Back when she was a teenager, she would have relished having his attention—but now it just felt forced and awkward.

"Mei dat is taking care of the front for us." He opened his lunch bag and pulled out a baloney sandwich and a small bag of chips. He opened the bag and held it out to her. "Would you like a chip?"

"Danki." She took one and popped it into her mouth.

"What are you reading?" He raised an eyebrow and nodded toward the catalog.

"I'm learning about hammers." She pushed the catalog toward him.

"Sounds exciting." He chuckled.

She couldn't stop her smile as she studied his face. He was truly handsome, with milk chocolate eyes and chiseled cheekbones. Why hadn't he settled down with one of the pretty young women in his community?

"Is something on your mind?" he asked after swallowing a bite of sandwich.

"Uh, not really." She cleared her throat and prayed that the heat crawling up her neck didn't show on her cheeks. "Was it still busy out there?"

He shook his head as he took another bite, chewed, and swallowed. "It was actually slowing down, so *Dat* told me to go ahead and eat. I think he was worried you were lonely in here."

"He was concerned that I was lonely?"

Rudy shrugged. "He wants to make sure you feel welcome. He doesn't want you to quit on your first day."

"Oh." She looked down at her sandwich as the conversation with her father at supper last night echoed through her mind.

Her face crumpled as she recalled *Dat*'s frown when he dropped her off at the store this morning. He'd been silent during their journey to town, and his disapproval felt like another person sitting in the buggy with them. Marlene had only wanted to help her father get back on his feet, but her efforts seemed to be more of a hindrance than a support.

And her worst fear was settling into her bones—that *Dat* wanted to return to Indiana. How could she convince him to stay and rebuild their lives in Bird-in-Hand? Didn't living here make him feel closer to *Mamm* the way it did for her?

"Penny for your thoughts."

"What?" Her gaze snapped to his, and the warmth in his dark eyes stole her breath for a moment.

She absently folded a paper napkin as she considered her response. She didn't want to dump her problems on Rudy, especially since it was her first day working at his father's store. She peeked up again and he continued to watch her as he chewed more of his sandwich.

When he held up his bag of chips, she took another one and smiled. A calm settled over her. It was as if Rudy could be the friend she needed today.

"What's it like being back after so many years?" he asked.

She shrugged. "I don't know. I guess it's strange."

"What do you mean?" He took a drink of water.

She tilted her head, considering her response. "I have always thought of Bird-in-Hand as my home since I was born here. Still, I feel like a stranger, even though I know people and grew up here. So I'm a stranger, but I'm not. Does that make sense?"

"*Ya*, it does." He set the bottle on the table. "Have you had the chance to see any old *freinden*?"

She shook her head while chewing. "I haven't, but I will at church tomorrow." Her mind wandered through memories of her friends from school and youth group, wavering between nervousness and excitement. Would any of her old friends recognize her at church? Would they welcome her back? She took a sip of water. "Do you see Laura Riehl at all?"

Something unreadable flashed in his expression, but then it was gone. "*Ya*, I see her at church."

"How is she?"

"She's *gut*." He leaned back in his chair and drummed his fingers on the table. "Her name is Laura Lambert now. She's been married for about three and a half years, I think. She has a *dochder*."

"Wow." Marlene smiled. "I'm *froh* for her."

"*Ya*." He cleared his throat and met her gaze. Something flickered in his eyes. Was it sadness or possibly regret? "Her family has been through a lot. She lost her *mamm* five years ago, and then her best *freind* Savilla passed away shortly after."

Marlene gasped, cupping a hand to her mouth. "Laura lost her *mamm* and Savilla?"

Rudy frowned. "It was a difficult time."

"I'm so sorry to hear that." Tears prickled the corners of her eyes. "I know how difficult it is to lose a *mamm*. My heart goes out to her."

A heavy silence settled over them as they ate. Marlene swiped a few more potato chips from Rudy, contemplating Laura and her family. She was grateful that her old friend was married and had a *dochder*—surely a source of comfort for Laura during a painful time.

"I thought I'd be married by now." The words slipped from Marlene's lips without forethought.

To her surprise, Rudy snorted. "*Mei mamm* would be delighted if I were married. All I hear about is how she wants grandchildren."

"Really?" Marlene couldn't hold back her grin.

He rolled his eyes. "You have no idea."

As if on cue, they both laughed—and she knew the ice between them had been broken.

Rudy wiped at his eyes with a napkin before finishing his sandwich.

"I guess it must be difficult being an only child," Marlene said.

Rudy nodded. "All of *mei mamm*'s focus is on me." He crunched another potato chip. "*Mamm* once told me that she wanted more *kinner* but couldn't have them. I know I'm a blessing to her, but sometimes I wish I had a sibling to absorb some of her attention."

"I always wanted an older *bruder*." Marlene rested her chin on her hand.

"I can relate to that."

"Really?" she asked.

"If I had an older *bruder*, then I'd have someone else to help me with the store." He gestured around the room. "*Mei dat* wants to give it all to me, and some days it's a lot of pressure. It feels like an impossible standard to live up to, you know?"

She considered that and then smiled. "I bet you make your *dat* very proud."

He cocked an eyebrow. "You do?"

She nodded. "Surely your *dat* is satisfied with your work ethic."

A smile played at his lips. "Thanks, Marlene." He glanced at the clock and then back at her. "But we'd better finish up and get out front before he fires us both."

"Okay." As Marlene stole another chip, she felt her shoulders relax again. After all of these years, she might actually become friends with Rudy Swarey.

-⋘-

"How did Marlene do at the store today?" *Mamm* asked as she sat across from Rudy at supper later that evening.

"She did well." Rudy glanced over at *Dat*, who nodded. "She caught on quickly and was very courteous with the customers."

"She has experience working at a market, so she knows how busy a store can be," *Dat* chimed in as he cut his piece of steak.

Mamm scooped a pile of green beans on her plate and then passed the bowl to Rudy. "What brought her family back to Bird-in-Hand?"

"Her *dat* lost his job at a factory, so they came back to live with her *aenti* and *onkel*." Rudy recalled how quiet she'd been when she'd first arrived at the store this morning, but by the end of the day, she seemed happier. Maybe he'd managed to encourage her when they ate lunch together.

"That's *bedauerlich*." *Mamm* clicked her tongue. "Their family went through so much when Rosa Lynn died of cancer all of those years ago. I'm surprised Elias didn't remarry when they moved to Indiana. Maybe he'll meet someone here and start a new life. It would be hard for anyone to measure up to Rosa Lynn though. They were so in love."

Rudy nodded as he bit into his steak. His thoughts meandered back to lunch and how Marlene had laughed with him as they discussed their romantic lives—or lack thereof. She had such a pretty smile and a sweet laugh. Why hadn't he noticed her when they were in youth group together? Could they possibly become good friends? Or maybe even more?

He forced his mind to change course. He had no business even considering having a relationship with Marlene—or anyone else, for that matter. He'd learned his lesson nearly four years ago when his relationship with Laura Riehl had fallen apart and she'd fallen in love with Allen Lambert. After dating for four years, Rudy and Laura had grown apart, and their breakup had turned his world upside down.

Although Rudy had been guilty of allowing their relationship to deteriorate, he still wasn't ready to face another painful breakup. He had no interest in risking his heart again, no matter how much his mother pressured him to settled down and bless her with grandchildren. Maybe he was better off alone. Besides, his father's store demanded nearly all of his focus.

"Did you hear me, Rudy?"

"What?" His attention snapped to his mother's curious brown eyes.

"I asked if you were going to introduce Marlene around the community again." *Mamm's* lips curled with a smile. "It's been a long time since she's seen everyone, so she needs a *freind*."

Rudy frowned. *Mamm* clearly had designs on him and Marlene that went beyond friendship.

"I'm sure Marlene will find her way in the community just fine," Rudy quipped.

Mamm's smile broadened. "*Ya*, but you two have a history. You went to school together, and you're the same age." Her eyes rounded.

"Maybe Marlene will be the one, Rudy! You'll finally settle down, and I'll get some grandchildren."

Rudy swallowed a groan and glanced at his father, who stared at his plate and continued to cut up his steak. *Please save me, Dat. Say something—anything—to change the subject!*

"I suppose we'll see Marlene, her *schweschder*, and her *dat* at church tomorrow since her *aenti* and *onkel* are members of our church district. I remember Marlene was always a *schee maedel*," *Mamm* continued. "She looked like her *mamm* with her pretty green eyes and that bright blond hair. I'll make sure I talk to her and introduce her to some of her *mamm's* old *freinden*."

Then she snapped her fingers as if an idea had captured her. "You should ask her out now since I'm certain the other young men in our community will be *froh* to see her back."

"I think Marlene is more concerned with finding her way in the community than landing a boyfriend," Rudy said through gritted teeth. "She said it's awkward coming back after ten years."

"I suppose I can see that." *Mamm* tapped her chin, and her eyes brightened once again. "So, I saw Lydia Smucker the other day. She told me that her eldest *dochder* just got engaged."

As *Mamm* recounted the goings-on of other friends in the community, Rudy's thoughts once again returned to Marlene's pretty smile. While he'd never admit it to his mother, Rudy did want to be Marlene's friend. In fact, he hoped he could make her feel welcome in the community and have the pleasure of seeing her smile often.

— CHAPTER 3 —

Marlene walked up the path toward the Glick family's farm-house with Anna, Betsy, and *Aenti* Feenie the following morning. She smoothed her hands down her white apron and pink dress and turned toward the barn, where she spotted her father and uncle talking to a group of men all dressed in matching crisp white shirts, black vests, and trousers.

The Glick family was hosting the Sunday service today, and Marlene glanced around the crowd near the barn in search of faces she recognized. A few of the men looked familiar, but their names had escaped her.

Marlene felt the breath tightening her lungs as she followed her sister, cousin, and aunt up the porch steps and toward the back door. Voices sounded from the kitchen, and as she made her way through the mudroom and into the large kitchen, the women were gathered in a circle to visit before the church service began in the barn.

Marlene closed her eyes and tried to gather her wits. As her sister, aunt, and cousin walked together toward the far side of the room to greet friends, Marlene remained in the doorway, cemented in place by her swirling anxiousness.

She scanned the kitchen hoping to see someone she knew, but she only saw vaguely familiar but nameless faces. How could she assimilate back into the community when she couldn't recall the names of any of her friends?

She bit her lower lip and considered walking back out the door, then going out to the barn to look for Rudy since *Aenti* Feenie had mentioned he was a member of their church district. But what would the other members say if they saw Marlene talking with Rudy instead of the women before the service? She didn't want to encourage rumors before reacquainting herself with the members of the community.

"Marlene!" *Aenti* Feenie approached and reached for her arm. "Come meet everyone."

Marlene smiled as her aunt introduced her to old acquaintances. Her heart warmed when people she hadn't seen in years offered her bright smiles and warm handshakes. All of her worry evaporated, and the muscles in her shoulders loosened. Oh, it was so good to be back in Bird-in-Hand!

"Marlene! There you are!" Ada Swarey appeared beside her and shook her hand. "I heard you're doing a great job at the store."

"*Danki.*" Marlene's smile widened. "I'm so grateful for the job."

"It's so *gut* to see you." Ada gave her hand another gentle squeeze, and Marlene enjoyed the sweet gesture.

"Marlene? Is that you?"

Marlene spun and came face-to-face with Laura Riehl Lambert. "Laura?"

"Hi!" Laura opened her arms and pulled Marlene into a hug. "How long has it been?"

"Ten years." Marlene took in her friend's pretty face. Although they were ten years older now, Laura looked the same as Marlene remembered with her beautiful dark brown hair and striking, bright blue eyes. "You look fantastic."

"You do too." Laura clicked her tongue. "I had no idea you were back."

"*Mei dat*, Anna, and I just came back this week."

"Are you back to stay?"

"I hope so." Marlene looked down at a little blond girl standing next to Laura, twirling her finger around the tie to her tiny prayer covering. "This must be your *dochder*."

"*Ya*, it is." Laura's smile was wide as she looked down at the girl. "This is Mollie. Her *mutter* was Savilla. I married her *dat*, Allen, a little over three years ago."

Marlene's smile faded and she touched Laura's hand. "Rudy told me that you lost your *mamm* and Savilla. I'm so sorry for your loss."

"*Danki*." Laura cocked her head, looking closely at Marlene. "When did you see Rudy?"

"I'm working at his *dat*'s store part-time. I just started yesterday."

"Oh." Laura touched Mollie's arm. "Mollie, this is *mei freind* Marlene. Can you say hello?"

"Hi." Mollie waved at her.

"She's beautiful." Marlene smiled at the girl, taking in her baby-blue eyes. She recalled Savilla's chocolate-colored eyes and surmised that Mollie's father must have blue eyes.

"How are the rest of your siblings?" Marlene asked.

"They're doing well." Laura nodded.

Marlene smiled as Laura filled her in on what her older brother, twin brother, and younger sister were doing. She also mentioned that her father had remarried, so now she had three stepsiblings.

When the clock struck nine, the women began filing out of the kitchen on their way to the barn for the service.

"I'm so glad you're back." Laura gave Marlene's shoulder a squeeze.

"I am too," Marlene said.

"I'll see you after the service," Laura said before disappearing into the crowd.

Marlene found her sister and Betsy and then walked with them into the barn, where Anna sat between them on the backless benches in the unmarried women's section of the space.

As Betsy and Anna whispered, Marlene looked around the barn for more familiar faces. She spotted Laura sitting between a middle-aged woman and a pretty blond, whom Marlene assumed was Laura's stepmother and her older brother's wife. Marlene breathed sighs of relief when she found a few more people she recognized as former friends.

When her eyes moved to the unmarried men's section, she also saw Laura's twin, Mark, who looked almost exactly as she'd remembered. Finally she found Rudy sitting a few spots away from him.

Rudy looked handsome dressed in his Sunday suit. His dark eyes were bright and cheerful as he spoke to the young man sitting beside him who looked to be about their age. Could the man be one of his cousins he had mentioned to Marlene?

The man said something to Rudy, who laughed before turning toward Marlene. When his gaze tangled with hers, his smile widened, and he lifted his hand in a wave. She returned the gesture with a nod.

"Who is that?"

"Hmm?" Marlene faced her sister.

"That man." Anna angled her head toward Rudy.

"Stop nodding toward him." Marlene heard the hint of embarrassment in her voice. "That's Rudy."

"Oh." Anna sang the word. "Now I see why you wanted to work at the hardware store."

"What's that supposed to mean?" Marlene whispered, trying to quiet the chatter between them.

"He's handsome." Anna grinned as humiliation threatened to set Marlene's cheeks aflame.

"Who's handsome?" Betsy leaned over Anna to join the conversation.

Marlene wanted to bury her face in her hands. Could this get any more embarrassing? If Rudy witnessed this conversation, he'd certainly notice the commotion. She only wanted to be his friend, but surely he'd think she had a crush on him!

"Rudy Swarey." Anna lifted her chin toward the unmarried men's section of the barn.

"Oh, *ya*," Betsy said. "He's very handsome."

Marlene stared down at her lap and hoped the service would start soon. If not, then she'd have to crawl under the bench to escape this exasperating display by her sister and cousin.

She breathed a deep sigh of relief when the song leader for the service began to sing. The young man sitting on the other side of the barn sang the first syllable of each line, and the rest of the congregation joined him to finish each line.

Opening her hymnal, Marlene turned her thoughts toward the hymn. She opened her heart to hear God's Word for the first time in a decade amid the company of her former church district. It was so good to be back home!

--<<<<--

"So Marlene did a *gut* job at the store yesterday?" Neil asked, sitting across from Rudy at the long lunch table after the service.

"*Ya*, she did." Rudy swiped a pretzel from his cousin's plate and popped it into his mouth. "She worked hard and wasn't frazzled when the store got busy."

Neil lifted his eyebrows. "Am I out of a job?"

"Not unless you quit." Rudy glanced toward the other side of the long table created out of the benches, where Marlene filled coffee cups and smiled at the men seated along the table. She looked pretty in her pink dress, and her cheeks blushed as she said something to another man.

His interest had been piqued when he watched her interact with her younger sister and cousin in an animated conversation before the service began. He'd longed to sneak across the barn and eavesdrop as Marlene had blushed and looked down at her lap. If only he could know what they'd been discussing. Maybe he would ask her tomorrow at work.

"Are you going over to Paul's later today?"

"*Ya.*" Rudy looked over at his favorite cousin. "Don't we always go to Paul's after church?"

"*Ya*, I guess we do." Neil shook his head. "Who would've thought we'd still be in a singles group at our age?"

Rudy snickered. "Funny you should say that. I had a similar conversation with Marlene yesterday."

"Oh *ya?*" Neil leaned forward on his elbows. "What else did you discuss with her?"

Rudy shrugged. "Not much. We talked about the community and *freinden*. No big deal."

"Huh." Neil raised his eyebrows. Then his brown eyes darted to something behind Rudy and then back again.

"What?" Rudy asked.

"*Kaffi?*"

Rudy craned his neck over his shoulder as Marlene appeared holding a carafe. Her green eyes focused on him, and he was almost certain his pulse ticked up a little.

"Would you like some *kaffi?*" she repeated.

"*Ya, danki.*" Rudy handed her his cup, and she filled it. Then he pointed to Neil. "Marlene, this is my cousin Neil Byler. He works part-time in the store too."

"Hi." Marlene nodded at him. "It's nice to meet you."

"It's nice to meet you too. I've heard a lot about you." Neil gave Rudy a sideways look, and Rudy did his best not to glare at him.

"Would you like some *kaffi* too?" she offered.

"*Ya,* please." Neil handed Marlene his cup. "*Danki.*"

"*Gern gschehne.*" She lifted the carafe, then met Rudy's gaze again. "I guess I'll see you at work tomorrow."

"I'll be there," Rudy said.

After she served coffee to the men surrounding him, Rudy turned to watch her move down the line. When he realized he'd been watching her too long, he swiveled around and picked up his coffee cup. He glanced over at Neil and found him grinning.

As he sipped his coffee, Rudy braced himself, waiting for Neil to make a sarcastic comment. Instead, his cousin remained silent.

"What?" Rudy finally demanded.

Neil wagged a finger at him. "I can see why you told your *dat* to hire her."

"What is that supposed to mean?"

"She's really *schee* and sweet." Neil rubbed his clean-shaven chin. "Maybe I should change my hours so I can work with her too."

Rudy rolled his eyes. "Are you done teasing me?"

Neil looked toward Marlene as she worked. "You should invite her to come to Paul's with us."

"I'm sure she has plans with her *schweschder* and cousin."

"They can come too," Neil offered.

Rudy took another sip as he considered the idea. If he invited Marlene to Paul's, would she consider going? Sundays were for visiting family and friends, and he already considered Marlene a friend. But he would also see her at work tomorrow. Would it appear forward if he expected her to spend time with him at work and also on the weekends?

"If you don't invite her, then I will," Neil said.

"I don't think it's a *gut* idea," Rudy warned.

Neil's brow furrowed. "Why not?"

"Because I'm going to see her at work tomorrow." Rudy picked up another pretzel.

"So?"

"I don't want her to think I'm pushy." Rudy looked over at Marlene as she said something to her sister before walking toward the barn door.

"If you aren't pushy, another guy will be," Neil said. "I don't think she'll be single for long."

"I'm not looking for a relationship," Rudy said.

Neil snorted. "I wouldn't let an opportunity pass me by."

As Marlene disappeared through the barn door, Rudy couldn't help but wonder if she would ever be interested in him as more than a friend.

⟨⟨⟨⟨–

Marlene stepped out on the back porch later that afternoon and sank down onto the rocking chair beside *Dat*'s. Her stomach coiled into a knot as she turned toward him and took in his stoic expression. As he stared out toward *Onkel* Leonard's pasture, she wondered what was on his mind.

"Where's Anna?" *Dat* asked without meeting her stare.

"She and Betsy went out with the youth group." Marlene settled back in the rocker and pushed it into motion with her toe.

"Why didn't you go?"

"I'm older than they are. I doubt they'd want me there."

Dat kept his eyes focused straight ahead, and the silence stretched between them like a chasm. Marlene struggled to think of something more to say to encourage conversation with her father.

"It was nice to be back at our old church district," she offered.

He nodded.

"Did you talk to some of your old *freinden?*" she asked.

"*Ya.*" He ran a hand over his beard.

"That's *gut.*" She paused, hoping he'd say more—but when he remained silent, her heart sank. She couldn't handle this distance between them and needed to clear the air. "*Dat,* are you upset with me?"

He looked over at her and shook his head. "No. Why do you ask?"

"You've been cold to me ever since I told you about my job. I was just trying to help." Her voice sounded thick to her own ears. "We're a family, and we should take care of each other. That's what *Mamm* would want us to do."

He blew out a puff of air, and his hazel eyes seemed to shimmer. "I know, but it's my job to take care of you and your *schweschder.* Lately I haven't done a very *gut* job of that."

"That's not true." She reached out and touched his arm. "It's not your fault that the factory laid you off or that you couldn't find another steady job. We're just doing the best we can, and that's why I want to help by working at the hardware store."

Dat's expression warmed. "You've always been such a *gut dochder.*"

She sucked in a breath as her throat dried, and a tender emotion rolled through her.

"Your *mamm* would be so proud of you and Anna." *Dat* patted her shoulder, then looked out toward the pasture once again.

Marlene wiped at her eyes, trying to stop the wetness that filled them. She and her father sat in silence for several moments, the only sounds coming from their rocking chairs moving back and forth on the porch.

"Does that mean you approve of my job at the store?" she finally asked.

"*Ya*," *Dat* said. "As long as it doesn't interfere with your chores at home." His expression became grave. "But don't forget that this is only temporary. My goal is to get us back to Indiana."

"Why can't we stay?" she asked, her voice as hesitant as her heartbeat.

"Because we belong in Shipshewana," he said.

"But I like here, and I want to stay."

"It's not up for discussion," *Dat* said, his tone warning her not to disagree.

Marlene took in the lines on his face and rested her head against the back of the chair. Why didn't he see that Pennsylvania was where they belonged?

As sadness gripped her, she prayed that her father would start to see how Bird-in-Hand was their true home—and that his job at *Onkel* Leonard's store was good for all of them.

— CHAPTER 4 —

H ow was your Sunday afternoon?" Rudy asked Marlene as he stepped into the break room at lunchtime.

Marlene shrugged as she wiped her mouth with a paper napkin. He'd attempted to make conversation with her throughout the morning, but she'd only responded with terse replies. He was determined to encourage her to talk to him since thoughts of her had drifted in and out of his mind throughout the weekend.

"It was *gut*." She crumpled the napkin as she spoke. "I visited with *mei dat*, *aenti*, and *onkel*, and then I took a nap."

He retrieved his lunch bag and two bottles of water from the refrigerator, then sat down across from her at the table. "What did Anna do?"

"Anna?" Marlene seemed surprised by the question. "She and Betsy went to the youth group gathering. She said they played volleyball most of the afternoon."

He passed her a bottle of water. "Why didn't you go with them?"

Her blond eyebrows lifted. "I'm a little bit too old for a youth group. I'm not twenty anymore."

He snorted. "You make it sound like you're forty."

"I feel that way sometimes." She sighed, her shoulders wilting as she picked up her ham-and-cheese sandwich and took a bite.

"I do too." He unwrapped his liverwurst sandwich, then bowed his head in silent prayer.

"What did you do yesterday?" she asked after he finished praying.

When he looked up and found her green eyes focused on him, happiness flooded him. It was the first personal question she'd asked him all day. Perhaps he was making progress with his efforts to encourage her to talk.

"Neil and I went to visit *freinden*. We go just about every Sunday. There's a group of us who are all around the same age who visit, both men and women. We're the late-twenties singles, I suppose." He held out his potato chips to her, and she took one. "You should come with us sometime." Regret filled him as he recalled his conversation with his cousin yesterday. Maybe Neil had been right. Why hadn't Rudy invited her?

Marlene looked down at her sandwich. "*Danki*, but that's okay."

"*Was iss letz?*"

"You don't have to go out of your way with me. I'll be fine."

"How is inviting you to meet *mei freinden* going out of my way? We're in the same church district, and you and I grew up together."

"I know." She absently took another bite of her sandwich. Something was wrong, and his curiosity was driving him to near distraction.

"Do you want to talk about what's bothering you?"

She looked up at him, and he was almost certain he saw tears in her eyes. Worry shot through him.

"Marlene," he began, "I know we were never close, but you can trust me."

"I appreciate that." She sniffed and wiped at her eyes. "It's *mei dat*. He's so *bedauerlich*, and I don't know how to help him. When he was laid off from the factory, he tried for months to find another job. He was determined not to lose the little *haus* we rented in Shipshewana, and he didn't want to come back here to relive all of the memories of how we lost *mei mamm*. He found a few jobs in Indiana, but none of them were steady. Coming here was his last resort."

She looked down at the table and drew circles on the wood grain with her fingertip. "When he ran out of money, we had no choice but to come back and move in with *mei mamm's schweschder*. I know *mei dat* appreciates *mei onkel's* generosity, but I don't think *mei dat* is *froh* working at *mei onkel's* store. I got this job to help him get back on his feet financially, but I think *mei dat* is ashamed of needing help."

She set her bent elbow on the table, then rested her chin on her palm as she looked over at him. "My plan was to give *mei dat* my paycheck to put toward a rental *haus*, but that plan backfired. He got so angry with me."

"He was angry?" Rudy leaned forward as he tried to understand.

"*Ya*." She slumped back in the chair. "When I broke the news to him, he was worried I wouldn't complete chores at home. Thankfully Anna defended me and said she'd make sure my chores were done. *Dat* says it's his responsibility to support us, so I guess he thought I was undermining his role." Her lip trembled. "I wasn't trying to make him feel like less of a man or a *dat*. I just want to help take care of my family."

The urge to reach out and touch Marlene's hand nearly overwhelmed him, but he tamped it down. He wished he could take the pain he saw in her eyes onto himself.

"Yesterday I finally convinced him to talk to me. He said I was a *gut dochder* and that *Mamm* would be proud of me. Then he gave me his blessing to work here." She sniffed again. "I know he's not upset with me, but I hate to see him so *bedauerlich*."

Rudy sat silently as she spoke, grateful Marlene was confiding in him. But how on earth could he possibly help her?

"But that's not the worst of it," she added.

"What is it then?"

"He wants to go back to Shipshewana." She wiped at her eyes. "He doesn't see Bird-in-Hand as our home, but I do. I don't want to go back to Indiana. I want to stay here, and I don't understand why he wants to leave again."

"I'm sorry." He tried to shake off the sadness he felt at the idea of her leaving. She was becoming a friend to him, and he dreaded the idea of losing the chance to get to know her.

She squeezed her eyes shut and shook her head. "I'm sorry. You didn't ask me to pour my heart out to you."

"It's fine," he insisted. "In fact, I'm glad you did."

"Really?" She peered up at him.

"Ya." He forced a smile. "You've been so quiet all morning that I was worried about you."

"You were worried about me?" Her nose scrunched in a funny way, and he bit back a laugh. She was adorable.

"Aren't we *freinden?*" he asked.

"*Ya*, I suppose we are."

"Well, *freinden* worry about each other. So you can tell me whatever is bothering you, and I'll do the same."

"Okay." When she smiled again, relief flooded him. "What's bothering *you* today?" she asked.

"Hmm." He rubbed his chin as he tried to fabricate something to share. He couldn't possibly tell Marlene that his mother had been pressuring him to date her. That would be much too awkward. Then he snapped his fingers when an idea came to him. "I know. We received a huge shipment of fasteners, nuts, and bolts, and I have to price them all and put them out for the display."

"That's what's bothering you?" She laughed, and he savored the sound.

"Yup." He grinned.

"Well then, I suppose we'd better finish our lunches and get hopping on it."

"That's a plan."

-⫸⫸⫸-

Thunder rumbled as Marlene walked toward the store's exit later that afternoon.

"I'll see you Wednesday," she called over her shoulder to Rudy and Jeptha.

Rudy waved and smiled. "Take care, Marlene!"

"Have a *gut* evening," Jeptha chimed in.

"*Danki.*" Marlene hesitated at the door as raindrops peppered the sidewalk and street in front of her. She fished her umbrella out from the bottom of her tote bag, took a deep breath, and pushed the door open.

The sweet scent of rain filled her senses. She hurried out onto the sidewalk, dodging small puddles as the rain began to beat a steady cadence on her umbrella. As she rushed down the road, the raindrops grew heavier, soaking her black shoes and splashing onto her black apron and blue dress.

She picked up her pace and gritted her teeth as the rain continued to drench her feet and legs. She considered going back to the store and calling a driver to pick her up, then decided against it. The point of working at the hardware store was to save every penny she earned.

She stopped at the corner and waited for traffic to pass before crossing the street. As she stepped up onto the sidewalk, a strong gust of wind blew her umbrella inside out, causing her to stumble as the rain continued to soak her. With a screech of frustration, Marlene struggled to fix the umbrella despite another gust of wind. As she righted the umbrella, a car rushed by, hitting a large puddle and splashing water all over her like a tidal wave.

Marlene brushed her hand down her drenched dress and let out another cry of aggravation. Tears stung her eyes, and her shoulders wilted at the sight of her dripping dress. She was soaked, humiliated, and disheartened. A tear dribbled down her cheek, and she brushed it away. She was certain she looked like a drowned rat. How mortifying!

Get it together, Marlene! You're stronger than this!

The little voice in her mind took her by surprise. Squaring her shoulders, she started down the flooded sidewalk, her shoes squeaking with every step.

She turned down another road and had to step into the slippery mud to avoid an oncoming car. In her peripheral vision, she noted an oncoming horse and buggy but kept walking. With her head down, she might avoid seeing someone she might know. The thought of a community member seeing her like this sent a swell of humiliation over her.

"Marlene!"

She cringed at the sound of her name. Who had recognized her? Could this day get any worse?

"Marlene! Marlene, it's me, Rudy!"

She cut her eyes to the side and suppressed a groan when she found Rudy calling to her from his buggy. Her cheeks heated with her rising embarrassment. Why did he have to come along when she was such a wreck?

"Marlene." He halted the horse. "Get in the buggy."

Closing the umbrella, she climbed into the buggy beside him and shivered.

"Why didn't you say you needed a ride?" He pulled a quilt from the back of the buggy and handed it to her. "I never would have let you walk home in this rain."

She patted her face dry with the quilt and wrapped it around herself.

"I can pick you up in the morning and then bring you home after work," he offered, guiding the horse down the road. "You only live a couple of blocks from me."

"It's okay. *Mei dat* drops me off in the morning on his way to work. He works later than I do, so that's why I walk home."

"Well, I can take you home. It's not a problem."

She opened her mouth to respond, but her words were trapped in her throat. A new round of tears overcame her—and though she held her breath to stymie them, her tears broke free.

"*Ach*, Marlene."

As the tears fell, she held the quilt over her face to shield her grief from Rudy.

The buggy came to a stop. Then she felt Rudy shift closer to her.

"Marlene. Talk to me." Rudy's breath was warm and close to her ear, sending a shiver of awareness cascading up her spine. "Please tell me what's wrong."

She took deep breaths in order to calm her frayed nerves. She wiped at her eyes but kept her gaze trained on her lap.

"I'm humiliated that I had to walk home in the rain. I hate that you have to see me soaked like this." She heard the tremble in her voice but pushed on as she hugged the quilt closer to her chest.

"I'm happy to give you a ride, Marlene." His thigh brushed against hers, and her pulse skittered. "You don't have to walk home in the rain anymore."

"*Danki*." She looked out the window to avoid his eyes as fat raindrops pelted the glass.

"Is that all that's upsetting you?"

Beneath the shelter of the buggy, she felt the urge to share what was burdening her heart. "No. It's just that I felt terrible when *mei dat* lost his job, but I was excited when he said we were coming back here. But I also feel guilty because I almost didn't come with *mei dat* and Anna. I considered staying behind in Indiana."

"Where were you going to stay?"

"Right before we left, my boyfriend proposed to me. I almost said yes to him. If I had married Colin, then I'd still be in Indiana, which means I wouldn't have to feel the heartache of leaving Bird-in-Hand for a second time."

She closed her eyes against the nagging guilt. She was a dreadful person for even considering leaving her father and sister behind. She was a sinner who didn't deserve Rudy's friendship or her family's kindness.

"Did you love Colin?"

Marlene turned to face Rudy, then shook her head. "Not the way a *fraa* should love her husband."

Something that looked like understanding flashed across his face. How could Rudy possibly understand her complicated feelings for her ex-boyfriend?

"I'm a horrible person," she whispered. "Colin would have been an easy way out."

"You're not horrible." Rudy reached out his hand as if he might touch her arm, but then he pulled it back.

"You're wrong." Her voice quaked. "I am horrible. If I had said yes to Colin, then I would be stuck in a loveless marriage. Only a bad person would consider doing that instead of working hard to help her family."

Rudy leaned back on the door behind him and crossed his arms over his chest. "I almost did the same thing four years ago."

"What do you mean?" She pivoted her body toward him.

His expression warmed as he held fast to the bench seat. "I dated Laura Lambert for four years. Well, she was Laura Riehl back then."

"You did?" Curiosity nipped at her. Was that why he seemed surprised when she'd asked about Laura?

"*Ya.*" He ran his finger over the back of the seat as he spoke. "It was fun in the beginning. We had a great time with our *freinden* at youth group. We went on picnics, spent days at the lake, played games late into the night, and laughed a lot. We were carefree and life was *gut*. But then she lost her *mamm* and everything changed. It was as if we couldn't relate to each other at all. We started growing apart."

His lips twisted into a frown and he looked down at his lap as if to shield himself from her gaze. "I wasn't much of a boyfriend to her when she needed me most. I was too selfish and immature to realize I was putting my own wants and needs before hers. It's really my fault that we grew apart. Then she lost Savilla, and she pulled even further away from me. I became even more selfish and thoughtless, instead of asking Laura what she needed from me. Savilla's *mamm* was hurt in an accident, and Laura started helping Savilla's widower, Allen, take care of his *dochder.* They grieved together and fell in love along the way. Then they got married."

He paused, shaking his head. "I'm not envious of their relationship, but looking back, I see the mistakes I made. Still, it's obvious that she and Allen belong together. From what I can tell, they're really *froh* and have a *gut*, solid marriage."

Her eyes met his, and she was almost certain she saw regret there. "*Mei mamm* had pressured me for years to marry Laura, and I had considered it for all of the wrong reasons. I knew dee in my heart Laura wasn't the one for me. *Mei mamm* wanted grandchildren so badly, but I couldn't ask Laura to marry me if it didn't feel right."

Marlene nodded slowly. "You're right. I'm thinking about the stability Colin could have given me, but that's not enough to make a marriage work."

Rudy held a finger up. "Exactly."

They both grew silent, and something unspoken passed between them. It was as if Rudy truly understood her, more than her family members ever had. Did he feel that connection, too, or was she imagining it?

"Don't feel guilty for considering what would have happened if you had stayed behind in Indiana." His words were soft and warm, like the quilt she held tight around her body. "You're allowed to wonder what could have been. We're human and we all wonder about decisions we didn't make."

He leaned toward her. "But you shouldn't worry about what you left behind in Indiana. You have *freinden* here, and we're all *froh* that you're back." He pointed to his chest. "You have me. Come out with *mei freinden* on Sunday. I know they'd love to meet you." He grinned sheepishly. "*Mei freinden* really aren't that bad."

"I never said they were."

"I know." He gave her shoulder a little shove, and she laughed. Then he grabbed the reins. "I'd better get you home before your family starts to worry about you."

Marlene stared out the window as the raindrops subsided. By the time Rudy guided the horse up her aunt's driveway, the rain was gone and the sunshine had begun to peek through the clouds.

"*Danki* for the ride," she told him when he halted the horse.

"*Gern gschehne.*"

She pulled off the quilt and held it up. "I can wash this for you and bring it to work."

"No need." He took the damp quilt and tossed it into the back of the buggy. "I'll ask *mei mamm* to wash it."

She pushed the door open and then hesitated. "Would you like to stay for supper?"

"*Mei mamm* is expecting me. Maybe some other time?"

"All right. *Gut nacht.*" She climbed out of the buggy and shut the door.

As his horse and buggy made its way down the driveway, she considered that maybe Rudy was right. She needed to take him up on his offer to meet his friends. With Rudy's help, maybe she would make even more friends within the Bird-in-Hand community.

But what if Rudy's friends didn't like her?

—◄◄◄—

"So you gave her a ride home in the rain?" *Mamm*'s eyes were wide as they ate the pot roast she had made.

Rudy swallowed an aggravated puff of air. "*Ya*, I did. She was soaked."

Mamm clicked her tongue. "You should have accepted her offer to stay for supper."

"Is that right?" Rudy set his glass of water on the table. "I thought you'd be upset since you made a point of telling *Dat* and me that you were making pot roast tonight and that we'd better be home on time."

"Well," *Mamm* hesitated. "I would have understood if you were having supper with Marlene. After all, she's a lovely *maedel*, and neither of you is getting any younger. You have to seize every opportunity to get to know her before another young man wins her heart and marries her."

"*Mamm*." Rudy squeezed the bridge of his nose. "I'm not looking for a relationship right now."

"You should be." She pointed her fork at him. "You're almost thirty, and I want grandchildren before I'm too old to play with them."

Rudy turned to his father and offered his best pleading expression.

"I appreciate that you and Marlene got all of that new stock out onto the floor today," *Dat* said without missing a beat. "That was a big project done."

As *Dat* continued to discuss the store, Rudy replayed his conversation with Marlene in his mind. The emotion in her voice had taken him aback, and when her tears began to fall, he'd longed to pull her into his arms and console her.

Where had this sudden urge to protect her come from?

He really didn't know her very well, and he had no right to even consider touching her. Still, he felt her tugging at his heartstrings.

Talking to her was so easy. He'd never shared with anyone his innermost feelings about his breakup with Laura. When his friends had asked about it, he'd only said that they'd grown apart. But when he'd opened up to Marlene, he had spoken the honest truth using words he'd never before been brave enough to utter. To no one else had he admitted his regret for not being the boyfriend Laura had needed and deserved when she'd lost her mother and best friend.

Rudy pushed his peas around his plate with his fork as he remembered Marlene's beautiful face as she listened to him. In the moment he'd felt as if Marlene understood him better than any of his friends. Perhaps he needed Marlene's friendship as much as she'd needed his today.

His chest filled with warmth at the idea of knowing her better. He'd have to insist she join him on Sunday when he went to see his friends. He just hoped that her father would soon realize that moving back to Bird-in-Hand was a blessing and not a burden—and that Marlene's reunion with the community would become permanent.

— CHAPTER 5 —

Rudy came around the counter at the front of the store as Marlene rang up another customer, bagged his items, and handed the Amish man his receipt.

"*Danki* for coming in today, Wilbur." Her pretty face lit up with a smile as she held out his bag. "I hope you'll come see us again soon."

"*Danki.*" Wilbur took his bag and nodded before heading to the door.

"You are officially an expert," Rudy said as he approached her.

"Well, I sure hope I am after two weeks of working here." Marlene closed the cash register drawer, then looked around the store. "Is everyone gone?"

"Yup." Rudy hopped up on a stool and faced her. "It's actually time to close up."

"Wow." She looked up at the clock. "Today flew by."

"I told you Saturdays were busy." He rested his right ankle on his left knee.

"You weren't kidding." She pushed a couple of buttons on the register, and it popped open. "I guess I'll start closing."

"No, I'll do it." He leaned forward and pushed the drawer closed. "I have a question for you."

"Oh. What's your question?" Her green eyes rounded as she looked over at him.

She'd been pleasant to him all day, but they hadn't had much time to talk since the store never slowed down. In fact, they had taken their lunches in shifts, which was disappointing. Rudy enjoyed eating with her on the quieter days during lunch the last two weeks, but today their constant stream of customers had other plans.

"What are you doing after church tomorrow?" he asked.

"What do you mean?" She pushed the ribbons on her prayer covering behind her slight shoulders.

"I'm wondering if you're actually going to come with me to visit *mei freinden* tomorrow after the service. You said you were interested, but you turned me down last time. Will you come with me tomorrow?" He held his breath, praying she'd agree to join him at his friend's house.

"Oh." She fingered the counter and swallowed. "I guess so."

He narrowed his eyes and studied what appeared to be her jitters. "Are you *naerfich?*"

She chewed her lower lip and gave him a half shrug. "Maybe."

"Why are you nervous?" He couldn't stop his smile. She was so cute.

"What if your *freinden* don't like me?"

He clicked his tongue as he stood. "You can't possibly be serious."

"What do you mean?" She took a step toward him.

"How could they not like you?" He gestured toward her. "Marlene, you're sweet, funny, and *schee*. They're going to love you." *In fact, I'm a little concerned about how much they'll like you*. He grinned at Marlene and headed toward the front door, hoping to leave his errant thought behind him at the counter.

"I'll lock up so that no more customers decide to come in." Rudy locked the door and flipped the sign to Closed before turning back toward the counter. Marlene still stood there motionless, her eyes wide once again.

"So, what do you say?" he asked.

"*Ya*, I will." She nodded, but her expression still seemed surprised.

"Great." He felt some of the tension in his shoulders release. She'd finally agreed to meet his friends.

If only he could figure out why he was so determined to convince her to like his friends.

-⟨⟨⟨⟨-

After church the following afternoon, Rudy smiled up at Marlene as she filled his coffee cup. "Are we still on for this afternoon?"

"*Ya*." Marlene gave a little smile and then reached across the table for Neil's cup.

Neil divided a look between Marlene and Rudy as his dark eyebrows rose. "What's this about?"

"Marlene is coming with me today," Rudy explained.

"Really?" Neil took his filled cup from Marlene. "You're going to join us at Paul's *haus*?"

"*Ya*." She lifted the carafe. "I'll see you after lunch."

"I look forward to it," Rudy called after her as she moved on to the next table. She looked so pretty today clad in a yellow dress that reminded him of butter. Her eyes seemed greener and her smile genuine when she saw him across the barn during the sermon.

Neil leaned forward and lowered his voice. "You finally did it. You asked her out!"

Rudy's smile faded as he looked across the table at his cousin. "It's not a date."

"*Ya*, it is." Neil pointed at him. "It's a date, and it's about time." He tapped the table. "*Gut* for you. You've been single too long. You haven't dated anyone since you broke up with Laura, and that was almost four years ago."

Rudy groaned. "You sound like *mei mamm*."

"Maybe that's because she's right. It's time for you to move on."

Rudy looked over to where Marlene filled another man's cup, and he found himself contemplating what it would be like to date her. They were good friends already. She seemed to open up to him, and he certainly didn't have any trouble talking to her.

But he wasn't looking for a relationship, and neither was she. And if he were looking for one, he wouldn't want to ruin their special friendship by dating her. What if they broke up? Working with her would become awkward, and their friendship would dissolve—just as his friendship with Laura was destroyed by their breakup.

"Admit it," Neil began, breaking through Rudy's thoughts. "You like her—*a lot*."

"*Ya*, I like her as a *freind* and nothing more." Rudy tried to stress his words.

"You're *narrisch*."

"Why am I crazy?"

"Because a *maedel* like her won't stay single for long." Neil gestured toward Marlene. "You should act now. If not, then you'll be bellyaching when someone else asks her out."

"Once again, you sound like *mei mamm*," Rudy groused.

"Maybe that's because your *mamm* is right yet again."

As Neil took a long drink of coffee, Rudy let Neil's words filter through his mind. No matter what his friend said, Rudy couldn't convince himself to risk his friendship with Marlene, because she had somehow become important to him—and he couldn't risk losing her now.

-◄◄◄◄-

"I'm going with Rudy to visit some *freinden* this afternoon," Marlene told Anna and *Dat* as they stood by *Dat*'s buggy after lunch.

"And I'm going to youth group with Betsy," Anna chimed in.

"Okay." *Dat* opened the buggy door. "You both be safe."

Anna looped her arm around Marlene's shoulder and steered her back toward the barn. Her pretty face broke out into a grin. "You have a date?"

"No," Marlene said, trying to hush Anna. "It's not a date. Rudy just invited me to visit with *freinden*. That's all it is, so don't make more of it than that."

"I think he likes you."

"Why would you say that?" Marlene tried to ignore how her heart danced at the idea.

"He was watching you during the service."

"No, he wasn't."

"*Ya*, he was." Anna spun to face her. "He was watching you *a lot*." She wagged a finger at Marlene. "He likes you, and I think it's *wunderbaar*. He's a really nice man. He'd be *gut* for you."

Marlene grabbed her sister's finger to stop it from wagging. "Stop it. Just knock it off. Rudy is *mei freind*, and that's it."

"If you say so." Anna grinned and then hugged her. "See you later. Go have some fun."

"You too." Marlene turned and headed toward where Rudy stood, leaning against his buggy door and talking to Neil. He looked so handsome in his Sunday black-and-white suit. He seemed taller, and his shoulders seemed even wider and broader than usual. The thought sent a tingly wave of warmth through her.

Where was this attraction coming from? The last thing she needed was a relationship to complicate her already complicated life. She needed Rudy to be her friend and nothing more.

He turned toward her and smiled, his handsome face brightening. "Are you ready?"

"*Ya.*" She straightened the hem of her apron as she approached him.

"Great." Rudy looked at Neil. "We'll see you there."

Neil smiled at them both, then headed to his buggy.

Marlene climbed into the passenger side and crossed her arms over her waist as Rudy hopped in and grabbed the reins.

"Did Anna and Betsy go to their youth group?" Rudy asked, guiding the horse toward the road.

"*Ya.*" Marlene turned toward him. "Anna was *froh* to see me actually getting out of the *haus* today."

"Oh *ya?*" He grinned. "That's *gut.*"

"Sometimes I feel like the odd one out, you know?"

He gave her a sideways glance. "Why is that?"

"Well, Anna and Betsy are both the same age, and I'm the older one. It's as if they're *schweschdere* and I'm not." Why was it so easy to confess her innermost thoughts and feelings to him?

He nodded slowly. "That makes sense, but you're here with me. We'll have our own fun this afternoon."

"Right." She settled back in the seat and smiled. She wouldn't let her worries get her down today.

An amiable silence settled over them as she watched the traffic and farmland speed by outside the buggy. When Rudy guided the horse onto the road that led to her former farmhouse, her heart lurched and she gasped.

"Are you all right?" Rudy asked.

She nodded, but a pang lit in her chest—a mixture of grief, long-ing, and panic—when the little white farmhouse came into view. How had she not realized they were driving this way?

"This used to be our farmhouse, Rudy."

"Oh, Marlene, I'm sorry. I didn't even think about—"

"It's okay." She turned toward him. "Can we stop for a minute?"

"Of course." Rudy guided the horse to the grass in front of the house and halted. "Take your time."

"*Danki.*" Marlene climbed out of the buggy and came around to the grass. Her legs wobbled as she took in the little two-story house with its wraparound porch and red barn. A knot of emotion tight-ened inside of her as memories of her mother overtook her mind. She recalled her mother humming as she made breakfast and smiling as she hung out the laundry from the back porch. She could almost see her mother standing in front of her, could almost hear her voice. Her body thrummed, and wetness gathered beneath her eyes.

Marlene blinked away a tear when she realized Rudy had come to stand beside her. She gave him a sad smile as heaviness settled around her heart. "I could get lost in the memories. I have been too nervous to come by here." Her eyes closed. "You must think I'm a coward."

"No." He shook his head. "I don't think that at all."

"It feels like we lived here just yesterday." Marlene turned back toward the house. "I can still smell the kitchen when she was baking bread. Hear the sound of her voice when she sang, believing no one was listening."

Her hand shook as she rubbed at a knot forming in her shoulder. "She was the most beautiful woman I've ever known. She gave the best hugs. She always knew how to make me smile, even when I'd had a bad day or someone at school had hurt my feelings."

"Who hurt your feelings?"

When she turned to face him, his expression was bold. Why was Rudy worried about something that had happened when they were children?

"Oh, it was nothing." She waved off the comment as more memories doused her. Then something deep inside of her unlocked, allowing a torrent of words to flow from her lips. "When we found out she had cancer, the doctors said it was too advanced for the treatments to work. I prayed and prayed for her, begging God not to take her, but she was gone in only a matter of months."

"I'm so sorry." Rudy reached for her hand, and Marlene gasped when their skin brushed. A startling pulse zipped up her arm as his fingers enveloped hers.

Marlene studied his milk chocolate eyes. Had he noticed the sizzle between them, or was she the only one to feel it?

Then he let go of her hand and stepped away from her. "Sorry. What were you saying?" When he swallowed, his Adam's apple bobbed.

Marlene's hand still tingled where Rudy's hand had been. "She was gone so quickly, and *mei dat* changed. He worked later hours at his roofing jobs. He hardly ever spoke and he never smiled." She sniffed and shook her head. "And then one day he said we were moving. There was no discussion. I think he wanted to escape the memories."

Closing her eyes, she spoke through the rawness. "Some days I wonder what life would be like if *Mamm* had never gotten sick. Would my parents still live here? Would I have met someone in my former church district and gotten married? Would I be living on a farm and starting a family right now?" She turned toward Rudy and found him studying her. The intensity in his eyes sent a shiver through her.

She turned toward the buggy to escape his eyes and the unfamiliar feelings they rendered. "We should go. I'm sorry for holding us up."

"Marlene. Wait."

She spun to face him, and he gestured back toward the house.

"We can stay here as long as you want." He pointed to the ground. "If you want to sit here and talk all afternoon, we can. Whatever you want to do is fine with me."

His thoughtfulness surprised her, and she paused to gather her thoughts. "*Danki*, Rudy. But I'm ready to go."

He raised an eyebrow. "Are you sure?"

"I'm positive. I really want to meet your *freinden*." She turned her back on the house and climbed into the buggy as he hopped up on the other side.

He took hold of the reins and faced her. "They're going to be your *freinden* too before the end of the day."

"I hope so." And she did.

-◄◄◄-

Marlene sipped her lemonade and sat on a bale of hay while Rudy and Neil played Ping-Pong in the middle of Paul's barn. She set the cup next to her on the bale and looked toward three young women talking in the corner. Across the barn, four more young men stood clustered near the Ping-Pong table, laughing and heckling each other good-naturedly.

Folding her arms over her apron, Marlene watched Rudy as he hit the ball so hard it launched over Neil's head and flew to the other side of the barn. When Rudy bent at the waist and laughed, Marlene delighted in the sound.

Though she was grateful he had invited her today, she still felt like an outsider. Everyone had said hello to her, but she had faded into the corner as conversations about people she didn't know filled the air. She couldn't possibly catch up with the years of friendship and closeness that connected the other members of the group.

While Rudy continued playing Ping-Pong with Neil, Marlene stood and headed outside of the barn. She wandered toward the pasture fence, breathing in the mid-June evening air as the sunset above her stained the sky with brilliant streaks of orange and yellow. She leaned forward on the split rail and watched Paul's father's horses frolic in the lush field. She was admiring one of the mares when an arm brushed against hers.

"Were you going to steal my horse and buggy and sneak home while I was busy beating Neil?"

She looked up at Rudy and chuckled. "Of course not!"

"Likely story." He leaned back against the fence and pursed his lips. "So, what's going on in that pretty head of yours?"

She blinked. That was the second time in two days that Rudy had called her pretty. Did he truly believe it, or was he simply being kind?

The thought sent excitement fluttering through her like a hummingbird's wings. After all of these years, maybe Rudy Swarey had finally noticed her.

"Are you going to make me guess?" He rubbed his chin, oblivious to her inner turmoil. "Let's see. You're bored out of your mind and you regret your decision to come today."

"I'm not bored."

"*Ach*. But you do regret coming with me." He placed a hand on his chest. "That hurts."

"Not exactly." She turned back toward the horses. "I just feel so out of place. I was born here, but I haven't lived here for ten years. I barely know anyone, and I can't compete with the history you and your *freinden* share."

"Well, you won't get to know anyone until you try talking to them." He gestured toward the barn. "Why don't you come back inside, and I can introduce you around again?" When she hesitated, he bumped his shoulder against hers. "Come on, Marlene. Please do it for me."

She looked up at his puppy dog expression and couldn't suppress her laugh. "Okay."

"Great." He held out his hand, and she took it, enjoying the warmth and comfort of his skin. Had she ever felt so protected and cherished when she was with Colin?

The thought left her dizzy with confusion for a moment—but then she chided herself. *Stop thinking of Rudy as more than a friend, Marlene!*

When they reached the barn, he steered her over to the group of young women.

"Aary Mae," he said. "Don't you have relatives in Shipshewana?"

"*Ya*, I do." A pretty brunette turned toward them. "I have a few cousins there. I was just there to visit last fall."

"Really?" Rudy drew out the word. "Well, Marlene lived there for ten years."

"No kidding." Aary Mae smiled at her as the other young women gathered around them. "Where in Shipshewana did you live?"

Rudy walked back over to the Ping-Pong table as Marlene began to chat with the other young woman.

When Marlene glanced over at Rudy, he winked at her and returned to the game.

— CHAPTER 6 —

"Did you have fun today?" Rudy glanced over at Marlene as he guided the horse down the main road toward the street where her aunt's farm was located.

"I did." She nodded with enthusiasm, her face lighting up with a smile. "*Danki* for inviting me."

"*Danki* for coming with me." He directed the horse onto her aunt's road. "Did you have a good conversation with Aary Mae?"

"*Ya.*" She offered an adorable, sheepish expression. "Talking about Shipshewana broke the ice. We wound up discussing all kinds of other subjects, like recipes, sewing, and our favorite kinds of books. The other *maed* were nice too. I feel like I made some new *freinden* tonight."

"Great." Relief flooded him. Even if she'd only made one friend, then she'd made a connection to the community. Perhaps she wouldn't feel like a stranger in Bird-in-Hand anymore.

"Why haven't you dated any of them?"

"What?" Rudy gave her a quick glance before turning into her aunt's driveway.

"I asked why you haven't dated any of the *maed*. They all seem to like you. Aary Mae is really *schee*, and so is Suzanne. They all spoke very highly of you when I told them you had invited me to come today." She touched the buggy door as she looked at him. "I'm surprised you haven't asked one of them out."

His mouth moved, but he was unsure of how to respond. He'd never once considered asking out Aary Mae, Suzanne, or any of the young women who had been at Paul's house today. The idea had never occurred to him.

"I don't like them that way," he said.

"I'm surprised." When he halted the horse by the back porch, she picked up her purse from the floorboard of the buggy and turned to Rudy. "I had a really nice time today."

"I did too. Thanks again for coming with me."

"*Gern gschehne.*" She smiled warmly at him, and the tendril of hair that she'd brushed out of her face several times today cascaded down her cheek.

Without any forethought, Rudy reached out and brushed the lock of hair back, anchoring it behind her ear. She sucked in a breath at his touch, and warmth spread through him as he breathed in the flowery scent of her perfume.

When he felt a sudden, overwhelming urge to kiss her, he leaned down and then froze.

What am I doing? We're not dating! She's only mei freind!

He shifted away from her and cleared his throat, but she continued to stare up at him—her chest moving up and down as she breathed deeply.

"*Gut nacht.*" He grabbed the reins and looked out the windshield. "I'll see you tomorrow."

"*Gut nacht,*" she said, climbing out of the buggy. Then she hurried up the back porch steps and disappeared into the house.

Once she was gone, Rudy cupped his hand to his forehead and

tried to calm his racing pulse. Then he closed his eyes and tried to even out his breaths.

He had almost kissed Marlene! What had come over him?

When he touched her cheek, he'd felt an invisible magnet pulling him toward her. The thought of kissing her had felt natural, but it was wrong. Wasn't it?

They didn't know each other well, and she had even implied that he should date someone else. She'd even stated that she wasn't sure if she belonged in Bird-in-Hand. Trying to date Marlene would only end in heartbreak.

"I'm losing my mind," he whispered as he guided the horse back down the driveway and toward the road.

He had to put all thoughts of dating her out of his mind. She was his friend—his good friend—and also his coworker. To see her would complicate things too much, and he'd run the risk of ruining both their friendship and their working rapport.

The horse trotted onto the road where his parents' farmhouse was located. Rudy knew as he maneuvered toward a stopping point that he had to erase all romantic thoughts about Marlene from his mind.

But somehow, he already knew how hard that task would be.

-««<-

Marlene rushed up to the bedroom she shared with Anna and flopped on their bed. Staring up at the ceiling, she cupped her hands to her burning cheeks. She was almost certain Rudy had nearly kissed her in the buggy. And she'd wanted him to kiss her!

Hold on a minute, Marlene. You aren't a teenager with a crush any-more. Rudy is a grown man!

She rolled over and moaned into her pillow. What was she

thinking? Rudy was wonderful. He was handsome, funny, kind, thoughtful, and understanding. He was almost perfect. He had become her best friend in Bird-in-Hand, and he'd gone out of his way to make her feel at home. But wanting more than that from Rudy would run the risk of destroying their very special friendship.

After all, they both had long-term relationships behind them that had ended with painful breakups. Why would she want to chance dating Rudy if losing him forever were a possibility?

With a sigh, Marlene leaned forward, stood up, and changed into her nightgown. After brushing her teeth, she returned to the bed and scooted under the sheet.

As she rolled to face the window, her thoughts lingered on Rudy and the fun afternoon she'd spent with him and his friends. She was so grateful for his friendship, and she hoped one day he would understand just how much it meant to her.

She also hoped her friendship meant a lot to him.

-◄◄◄-

A month later, Rudy came up behind Marlene in the tool aisle. "Is that what you call stocking shelves?" he teased.

"Excuse me?" She spun to face him, her hand jammed on her small hip. "You think you could stock it better?"

"I most certainly do." He reached for the tape measure in her hand, but she waved it above her head. "Give me that!"

"Nope!" She stepped to her right and then her left. "It's mine."

"Hand it over." He went after her, and she squealed when he grabbed her arm. "Give it to me."

"No! No!" She giggled and tried to free her arm. "I'll never let you have it! Let me go!" She giggled again.

"Ahem."

When someone cleared his throat behind them, Rudy spun to find Neil watching with a wide grin on his face.

"Hi, Neil," Marlene said.

"Hey, Neil." Rudy did his best to sound casual. "What are you doing here?"

"I just came for my paycheck." Neil's grin widened. "Apparently I interrupted something."

"No, you didn't." Marlene stuck her tongue out at Rudy, then hurried to the tape measure display and resumed stocking the shelves.

Rudy resisted the urge to continue their little game. How he enjoyed teasing her and laughing with her!

For the past month, he had done his best to put the notion of dating her out of his mind. Instead, he just relished her company. He cherished the days they worked together since she made them more enjoyable. She brightened up the store with their conversations at lunch, and as they worked out on the floor together, they often found themselves joking around.

Since the first Sunday she'd gone to Paul's house, she had joined Rudy to visit friends on Sundays when her family didn't insist she and Anna stay home. Rudy knew their friendship had grown by leaps and bounds, and he couldn't shake the feeling that they could be more than friends. Still, his worry about losing her kept him from pursuing something more.

"So, could you get my paycheck for me?" Neil asked, slamming Rudy back to the present.

"Sure." Rudy walked with Neil to the office, where he retrieved Neil's paycheck from the safe. "Here you go."

"*Danki.*" Neil shook the envelope containing the check at Rudy. "You and Marlene were awfully cozy out there, huh?"

"We were just messing around." Rudy waved off the comment.

"No, it was more than that." Neil folded the envelope in half and slipped it into his pocket. "When are you going to ask her out?"

"Knock it off, Neil. You know I'm not interested."

Neil snorted. "You couldn't be more interested. It's been written all over your face for weeks now. You stare at her in church, and whenever she's in the room, she's got your full focus. Just admit it, Rudy. You're in love with her."

"In *love* with her?" Rudy scoffed. "Now you're just being dramatic."

"Is that so?" Neil jammed a finger into Rudy's chest. "Well then. How would you feel if Paul or I asked her out?"

Rudy gritted his teeth with enough force to flex a muscle in his jaw. The truth was, the idea of another man asking her to be his girlfriend left envy boiling in his gut. He dreaded it whenever he saw one of his friends talking to her at church or at one of their Sunday afternoon gatherings. Nightly he prayed she wouldn't fall in love with anyone else. And he was completely aware of how immature and selfish his feelings were.

But he couldn't admit that to Neil or anyone else.

"It's her business if she decides to date someone. I can't stop her." The words tasted bitter on Rudy's tongue.

"Look, Rudy." Neil lowered his voice. "Marlene is terrific, and you'd be *narrisch* to let her slip through your fingers. What are you afraid of?"

Rudy lifted his chin. "I'm not afraid of anything."

Neil seemed to study him. "It's been almost four years since you and Laura broke up."

"Neil, stop it. I don't want to talk about this anymore." Rudy slipped past his cousin and moved out to the stockroom. "I have things to do before *mei dat* gets back from the bank."

"Wait." Neil rushed after him. "Please don't forget that what happened between you and Laura wasn't your fault. You just outgrew each other. You can't let that stop you from trying again with someone else."

Rudy spun toward him. "Why don't you worry about your own life and leave mine alone, okay?"

Neil held his hands up. "I'm just saying, Marlene obviously cares about you as much as you care about her. You should tell her how you feel before it's too late."

"Are you done?" Rudy nearly spat the words at him.

"*Ya.*" Neil frowned. "I'm done. I just hope you're not."

As Neil headed back out into the store, Rudy scrubbed a hand down his face. He didn't want to believe that his cousin was right about Marlene. Life would get too complicated if they were more than friends. But how much longer could he deny that his feelings for her were growing each day?

-◄◄◄-

Marlene hummed as she pinned a pair of her father's trousers to the clothesline and pushed the line out toward the barn. Birds sang in a nearby tree as the July afternoon sun warmed her skin. It was the perfect day, and she couldn't stop smiling.

She'd enjoyed doing chores with her aunt, sister, and cousin today, and tomorrow she would see Rudy for their Saturday shift at the hardware store. She couldn't wait to see him again. She hoped he would tease her and make her laugh. They had so much fun working together, even when the store stayed busy from the time it opened until it closed.

"Listen to you." Anna appeared beside Marlene on the porch and set another basket of wet clothes at her feet. "You're humming like a *maedel* in love."

Marlene stopped humming and glared at her. "I'm not a *maedel* in love."

"*Ya*, you are." Anna pointed at her. "You're in love with Rudy. Why don't you just face the fact?"

"Please." Marlene picked up another pair of her *dat*'s trousers and hung them on the line to avoid Anna's accusing look.

"Clearly, you two are crazy about each other. Why aren't you dating?"

"He doesn't care about me that way. We're just really *gut freinden* who enjoy each other's company."

Anna handed her a pair of their *onkel*'s trousers. "Well, you can't keep your eyes off each other at church, and you never stop smiling when he's around. You tease each other like a couple who has been together for years. You remind me of how *Dat* and *Mamm* used to act before she got sick."

Marlene bristled at the quip as she straightened the wet trousers on the line.

"Don't you want to date him?" Anna asked gently.

Marlene was stumped by the question. Deep in her heart, she did want to date him. He was everything she'd ever dreamt of having in a boyfriend, but dating would change everything. She and Colin had been good friends, and their relationship grew complicated when he asked her to be his girlfriend. She couldn't run the risk of upsetting things between her and Rudy when what they already had was so easy and fun.

"He's handsome, funny, and nice. Why wouldn't you want a boyfriend like him?" Anna handed her another pair of *Onkel* Leonard's trousers.

"I don't think I'm what he's looking for," Marlene admitted. "He seems *froh* living his life as a bachelor. He's never said a word about dating me, so why would I assume he wants to?"

Anna was silent for a beat as she handed Marlene a white shirt. "If he asked you out, what would you say?"

Marlene turned toward her. "I don't know. Part of me would be *froh*, but another part would be *bedauerlich*."

Anna's brow furrowed. "Why would you be sad?"

"Because everything would change." And change was what scared Marlene the most.

— CHAPTER 7 —

The bell above the front door rang, announcing a customer. Marlene looked up from the counter and smiled when she spotted Rudy's mother walking toward her. "Hi, Ada! *Wie geht's?*"

"I'm doing fine, *danki*. How are you doing today, Marlene?" Ada asked.

"I'm doing well. It's a *schee* Monday here at Lancaster Hardware and Supply." Marlene leaned forward on the counter. "Did you need me to find Jeptha or Rudy for you?" She pointed toward the aisle where Rudy had been stocking painting supplies.

"No, I actually came to see you."

"Oh." Marlene gripped the corner of the counter as questions filled her head. Was Ada going to fire her? "What do you need to discuss with me?"

"I've heard so many *wunderbaar* things about you that I wanted to come and visit." Ada's smile was bright, and Marlene couldn't help but think that Rudy had inherited his smile from Ada. "Rudy and Jeptha talk about you incessantly at home. They both say you work so hard and that you're helpful and pleasant to the customers, no matter how busy the store gets."

"*Danki*." Marlene stood up a little straighter. "I appreciate the compliments."

"Oh, *mei sohn* thinks the world of you. He talks about you all the time."

"Does he now?" Marlene looked over to the aisle where Rudy stood and spotted him rubbing a hand down his face, which looked to be stained the color of red delicious apples. She bit the inside of her lip to prevent a giggle from bursting forth. "That's awfully nice, Ada."

"That's why I wanted to invite you over for supper tonight."

"Oh." Marlene looked over at Rudy and found him frowning, his shoulders hunching as an apology spread across his face.

"I'm making my special chicken potpie casserole. It's Rudy's favorite." Ada leaned forward. "And I won't take no for an answer. I want to thank you for making my Rudy smile again."

Marlene stilled. She'd made Rudy smile again? Was that true?

"Please say yes." Ada folded her hands as if she were praying.

Marlene glanced at Rudy as he walked up behind his mother. "Well, I don't know, Ada. It's Monday, and—"

"Please, Marlene," Ada said again.

Marlene met Rudy's gaze, and his eyes pleaded as he mouthed the word, *Please?*

Marlene looked back at Ada. "*Ya*, I'd be delighted to join you for supper."

"Great." Ada clapped her hands.

Behind her, Rudy mouthed a thank-you.

Ada spun to face Rudy and patted his chest. "You bring Marlene home for supper tonight. I'm going to make her something special to thank her for being such a *gut freind* to you."

"*Ya, Mamm.*" Rudy gave her a quick hug, and Marlene's heart swelled with admiration for him.

"Well, I'm off to the market," Ada said over her shoulder as she headed toward the door. "I'll see you all tonight."

"Good-bye, Ada," Marlene called after her.

Rudy shook his head as he came up behind the counter to Marlene. "I'm sorry about her."

"Don't be." Marlene opened a bottle of water and took a sip. "It's an honor to be invited for supper with your family."

"Just ignore her pushiness." Rudy leaned against the counter behind him. "She means well, but she gets a little overexcited."

"I think she's great, and you should be thankful to have her."

Rudy's eyes widened, and he leaned toward her as he gasped. "I'm sorry, Marlene, I didn't mean to—"

"It's okay." She nudged his foot with hers. "I know what you meant, and I meant it when I said it is a privilege to be invited." She walked to the back wall and picked up the phone. "I'll leave a message for my family so they'll know I won't be home for supper. Tonight will be fun."

As she dialed the number, happiness bubbled inside of her. She couldn't wait to have supper with Rudy and his family. Eating with him would be a new step in their special friendship.

-‹‹‹-

Rudy savored the delicious chicken potpie casserole as he looked across his mother's kitchen table at Marlene. She was stunning as she smiled and talked about how much she enjoyed being back in Bird-in-Hand. Her gorgeous green eyes seemed to sparkle in the natural light streaming in through the kitchen windows. She wore her kelly green dress—the one he liked best on her—and her cheeks were flushed pink. He studied her, memorizing every line of her face and every intonation of her voice. She was perfect to him, beautiful inside and out.

He was falling for her, and it scared him deeply. She was on his mind throughout the day, and she invaded his dreams at night. He felt a spark any time their hands brushed, and his heart swelled every time she laughed.

The thought of losing her to someone else nearly ripped him to shreds. Yet nothing he could do would stop his emotions for her, which grew deeper as the days wore on.

"Did you like Indiana?" *Mamm* asked as she scooped more casserole onto her plate.

Marlene nodded. "I did. But Bird-in-Hand feels like home again." She looked over at Rudy. "Thanks to your *sohn*."

"That's *gut* to know." *Mamm* winked at Rudy.

"This is *appeditlich*, Ada." Marlene pointed her fork at her plate. "I have to get the recipe. I think *mei dat* would enjoy it too."

"Oh *ya*." *Mamm* wiped her mouth with a paper napkin. "I'll be sure to write it down before you leave tonight."

"How do you like working at the store?" *Dat* asked Marlene. "You never seem to complain, but I don't know if you're just being polite."

Marlene gave a little laugh, and Rudy couldn't hold back his grin.

"I love working there," Marlene insisted. "I worked at a market in Shipshewana, so I was used to retail. I enjoy interacting with the customers."

"You worked at a market?" *Mamm* leaned forward. "What kind of things did you sell?"

As Marlene told tales about living in Indiana, Rudy looked down at his plate. He had to find a way to manage his feelings for her before he wound up with a broken heart, though he feared it was already too late. She'd already won him over, and now his parents were falling for her too.

Rudy suddenly realized that his heart was doomed.

-‹‹‹‹-

"Everything was lovely tonight, Ada," Marlene said as she dried a dish and set it in the cabinet. "*Danki* again for inviting me over."

"*Gern gschehne*," Ada tossed over her shoulder. "I'm so *froh* you could join us for supper. I wanted to get to know you better since Rudy seems smitten with you."

"Oh, I don't think that's the case." Marlene picked up another dish from the drying rack, and her hands trembled at the prospect of winning Rudy's heart. "We're just really *gut freinden*."

"Marlene, I'm not blind," Ada said, scrubbing a dish. "I know *mei sohn*, and he definitely has feelings for you. He's a little shy since he went through such a bad breakup years ago. I think he blames himself for the problems he had with Laura, but it wasn't his fault alone. They were young when they got together, and they just grew apart after she lost her *mamm* and her best friend, Savilla. It has taken him a long time to heal from that, but I think he might finally be ready to move on, thanks to you."

Marlene shook her head. "He and I get along great, but I don't think he wants to date me."

"Rudy is a very *gut* man," Ada continued. "He has a *gut* heart even though he's a little reticent when it comes to sharing his feelings. He's a hard worker, and he's going to take over his *dat*'s store someday soon. Jeptha has been grooming him for years. When the time is right, he'll take this *haus* and we'll build a little one for ourselves in the back." She pointed to the window over the sink. "Just give him time, and he'll tell you how he feels."

Marlene studied Ada as confusion swirled through her. Did Ada truly understand the situation as well as she thought? Surely she was misguided. Rudy had never even said he cared about Marlene.

But Marlene didn't want to hurt Ada's feelings. Maybe it gave Ada hope to believe she'd welcome the grandchildren she prayed for sooner rather than later.

Ada turned to face Marlene, her expression suddenly serious. "Don't you have feelings for *mei sohn*?"

Marlene opened her mouth and then closed it. How could she admit she cared for Rudy when she wasn't sure he would ever share those feelings?

"You know, Jeptha and I were *gut freinden* before we started dating. We knew each other in school and then youth group. We talked occasionally, but we didn't start dating until we were around your age." Ada turned back toward the sink. "Sometimes love takes a little longer to develop."

Love?

Marlene swallowed as a ball of unease formed under her ribs. She had to stop this conversation before Ada starting planning their wedding!

The back door opened and then clicked shut, and Rudy sauntered into the kitchen. As confusion trampled her like a team of horses, Marlene could only stare at him.

Could she possibly love Rudy? Could he love her too?

He stepped over to the counter and leaned against it before lifting an eyebrow. "What are you two ladies discussing?"

"You," Ada quipped, and Marlene cringed.

"Really!" Rudy stood up straight. "I hope you've been saying *gut* things about me."

"Only the best," Ada said as she scrubbed a handful of utensils.

Rudy touched Marlene's arm. "I'd better get you home before your family thinks I've kidnapped you."

"Oh." Marlene looked at the drain board, which contained

glasses and another pile of utensils. "I need to help finish with the dishes."

"No, no." Ada dismissed her with a wave of her hand. "You go on. I can handle this."

"Are you sure?" Marlene asked.

"Of course I am." Ada gave her a knowing smile. "I'll see you again soon."

"*Danki* for supper," Marlene said before following Rudy outside.

When she stepped out onto the porch, she said good night to Rudy's father as he swayed back and forth in a rocker. Then she walked down the steps and climbed into Rudy's waiting buggy.

"I'm sorry if *mei mamm* was a bit blunt," Rudy said as he led the horse toward the road.

"She was fine," Marlene said, settling back in the seat. "I had a lovely time."

"I'm glad."

They rode in silence for a while as her conversation with Ada spun through her mind. Possibilities consumed her as she considered what it would be like to date Rudy. Would he tell her that he loved her? Would *Dat* give him permission to date her? If so, would *Dat* allow her to continue working at the store if she and Rudy were a couple?

The questions echoed through her mind as she stared out the window at the passing traffic.

She glanced over at Rudy and found him also staring out the front windshield, seemingly occupied in thought. Was he thinking of her and imagining what a future together would look like? She desperately wished he would tell her how he felt.

Marlene dismissed the thought and chewed her lower lip as her aunt's house came into view. The ride home had been too short.

She wanted more time with him, but she would see him again on Wednesday when she came to work. How would she manage without talking to him tomorrow? She was already too attached.

Rudy halted the horse at the top of her driveway and then turned toward her. "The evening wasn't long enough."

She smiled. "I was just thinking the same thing."

Leaning over, he tenderly pressed his hand to her cheek, and her pulse galloped. "I had a nice time tonight."

"I did too," she whispered, her words vibrating within her.

"*Danki* for coming over to have supper with my family." His husky voice made her wonder if he were holding something back.

A moment passed between them, and his nearness made her dizzy. Did he feel it too?

When Rudy didn't speak, Marlene knew she had to get out of the buggy before she confessed her feelings to him. She couldn't bare her soul until she was certain he cared for her in return.

"*Danki* for driving me home," she said, breaking the moment in two. She touched his shoulder and pushed open the door. "I'll see you Wednesday."

"I can't wait," he said. "*Gut nacht.*"

She climbed out of the buggy and then hurried up the porch steps, her steps so light she felt as if she were floating on a cloud.

Marlene ran into the kitchen and then stopped dead in her tracks when she found her father at the kitchen table, scowling. Anna and Betsy wiped tears from their cheeks as *Aenti* Feenie and *Onkel* Leonard looked on, their faces etched with concern.

"What happened?" Marlene asked as her happiness dissolved.

"My cousin Floyd called me earlier today and offered me a job at his shop," *Dat* announced.

"What?" Marlene's voice cracked. "Floyd in Indiana?"

"We're moving back to Shipshewana next week," *Dat* continued. "It's all set. I'm going to rent a *haus* from him, and we're going to—"

"No!" Marlene cried as the floor dropped out from under her. She had to be dreaming. This couldn't be real!

"No, no, no! I don't want to go back. I want to stay here." Marlene gestured around the kitchen as dread poured into her. "We've made a life here, and we belong here. We've been reunited with this community after all this time. You can't do this to me. You can't make me leave."

"Marlene." *Dat* stood and held his hands up. "Please calm down and listen to me. It's all settled. Floyd is going to pay me a decent salary in Indiana." His words shot across her nerves like shards of glass, cutting and fraying them.

"No!" Tears rushed down Marlene's hot cheeks, and she let out a sob. "I don't want to go. I want to stay here."

Dat glanced at her aunt and uncle. "I appreciate all that Feenie and Leonard have done for us, but we belong back in Indiana."

"I don't! I want to stay here!"

Before *Dat* could respond, Marlene rushed into the mudroom, grabbed a flashlight from the shelf on the wall, and dashed out the back door into the darkness.

— CHAPTER 8 —

Marlene dropped to her knees in front of her mother's grave as tears continued to flow down her cheeks. She hadn't stopped running until she reached the cemetery, then weaved through the headstones until she found her mother's name.

Reaching up, she ran her fingers over the cool concrete as her heartache rushed through her.

"*Mamm,*" she whispered, "I need your help. *Dat* wants to take Anna and me back to Shipshewana, and I want to stay here. It's comforting to be back here in Bird-in-Hand. I feel closer to you, and not just because your grave is here. The memories of the four of us together as a family make me *froh*. This is where I belong. This is home."

She sat back on her heels while pressing her fingers onto the gravestone. "I miss you, *Mamm*. I miss your voice, your laugh, and your hugs. I miss your patience and your sage advice. For the first time in years, I'm *froh*. I've met someone. I don't know if you remember Rudy Swarey, but we grew up together. I had a crush on him when we were teenagers, but we were never close. We were barely acquaintances back then, but he's my *freind* now. In fact, he's my best *freind*, and I think I'm falling in love with him."

Her own words rang loudly in her ears, and she gasped, covering her mouth with her hand. Her heart twisted with renewed grief at the thought of losing him.

"I do love him, *Mamm*," she continued. "When I'm with him, I'm happy. In fact, I'm happier than I've been in years. He's different from Colin. He understands me in a way Colin never did. Rudy is handsome, funny, thoughtful, and genuine. I also feel this attraction that I've never felt before. Rudy is the man I've always prayed to find."

Her lip quivered as sorrow coursed through her. If only her mother could have seen Rudy and Marlene together.

"And now that I've fallen in love—true love, for the first time—I have to say good-bye to him. I don't know how to do it. Please help me. Please send me a sign. How do I make *Dat* realize that we belong here? How do I convince him not to take me away from my life here and a possible future with Rudy? Help me, *Mamm*. Please."

Hugging her arms to her chest, Marlene leaned forward and sobbed as a wave of anguish pulled her under.

-<<<-

Rudy stepped out of the barn after stowing his horse and buggy and froze. He blinked to make sure he wasn't imagining Marlene walking up his driveway with a flashlight guiding her way.

"Marlene?" He rushed over to her, and his heart clenched when he spotted tears streaming down her face. "Marlene! *Was iss letz?*" He reached for her and swiped the tears away with the tip of his finger. "Tell me what's wrong." Alarm roared through him as she took deep breaths and sniffed.

"It's *mei dat*." She looked up at him, and her lip trembled. "When I got home, he said he got a job offer back in Shipshewana. His cousin offered him a job and a *haus* to rent. He wants to go back there, says we belong in Indiana. I ran out of the *haus* and went to the cemetery to see *mei mamm*. Then I came here to tell you."

"No." Rudy shook his head as dread pooled inside him. "No, you can't go."

"I don't want to go." She sniffed as more tears leaked from her eyes.

As he examined her tearful face, a new emotion burned through him. He knew in that moment that he loved her.

He truly loved her, and he could not lose her.

He was in love with Marlene Bawell, and he felt it to the marrow of his bones. He couldn't let her go—not now, not ever.

"You can't go." He rested his hands on her shoulders and took a deep breath as determination surged through him. "You can't leave me, Marlene. I'm in love with you, and I can't lose you."

She gasped as she looked up at him. "I love you, too, Rudy."

He pulled her to him and brushed his lips over hers. The contact sent liquid heat shooting from his head to his toes. Finally he understood. This is what love was supposed to feel like!

When he broke the kiss, she rested her head on his shoulder. "I can't lose you either, Rudy. Not when I finally have you."

He searched her eyes. "What do you mean?"

"I had a crush on you when we were teenagers." She gave a little laugh as she wiped at her eyes.

"What?" He gasped. "I never knew you liked me."

"I know." She shrugged. "You never noticed me, but I noticed you."

"I may have been blind back then, but I don't want to let you go now."

"*Ich liebe dich.*" Her words were music to his ears.

"I love you too." He shook his head. "Look at us. We're nearly thirty, and we've finally found each other. Remember when you said you feel old? Well, I do too."

"Does that make us late bloomers?" She smiled tenderly, but then it faded. "I hope it's not too late, Rudy."

"It isn't. I refuse to let you go." He set his jaw as resolve gripped him. "Let's go talk to your father. We have to convince him to stay."

"Okay."

"Let me hitch up my horse." Threading his fingers with hers, he steered her toward the barn.

-◄◄◄-

"What are you going to say to *mei dat* to convince him to stay?" Marlene asked as they rode in the buggy to her family's house.

"I'm not sure." A muscle in Rudy's jaw ticked as he kept his eyes trained on the windshield. "Maybe we can ask him if you can stay with your *aenti* and *onkel* while he and Anna go back to Indiana."

Marlene nodded as she considered it. "That might work. I'd miss them, but I could always visit them, and they could visit me."

"Right." He gave her a kind glance, then looked back toward the road. "I'm not sure what else I can say unless we just beg him not to go."

"I pray it works," she whispered, her heart swelling with hope.

Closing her eyes, Marlene opened her heart to God:

Please, God, don't make me leave Rudy. I love him and I can't endure the thought of losing him. Please convince Dat *to let us stay and continue building a life here. Only you can warm his heart.*

She opened her eyes as her aunt and uncle's house came into view. When Rudy halted the horse, she turned to him and touched his hand. "*Danki* for coming with me."

"I wouldn't dream of letting you face this alone." He brushed his thumb across her cheek. "We'll get through this together."

She leaned into his touch and closed her eyes. "Thank you."

Then she pushed open the buggy door and hurried toward the house. Rudy caught up with her and took her hand in his. They walked up the porch steps and in through the mudroom, where they found her father sitting at the kitchen table alone.

"Marlene!" *Dat* stood, his voice echoing off the kitchen walls. "How dare you run off like that. I was worried sick about you!"

"Elias," Rudy began, still holding onto her hand. "Please listen to what I have to say." He glanced at Marlene and then back at *Dat*. "I'm in love with Marlene, and I don't want you to go. Please stay here and let us build a life together. You haven't been here two months yet, so there's still time for you to make this feel like home again."

Dat shook his head. "It's not that simple."

Onkel Leonard appeared in the doorway. "Actually, it is."

"What do you mean?" *Dat* turned to face him.

"What if I offered you a partnership in my business?" *Onkel* Leonard came to stand beside *Dat*. "I'll double your salary, and I'll help you find a *haus* to rent. I know of one nearby, and I'll loan you the money for the deposit. I wanted to offer you this sooner, but you seemed so determined to return to Indiana. We've only just been reunited, and I want you to stay. I'd be honored to make you my partner."

Hope lit in Marlene's chest as she looked up at Rudy. He nodded at her as if to tell her to keep the faith.

"I couldn't take more from you, Leonard." *Dat* shook his head. "You've already done so much."

"That's what family is for." *Onkel* Leonard sighed. "Feenie and I have always wished we'd done more for you after Rosa Lynn died. Let us help you now." He offered his hand to *Dat*. "What do you say?"

Dat hesitated, then took his hand and shook it. "*Danki*. I'll accept your offer."

Marlene clapped as she jumped up and down. "Does this mean we're going to stay?"

Dat turned to her and nodded. "*Ya*, I guess it does."

"*Danki! Danki, Dat!*" She hugged her father as happiness blossomed in her soul. Then she turned back to Rudy and wove her fingers through his.

Dat cleared his throat and faced Rudy. "And you. Do you have something to ask me?"

"*Ya*, I do." Rudy squeezed her hand as he looked at *Dat*. "I would like your blessing to please date Marlene. She means a lot to me, and I'd like to get to know her better."

Marlene held her breath as her *dat* looked between them.

"*Ya*, you have my blessing," *Dat* said, and Marlene blew out the breath she'd been holding. "Well then, I suppose it's late. You need to get back home, Rudy."

"I do." Rudy looked down at her. "Will you walk me outside?"

Marlene held tight to Rudy's hand as they stepped out onto the porch. "I thought I was going to lose you."

"You'll never lose me," he whispered, his gaze burning down on her and a smile turning up his lips. "I'm so *froh* right now I think I might explode."

She laughed as her heartbeat leapt. "I feel the same way."

"I thought you would never consider dating someone like me."

"I didn't think you'd be interested in me," Marlene admitted. "Aren't we a pair?"

"*Ya*, we are." As her arm reached around his waist, he leaned down and brushed his lips against hers, sending electric pulses singing through her. She closed her eyes and savored the feel of him.

Rudy leaned his forehead against hers. "I'm so glad you're my girlfriend. I love you, Marlene."

"*Ich liebe dich*," she said. "Thank you for choosing me."

As Rudy pulled her close for a hug, Marlene felt overwhelming gratitude—and silently thanked God for helping her find her true home.

— DISCUSSION QUESTIONS —

1. Marlene feels like a stranger when she moves back to Bird-in-Hand after living in Indiana for ten years. Think of a time when you felt lost and alone. Where did you find your strength? What Bible verses would help?
2. Rudy is reluctant to date after his painful breakup with Laura Riehl nearly four years ago. Instead of dating, he tries to convince himself that he doesn't have feelings for Marlene. What do you think changed his point of view throughout the story?
3. Ada is determined to convince Rudy to get married so she can finally welcome grandchildren into the world. While her intentions are good, she tends to meddle and make Rudy crazy. Can you relate to his feelings toward his mother?
4. After Marlene's mother died, her father insisted they move away in order to escape the memories. Have you ever faced a difficult loss? If so, where did you find comfort during that time?
5. Which character can you identify with the most? Which character seemed to carry the most emotional stake in the story? Was it Marlene, Rudy, Elias, Anna, or someone else?

6. Elias decides to stay in Bird-in-Hand at the end of the story. What do you think causes him to change his heart and mind?

7. What role did the store play in the growth of Marlene and Rudy's relationship?

— ACKNOWLEDGMENTS —

As always, I'm grateful for my loving family, including my mother, Lola Goebelbecker; my husband, Joe; and my sons, Zac and Matt.

Special thanks to my mother and my dear friend Becky Biddy, who graciously proofread the draft and corrected my hilarious typos.

I'm also grateful for my special Amish friend who patiently answers my endless stream of questions. You're a blessing in my life.

Thank you to my wonderful church family at Morning Star Lutheran in Matthews, North Carolina, for your encouragement, prayers, love, and friendship. You all mean so much to my family and me.

Thank you to Zac Weikal and the fabulous members of my Bakery Bunch! I'm so grateful for your friendship and your excitement about my books. You all are awesome!

To my agent, Natasha Kern—I can't thank you enough for your guidance, advice, and friendship. You are a tremendous blessing in my life.

Thank you to my amazing editor, Jocelyn Bailey, for your friendship and guidance. I'm grateful to each and every person at

ACKNOWLEDGMENTS

HarperCollins Christian Publishing who helped make this book a reality.

Thank you most of all to God—for giving me the inspiration and the words to glorify you. I'm grateful and humbled you've chosen this path for me.

A REUNION OF HEARTS

Beth Wiseman

To Rae of Sunshine, always remembered, never forgotten.

— CHAPTER 1 —

Ruth Beiler stepped out of the red Buick Enclave she'd rented at the airport and pressed her feet on the dewy grass that twinkled in the early-morning light. Her brown loafers sank into the lush green yard where she'd spent her childhood. Memories of wonderful times flooded her mind—playing in the sprinkler with Esther on hot summer days, hosting Sunday singings, collecting eggs, planting a garden, and hanging clothes on the line, only to argue about who would take them down later.

Ruth had missed her family, especially her sister. Esther and Amos had lived in their family home for two years now, since their parents relocated to the *daadi haus* on the north end of the property. The house had been in the Stoltzfus family for four generations.

Coming back to Lancaster County, even after five years, still fueled the grief Ruth carried around like a cement backpack, an unwanted accessory that would forever be a part of who she was now. Losing a child did that to a person.

She stood in the grass, feet rooted to the ground, as she scanned her surroundings. The barn sported a fresh coat of red paint. The chicken coop had been overhauled with new wiring, and there was a wooden house with a ramp inside. Several hens pushed for space to crane their necks out to squawk a disgruntled welcome.

The white farmhouse looked exactly the same. The porch was painted a light gray, and two white rockers rested beside each other with a small table in between. Green blinds in the windows were drawn halfway. The flowerbeds were in full bloom with begonias, lilies, freesia, and daffodils—their mother's favorite.

Ruth breathed in the familiar scent of the flowers mingled with freshly cut hay and manure. Altogether, the smells of springtime created an aroma Ruth had found herself trying to remember at her new home in Florida.

Like a mirror cracking before her eyes, the pleasant memories broke and fell in pieces, giving way to the dark part of her mind where the pain was still fresh. The sirens, the bright lights on the cars spinning red and blue, and the police marching up the porch steps.

She and Gideon were having supper with Esther and Amos when they received the news that Grace had been killed. Their only child. Beautiful, ten-year-old Grace was riding in a buggy with Mae Beiler, Ruth's mother-in-law, when she was killed along with her grandmother. Onlookers said a fire alarm sounded nearby, and Mae's horse got spooked and darted into traffic on Lincoln Highway.

Ruth squeezed her eyelids closed as the images of that night resurfaced, causing tears to fill her eyes. For the week she would be here, she'd promised herself she would try to focus on happy memories and not let her grief overshadow this time with her sister and other family members who were coming from out of state for the reunion.

She opened her eyes, took a deep breath, and pictured two little girls playing in the sprinkler not ten feet from where she was standing. It was a technique she learned from her support group, to quickly replace the bad memory with a good one. Ruth would need to practice a lot to get through this week.

In Florida she was able to compartmentalize and keep the sadness out of sight and out of mind, even if only for a while. That might prove to be a difficult task here, where the good and bad memories collided. She hoped that by coming for a visit, she would return filled with an abundance of new memories to offset the bad.

Staying with her sister's family would be better than staying at the house she and Gideon had abandoned when they left the Old Order Amish community, each hauling a grief that divided them as they went their separate ways.

Gideon lived in Ohio now. He'd relocated near cousins there after running away, the same way Ruth had when she reconnected with distant relatives in Florida. She hadn't seen him since then. They talked on the phone several times and exchanged a few letters the first year, but the communication was too painful. The phone calls and letters slowly stopped.

She'd heard from Gideon for the first time a few weeks ago. He asked if she would mind him coming for the reunion, and she told him that was fine. He was still her husband, and this was his family, too, so the reunion would give them a chance to see family again and get the house ready to sell. Gideon said he'd been mailing checks to a local teenager to keep up with the yard, and Ruth told him Esther went inside occasionally to check for mice or vandals. She knew going in the house was painful for her sister, too, and Ruth appreciated her sister's kindness. Esther had even covered the furniture with sheets and given everything a good wipe down once a month. The call with Gideon was awkward, businesslike, and Ruth wondered if he had moved on. Perhaps he was even dating.

Ruth and Gideon were shunned when they left each other and the community. Even though her communication with Gideon had ceased, Ruth continued to correspond with her loved ones, mostly her sister, mother, and father-in-law. Her mother said the bishop was aware but wasn't making a fuss about it.

Bishop Lapp had further extended his grace by allowing Ruth to come home. Most likely her family hoped she was here to stay—if the bishop would even allow it. She'd already prepared for the onslaught of reasons they would offer for her to return to the life she'd loved and left. But no amount of best-intended coaxing would ever lure Ruth back to this place permanently. Everything she once found so beautiful was now tarnished.

She jumped when the screen door opened and a young girl bounced down the porch steps and skipped barefoot across the yard. The child wore a light-blue dress, and a few strands of curly blonde hair were flying around the sides of her *kapp*. At Esther's insistence, Ruth had arrived before anyone else, so this bundle of energy must be Esther and Amos's daughter, Becky. *My niece.* She was carrying a bundle of daisies wrapped in paper towels and stopped in front of Ruth, smiling. Ruth had never seen the little girl before. She was as beautiful as her mother had been at that age, and she even had the same dimples as Esther.

"You are *mei aenti* Ruth." Becky bounced up on her toes as she offered the flowers.

Squatting down to the child's level, Ruth accepted them. "*Ya*, I am. *Danki* for these." She was surprised how easily the dialect rolled off her tongue. She hadn't used it in years. Pennsylvania *Deitsch* was the first language an Amish child learned. They didn't usually learn English until they started school, but Esther had told Ruth she wanted Becky to get a jump on it before school started in the fall. Esther didn't take to English very well her first year, so she might be worried Becky would have trouble with it too.

A squeal came from the porch before Ruth's sister rushed down the stairs and across the yard. She flung her arms around Ruth and kissed her on the cheek.

"I've missed you so much." Esther squeezed her so hard she almost couldn't breathe. "I made all of your favorites for dinner." She eased out of the hug and locked eyes with Ruth. "You look so pretty."

Ruth's younger sister had never seen her in English clothes or wearing a small amount of makeup. Ruth had kept her dark hair long over the years and it was pulled into a ponytail. She'd chosen jeans and a long sleeve tan blouse for today, out of respect for her family. It was hot enough in Florida, and here, to wear shorts, but it was frowned upon by the Amish to expose that much of yourself.

As they crossed the yard, Ruth glanced over at the swing hanging from the large oak tree. How many times had she pushed Grace in that swing when they'd come to visit her parents?

She thought again about the house Gideon built for them, the one they moved into after they'd been married about a year, the house they raised Grace in for ten years.

Gideon left the community about two months after Ruth, leaving most of their belongings behind. Even though they agreed to go through everything together this week, Ruth feared that part of this trip. Would seeing everything again set back the progress she'd made? She was equally fearful about seeing Gideon for the first time in all these years. Her stomach churned every time she thought about it. Would he look the same? Would he act the same? Had he shaved his beard? An endless list of questions ran through her mind when it came to Gideon.

In hindsight Ruth knew his pain was probably worse than her own. He'd lost his only child and his mother. Ruth had loved Mae, too, but she was Gideon's mother. At the time, Ruth couldn't see past her own grief, and she had no sympathy to give anyone else, not even her husband. Her support group in Florida for grieving parents had helped a lot, but it took her a while to feel strong enough to talk about losing Grace. Again she worried if this trip was a mistake. She prayed that being here would help her to continue healing.

As Ruth crossed over the threshold, the wonderful smells of home wafted up her nostrils—freshly baked bread and something simmering on the stove. Maybe it was Esther's special beef stew. Her sister had mentioned preparing Ruth's favorites for dinner, the noon meal. Ruth had grown used to dinner being the nighttime meal in the English world, but here, dinner meant lunch.

Amos greeted her with a hug in the living room. "So glad to have you home."

She forced a smile as she eased out of his arms. "It's *gut* to be here." Her brother-in-law was a wonderful man, a good husband to Esther, and a great father.

Esther motioned around the living room. "What do you think of our new furniture? *Mamm* was attached to their couch, and can you imagine *Daed* not having his recliner? They left almost everything else when they moved to the *daadi haus*, but they wanted those two pieces." Esther smiled.

Ruth didn't think her sister had aged a day since she'd been gone, but there was a maturity that showed in her expressions. Motherhood. Ruth had worried things might be awkward after not seeing everyone for so long, but Esther carried on in the same upbeat manner as always.

"I love it." The beige couch had large cushion backs with a dropdown table in the middle. The new recliner was a dark shade of tan and beautifully complemented the multicolored rug with its shades of brown. The coffee table had a glass top and a vase filled with daisies in the middle. Glancing around, Ruth noticed a calendar hanging on the wall, as well as a framed picture of a lovely landscape that looked like it could have been taken right out the back door. There was also a beautiful clock on the mantel and figurines of angels on either side of it.

"I know what you're thinking." Esther sighed as she blew a strand of hair away from her face. "It's a bit fancy."

That was what Ruth was thinking. "It's lovely. What did *Mamm* say?"

"That it was a bit fancy." Esther chuckled.

Laughter. If the walls in the house could talk, they'd tell of wonderful times filled with cheerfulness. Those were the memories she wanted to take back with her.

"When will *Mamm* and *Daed* be here?" Ruth felt a tinge of disappointment that her parents hadn't come to welcome her.

"They should be here any minute." Esther looked at the clock, then frowned. "Where is Becky?"

Amos glanced around. "She was just here." He shrugged. "Maybe she went outside."

Esther shook her head. "I think she would live outside if we'd let her. She's supposed to let us know if she's going out to swing." She nodded to her husband. "Will you find her and remind her not to just disappear?"

Ruth drew in a deep breath, recalling how much Grace had loved the outdoors. Ruth had looked forward to meeting her niece, but seeing the girl also brought on a surge of pain she should have expected. Memories of Grace at that age filled her mind.

After the screen door closed behind Amos, Esther drew closer to her sister and touched Ruth's arm, her eyebrows knitting together. "Gideon is already here. I thought he wasn't coming until tomorrow, but he stopped by this morning. He's staying at his *daed's haus.*"

Ruth's heart pounded against her chest.

Esther smiled a little. "He looked good."

Ruth put a hand to her chest and locked eyes with her sister. "I'm so nervous about seeing him. We've barely communicated over the last five years, and not at all in the last four. It's hard enough for me to be here, Esther, and . . ." She paused when her voice cracked. "As much as I've missed my family, facing Gideon, our house"—she blinked back tears—"I thought I was ready, but now I'm not sure."

"Ruth . . ." Esther spoke with tenderness in her voice. "You said you wanted this trip to help you heal. Let *Gott* do His work."

Ruth blinked again, pushing back more tears that threatened to spill. "I'm scared," she said, barely above a whisper.

Esther wrapped her arms around her and kissed her on the cheek again. "I know you are." Her sister's eyes were watery now too. "But fear blocks the voice of *Gott*. Listen to Him, and everything will be okay, *ya?*"

"I hope so." Ruth forced a smile. "But I am so happy to see you, and I'm anxious to see *Mamm* and *Daed*."

Esther's expression sobered.

"What is it?" Ruth swallowed a knot in her throat. "Is it *Mamm* or *Daed?* Is one of them sick?"

Esther shook her head. "*Nee*, they're fine. I would have told you in a letter or by phone if they were ill." Her sister scratched her cheek and sighed. "I just remembered something Gideon said this morning, and I don't want you to be caught off guard."

Ruth held her breath, waiting, as she thought about things Gideon might say to catch her off guard. There were too many to list. They didn't know anything about each other's current lives. Would he tell her he wanted them to try again, to recapture the love they once cherished? Was he moving out of the country? Was he sick? Her mind was spinning ideas faster than Ruth could process them.

"He wanted to know what time you would be here." Esther paused as she dropped her gaze. "He said he has some important papers he needs you to sign."

Ruth couldn't breathe. Hands might as well have been around her neck, choking the life out of her. "I should have seen this coming," she said, her voice breaking. But she hadn't, and the wind was knocked out of her, for sure.

"He must have divorce papers for me to sign."

— CHAPTER 2 —

Gideon sat across the table from his father as they ate the noon meal. They had said very little to each other following Gideon's arrival yesterday.

John Beiler was fifty when Gideon left the community. Now he looked like a man in his early seventies, his dark hair an equal mixture of brown and gray, his beard the same blended hues. The lines of time feathered from the corners of his eyes, attaching themselves to a road map of deep crevices. His body was worn from decades of hard work, but mostly from the last few years of grief. He'd stopped attending worship service the day his wife and granddaughter were killed, his faith shattered.

Gideon understood the angry feelings and loss of faith. Temporarily, he carried ill will toward the Lord as well. But over time he was able to accept that his mother's and child's deaths were the will of God, which was what he'd grown up believing—that everything that happened was part of God's plan, His will.

He hadn't been in the English world long before he learned that trusting solely in God's will was not universal. He'd met plenty of people grieving, and a lot of them had walked away from God. Gideon understood his father's initial reaction to the tragedies they'd faced, but he thought his father would have eventually turned back to God.

"The meatloaf was *gut*," Gideon said after he finished the last bite on his plate. His father nodded. Gideon wondered how often his father ate meals that came frozen in a box. It tasted better than Gideon would have thought, but maybe that was because it was heated slowly in the oven and not microwaved in a minute or two. He recalled the many home-cooked meals he'd had in this house over the years.

Gideon inquired about various cousins he hadn't seen since Grace's and his mother's funerals.

His father shrugged. "I'm not sure how many are coming." Narrowing bushy eyebrows and squinting at Gideon, his father stroked his beard. "Why are you here? You wrote that you weren't coming. What made you change your mind?"

Gideon wiped his mouth with his napkin. He already knew his father had no plans to attend the family reunion. Even though it was for Ruth's side of the family, Gideon's parents had attended in the past.

"I missed everyone. And I need to take care of some loose ends here. You know . . . the house, stuff like that." He also needed to face Ruth, to apologize for the way he'd acted in the months following the accident. He'd also met someone, a woman in Ohio, who he'd been out with a few times. Technically he and Ruth were still married, and they needed to address that fact. Ruth had been the love of his life, yet they'd destroyed each other after Grace's death, each picking off chips of the other's last bit of sanity. Instead of clinging together, they tore each other to shreds.

As he looked at his father, Gideon knew it would have been him if he'd stayed—a bitter, lonely man without faith. He had needed distance from this place to heal.

He wasn't sure how long he'd been lost in thought when his father cleared his throat. "I take a nap this time of day." The chair dragged against the wood floor as he pushed away from the table and stood. He shuffled across the room but turned back as he crossed the threshold into the living room. "I'm glad you're here, *sohn*." He didn't wait for a response but continued toward his bedroom and closed the door behind him.

Gideon sighed as he stared at the wall. He sat there for a while before he stacked the dishes and carried them to the sink. He'd wash them when he got home from the cemetery. The delay wouldn't bother his father. The house was a wreck, and dishes filled the sink when he first arrived.

He pulled his keys from his pocket and walked outside toward his white Chevy Silverado pickup truck. He'd joined a wonderful Christian church a few months after he moved, and he got a driver's license and bought the truck a couple weeks later, after he saved enough money from working at the hardware store his cousins owned. He was blessed to have work shortly after he arrived. Staying busy helped him through his grief in the beginning, and he made a good life for himself in Ohio. But being back in Lancaster County filled him with a sense of regret about what could have been.

Gideon drove to a local florist and browsed the displays before he chose two arrangements, each a dozen yellow roses. He was thankful he didn't know the young clerk who waited on him. He wasn't in the mood for small talk. His first order of business would be the hardest. After he visited Grace and his mother, he would go to the house where he, Ruth, and Grace had lived and assess what needed to be done.

He parked at the cemetery next to the only other vehicle in the small dirt parking lot, a red SUV. Forcing the door open, he stepped onto the dirt, then gently closed the door. Taking deep breaths, he eyed the rows of plain headstones with no more than a name and date carved into the wood. They were all exactly the same, and Gideon allowed shame to latch on to him because he didn't remember which row was Grace's. That day had been a blur. He trudged forward.

He wouldn't have brought flowers to a grave in his past life, but he'd been to several English funerals in Ohio, and there was an abundance of flowers at each one. It might not be the Amish way, but Grace and his mother had loved roses. They'd had several rose bushes when he was growing up and at the home he's shared with Ruth and Grace.

In the distance, he saw a woman kneeling in front of a headstone. She wasn't Amish. He could tell because she wasn't wearing a head covering or a dress, but jeans and a tan shirt. Her face was buried in her hands as her shoulders shook.

Gideon shuffled forward, the roses dangling in one hand at his side. His chest tightened as he neared what he thought was Grace's grave. When the woman turned around, wiped her eyes, and locked eyes with him, Gideon became caught in a magnetic field pushing and pulling him at the same time.

He fought the heaviness in his chest as he blinked at the woman. He took a few more slow steps, and as his wife's eyes held his, he wanted to turn and run back to his truck. Or into her arms. He wasn't sure. He stopped only a few feet from her, unprepared for this meeting. Gideon thought he'd at least have tonight to think about everything he wanted to say to her.

Dabbing at her eyes again, Ruth rushed to her feet, then moved quickly toward him.

"Ruth," he whispered. "I-I can come back if . . ."

She shook her head, sniffling. Even with dark circles under her eyes and tearstained cheeks, Gideon thought she was the most beautiful woman on earth. Strands of her long dark hair flew below her ponytail as a strong breeze cut through the space between them.

She looked at the ground for a moment, then raised her head and gazed into his eyes, tipping her head slightly, like she might be trying to see through him, to read his thoughts. Gideon wondered if she would like what she saw. His journey was fraught with pitfalls, times when he'd lost his footing. What had her last five years been like?

Her eyes drifted to the roses at his side. "Grace's favorite." She blinked, then sniffled again before she locked eyes with him. "It's good to see you."

He took a deep breath. He'd made love to this woman, had a child with her, and loved her with all of his heart for so many years. But as he gazed at her now, he saw a stranger. A ghost from his past. He didn't know anything about her, except that she lived in Florida. She didn't know anything about him either.

"I-I've been here a while." Ruth glanced back at Grace's grave. There was a bouquet of yellow roses laid across the grass. "I can let you have some time with her."

"No. Stay." The words jumped from his mouth before he had time to think. He wouldn't be able to hold back his tears much longer, and he hadn't even been able to look directly at his daughter's headstone yet. Did he want Ruth to see him this way?

Being alone seemed terrifying all of a sudden, though. As a tear trickled down his cheek, he placed one of the bouquets next to the flowers Ruth had left. Gideon knew Grace wasn't there. She was in heaven. He wondered if she could see him. Did God give her glimpses of the lives that went on without her? Gideon hoped not. Grace would surely be disappointed in her parents.

"I miss you every single day of my life." He squatted down and placed his hands on the grass where her body was laid to rest, recalling the images of his father, father-in-law, Amos, and two cousins lowering his beloved little girl into the ground. The tears came full force then, and even harder when Ruth knelt beside him and put an arm around him. She lay her head on his shoulder, weeping along with him. Then she tearfully reached for Gideon's hand and began to recite the Lord's Prayer.

There were things to be said, situations to handle . . . but right now, they were two parents praying over their daughter's grave. Everything else could wait.

After a few moments of silence, they both stood. Gideon pulled a handkerchief from his pocket and dried his eyes, embarrassed that he was trembling and crying in front of Ruth.

He wanted to tell her how sorry he was that he'd failed her, that he was sorry he hadn't had the strength to provide the emotional support she needed back then. Did he tell her that during one of their phone calls that first year they stayed in touch? Surely he did. But his thoughts were scrambled, and he still needed to do one more thing while he was here.

"Do you want to come with me?" He nodded four headstones to his left. His mother was buried on the other side of his grandparents.

"If that's okay. I've already visited her grave, but I'd like to go with you." They'd both stopped crying, and the soberness and silence were deafening. Too many thoughts and memories slammed around in his head. He walked alongside Ruth to his mother's grave, determined not to cry again, but his best efforts failed him. Ruth reached for his hand, and together they knelt and prayed. She trembled right along with him as he placed the other dozen roses beside the arrangement Ruth must have left earlier.

"Even after five years, the pain feels fresh." He stared at his mother's grave for a few seconds before he stood and offered a hand to Ruth. Gideon wondered if this trip would undo all his hard work to control his grief. He supposed it never went away, but time and prayer had helped. Being back here, seeing Ruth, it was all painful and confusing.

"I hope you're doing well in Florida." He cleared his throat and thought about what a dumb and casual thing it was to say when there was clearly so much more they needed to talk about. But now probably wasn't the right time for anything heavy.

Ruth nodded. "I am." She smiled a little, and he caught her looking him up and down. She'd never seen him in blue jeans and a T-shirt before. "I guess you chose not to join another Amish community." Waving a hand at her own attire, she said, "Obviously, neither did I."

"It didn't feel right, even if another district had accepted me, I . . ." He shrugged. "I had forsaken God. But I found Him at a non-denominational church."

"That's good." She kept her eyes cast down as they inched back to their vehicles. "I found a church, too, but . . ." She lifted one shoulder, then dropped it. "It's not the same."

Gideon wondered what was going through Ruth's mind. His own thoughts were all over the place. Why did they stop talking and writing letters? The cease in communication wasn't abrupt. The phone calls and letters became less and less until they just no longer existed.

As they walked, they didn't touch each other, didn't hold hands like earlier. Each stride felt shaky and awkward, but only a few minutes ago, they'd shown the most intimate parts of themselves when they'd cried over their lost loved ones. Should he hug her before they left? He wished their first meeting hadn't been a surprise for either of them, but maybe this was how it was meant to be. Perhaps God knew they would need each other for this visit to Grace's and his mother's final resting spots.

Gideon walked her to her car and opened the door for her. She got in and turned back to him. "Esther said you had some papers for me to sign."

He nodded over his shoulder toward his truck. "Oh, yeah. I do. They're actually in my backseat. Hang on. I'll get them."

Returning with a large white envelope, he handed it to her. "I'll give you time to look these over and see if there is anything you want to change or don't agree with."

She took the envelope but avoided looking at him as she set it on the passenger seat by her purse. "Okay."

Ruth started the car, but Gideon wasn't ready for her to go. "I feel like we have some things to talk about." At the very least, Gideon wanted to hear about her life, where she worked, if she was happy. On a more personal note, was she seeing anyone? Had she been with anyone else? He probably didn't have a right to ask about that.

She glanced at him briefly, then looked at the white envelope to her right. "There's probably nothing for us to talk about. I'll get this back to you soon."

Gideon's jaw dropped. How could she say that? She clearly didn't have an inkling of love left for him. And just the opposite was true for him. He still loved her, as much now as ever, which could be a problem for him and the woman he was dating back home, but Gideon was willing to work through it to have another chance with Ruth.

Reuniting hadn't been on his mind prior to seeing her today, but he'd begun to ponder the possibility the moment he laid eyes on her. If she didn't think they had anything to talk about, he'd take care of business here and head back to Ohio.

But then she started to cry again, and Gideon was more confused than ever.

— CHAPTER 3 —

Ruth forced herself to stop crying. She'd known they couldn't stay in limbo forever, but she hadn't expected divorce papers on this trip.

She finally gazed into Gideon's eyes. He was the only man she'd ever loved, and her chest tightened until she struggled to breathe. "Are you seeing someone?" she whispered.

"Ruthie . . ." Gideon took off his hat and pulled a handkerchief from his pocket, then dabbed at the sweat pooling on his forehead.

Ruth squeezed her eyes closed, wishing she hadn't asked, and wishing he hadn't called her Ruthie. He'd been the only one to ever call her that, and it made his hesitation to answer hurt even more.

"We haven't communicated in over four years, not even a letter." He paused as he put his hat back on. "Why are you even asking me that when you don't think we have anything to talk about?"

Gideon had moved on. She could tell by his continued avoidance of the question. She looked at the white envelope. Why prolong the inevitable by hashing everything out? This trip was about reconnecting with her family and trying to capture moments of joy and focus on the good memories. Esther warned her about the papers so she wouldn't be caught off guard. But she'd completely unraveled, and she'd done so in front of Gideon.

Ruth thought her heart might explode, and she wondered if Gideon could see it pounding against her chest. She had chosen not to date anyone, but it was wrong of her to assume Gideon hadn't found someone to share his life with.

"I'll look over the papers and get them back to you." Her voice sounded small and fragile, even to herself. She always thought if she ever saw Gideon again she would portray herself as the strong woman she was before Grace's accident.

"Ruthie . . ."

She squeezed her eyes closed again, then opened them wide as her chest tightened even more.

Gideon rubbed his forehead. "Does it even matter if I'm seeing someone else?"

Her husband still had a long dark beard. She'd noticed it when she first saw him. It had given her hope that he wasn't pretending to be single. She wondered if he would shave it after they were divorced.

She wanted to tell him that it did matter, but this was all too much to process. Visiting Grace was hard enough. Seeing Gideon was a welcomed reunion at first. No matter how badly they treated each other after Grace and Mae died, there was a bond between them. Parents have an unbreakable connection, but also an understanding when bereaved. Facing divorce, something she didn't even believe in, should have been on her radar, but couldn't it have waited? *He must be in love with someone else.*

She said good-bye and closed her door, then backed out of the small parking area without looking back. She drove around for thirty minutes, long enough to stop crying.

Even though she and Gideon weren't living a married life God would approve of, they were still married. She'd been asked out plenty of times in Florida, but she declined every invitation. She was married. But apparently being legally and spiritually bound hadn't stopped Gideon from finding someone else. His evasive answer—Does it really matter?—seemed to confirm he was in love with another woman, thus the need for a divorce.

When she turned into Esther and Amos's driveway, her heart sank. There were buggies everywhere. Ruth forgot Esther and her mother had a group of women coming today to work on wedding preparations for their childhood friends, Ben and Annie. Even though the wedding wasn't until October, an Amish wedding was a big deal, and there was a lot to be done, just like weddings in the outside world. This was the last thing Ruth wanted to be around, but she was sure her sister and the other women already heard her pull in the driveway.

She shuffled toward the front door, which was open, and as she stepped across the threshold, the breeze at her back, she inhaled the smell of cookies baking. Her mother was the first to greet her with a hug. Ruth told her last night at supper that she would be visiting Grace today.

"I think everyone knows *mei dochder*, Ruth, *ya?*" Her mother waved an arm around the room.

Ruth forced herself to smile as she glanced at the women. In unison the ladies and girls—about twelve of them—flashed a smile as if on cue.

"It's great to be here," Ruth said, wishing she could get back in the car and head to the airport. But then she locked eyes with Esther, who wasn't smiling. She knew Ruth well enough to know something was wrong.

After everyone settled back into a conversation about the wedding, Ruth sat quietly, her insides swirling with anxiety, her heart pumping faster than it should. Occasionally, the women brought her into the conversation and asked an opinion about the meal to be served or items the bride and groom might need to start their lives. Ruth had known Annie and Ben all her life, and she wanted to be happy about this wedding, but her own marriage was ending, and the chatter was becoming torturous. *But didn't my marriage end five years ago?*

Every time the conversation shifted to anything about children, someone quickly redirected the topic. They didn't want to say anything about Grace. Even last night with her parents, Esther, Amos, and Becky—her immediate family—no one mentioned Grace.

Ruth wanted to remind everyone that Grace had lived, been loved, and existed. It was worse for everyone to work so hard at avoiding any mention of her. People back in Florida didn't know Grace. Friends and coworkers listened, commented, and were generally sympathetic when Ruth spoke about her only child. But this was Grace's family and people who knew her well, the diary keepers of the short life she'd lived. These loved ones held the fond recollections and happy memories Ruth wanted to take home with her.

After what seemed like hours, Becky came bouncing down the stairs, her unmanageable blonde curls flying loose from her prayer covering, the way they'd done since Ruth arrived. Esther met her daughter at the stairs and whispered something in her ear. Becky walked directly to Ruth while the ladies continued talking.

Becky whispered in Ruth's ear, "I collect the eggs in the mornings, but I didn't this morning because there was a snake in front of the coop." She glanced around and saw that no one was paying attention to her. "Will you come with me?" The child reached for Ruth's hand.

Ruth glanced at Esther, who offered her a weak smile. This was surely Esther's idea to save her, and Ruth was more than happy to oblige Becky's request.

Her niece held her hand tightly all the way to the chicken coop, then squeezed as she pointed with her other hand. "That's where the snake was."

Becky's hand trembled in Ruth's, but the instincts of motherhood were still there. Ruth was equally as afraid of snakes, but it was her job to squash the girl's fear. She squatted down in front of her beautiful niece.

"I know snakes look very scary, and some of them are dangerous, but the only snakes I ever saw when I lived here were chicken snakes, and they won't hurt you."

Becky sighed, then swatted at a fly buzzing their heads. "Will you be here for Ben and Annie's wedding?"

Ruth stood and brushed off her jeans. "Um, *nee*." Again she slipped into her native dialect. "I'm only going to be here a week."

Becky pushed her lips into a pout. "That's not very long."

"I know. But maybe I'll visit more often." It was much too soon to know when she would return. A lot of things could happen while she was here. She thought about the white envelope in the car that she hadn't opened yet. Would divorce give her some closure and allow her to move on, the way Gideon had? Would it be easier to visit this place where she grew up? Or did divorce have less to do with it? Would the healing forces of time make things easier? She wasn't sure.

After Ruth searched around the coop for snakes, she and Becky went inside. Her niece picked up a small basket and they collected the eggs. They worked quietly for a while before Becky spoke.

"Why don't you and Gideon live in the same place?" Becky stretched her neck up to look at Ruth. "Is it because your daughter, Grace, died?"

Ruth blinked a few times. "I suppose that's part of it." She had no plans to divulge her marital issues to a five-year-old and hoped to redirect the conversation, but Becky spoke up again.

"*Mamm* said Grace was beautiful and very smart and *gut* at numbers. *Daed* said a terrible thing happened to her and her *mammi*, but that it was *Gott's* will for them to go to heaven." She cocked her head to one side, frowning. "Do you think so?"

Ruth had spent a long time struggling to accept that Grace's and Mae's deaths were God's will, but she finally had. She learned in her support group that not everyone believed the way the Amish did. Part of Ruth would always be Amish no matter where she lived or what religion she practiced.

"*Ya.* I guess I do."

When the basket was full, they secured the chicken coop and started back to the house, the last place Ruth wanted to go. Becky stopped abruptly, looking up at Ruth again.

"Do you want to see *mei* garden? It's not big like *Mamm's*, but she let me do it by myself."

"I'd love to see your garden."

Ruth carried the basket of eggs, and Becky latched on to her free hand. "Will you tell me about Grace? She is *mei* cousin, right?"

Ruth's first instinct was to shelter the child from the tears that would surely spill. Instead she pictured Grace skipping across the yard and kicking her feet high in the swing to Ruth's right. Talking about Grace would create happy memories of this time with Becky—a winning combination.

"I would love to tell you all about Grace." She smiled down at the precious little girl.

For the next half hour, Ruth sat with her niece in the grass beside Becky's small garden and told her about Grace. Her niece glowed the entire time, asked questions, and laughed at some of Grace's adventures. She especially liked the story about how Grace taught herself to ride a unicycle.

"Her *daed* found the one-wheel bike at a yard sale," Ruth said as she finished the story. "Grace wanted to ride it to school, but she couldn't keep her balance since she had books and a lunchbox." She chuckled. "But it didn't keep her from trying for over a week."

They were both laughing when a white truck turned in the driveway. Ruth's mood sobered right away.

Gideon.

— CHAPTER 4 —

Gideon eyed all the buggies and wondered what he had interrupted. He considered leaving until he saw Ruth and a little girl walking hand in hand toward him. Gideon didn't know the child, but all he could see was Ruth and Grace walking together. He blinked his eyes a few times to clear the image.

He waved toward the line of buggies and the horses tethered to the fence side by side. "I must have come at a bad time."

"Esther and my mother are hosting a group of women to finalize plans for Ben and Annie's wedding. If you've come to talk about the papers, now isn't the best time." Ruth glanced at Becky, who smiled.

"Are you Gideon, Ruth's husband?" The child still held Ruth's hand as her expression dimpled.

Gideon's gaze met the little girl's bright blue eyes. "Yes, I am." It felt odd to admit he was Ruth's husband since they hadn't lived as husband and wife for so long. "And are you Becky?" The child had Esther's features, but he didn't remember Ruth's sister having blonde curls when she was young.

The girl nodded. "That's what I thought. You're handsome like *Aenti* Ruth said."

Gideon glanced at Ruth, but she wouldn't meet his eyes as she blushed.

Becky stood up on her toes and grinned. "*Aenti* Ruth told me all about Grace. I wish I had known her. But she's in heaven with *Gott*."

Gideon loved how Becky's eyes lit up as she talked about Grace. His father changed the subject every time Gideon mentioned Grace's name. The few folks he'd run into since he arrived seemed to steer clear of mentioning Gideon's daughter as well.

"She was very special." He refocused on Ruth, her eyes looking somewhere past him. He regretted her abrupt exit from the cemetery earlier. It wasn't how he'd wanted their first meeting to go. "Grace was very beautiful, like her *mudder*, inside and out."

He was surprised how easily he made the comment. There was no denying that Ruth was attractive, but it was her heart that captured Gideon all those years ago. She was kind and compassionate, helpful but not overbearing, and she was happiest when she was with Grace.

"Do you want to see *mei* garden?" Becky bounced up on her toes again, her grin bringing out her dimples again.

Gideon started to answer, but activity on the front porch caught their attention. A bunch of women poured out of the house and started down the porch steps. Some were smiling and whispering. Gideon recognized most of the ladies, and they all greeted him on the way to their buggies. Esther and Ruth's mother waved from the porch as the buggies headed down the drive, then walked slowly toward Gideon.

"It's *gut* to see you, Gideon." Esther wrapped her arms around his neck as he told her it was nice to see her too. "I see you've met Becky," Esther said after she eased away.

"Yeah, I missed her this morning. She was out running errands with Amos. She's a beautiful little girl." Gideon smiled. It wasn't just Becky's blonde hair, dimply cheeks, and bright eyes that brought forth the compliment. The little girl had what he and Ruth used to call "the light"—it was a term they coined when they were dating and described a person who seemed to shine with goodness through the grace of God.

Gideon saw it in Ruth when she was a little girl. She admitted to seeing it in him, too, when they were teenagers. After he and Ruth married and Grace was born, he could still remember the way Ruth held Grace in her arms for the first time and said, "Look, Gideon. She has the light."

Gideon saw only a hint of that light in Ruth earlier today. He wondered if she saw any at all when she looked at him.

Ruth and Esther's mother stepped forward next and gave Gideon a quick and gentle hug. He'd never been close to Judith, but mostly because she was a quiet woman who seemed most comfortable at her husband's side. Gideon remembered Ruth being like that with him when they were dating and even early into their marriage.

Over time, love changes and grows. Maybe Judith and David had gone full circle after raising their family and were back in the same place they started, happiest at each other's sides.

When Grace came along, Gideon and Ruth recaptured some of the euphoria of a new couple and also became a triangle of love. They were happiest when the three of them were together. When the triangle broke, Ruth and Gideon couldn't seem to find their way back to the couple they were before.

Esther touched Becky on the shoulder. "Come along, Becky." Esther glanced knowingly at Ruth and offered a smile to her sister.

Becky waved as Esther and her mother walked with her back toward the house.

After they were inside, Gideon ran his hand over his beard, with no clue what to say to Ruth. He'd already hurt her feelings by letting her assume he was seeing someone. And he was, but he'd only been out with Cheryl a few times, so he wasn't sure that qualified as seeing someone. Cheryl knew he was married but had been separated from his wife for a long time. Maybe he was just trying to justify the way he was drawn to Ruth right now?

"I'm surprised you haven't shaved your beard." She raised a hand to her forehead, squinting to block the sun. Gideon stepped sideways, putting her in his shadow.

"I thought about it." He shrugged. "But I've had it so long, I just . . ." He'd held on to some of his Amish beliefs, and, in truth, it would feel wrong to shave.

"Does your lady friend like it?" Ruth folded her hands in front of her, now that the sun was no longer in her eyes.

Gideon hung his head for a couple seconds. If he denied he was spending time with someone else, even if it was only a few dates, not only was it lying, but it would be unfair to Cheryl. He liked her. "No. She doesn't really care for it."

They were quiet. Gideon's eyes were on his feet again as he kicked at the grass, his hands in his pockets. Eventually, he locked eyes with her. "I feel like there are things that need to be said, but you kind of threw me for a loop earlier when you said you didn't think we needed to talk."

She stared at him for a while. "I'll sign the papers, Gideon, so you can get on with your life."

He sighed as he scratched his forehead. "Ruthie, is there a problem with the papers? Is it money? Do you think it should be more?" He shook his head. "I'm confused. We can make any modifications that you want."

She lifted her chin and did that thing she did with her eyes when she was mad. They turned to tiny slits beneath her furrowed eyebrows. "Gideon, I wouldn't even know what to change. I know very little about divorce papers."

Gideon could feel his eyes rounding before he blinked them a few times. "What? Divorce? Who said anything about divorce? Is that what you want?" He stepped closer to her, frowning. "Ruthie, did you even open the envelope?"

"No. But I'm sure however you chose to handle things is fine." She shook her head. "I never thought I'd be a divorced woman, but then . . . I never thought . . ."

We'd lose Grace? Or I'd be contemplating a relationship with another woman? Or that we'd be discussing divorce?

"This is none of my business." Ruth chewed her bottom lip. "But are you planning to remarry?"

Gideon was still reeling from the mention of divorce. "Let's get back to the papers . . ." He grinned slightly. "That would be the agreement you need to sign to put the house on the market."

Ruth raised both eyebrows. "It's not divorce papers?"

Gideon shook his head. "No. And, even if it was, I wouldn't have given them to you at the cemetery. The agreement needs your signature, but if you think I've priced the house too low, we can talk about it. And, do we want to add electricity before we sell it? I wrote a list of notes." He paused, trying to read her expression, thinking he saw a little relief when she took a deep breath.

"I'll look over your notes." Ruth lowered her head as she folded her arms across her chest, then sighed before she looked back at him. "But is divorce something we need to talk about too?" She eyed him up and down, then gestured between them. "Look at us. We aren't Amish, and most of the time, I still don't feel completely *Englisch*. I don't even believe in divorce."

When she looked back at him, tears were in her eyes, and Gideon's emotions bubbled to the surface. He thought about their time at the cemetery earlier this afternoon, the bond he felt just holding her hand as they visited his mother and Grace. Now they were back to being strangers and talking about divorce. He wanted to know what life had been like for Ruth the last five years.

"Maybe we do all of this in baby steps. It's been a long time since we've seen each other. We visited our daughter today." He paused to swallow back the lump forming in his throat. "And we need to sell the house and tie up any loose ends. I think we still have a couple hundred dollars in an old savings account at the bank."

She nodded.

"And to answer your question, no. I'm not planning to remarry."

"Not yet," she said as she dropped her arms to her side. "But I agree that we can shelve any talk about divorce until we get these other things taken care of."

Gideon couldn't stand it anymore. His heart hammered against his chest as he blurted, "Are you seeing someone?"

"No."

He breathed a sigh of relief, even though her answer was curt enough for him to read between the lines. She was insinuating that she had remained faithful and he hadn't. When she didn't elaborate, he wondered how much of the last five years she would be willing to share with him.

"Do you want to go on a picnic with me tomorrow? We could go down to Pequea Creek." He raised a shoulder and dropped it slowly. "It's peaceful there. It isn't supposed to be too hot. We could look over the papers and . . . talk."

Ruth ran a hand along the back of her neck as she twisted her mouth back and forth. "Ok. I'll bring the food." She smiled a little. "If left up to you or your father to feed us, I fear the outcome."

Gideon chuckled, welcoming the shift in the conversation. "You have a point. Pick you up at eleven?"

Ruth nodded, then tilted her head to one side. "Could we bring Becky with us? I'd like to get to know my niece while I'm here."

Ruth was setting boundaries. With Becky present, the conversation couldn't stray beyond readying the house to sell and maybe a few details about how they'd each lived since leaving Lancaster County. They wouldn't be able to venture into territory they weren't ready for yet.

"I'd like that. I'd enjoy getting to know Becky too."

Ruth smiled a little, but the light she once held was barely visible. "She's a lovely child."

Gideon finally offered a quick wave before he started toward his truck. "See you tomorrow." He was a little fearful Ruth would change her mind if he stayed much longer.

He wondered if she'd made the connection about Pequea Creek.

-◄◄◄-

When Ruth walked back in the house, her mother stood from where she'd been sitting on the couch. "Did you have a nice talk with Gideon?"

Ruth kicked off her shoes by the front door like she'd been doing since she arrived. The old habit came as naturally as slipping back into the Pennsylvania *Deitsch* dialect.

"I guess it went pretty good, all things considered." It was silly not to open the envelope. She could have avoided a lot of heartache if she'd just opened it. Or was that part of God's plan? The thought of divorce ripped at her insides now that she thought it might become a reality.

Her mother nodded, then yawned. "I think it's nap time for me. All this activity today has me worn out." As she passed by Ruth, she touched her on the arm. "Lean on the Lord, *mei dochder*."

Ruth sensed her mother was about to say more, but Esther came down the stairs with Becky right behind her.

"*Danki* for all the help, *Mamm*, especially the food." Esther walked their mother to the door, then turned to Becky. "Tell *Mammi* bye, and it's time for someone else's nap, too, *ya*?"

Becky gave her grandmother a big hug before she left, then the little girl rolled her lip into a pout. "I'm too big for a nap."

Esther chuckled. "You're never too big for a nap. Didn't you just hear your *mammi* say she was going home to take a nap?"

"But I want to talk to *Aenti* Ruth more."

Ruth cleared her throat. "Well, if it's okay with your *mamm*, Gideon and I would like to take you on a picnic with us to Pequea Creek tomorrow." She glanced at her sister who was grinning ear to ear.

"I think that's a wonderful idea." Esther winked at Ruth before she turned to her daughter. "Becky, how does that sound?"

Ruth's niece released a heavy sigh. "That sounds *gut*, but I still don't want to take a nap." Becky huffed before she stomped up the stairs.

"She's so much like you at that age." Ruth plopped down on the couch and smiled. "Overdramatic."

Esther sat in one of the rocking chairs, kicked it into motion, and grinned. "Maybe." Then she began twirling the string on her *kapp*. "Pequea Creek, *ya*?" She let the string go and began tapping a finger to her chin. "Isn't that where you and Gideon had your first kiss?"

Ruth felt her cheeks warming. "Yes. But don't read into that, Esther." Ruth had already read plenty into it on her own, thus the idea to bring Becky along. She wanted to get to know her niece better, but she also worried she might be tempted to relive that first kiss with Gideon. She was still as attracted to him as ever, but kissing him would be out of the question since he had another woman in his life.

"It sure seems significant that he picked that particular place for a picnic." Esther folded her hands in her lap. "Maybe it's not a *gut* idea for Becky to go tomorrow. That won't give you and Gideon much privacy."

"No, we'd both like Becky to go." She frowned at Esther. "We don't need that kind of privacy."

Esther rolled her eyes before she chuckled. "I meant talking, not kissing."

"Well, there are some things I don't think either of us is ready to talk about."

Esther pressed her palms together and brought her folded hands to her chin. "We've all been hoping and praying you two might reconnect. Do you think there's a chance?"

Ruth shook her head. "No. Don't you remember how horrible we were to each other those months that followed Grace's death? I'm not sure we can go back."

"But you were grieving." Esther left the rocker and joined Ruth on the couch. "People say all kinds of things when they're hurting."

Ruth shook her head. "It's not just that. Gideon is seeing someone."

Esther's eyes grew as round as saucers.

"Why do you look so surprised? It's been half a decade." She pointed to her blue jeans. "We clearly aren't Amish anymore."

Esther shrugged, frowning. "I just can't picture Gideon with anyone else."

"I don't know, but those are the kinds of conversations I'm not ready to have. Becky is a breath of fresh air to me, and I think to Gideon too. We'll enjoy spending time with her tomorrow, and she'll help keep the conversation light."

Esther laughed. "Taking Becky might be risky. You never know what will come out of that child's mouth. I hope she hasn't already said anything to make you feel uncomfortable."

"Actually, she's the only one who has not made me feel uncomfortable."

Esther stiffened. "What do you mean?"

"Esther, I love you, but I could tell that everyone in the room today had been asked not to mention Grace." She blinked, but it didn't stop the tears. "Becky is the only one who dared to ask about her when we were by ourselves, and we spent our time talking about Grace. My daughter, Grace. She lived for ten years, and she will always be a part of my life. It hurts when no one even mentions her, like she never existed."

Esther pulled Ruth into a hug as she started to cry too. "I'm sorry, Ruth. I'm so sorry." She eased away and swiped at her eyes. "I just wanted to make your stay as pain free as possible. I thought talking about her might upset you too much."

"Not talking about her upsets me. In Florida, I talk about her to anyone who will listen. But they didn't know her the way people here did." Ruth sniffled, then shook her head. "It's not your fault. I know you were just trying to do what you thought best, and *Mamm* and *Daed* too."

"I was also worried that spending too much time with Becky might cause you heartache too." She leaned her head back against the couch and closed her eyes. "I miss Grace, too, and I still think about her every day. I see her in things Becky does, and it makes me miss her so much." She turned to face Ruth. "I can't imagine how it must be for you."

"Like I said, Becky is a breath of fresh air. She's a beautiful child, and I love sharing stories about Grace with her. I want to always remember everything about her." She paused and locked eyes with her sister. "One of my many regrets is that I don't have any pictures of Grace. I know it wasn't allowed, but I'd do anything to see her face again. With each passing year, her image slips a little further away. What happens if it disappears forever?"

Esther pulled her knees to her chest and wrapped her arms around her legs like she did when they were kids. "It won't. And I want to talk about Grace too."

Ruth leaned an ear toward the stairs. "Is Becky awake? I thought I heard something."

Esther smiled. "If I rush up there right now, she'll pretend to be asleep, but she won't be."

"Just like you used to do." Ruth knocked her shoulder playfully against her little sister's.

"Do you remember the time Grace found those baby rabbits? The mother was nowhere around and she brought them all home?"

Ruth laughed. "Remember? They were so small we had to feed them with little droppers every few hours. It was like having four premature babies to tend to." She loved that recollection. "Grace was so dedicated. She would have made a wonderful mother."

And from there, Esther began to recall more and more stories about Grace, some that Ruth didn't even know about. Ruth packed each one into her memory bank to take back to Florida with her. This was what she'd hoped for.

— CHAPTER 5 —

Gideon pulled into Esther and Amos's driveway. Ruth and Becky were sitting on the porch steps with a picnic basket between them. Gideon's mind drifted back to when he was sixteen and on his first picnic with Ruth. They had their whole lives to look forward to, and he still remembered that first kiss like it happened yesterday.

He opened the truck door and walked toward them. Ruth stood, toting the basket. She was wearing a light blue shirt, jeans, white sneakers, and her dark hair flowed well past her waist. Even after all these years, he felt weak at the sight of her.

"Hello, ladies."

"I'm not really a lady." Becky scowled a little, her cheeks dimpling the same way as when she smiled. "I'm a girl."

Gideon squatted down in front of her and grinned. "And a beautiful girl you are. But one day you'll be a beautiful lady."

The child smiled before she twisted in circles, her light-blue dress catching in the wind beneath her black apron. "*Mei mamm* made me a new dress."

Gideon stood. "It's a very pretty dress." He walked around to the passenger side of his truck and opened the door for Ruth, then helped Becky into a booster seat he'd found at his parents' house.

It was a short drive to the creek. Once they parked, Ruth led the way while Gideon followed, picnic basket in one hand and Becky holding on to the other. Gideon might have suggested coming to the creek, but Ruth seemed to be following his lead. She chose the exact spot where they shared their first kiss and frequented throughout their courtship. They brought Grace here countless times as well.

"Is this okay?" Ruth avoided his eyes as she took the picnic basket from him.

"Uh, yeah. This is fine." Gideon didn't want to analyze her intentions. He would focus on the beautiful day the Lord had gifted them. There wasn't a cloud in the sky, and a cool breeze rustled the leaves as it blew through and met with the babbling creek. Ruth spread out a red-and-white checkered blanket, then sat and unpacked the basket.

Gideon instinctively followed Becky. He remembered how Grace would get too close to the water's edge. It wasn't deep in this area, but falling in would yield some nasty scrapes from the rocks barely peaking above the ripples of water.

"Careful," he said as he reached for her hand.

They sat on a rock facing the creek. "*Mamm* and *Daed* brought me here once for a picnic too. It's pretty here."

Gideon gazed at her profile, and once again he saw Grace. Esther and Ruth looked a lot alike, so maybe it wasn't surprising that he kept seeing Grace in Becky. Or maybe he just wanted to see Grace. For months after she was gone, he'd dreamed about her. Each time, she was happy and smiling, and Gideon tried to hold on to that image through the darkest days.

"Everything's ready." Ruth had the food spread out in front of her, and her feet were tucked beneath her as she smiled at them.

Gideon had taken plenty of pictures since he moved away. He wanted to take out his cell phone and capture this moment, the way Ruth's hair blew free in the breeze, her smile. The last time he saw his wife, her face was contorted into an expression that didn't even resemble the woman she was. This was his Ruthie, a postcard vision of the way things used to be. Then he glanced at Becky, their niece, and wondered if it would be possible to cherish the old memories but also make new ones.

-≪≪-

After they bowed their heads in silent prayer, Ruth helped Becky spread chicken salad on her two pieces of bread. Ruth had gotten up early and found all the ingredients, and Esther baked an apple pie the day before so Ruth snagged three slices.

"This is the best chicken salad ever," Becky said with a mouthful. After she swallowed she asked, "What's different about yours? *Mamm's* doesn't taste the same."

Gideon chuckled. "There's a secret ingredient in it." He picked up his own sandwich and pretended to study it, squinting and holding it at eye level. "At least, that's what your mother tells everyone."

Ruth froze, even stopped chewing, as she wondered if Gideon realized his blunder.

Becky giggled. "She's not *mei mudder*, she's *mei aenti*."

Gideon's cheeks turned a rosy shade of red. "Uh, yeah." He looked at Ruth, his eyebrows furrowed. "Sorry about that."

Ruth finally finished chewing and swallowed. "It's fine." Becky obviously reminded Gideon of Grace too.

"What's the secret ingredient?" Becky's eyes sparkled with curiosity.

"Well . . ." Ruth tapped a finger to her chin. "It wouldn't be a secret if I told you, now would it?"

Gideon laughed again, and the sound of his voice melted away the tension that had built up about this trip. Even though she'd looked forward to it, she worried that at any minute things might explode. Ruth believed that part of the reason they'd split up was because the sight of each other reminded them too much of Grace.

"She won't even tell me her secret ingredient." Gideon grinned as he rolled his eyes.

Becky smiled. "And you're her husband."

Ruth lifted her eyes to Gideon's, but he looked somewhere over her shoulder, lost in . . . what? Memories? Regrets? Thoughts of Grace?

Becky set her sandwich on the paper plate. "If you're married, why don't you live together?"

It was an innocent question, but Ruth wanted to keep things light today. She looked at Gideon and hoped he'd answer the child in a way she could understand. But he had just put the last bite of sandwich in his mouth and merely raised an eyebrow at her.

"We just don't." Ruth forced a smile and tried to sound casual as she eased a plate with pie closer to Becky, eager to steer the conversation in another direction. "Your *mamm* made this yesterday."

Becky's doe eyes found Ruth. She blinked several times, a look of confusion on her face. Ruth thought about what Esther said, how you never knew what would come out of Becky's mouth. Or any five-year-old for that matter. Ruth needed to grab the reigns of this conversation.

She set down her plate and pressed her palms together, smiling. "You know what? I'm only going to be here a week, so I want to hear all about you. What are your favorite things to do? What's your favorite color? Or anything else you'd like to share with us."

Becky put the rest of her sandwich on her plate and pulled the slice of pie closer. Ruth should probably tell her to finish her sandwich first, the way she'd had to do with Grace, but redirecting the conversation seemed more important.

Becky shrugged, not looking at Ruth or Gideon. She forked a bite of pie then slowly raised it to her mouth, her eyebrows knitted as if she was in deep thought.

Ruth braced herself for more questions about she and Gideon. The wait seemed to go on forever, but Becky finally said, "Blue is my favorite color."

"Mine too." Ruth pointed to her dark-blue blouse and then to Becky's light-blue dress. She looked at Gideon. "It was Grace's favorite color too."

Gideon genuinely smiled, and Ruth was happy to see that he was open to talking about Grace.

"So, I remember you being named Rebecca," Gideon said after wiping his mouth with a napkin. "Do you always remember being called Becky?"

The child let out an exaggerated sigh before dramatically throwing her head back. Once she straightened, she sighed again and said, "I want to be called Beatrice."

Ruth bit her lip to stifle a smile, then she glanced at Gideon.

"Beatrice?" Gideon scratched his forehead.

Ruth was still getting used to seeing him without the cropped bangs he'd always had. Now his dark hair was combed to the side. But when the wind blew, it fell forward, resembling the cut of the man she remembered.

"Why do you want to be called Beatrice?" Gideon chuckled. "I don't think that's an Amish name." He looked at Ruth. "Is it?"

Ruth shrugged. "If it is, I've never known anyone Amish who has it. Where did you even hear that name?"

"I think a bird whispered it in my ear." Becky covered her mouth with both hands and giggled. She lowered her hands slowly, looking back and forth between Ruth and Gideon. She laughed so hard it was contagious, and within seconds Gideon and Ruth were guffawing as if they'd just heard the funniest joke ever.

The more they laughed, the more Becky giggled. And before Ruth knew it, tears of joy pooled in the corners of her eyes from the gut-busting laughter she hadn't experienced in a long time.

There is nothing more glorious than the laughter of a child.

When she finally caught her breath, she looked at Gideon. He'd stopped laughing, but Ruth recognized his expression. It was original to Gideon, a look that came into his eyes, the way his jaw twitched, the manner in which his mouth was slightly open. It was the look he'd given her every time he wanted to make love.

— CHAPTER 6 —

Gideon listened as Becky—or Beatrice, as she preferred—rattled off more of her favorite colors, how she could stand on her head for ten minutes, how she ate frog legs one time and jumped like a frog for days, and a host of other stories that had Ruth in stitches, laughing so hard, she had both arms wrapped around her middle.

Gideon laughed along with her, but he was distracted by seeing his Ruth again, the Ruth he remembered from before the accident. His longing for her caught him off guard. But it wasn't just a physical desire. Ruth's light seemed to grow brighter the more she laughed. He wondered if she would treasure these new memories the way he hoped to.

"Beatrice, you have done some amazing things." Ruth finally caught her breath and looked at Gideon with an expression he remembered. If he had to label the look he would call it joyful. A familiar twinkle in her eyes lit up her face when she smiled. She seemed to be feeling something, too, their eyes connecting more than once.

For the next hour, they roamed up and down the shore of the creek, stopping to skim rocks every now and then. Their niece kept them entertained with stories and childish antics.

By the time they headed home, it wasn't long before Princess

Beatrice fell asleep in the booster seat. After Gideon parked his truck and killed the engine, the little one awoke, yawning.

Gideon climbed out of the driver's side while Ruth helped Becky out and set her safely on the ground, then closed the passenger door.

"I need to use the bathroom." Becky yawned again, then waved before she rushed across the front yard and into the house.

"Thanks for the great meal," Gideon said as he walked around the truck to join Ruth. The creek seemed to take them back in time. Now they were stepping back into reality. But he wasn't ready for the day to end. And he wasn't looking forward to the next item on his agenda: facing their old house.

"It was a good day." Gideon swallowed hard and pushed away thoughts of intimacy between him and Ruth, even though his eyes kept drifting to her lips.

"*Ya*, it was a *gut* day." She smiled.

"It's easy to slip back into the dialect, *ya?*" Gideon's eyes found her lips again. He forced himself to look away, kicking at the grass with one of his Nikes. "Do you ever think of coming back here to live?"

Ruth shrugged. "Sometimes. What about you?"

Gideon lowered his gaze, thought for a few seconds, then looked up at her. "Sometimes."

Ruth had pulled her hair up in a ponytail again, but it was long enough for the breeze to blow strands across her face. She brushed the loose tresses away. He wished he could remove the band holding her hair, let it fall loose, and run his fingers through it. "How long will you be here?"

"I'm planning to stay for a week. We'll have the reunion Saturday, then I fly out on Tuesday."

Gideon nodded as he looked at the ground, then forced a smile. "I better go." He paused as dread churned in his stomach. "I'm going to the house, to see what needs to be done to sell it. After you read the listing agreement, let me know what you think."

He turned and walked back around to the driver's side of the truck.

-≪≪≪-

Ruth nodded as she chewed her bottom lip for a few seconds. "I should help you. With the house."

She had planned to make that part of her recovery process while she was here—visiting their former home. But she wasn't sure if it would be easier going alone or with Gideon. If she went alone, she was sure to melt in a puddle on the floor and stay there for hours crying. With Gideon, she'd at least try to corral her emotions.

Shaking his head, Gideon sighed. "You don't have to do that."

Ruth wasn't sure if he didn't want her to go with him or if he was just being kind. "I came here to see my family and friends, but I also need to face a few things while I'm here, and the house is one of them. It's not fair for you to do the work alone. I should help."

Gideon looped his thumbs in the belt loops of his jeans and rocked back on his heels once. "It might be easier on both of us if we do it together."

"Maybe." Ruth raised her eyes to his as she thought about their time together at the cemetery, the bond they still shared. She glanced over her shoulder. "I need to run in the house and let Esther know what I'm doing."

Ruth returned a few minutes later. Her sister had been way too happy that she was spending more time with Gideon. She hoped Esther didn't get her hopes up about them getting back together. There was just too much water under that bridge.

It was a quiet ride to the house. And that was okay. Gideon surely had the same apprehensions she had. What would it be like to see their furniture covered up, their possessions packed, and reminders of how they ran away? Gideon packed almost everything since he left two months after Ruth. Esther said it didn't look like he'd taken much. Ruth understood. She left with very little too.

The yard was recently mowed, but the flowerbeds were barren of blooms and full of weeds. She recalled the plush greenery mixed with the colorful flowers she used to plant every spring.

Her heart pounded like a bass drum as she hesitated on the porch steps. Gideon unlocked the front door with a key he pulled from his pocket, and Ruth lifted a foot, heavy as lead, and stepped onto the porch.

As the door creaked open, Ruth prayed something positive would come from this visit, that somehow it would prove to be a part of their healing. The musty smell of mold hit her hard as she stepped across the threshold, her feet crunching on dried leaves that must have blown in through the broken window. Esther hadn't mentioned a broken window, but her sister also said she hadn't been to the house in almost a month. She meant to clean right before Ruth arrived, but Becky had gotten sick last week.

With no electricity, and the predictable spring rains, Ruth wasn't surprised the mold was already starting.

Rays of sunshine streamed in through the windows, lighting up the living room where she and Gideon had played with Grace, held family devotions, and where she taught Grace how to knit. It seemed like another lifetime ago but was so familiar that Ruth wanted to go get a broom and begin cleaning. When she was done, she'd make supper for her family. But that life was gone. All that remained were memories of a shattered life that needed repairing as much as the house itself.

Gideon opened one of the windows and a breeze sailed through the room. Ruth followed suit and opened another window in the living room. They were delaying the inevitable.

Grace's room.

Ruth suddenly wished she hadn't come with Gideon. How silly she'd been to think she would be able to contain her emotions, whether Gideon was here or not. She made her way to the kitchen and ran her hand along the white counter, pulling back a thick layer of black dust. As she leaned against it, she eyed the table with six chairs and remembered how she and Gideon had wanted at least four children. God had seen fit to give them only one.

They were all here on borrowed time, but she never could have imagined when Grace was born that their time together would only be ten years. She and Gideon tried to have more children prior to Grace's accident. The doctor said there was no reason they couldn't conceive, but it never happened.

Gideon sidled up next to her, his hip brushing against hers as he leaned against the counter beside her. "We had a lot of good times here."

Ruth nodded, overly aware of Gideon's arm as he pressed it atop the counter behind her, bringing himself even closer to her. She wanted to latch on to his T-shirt, squeeze it in her hand, and bury her face in his chest. To have his arms around her, comforting her. But she didn't move.

"It's not as bad as I thought." Gideon walked to the sink, leaned over, and lifted the window pane. "Although, I don't really know what I thought. Please thank Esther for checking on the place."

He sounded as lost as Ruth. "Esther felt bad that she hadn't been by in a month, and I'm sure she didn't know the window was broken. I'm surprised the guy who mows didn't tell someone. Or maybe he didn't notice. If we let the house air out overnight, we could start cleaning tomorrow." She'd just committed herself to another visit.

Gideon nodded before he walked back into the living room. Their brown-and-white striped couch was covered with a sheet, and so was the rocking chair in the corner where Ruth had rocked Grace to sleep so many times. Boxes were stacked everywhere, and Ruth thought about how awful it must have been for Gideon, doing the task alone.

Gideon slowed as he looked left toward the door that led to their bedroom, then right at the staircase. After a few seconds, he moved to the left, inching open the closed bedroom door.

Taking tiny steps, she followed him into the room. She pictured the pastel wedding quilt in shades of blue, yellow, pink, and pale green that used to cover their bed and was now in one of the boxes that lined the walls. Her eyes drifted around the room as she eyed all that was strange and familiar, her feelings mixing into an emotion Ruth couldn't define.

Gideon turned around to face her, a look in his eyes as if he might pull her onto the bed. He walked toward her instead, and as he neared, the expression she thought she recognized wasn't sexual, but desperate and wild. His eyes watered.

"I'm so sorry for everything I did after Grace died, for everything I said, and"—he took in a deep breath—"and for everything I didn't do. I wasn't there for you at all."

Ruth was already shaking her head. "No, Gideon. I was equally to blame for the way things went. I've wanted to apologize to you for years, for being the one who left first, who abandoned you. I just didn't know how . . ." She waved a hand around the bedroom. "I left you with all of this to handle, along with your grief, and I'm sorry."

Gideon's bottom lip quivered. "As head of the household, it was my job to take care of you."

Ruth lifted a hand to her chest, her heart thumping wildly. Her lip trembled as she fought the tears pooling in her eyes. Right now, Gideon seemed to need forgiveness and understanding more than she did. She wondered if he'd had any sort of counseling or a support group to lean on.

"I know we were raised that way, that the man is the head of the household. But, Gideon, our daughter died. We couldn't take care of ourselves, much less each other."

He pulled her into his arms, his beard brushing against her cheek as he held her face against his chest, shaking so hard his tears were turning to sobs.

After a while, he eased her away, cupped her cheeks, and gently wiped away her tears. Then he brushed strands of loose hair from her face, his hands on her cheeks, his mouth close enough to kiss her. Ruth longed for his touch, but just when she thought he might kiss her, he only pulled her to his chest again, his hand on the back of her neck. Ruth wrapped her arms around him, clutching the back of his T-shirt, both of them crying.

Gideon kissed Ruth on the top of her head, which only made her cry harder. And they hadn't even been to Grace's room yet.

— CHAPTER 7 —

Gideon wasn't sure how much more he could take today. Ruth's flushed cheeks and tearstained face implied the same. But as they stood outside Grace's room hand in hand, Gideon squeezed, hoping to give her the strength he hadn't been able to five years ago or five minutes ago.

He looked at her, and she nodded. Gideon grasped the doorknob and inched the door open. The sun had begun its descent, and its light and warmth filled the room. Dust bunnies danced atop the late-afternoon sunrays that filled the room. Gideon fought tears again as he remembered boxing up his daughter's things.

"I'm sorry you had to do this alone." Ruth pulled away from him and looked around the room. A tear rolled down her cheek. As in the other rooms, the furniture was covered with sheets, and boxes were along the wall.

"It's okay." Maybe it was the one thing that he'd spared his wife from.

Gideon closed his eyes and pictured Grace's room as it had been. Some of her clothes hung from hooks along the rack on the far side of the room. Her rocking chair with her favorite faceless doll was in the corner. The bedspread Ruth had sewn and surprised Grace with on her tenth birthday was sage green with an ivory lace ruffle that met the wood floor on three sides.

Gideon sat on the bed and hoped he could keep his emotions in check.

Ruth shuffled to the rack where Grace's clothes used to be, then she circled the room, touching the sheet-covered dresser, moving to the rocking chair, running her hand over the white covering. Gideon couldn't stop watching her every movement, and even with her back to him, he knew she was also remembering the way their daughter's room had looked.

She turned to face him. "Sometimes I-I forget what she looks like." She hung her head, shaking it. "What kind of mother would forget her child's face?"

Gideon offered a weak smile. "I see her every time I look at you."

⫷⫷⫷⫷⫷

Ruth's eyes clung to his. "I see her when I look at you too." She looked away. "Back then, it was just too hard."

Gideon walked to where she was standing near the window. "And now?"

Ruth held his gaze. "I still see her when I look at you, in your eyes."

"Maybe it's the reflection of yourself you see." He smiled a little, which was nice to see again after the emotional afternoon they'd had.

Ruth froze in time, longing to move forward and terrified of moving backward. "We were so messed up during that time." She kept her eyes on his, aware of the vulnerability he'd shown today and not wanting him to fall backward either. "But time does have a way of helping people look at things differently. And now, when I see her in your eyes, I don't want to run away. I want to embrace the good memories and make new ones."

Gideon nodded. "I went to counseling for a while, and it helped. But I've always felt like I needed closure for two things. Asking you to forgive me and coming back here."

Ruth was glad to hear that Gideon had gone to a therapist. Her support group had helped her survive those first months in Florida and steadied her when the grief became overwhelming. "Me too. And now, here we are, facing the last two things on our emotional bucket lists."

He smiled as he stared out the window. "Do you remember when Grace was in her second year of school, and she carried a wounded bird into the classroom in her apron pocket?"

Ruth chuckled. "Yes. The bird got loose and all the students were screaming trying to catch it. I can still remember hearing about it for weeks later."

They were quiet for a few moments, both seemingly lost in their memories.

Gideon cleared his throat. "I was thinking we'd sell the house with the furniture in it and just remove our personal belongings." He glanced around the room. "We'll have to go through these boxes."

Ruth walked over to the rocker. She pulled the sheet off and was surprised to see Grace's doll sitting there. "I'd like to have the rocking chair in our bedroom if it's okay with you. Or I can take this one if you want the other one."

He eyed the chair for a few moments. Or maybe it was the doll he was staring at. "I'm fine taking this one. It seems the rocking chairs should stay in the family since they belonged to each of our grandmothers."

For a few seconds they sounded like a normal husband and wife just making decisions together. Ruth reminded herself that wasn't the case as she picked up Grace's doll and held it to her chest.

"I can think of one person who might enjoy this doll, someone who would treasure it even as she gets older. And I'm sure there are some other things in the nightstand. Remember that little red suitcase Grace kept under the bed with her trinkets in it?"

Gideon smiled. "I think Becky would like the doll, too, and yes, how could I forget the little red suitcase."

She walked toward him and as they faced each other, Ruth still clutching the doll, she gazed into his eyes as a warm feeling swept over her.

They'd been so in love. Then, poof. Gone. Everything. Yet something was bubbling to the surface between them.

Ruth got on her knees by the bed and pulled out the red suitcase, clumps of dust and dirt coming out with it. She coughed, then hauled it onto the bed. She'd found the piece of luggage in her grandmother's attic when she was about Grace's age and later gave it to her daughter.

"Grace said she kept her private things in here. I almost feel like we're trespassing. But we have to know what's in it, right? I mean, there might be other things Becky might like, or that we want to keep." Ruth sat on the bed, brushing the dust off the suitcase. Gideon sat on the other side of the suitcase.

"Yeah, I think we should open it."

Neither moved. They each rested a hand on top of the worn piece of luggage. Finally, Gideon popped the latch and slowly lifted the lid.

Ruth carefully reached for a piece of white paper with three stick figures drawn on it, two tall, one small in the middle. Smiling, she said, "I remember when she drew this in her first year of school." She ran a finger along the sketch. "I never knew she kept it."

"Look at this." Gideon chuckled as he held up a ticket from the county fair. "I remember this day like it was yesterday."

"That was a great day." Ruth reached for a small teddy bear. "You won her this shooting those play guns filled with water." She laughed. "You weren't very good. It probably cost you twenty dollars to win a five-dollar bear."

"Be nice." He winked at her. "Those guns were on wobbly stands, and probably that way on purpose."

Ruth raised a shoulder and dropped it slowly. "If you say so, dear." Her chest tightened as she raised her eyes to Gideon's. "Sorry. Old habit."

She'd always used the endearment playfully, and she was surprised how easily it slipped out. She lowered her gaze and set the teddy bear aside. "I think I'd like to keep this, if that's okay with you." When she looked at him again, he nodded.

They shuffled through more of Grace's keepsakes, laughing, remembering, and treasuring each of their daughter's prized possessions.

"This feels good. Talking about her. Remembering. Laughing." Ruth shook her head. "Maybe we should have done this a long time ago."

Gideon looked around the room before he stood. "Grace would want us to go on with our lives. She wouldn't want us to be sad forever."

A phone rang in the living room with an unfamiliar ringtone, so she knew it was Gideon's.

"It's probably a good thing it rang, or I might have forgotten it."

Ruth glanced around Grace's room, then took the doll and followed Gideon downstairs to the living room. He chuckled. "Now I just have to find it."

Instead of looking for his phone when they reached the bottom of the stairs, he turned back toward Ruth. She didn't jump when he cupped one of her cheeks, looking at her as if seeing her for the first time. He lifted his other hand to her face as well.

"You are still as beautiful as ever." He whispered the words as he tilted his head to one side. It had taken five years and a visit to their daughter's room for her and Gideon to reconnect emotionally, but Ruth couldn't deny the physical attraction still between them. They'd loved each other deeply for so many years.

She didn't move when Gideon's hands eased her closer. Ruth longed to feel his mouth on hers, a taste of the intimacy they'd shared as husband and wife. But just before his lips brushed against hers, Gideon's phone beeped. It was sitting on the back of the couch close enough for Ruth to see the screen. Instinctively, her eyes darted toward the sound, and before she could look away her mind registered the words on the display.

Missed call from Cheryl. And below that was a text message. I miss you.

Ruth's chest tightened and the doll slipped from her hand. Now she had a name to put with Gideon's girlfriend, and she took a step away from him as he picked up the phone and glanced at the text. Ruth had almost done something horrible. She'd nearly kissed a man she no longer had a right to be with. Married or not, Gideon was involved with someone else.

Gideon looked up and walked toward her, his eyes widening in false innocence. "Ruth—"

"No." Ruth shook her head, then she picked up the faceless doll. "You don't owe me any explanations." She bit her lip until she thought it might bleed. "I'm going to walk back to Esther's." She turned to leave, but Gideon grabbed her arm.

"It's not what you think. It's only been a few dates."

She cringed at the word dates and fought the vision of Gideon in someone else's arms. She shook loose of him and hurried to the front door. She didn't turn around, even when he called out to her.

She'd barely made it out the door before she started to run.

Then the tears fell full force.

— CHAPTER 8 —

G ideon sat in his truck and stared at the house where he, Grace, and Ruth had made so many happy memories. Then he looked down at his phone, thinking the timing couldn't have been any worse. Was that God's way of telling him that he and Ruth couldn't go backward? Or maybe it was a reminder that, while Gideon wasn't committed to Cheryl, he'd kissed her, more than once. He had only talked to her once since he arrived in Lancaster County to let her know he was safe. In Cheryl's voice mail, she said she missed him.

He'd been about to kiss Ruth. Then how would he have felt about himself, especially after seeing Cheryl's text and hearing her voice mail? He started his truck and slowly pulled out of the driveway.

By the time Gideon returned to his father's house, he was barely able to contain his emotions, which were all over the place and strangling him. When he walked inside, his father straightened in his recliner and lowered the newspaper.

"How did things go today?" Gideon's father removed his reading glasses.

Gideon pulled off his shoes at the door, although he didn't see what the point was. The place was a wreck. A little shoe dirt would go unnoticed.

He walked to the couch, sat down, and sighed. "As good as could be expected, I guess." It had been a long day packed with too much emotion. He and Ruth should have eased into things, maybe the cemetery today, visiting the house tomorrow, and so on. It was no wonder he was on emotional overload.

Since he'd been home, he thought about his mother a lot, too, and how much he missed her. Being back in the house he'd grown up in gave him comfort in some ways. Seeing his mother's trinkets and things around the house brought back fond memories. But seeing how the house and his father had deteriorated made him regret he hadn't visited sooner. Was this the way his father had processed his grief, by just shutting down? Would Gideon have ended up like his dad if he'd stayed?

His renewed affections for Ruth were causing his insides to swirl with confusion. He took a deep breath and tried to focus on the good parts of the day, like the picnic with Becky and facing some of his fears. He'd been afraid to visit his daughter's grave. Did God's perfect timing have something to do with Ruth being there? He thought about the not-so-perfect timing of Cheryl's call and sighed again.

He forced himself to push on and recalled the joy he'd found being with Ruth, laughing and sharing stories about Grace. And Becky had also been a bright light in the day. But even those precious moments were clouded with thoughts of Ruth and how she ran from him.

"I'm going to leave tomorrow." Gideon leaned against the couch and folded his arms across his chest. "I'm not going to stay for the reunion."

His father stared at him. Gideon waited for him to talk him out of it. "I thought you said it went as *gut* as could be expected."

Gideon shook his head before he ran a hand through his hair. "Yeah, well, I don't know what I expected." He'd known it would be hard to visit Grace and the house. What he hadn't anticipated was his rekindled feelings for Ruth.

In some ways, things had changed—geography, their jobs, they drove cars, and they lived with electricity. Their grief would always be present, but it seemed more manageable now. But they were the same in a lot of ways too. They'd both carried their faith with them and stayed true to the belief that everything is God's will, even the most difficult experience of their lives.

Gideon could spin it a dozen different ways. Too much time had gone by to try to reclaim his life with Ruth. Had she wanted that? Not only did she think he was coming here to put the house on the market and visit his mother and Grace but was she hoping for a reconciliation after all these years? He shook his head and tried to clear his mind.

"I'm going to pay someone to clean up the house and do the repairs. I'm not sure it's healthy for me to be here." Gideon thought about how Ruth had left him to pack up everything five years ago. Now he'd be leaving her to go through it all. He didn't feel good about that, but being around her and not being able to be with her the way he wanted to would be torture.

His father stared at him with questioning eyes. Part of Gideon wanted his father to talk him out of the decision. Probably just as much as Gideon wanted to scream at his father and tell him to start living again. But there seemed to be an unspoken respect that allowed a man to grieve however he saw fit.

Gideon turned around and shook his head. "There's nothing here for me." He started walking toward the front door. He needed to go outside and call Cheryl. Maybe if he heard her voice, he'd realize he missed her, too, and that going back to Ohio would allow him to see where things were headed with her.

"I'm here," his father said softly.

Gideon slowly turned around, and the glassy-eyed look in his father's eyes was almost enough to make him stay. "I'm sorry. I promise I'll visit more." He wasn't sure if it was a lie or not.

The old man's bottom lip quivered.

Gideon wrote to his father often, checked to make sure he was keeping doctor appointments and taking his medication. He raised his shoulders, held them there for a while, then dropped them until his arms sagged on either side of him. It wasn't until he processed the thought that he had to admit how little he had done for his father.

"I'm sorry I haven't done more." Gideon decided this day was never going to end, and the roller coaster of emotions caused a heaviness in his chest. As guilt about his father crept into the mix, he sat down on the couch, leaned his elbows to his knees, and held his head in his hands.

His father pressed his lips together as his chest rose and he took a deep breath. "I enjoy the letters from you and Ruth, but I would still like to see you more."

Gideon's mouth fell open. He should have known Ruth would keep in touch with her father-in-law even if she didn't visit.

"I'll visit more often." Gideon scratched his forehead, his eyes on his shoes, then he looked up at his father and knew that he wasn't lying to the man. He would come to Lancaster County regularly.

"The last thing I want is for you to end up like me. But you are well on your way if you don't do a little soul searching while you're here."

"Soul searching? I came here to visit my daughter's grave. I forced myself to go into her room today, to go through her things. I spent the day with the woman I still love." He looked up at his father, who raised an eyebrow. "How can that even be true after so much time has passed?"

His father looped his thumbs beneath his suspenders. "Why

can't it be true? With the exception of me and your *mudder*, I don't think I've ever known two people more in *leib* than you and Ruth. Even after twelve years of marriage, you carried on like giddy teenagers. You might be able to make a *gut* life for yourself where you live now." He held up a finger. "But is it the best life, the one *Gott* planned for you?"

Gideon's heart hurt on so many levels. No wonder he hadn't come home sooner. He looked at the ceiling, filled his lungs with musty air, then blew it out slowly. "*Daed* . . ." He spoke softly. "Are you living the life God planned out for you? Not going to church. Bitter all of the time." He waved a hand around the living room. "Living like this."

His father stared at him for several moments. "*Nee*, Gideon. I am not. And that is my burden to bear. But a parent doesn't want to see his or her child end up in such a state." His father hung his head before he looked back up at Gideon, his eyes moist. Then his father left and closed the door to his bedroom behind him.

Gideon just sat there and held his throbbing head. It was too late for him and Ruth, no matter what kind of hormones were acting up when they were around each other. Too much time had gone by. He squeezed his eyes together, and he could see her sitting next to him in Grace's room and the way she ran from him, maybe scared of what she was experiencing, like Gideon.

He reached for his phone when it buzzed. This time he answered Cheryl's call. She'd give him the sense of normalcy he needed right now. Maybe she'd tell him about her day or what she was making for supper.

And that's pretty much what she did. Then she asked about his day.

"It was hard, but I'm glad I came." He took a deep breath, unsure if that was true. "I've decided to hire someone to get the house ready to sell. I've seen most everyone I need to see, so I'm coming home tomorrow. I don't see a reason to stay for the reunion."

"Are you sure?" Cheryl's voice was sweet and concerned. She really was a good person.

"I'm sure." He squeezed his eyes shut, picturing him and Cheryl eating a pizza in front of the TV soon or going out for a burger. He was craving normalcy, a routine that was less confusing.

He thought about how God gives us pain and sorrow but also gifts us with unexpected and wonderful joy. Gideon had already experienced that. Was God giving him another chance at happiness? Was Gideon running away from it or toward it?

-<<<-

Ruth feigned a stomachache and skipped supper. It wasn't really a lie. Her stomach had been tied in knots since she'd run away from Gideon. All this time, she avoided him because she thought seeing him would be too painful. Now that she'd seen him, he was all she could think about.

When she awoke the next morning, after only a few hours of fitful sleep, she lay in bed for a while in the guest bedroom that had once been hers, Grace's faceless doll tucked in tightly beside her. Yawning, she got up and readied herself for breakfast when she smelled bacon cooking. She carried the doll downstairs, hiding it behind her back when she saw Becky already seated at the table.

"Where's Amos?" Ruth stood in the doorway to the kitchen as Esther flipped bacon.

"He went with two other men this morning to look at a horse." Esther peered over her shoulder and rolled her eyes. "I think the horses we have are fine, but . . ." She shrugged.

"What's behind your back?" Becky grinned up at Ruth from her spot at the table.

"Who me?" Ruth smiled and held the doll out to Becky.

"Was she Grace's?" The little girl's bright eyes widened.

"*Ya*, she was." Then she spoke to Becky in their native dialect and told her where they had gotten the doll and how much Grace loved it.

Becky let out a loud gasp. "I will love her forever."

Ruth reached for a piece of bacon as she slid onto a chair. She silently thanked God for His blessings before she took a bite, glad she had a bit more appetite this morning.

"I feel like your time here is flying by. I wish you could stay longer." Esther nodded at Becky, then looked back at Ruth. "And I want to hear all about yesterday when the time is right."

"Maybe I'll stay a few extra days after the reunion. I don't think it will cost much to change my ticket home." A tinge of guilt wrapped around her. As much as she wanted to spend time with Esther, Becky, and Amos, it was Gideon she wanted to see the most.

It felt like self-torture, which was the reason she ran from him the day before. If he had kissed her, things wouldn't have stopped there. There was still a spark leftover from a passionate marriage, and being with him fanned the flame. Gideon had someone else now, but her desire to see him pulled at her. Maybe she should rethink her decision not to help him clean the house tomorrow. They weren't teenagers, and they should be able to control themselves.

"It would be great if you can stay longer." Esther set a bowl of eggs on the table next to a plate of biscuits, then she sat down, and they all bowed their heads. When Esther looked up, she said softly, "I wish you didn't have to leave at all."

Ruth took a biscuit and put it on her plate, then glanced around the kitchen as she thought of the wonderful memories she had from this house. "My life is very different now."

Esther smiled. "Is it?" She paused to butter a roll. "Aside from your office job and living so far away, what's different about it?"

Ruth widened her eyes as her jaw dropped for a couple of seconds. Didn't her sister see the obvious? "Esther, I have electricity at my apartment. I drive a car. I go to movies. I wear jeans." She recalled the learning curve she'd had when it came to computers and the time she spent learning basic bookkeeping, one of the things Gideon had handled prior to their split. He'd always done construction work, but her husband had also handled the paperwork that went along with running a business.

Esther gave Ruth a gentle smile. "Those are things and circumstances that have changed, but it doesn't mean you've changed." She lifted a hand to her heart. "Inside, I don't think you've changed much at all."

Ruth was pondering her sister's comment when Becky held up the doll. "I'm going to call her Beatrice if that's okay with you." She looked at Ruth.

"Of course. You call her whatever you like." Ruth stood and retrieved her phone from where she'd left it on the kitchen counter. "I'll need to go charge my phone sometime today." She found and opened Google and pulled up the site she was looking for.

"Becky, I decided to look up the name Beatrice since you like it so much. Do you know what it means?"

Becky shook her head.

"It means 'she who makes happy' or 'bringer of joy.'"

Esther smiled. "That's *mei boppli*, someone who makes people happy just with her presence." She leaned over and kissed her daughter.

Ruth waited for the sting she knew would come after the reminder that she can't kiss Grace like that anymore. Instead, there was nothing but joy for Esther and Becky. So many times Ruth had wondered how she would feel if she came back here. She'd never forget Grace, but perhaps time had helped. Time and little girls like Becky and sisters like Esther.

As she watched Esther and Becky, a deep sense of sadness filled her. She had so many regrets that she hadn't visited over the years. Her parents were getting up in age as well.

"What's wrong *Aenti* Ruth?" Becky jumped up, toting her doll, and walked around the table to where Ruth was sitting. "You look like you're about to cry."

Ruth forced a smile. "I don't think it's anything a hug won't fix."

Becky wrapped her arms around Ruth's neck. "Everything's going to be all right. You'll see." She eased away and kissed Ruth on the cheek.

I hope you're right.

After Becky left the kitchen, Ruth helped her sister clean the dishes, then they each grabbed a cup of coffee and sat back down at the kitchen table.

Ruth chuckled. "Where in the world did Becky hear a name like Beatrice?"

Esther rolled her eyes. "It was in a book of Bible stories, and the narrator is named Beatrice. Every time I read it to her, Becky says she's going to name her first daughter Beatrice." She shook her head. "I'm hoping that by naming the doll Beatrice, maybe she'll decide on a more traditional Amish name by the time she has *kinner*."

Esther put a hand on Ruth's. "I know it must have been a long and exhausting day yesterday, and I want to hear everything."

Ruth shared the events of the previous day, not skipping a single detail. When she finished, Esther was almost in tears.

"It's so hard to understand *Gott*'s plan for our lives. Do you think there is a chance for you and Gideon? You don't know how serious it is with the woman he's seeing."

"He said they'd only been on a few dates. But, now that I know that, I don't know if we can recapture what we had." Ruth's voice cracked as she spoke.

"It sounds like you already have." Esther smiled.

— CHAPTER 9 —

On Saturday Ruth enjoyed visiting with relatives she hadn't seen in years. Some had arrived a few days ago, and others were just getting there this morning. Each family brought several dishes, and the variety was wonderful, although Ruth wasn't sure she'd ever seen so much homemade bread. It seemed like each family brought at least a couple of loaves. Ruth thought about how she still made her mother's bread recipe in Florida.

Everyone was hopped-up about a return visit in the fall for Ben and Annie's wedding. It would probably draw three hundred people, the same way Ruth and Gideon's had. There would be enormous amounts of food, and while the gifts wouldn't be expensive, they would be plentiful.

Even with wedding joy in the air and the reunion in full swing at Esther and Amos's house, two people were missing. Gideon and his father. Ruth hadn't seen John Beiler since her arrival. She already knew from the letters they exchanged that he was a bit of a recluse, even though that wasn't the word John used. He didn't go to church and was rarely seen outside his house. Occasionally, someone would mention seeing him at the market. Ruth wondered who cooked for him. Had he learned how to cook, do laundry, and other things Mae had done before she died?

Ruth stayed at the reunion long enough after the meal that she wouldn't appear rude when she found Esther. "I know I should help you clean all of this up, but I'd really like to go see John Beiler."

Esther waved a dismissive hand. "Go. Look around. All of these women will stay for cleanup. You won't be missed." She paused, sighing. "I didn't expect John to show up, but I'm surprised Gideon isn't here. I thought it was part of the reason he came home."

Esther gave Ruth a quick hug and whispered in her ear. "Follow your heart. I'm sure Gideon will be there. Maybe you'll have a chance to talk to him."

Ruth wondered how much work Gideon had done at the house. Had he gone through the boxes? Uncovered the furniture?

"I can see the wheels turning in your head, Ruth. Listen for the word of *Gott*. He will speak to you in ways you might not always recognize."

Esther smiled. "I'm going to hold out hope that you'll decide to stay, whatever the outcome is with Gideon. You're stronger now, and I know you've worked hard to get here. So I guess in some ways you have changed inside. But it's a good change. And, besides, I want Becky to know her *aenti*."

"I plan to visit more, but Bishop Lapp might not be tolerant if I'm here too often."

Esther smiled. "Bishop Lapp has mellowed in the past few years. And you have unusual circumstances. Talk to him."

Ruth sighed. "Maybe."

"*Ach*, well, scoot." She gave Ruth a gentle shove. "Go see Gideon and John."

Ruth said good-bye to several people on her way to her car. She hoped she didn't spook all the horses tethered nearby when she started the engine.

By the time she made the short trip to John's house, her heart was at it again as she tried to identify her intentions. Yesterday she ran from Gideon. Now she was about to be face-to-face with him again.

John Beiler opened the door and a smile filled his face. Her father-in-law had aged a lot since she last saw him. His beard was almost completely gray, his salt-and-pepper hair thinning, and his jowls sagged in a way Ruth didn't remember, like he'd been frowning for five years. She was happy to see him smile as she wrapped her arms around him. John held her for a long moment before he motioned for her to come in.

"Excuse the mess." He rolled his eyes. "I'm afraid cleaning was always Mae's area of expertise, and I've gotten used to things being like this."

Ruth knew from Esther's and John's letters that the house wasn't tidy, but she was surprised how bad it was. "I can help you clean this place up."

John chuckled. "I've had lots of offers over the years. But to tell you the truth, I wouldn't be able to find a thing if it was clean. I know where everything is."

"Sorry if I overstepped." Ruth cringed as she looked down at her running shoes, deciding she probably didn't need to take them off.

John shook his head. "No apology necessary. I've just turned into a sloppy and grumpy old man." He grinned before he walked to the couch and moved a blanket and pillow to the floor. "Sit. Tell me about your life in Florida."

Ruth told him about her job, her apartment, and how she enjoyed living near the beach.

"We had several *gut* vacations near there when Gideon was growing up."

Ruth forced a smile. "*Ya*, I remember him talking about those trips." Pausing, she glanced around. "Speaking of Gideon, I was surprised he wasn't at the reunion. I thought that was partly the reason he came back."

John tipped his head to one side and stared at her. "Gideon left yesterday. I thought he got word to you."

Ruth bit her bottom lip, willing it not to tremble.

"He said he was going to hire someone to clean the house and do the repairs." John seemed to be searching Ruth's eyes, his brows furrowed. "He said he didn't want anything in the house—except his grandmother's rocking chair—that he was going to let you have whatever you wanted." He pointed to the chair in the corner. "He brought the rocker over before he left."

Ruth blinked a few times and took a deep breath. "I see."

John stared at her for a long time again, still running his hand over his beard. "Tragedy affects all of us in different ways, *mei maedel.* But you and Gideon have always belonged together. I thought this reunion might help you both see that. I thought when the two of you saw each other, you'd see *Gott*'s plan for your lives wasn't over."

"Gideon has someone else." Ruth fought the tears burning in her eyes.

"Do you?" John raised a bushy gray eyebrow.

Ruth shook her head. She'd spent years thinking she wouldn't love anyone but Gideon, but maybe it was time to rethink that and at least open herself up to the possibility.

They were quiet for a few seconds, then Ruth heard the word *stay* in her mind as clearly as if someone were standing right next to her, breathing it into her ear. She remembered what Esther said about being receptive to the voice of God. Did He want her to stay here?

"I'm not sure how welcome I'll be here by Bishop Lapp, but I'd like to stay and do the cleaning and repairs on the house myself or contract out the things I can't handle." Suddenly the thought of others trampling through her old home caused her to shudder. The house had served as a part of her healing, and her return visit hadn't been the tormented experience she'd expected. Not until she fled from Gideon. Maybe more time in the house by herself was what she needed.

John smiled. "I'd enjoy having you around for a while. What about your job?"

Ruth hadn't thought anything through, but she wanted to stay and work on the house. Shrugging, she smiled. "I have no idea. I didn't know I was going to stay until just now. Did Gideon leave you the key?"

John stood up. "*Ya*, I'll go fetch it."

When he returned, he walked to the rack by the front door and put on his hat. "I suspect there are a lot of repairs you can't do by yourself."

"*Nee*, I can't let you do that. I'm sure Esther and Amos will help. *Mei* parents both have back troubles, but I'm sure they'll lend a hand too." Having less traffic and fewer strangers in the house sounded appealing.

John smiled. "It would get me out of the house."

That did it. Ruth smiled and stood. "Ok. Let's go."

John put an arm around her as they walked onto the porch. "Welcome home," he said softly.

Ruth helped him down the steps. She had no clue what she was doing. She had belongings, friends, a job, and a life back in Florida. She had a rental car to return and a flight booked—

"You are home," the voice whispered in her mind again.

She looked at John, smiled, and said, "*Danki*."

Following the long drive home and a night to decompress, Gideon went to see Cheryl. He'd called her and asked if she wanted him to come over with a pizza. He needed to see her, to clear the images of Ruth he couldn't seem to shed.

Cheryl met him at the door wearing jeans and a purple blouse. Her long red hair was pulled into a ponytail, the same way Ruth had worn hers the last couple days.

Gideon kissed her on the cheek and then handed her the pizza.

She set it on the coffee table and went back to him, hugging him tightly. "I missed you," she whispered. She kissed him as if she hadn't seen him in months. It seemed a bit excessive since they'd only been on a few dates.

As Cheryl kissed him, all Gideon could see was Ruth. He eased away from her and tried to smile.

"I'm exhausted from the long drive, but I wanted to see you." He wanted normalcy, distractions, anything to keep him from thinking about his wife. Ruth had assumed he was serving her with divorce papers. He hadn't realized it at the time, but the finality of such an action disturbed him. He snapped back to the present.

"Well, I was happy to hear that, and I'm glad you're here."

They cozied up on the couch. Cheryl had two paper plates already set out, along with some grated parmesan and napkins.

She tucked a leg beneath her and turned to face him as she handed him a plate. She blinked slowly, her long lashes brushing against her high cheekbones. She was a beautiful woman, and she had a look in her eyes that made Gideon wonder if pizza was the only thing on her agenda.

— CHAPTER 10 —

Esther put her hands to her hips in the middle of Ruth's den. "I absolutely cannot believe how much you've gotten done in here in a week." She glanced around the room. "Unbelievable."

"Well, I've had a lot of help." Ruth looked over her shoulder when a drill started up. "John insisted on being here every day and taking care of little things, like the loose knob on the back door." She pointed to the front window. "And he replaced the glass in that window."

Esther frowned, grunting a little. "I hate that I haven't been able to help you. Becky is still sick with a terrible cold. Amos caught it from her, and I heard *Mamm* and *Daed* coughing when I went to see them this morning, so I told them to stay in and rest. But I couldn't stay away any longer."

"No worries." Ruth leaned closer to her sister and whispered, "This has been *gut* for John. The house seems to have a healing effect on him too." She grabbed her sister's hand and pulled her into the kitchen, then let go and smiled before she walked to the counter to the left of the sink. "This is where Grace and I made bread and baked dozens of cookies together."

She walked over to the kitchen table and climbed up on a chair.

"What are you doing?" Esther arched an eyebrow.

"This is where I stood when a huge mouse was loose in the house." She pointed to the chair across from her. "That's where Grace was standing." Ruth laughed. "We stayed on these chairs squealing until Gideon finally heard us and came to our rescue." She waved her arms. "I feel Grace everywhere, Esther. My heart isn't full, but the emptiness I've carried for so long is slowly filling." She hung her head. "I stayed away much too long."

Esther stared at her for a minute before she climbed up on the chair Ruth had pointed to and squealed. Ruth squealed along with her. John rushed into the room, his wild eyes ping-ponging between them.

"What is it? A mouse? Where?" John looked around for the culprit.

Ruth and Esther laughed. "We were just playing." Ruth stepped back down on the floor.

Esther lost her footing and almost fell. "I guess I shouldn't be standing on a chair." She eased herself back to the wood floor. "I have a hard enough time keeping my balance on the ground."

John rolled his eyes, chuckling and shaking his head. "Silly *maeds*, I tell you." He went back to the bedroom where he'd been tightening some screws on the windowsills.

"I haven't seen him laugh like that in a long time. The few times I've seen him, he was so sullen." Esther walked to Ruth and touched her arm. "It's nice to see you laugh like that too."

Ruth smiled. "Bishop Lapp might not accept me back into the community, but he can't kick me out of *mei haus*."

Esther's eyes filled with tears. "Are you staying for *gut*?"

Ruth put both hands to her forehead for a few seconds. "I haven't thought things through, but I feel happier here than I've felt in a long time. I'm going to roll with it and keep listening to God. Maybe I'm here for a month or two, just to get the house ready to sell. Or maybe

God led me to the decision to return home so I would feel His healing hand on me."

She shrugged, then laughed. "I don't know, Esther. But I called my boss and quit my job this morning. Yesterday, I returned the rental car and took a cab back here." She chuckled again. "It's all crazy behavior, but Gideon and I had a nice nest egg when we split up. I had to spend some of it to get set up in Florida, but I have enough left to live on for a while until I figure everything out."

"Becky is going to be so happy." Esther latched on to Ruth's hands. "I have something to tell you."

Ruth's pulse sped up. "What's wrong?"

"Nothing's wrong." Esther paused as a smile filled her face. "I'm pregnant."

Ruth raised a hand to her chest and smiled as her eyes welled with happy tears.

"I'm not very far along. I haven't even told *Mamm* and *Daed* yet."

Ruth threw her arms around her sister. "I'm so happy for you and Amos."

When they released each other Esther sighed. "Becky says if we don't name the baby Beatrice she will run away from home."

Ruth laughed. She could picture Becky saying that.

"Go ahead and laugh." Esther grinned, but then took a deep breath and blew it out slowly. "She wants us to name her Beatrice Grace." She lowered her eyes. "I know it doesn't even go together, really, and I wasn't sure how you would feel about it . . ."

Ruth brushed a tear from her cheek. "I think it would be wonderful." They shared another hug, then Ruth stepped back. "What if the *boppli* is a boy?"

Esther shook her head. "*Ach*, she still wants Beatrice." Her sister held up a finger. "But Amos and I are pushing for Benjamin."

Ruth gazed at her younger sister, pregnant with her second child. She heard the voice in her head again, and she repeated the words aloud.

"I'm home."

— CHAPTER 11 —

Ruth rode with John to Annie and Ben's wedding. Last month she purchased a car, but it was a lovely fall day, and she missed riding in a buggy. She'd dressed conservatively in a long skirt and white cotton blouse, not the traditional Amish clothes that were still in her closet.

She longed to wear the kind of clothes she'd worn most of her life and have her own horse and buggy. But it was up to the bishop to decide if and when Ruth could be rebaptized and become a member of the district again. Until that time hopefully came, she chose to respect the fact that she'd been shunned.

Her predicament fell into a gray area since her people didn't believe in divorce. For now, she would continue to accept Bishop Lapp's grace, by allowing her to resume communication with others in the district. She'd chosen not to have electricity installed in the house to show the bishop she was serious about making a new life here and living the Amish way. The car was a necessity for now, but she'd happily sell it.

Ruth awoke every morning at four o'clock to bake bread. She'd purchased four chickens and a milking cow. In many ways, she'd resumed her old life. There were large voids, but slowly her heart was filling in other ways. Tending to the yard, working outdoors, collecting eggs, and continuing to fix up the house kept her busy.

Slowly, she'd been able to recall more and more good memories about Grace, and while there would always be a level of grief, she was finding joy again. She thought about Gideon often and envisioned him here with her, but she hadn't heard from him, so she was forced to face the fact that he had truly moved on. Whatever spark she'd thought they had was only that—a spark that ignited in Ruth's heart, but apparently not in Gideon's. At some point, she would have to figure out a way to pay Gideon for his share of the house.

She wasn't sure what the future held, but she had something she didn't have prior to coming here. Hope. She had a hopeful heart that she prayed would be full and at peace. It was a process, but as long as she kept moving forward, she would be closer to that peace.

The biggest question would be how the elders and Bishop Lapp decided to handle her return home. Even if she was rebaptized into the community, she wasn't sure if romantic love would be in her future. She didn't believe in divorce, and she didn't think she would love anyone the way she loved Gideon.

John turned on the road to Annie's parents' house, and Ruth saw dozens of buggies with horses tethered to the fence. She was sure Esther and her mother had already been there for hours preparing food for the wedding. Knowing there would be plenty of help and not wanting to push Bishop Lapp, Ruth chose not to join them.

"I'm surprised you aren't riding to the wedding with Barbara." Ruth grinned at her father-in-law. John had been seen around town eating out with Barbara, a woman his age who had recently become widowed. It was customary for an Amish person to remarry soon after the death of a spouse. John had repeatedly said in letters that he would never remarry, customary or not. But then Barbara became available.

He'd even returned to church. Ruth had been attending Amish worship too. Bishop Lapp, once again, chose to look the other way.

"*Nee*, no one knows about me and Barbara." John winked at Ruth, and she smiled back at him.

"Don't kid yourself. They know. People have seen you together."

John chuckled. He glowed with an expression Ruth hadn't seen since before Mae and Grace died. It was a gradual transformation. First, he stepped out by helping Ruth with the house. Then he started going back to church once a month, and now every two weeks. John said it was a start and that he still had some things to work out with the Lord. And then there was Barbara, who seemed to propel him toward the same goal Ruth had—peace. But if romantic love was the answer, Ruth worried if she'd ever find the peace she longed for.

"There's *mei daed*," Ruth said after John had tethered the horse. "I'm going to talk to him before the service starts."

John nodded, and Ruth walked to where her father was washing his hands at the pump by the fence. The men had set up a large tent outside the Millers's house with a lot of tables and chairs. Normally there wouldn't be a tent, but rain was in the forecast, and even the Millers's wraparound porch couldn't hold all the guests.

"*Wie bischt, Daed?*"

"*Gut, mei maedel.* Nice to see you. It's been a few days."

It had been over a week, but Ruth didn't correct him. "I've been getting ready for winter. You know, stacking firewood in the mudroom and making sure I have enough propane, things like that."

"A woman needs a husband to take care of those things." Her father scowled.

Ruth brushed the wrinkles from her blouse as she sighed. "Well, I'm making do."

It started to drizzle as she walked across the yard with her father.

The service would be inside the Millers's house. When she and her father walked into the room, people were packed like sardines, some sitting, many standing. There were probably three hundred folks. Panels that divided the rooms had been removed to accommodate the crowd.

It had been a long time since Ruth attended a wedding. She tried to recall if Esther and Amos's had been the last one, but she couldn't remember.

Becky waved to Ruth from where she was sitting next to her mother. All the chairs near them were taken, so Ruth chose one of the few empty chairs in the back row. As was customary, the men and boys were on one side of the room, the women and girls facing them on the other side, and the deacons and bishop were in the middle. The bride and groom were on the front rows, facing each other.

Ruth was glad to be in the back when her eyes filled with tears. She hoped not too many people would notice. As Ben and Annie exchanged vows, she saw only her and Gideon. Two people madly in love, light-years away from tragedy and heartbreak.

Thunder boomed outside as rain pelted the tin roof. Ruth had always heard that rain at a wedding was good luck and symbolized fertility and cleansing, and if there was a rainbow afterward, the union would be blessed with happiness. She prayed that Ben and Annie would have a good marriage and life together, a union blessed by God that would last forever. Ruth remembered the rain when she married Gideon. There was lots of rain, but no rainbow when the storm was over. She'd been blessed with happiness, but not for nearly as long as she'd hoped.

A minute later, tears were streaming down her face. She dabbed at them with a tissue before she made her way to the kitchen. A few women hurried around putting finishing touches on the food. She kept her head down as she swept through them and went out to the porch.

She covered her face and sobbed, wishing she hadn't come. But she'd known Ben and Annie her entire life. It would have been wrong to miss their special day. For all her steps forward, there were still steps backward, tender spots in her heart that would take longer to heal.

After allowing herself a good cry, she uncovered her face and sniffled. It was pouring now, and she stepped closer to the house to avoid the spray of water as the wind pushed the rain sideways and underneath the porch awning. She went around the corner to the front porch where an even larger spray of water blew under the rafters, soaking most of her dress.

Ruth was almost at the door when she thought she heard someone call her name. In the distance, she saw a man. He was standing in the middle of the yard staring at her. Ruth didn't recognize him with the downpour of water between them. She quickly swiped at her eyes so she wouldn't be caught crying by a late guest. The man took a few steps toward her, and Ruth would recognize that gait anywhere. Gideon.

Of course Annie and Ben would invite Gideon to the wedding. He had grown up with them too. But Ruth never considered the possibility that he might attend after his abrupt departure.

She strained to see his truck, but there wasn't a vehicle in sight. She went weak in the knees, but it didn't stop her feet from moving toward him. She was soaked immediately, but her pace picked up until she was right in front of him.

"What are you doing here?" Ruth's teeth chattered. It was warm for October, but cool enough that being drenched caused her to shake. Or was it Gideon causing her to tremble? "You missed the wedding."

"I know." He was breathless. "I ran most of the way here after my truck broke down on Lincoln Highway."

Ruth just stared at him, at a loss for words. As they stood in the rain, soaking wet, Ruth couldn't move. She was afraid she'd lose the moment, the look on Gideon's face, the way his eyes blazed with a passion she remembered well. But there was something different about his expression now, more determined.

"I've spent so much time thinking about how we're different people from who we used to be and how we can't move forward together." Rainwater poured down Gideon's face, but he didn't flinch. "We had to move backward before we could go forward as new and better people." He shrugged. "Did we handle things the best way that we could? Probably not. But we lost a child. And we lost each other along the way. But the differences in our lives were more about what we had to face within ourselves. The people we were, the core of our souls never left us. We just had to find our way back. We both faced the challenges of a new life in the English world while grief gnawed at us from the inside. But we're different in other ways too."

He took a step closer to her and put his hand over his heart. "We're better. We've found ways to cope with our grief, and we've stayed in touch with God." He pounded his fist lightly against his chest. "And inside, I am still the man you married, who fell in love with you, who had a child with you. I love you now just as much as I did then." He shook his head. The rain was slowing. "I don't want anyone else. I don't love anyone else. I love you, Ruth."

Ruth blinked as she fought to control her tears, her heart pounding against the wall of her chest. Her face was so wet from rain that she barely noticed the tears pouring down her cheeks as Gideon latched his hands onto her shoulders.

"So, Ruth Marie Beiler, will you be my wife again, to love and cherish forever? I know we might need to ease into things, but I know I love you."

She nodded and held on to him tightly when he pulled her into a hug. They stayed in each other's arms for a while. The rain had stopped when he eased her away.

Ruth couldn't hold back the flow of tears as she nodded. "I'd like that."

Gideon kissed her with all the passion she remembered. "I *leib* you," he whispered in her ear as he held her.

"I *leib* you too." Saying it in *Deitsch* sounded as natural as being in Gideon's arms. She smiled when she saw a rainbow behind him. "Look."

Would blessings and happiness follow Ben and Annie on their wedding day and forever? Or was the colorful display God's way of saying He was giving Ruth and Gideon another chance? Either way, she silently thanked God for this day, for this moment. She prayed she and Gideon would face the future together, no matter what it held for them, and that they would continue to pull their strength from God and each other.

"Now, that's what I call a reunion!"

Ruth spun around just in time to see Esther lowering her hands from her mouth, evidently the person who yelled. She was surrounded by at least a dozen others who all began to clap.

Ruth turned back around to face her husband.

Thank you, *Gott*.

— EPILOGUE —

Beatrice Grace Stoltzfus was born three months later, and as Ruth held the tiny bundle in her arms, she could feel Grace smiling from heaven.

"She's beautiful." Ruth gazed upon her new niece. She'd waited until Amos left, along with Becky and the midwife, and even her parents before she entered the bedroom. "I'm so glad I'm able to be here this time." She looked up at her sister and grinned. "Becky got her wish for a girl."

"*Ya.* I didn't want her to run away from home." Esther smiled. "And I can already see the bishop baptizing her as Beatrice, but Amos decided we should call her Bea. Becky didn't care for that idea, but we're compromising. I remember you telling us what the name meant. I had to talk Amos into it a little, but he said he'll get used to having a daughter named Beatrice." She paused to take a deep breath. "This one was easier than Becky, but it still wasn't a picnic." Her sister lay a hand across her stomach.

"Well, I hope my second pregnancy will be easier too." Ruth smiled before she kissed Beatrice on the forehead, then she looked up at Esther, whose mouth was agape.

"I know. We were as shocked as you are. It took so long for me to get pregnant with Grace that we didn't see another child in our future."

"*Gott* is good," Esther said softly. "What a beautiful miracle He blessed you with after all you've been through."

"But we're going through it all together this time."

As Ruth thought about their journey, she was confident about her statement. She and Gideon had dated for a month, then they held a small ceremony to renew their vows. She and Gideon had been living in their home for almost two months as husband and wife. It wasn't without adjustments, some serious, some funny.

Gideon walked in his sleep now, which unraveled Ruth every time she heard him up and around during the night. Gideon said Ruth snored now, which she continued to deny. Changing Grace's room had been heartbreaking, and they'd argued a little about what to do with it. They agreed to leave it alone, but when they found out Ruth was pregnant, they tackled the project with a combination of bittersweet joy and sadness. Together it represented hope and faith.

As Ruth gazed at her sister, she thanked God again for His many blessings. Then she chuckled.

"I hope Becky won't be mad if we don't name a baby Beatrice too." Ruth chuckled.

"She's going to be beside herself excited and happy." Esther found Ruth's free hand and squeezed. "We don't always understand *Gott's* plan, but He never forsakes us."

Ruth handed tiny Beatrice back to her mother and smoothed the wrinkles from her black apron. "*Ya*. I know. I'll never forget Grace. She is in my heart forever. I was blessed to have her for ten years, and that's how I choose to think about it. I didn't lose her after ten years, I was blessed to have her for ten years."

"I'm so happy for you." A tear rolled down Esther's cheek, still rosy with exhaustion.

"I need to go talk to Becky and tell her the news." Ruth tapped a finger to her chin. "But first, there is one more thing I need to tell you."

Esther raised an eyebrow.

"Becky may actually need to help us pick out two names." Ruth's eyes welled with happiness as her sister's jaw dropped again. "The midwife thinks it could be twins, but it's too early to know for sure."

Esther was in the middle of congratulating Ruth when a loud squeal came from the den. Ruth went to the closed door and peeked out to see Amos, their parents, the midwife, and other family members watching an excited Becky as she hugged Gideon. Ruth looked back to her sister. "*Ach*, well, someone beat me to it. Gideon must have told Becky and the rest of them."

Ruth smiled at her husband as Becky jumped up and down, then finally turned around and waved to Ruth. Her niece cupped her mouth with her hands and yelled, "I can already think of so many names!"

Esther chuckled. "Oh, dear. I wonder what she'll come up with."

Ruth gazed at her husband and niece, thanking the Lord again for an abundance of peace, happiness, and hope for the future. She turned back to Esther again, closing the door behind her. "I'm sure we'll all settle on *gut* names."

"Ha. That's what you think. She's already mentioned Myrtle and Hilda for my future babies. She might suggest those for yours."

Ruth rested a hand on her stomach. "I have a funny feeling we are having boys."

Giggling, Esther rolled her eyes. "Our Becky has boy names picked out too. I'm hoping she outgrows this obsession with odd names that aren't common to our people."

"I'm afraid to ask what boy names she has in mind." Ruth winked at her sister. "But those names will be for your future *kinner*, I'm sure."

"She has six boy names. I'm sure I'm not having six boys." She pushed her lips into a pout. "Well, I guess I can't be sure about that. Amos is hoping for a lot of boys."

Ruth walked to the bed and kissed baby Beatrice on the cheek. "Be well, little one." Then she kissed her sister on the forehead. "Well done. She's beautiful." Standing, she took a deep breath. "Now, I'm going home with my husband, and we thought we'd take our niece for a while so her mother can rest."

Esther nodded, then locked eyes with Ruth. "*Gott* is good, isn't He?" Esther said again.

"In so many ways." Ruth blew Esther a kiss and opened the door that led to her husband and niece.

Husband. It was a word she would never tire of saying. She thanked *Gott* for gifting her with more children and for this second chance at happiness with Gideon. She paused before stepping over the threshold and closed her eyes.

I love you, Grace. Always and forever.

In her mind, she heard "I love you too, *Mamm*," and she smiled.

Everything was going to be okay. Better than okay.

Blessed.

— DISCUSSION QUESTIONS —

1. The loss of a loved one at any age is difficult, but especially when a child dies. Statistically, grief often causes the parents to split up. Has this happened to you or to anyone you know? Did the couple reunite or remain separated?

2. What do you think would have happened if Gideon and Ruth had stayed together? Or what might the outcome have been if they had returned home sooner? Did they possibly need their time apart in an effort for each of them to heal before they were able to console each other?

3. At the end of the story, I could almost see Grace smiling down on her parents. Did you have a sense of Grace's presence throughout the novella? If so, what were some of the recollections and memories that led you to feel like you knew Grace?

4. Ruth and Gideon both returned home to face people and painful situations they had avoided. But, in the end, it is people and situations that ultimately help them to continue the healing process. What are some examples of this?

— ACKNOWLEDGMENTS —

This was a difficult story to write, but one that God placed upon my heart. Much thanks to my publishing team at HarperCollins Christian Fiction. Special thanks to my editor, Kimberly Carlton, for encouraging me to go deeper with this novella. Your keen insight about the importance of a story like this led me to push myself harder in an effort to get it right. I always pray that my stories get into the hands of the right people, and it's especially true with this novella.

Raelyn, you are forever missed, but I felt your presence as I wrote about Grace and her family. Thank you for allowing me to be a part of your journey. Dance with the angels, sweet girl, and save some Jelly Belly jellybeans for me!

To Natasha Kern, my agent, you knew this would be a challenging story for me to tackle. Thank you for understanding how personal this novella is to me. And, of course, you continue to rock as my agent and dear friend. I'm blessed to have you in my life.

To my family and friends, what an amazing ride this continues to be. Thank you for supporting me and loving me.

And to God the Father, thank You for all that You are in my life.

A CHANCE TO REMEMBER

-‹‹‹-

Kathleen Fuller

To James. I love you.

— CHAPTER 1 —

Cevilla Schlabach pressed the damp potting soil in her flower box. She smiled and stepped back, admiring her work. Four impatiens plants bloomed there—each one purple, coral, pink, or white. The box was small and modest, but at least she could keep up with it on her own.

"We finished weeding the flower beds."

She turned to see Judah Yoder at the bottom of her porch steps. She picked up her cane and hobbled to the edge. "Every last weed?"

He grinned. "Every last weed."

"Where are Malachi and Perry?"

"Raking up the last of the leaves left over from last fall."

She nodded. This was the second year Judah, Malachi Chupp, and Perry Bontrager had spring cleaned her yard. The boys, who were all related to each other, did a good job. Judah, at twelve years old, had taken the lead and made sure Malachi, eight, and Perry, ten, finished their assigned tasks. That didn't stop her from wishing she could do it herself. She'd had quite the green thumb in her day. But arthritis and time had slowed her down, and now in the latter part of her eighties, she felt that slowing down more than ever.

No need to let these young people know that, though. She grinned and tapped her cane on the wooden porch planks. "*Gut* work deserves some fresh lemonade. And possibly a cookie or two."

"Cookies?" Malachi said as he and Perry rounded the corner of the house and hurried to stand by Judah. The older Yoder boy was taller, but Cevilla was sure Malachi would catch up to him soon.

"Did you say cookies?" Perry asked.

"I did. Two kinds." She held up two fingers. "Peanut butter and chocolate chip. Straight from Judah's *aenti*'s bakery."

"If *Aenti* Carolyn made them, then they're delicious." Judah started up the steps.

Cevilla held up her hand. "I need you *buwe* to do one more thing while I get the lemonade and cookies ready."

Judah stepped back. "What's that?"

"A few slats in the back of the barn are loose. They need to be nailed down. The barn floor could also use a good sweeping." The chores wouldn't take them long. She'd had to give up driving her own buggy and owning her own horse. She just couldn't keep up with caring for an animal. The buggy and Shep had a good home with Adam and Karen Chupp, but she missed her independence.

The boys nodded and took off. Cevilla went back in the house and headed to the kitchen. She washed the dirt from her hands, dried them on a towel, and removed the plastic wrap from the Styrofoam plate filled with bakery cookies. As she set the plate on the table, Malachi dashed into the kitchen.

"Someone's here to see you."

"Who?"

"I don't know."

Cevilla raised an eyebrow. Malachi knew everyone in the district, and Cevilla didn't get strangers for visitors.

"There's a woman with him too. They drive a fancy car. Fancier than I've ever seen."

She nodded, her curiosity piqued. "Tell him I'll be right out."

"Okay." Malachi looked longingly at the cookies. "We're almost finished in the barn."

"*Gut.* Then you're that much closer to getting *yer* snack."

Those words caused him to scurry out of the kitchen. Cevilla smiled at how the promise of a cookie or two could make a boy eager to work. She grabbed her cane and slowly headed for the front door. Malachi would probably be at the barn by the time she reached the porch. She frowned. Getting old wasn't for the fainthearted.

Who would be coming by that Malachi didn't recognize? Probably a salesman, although she couldn't recall the last time she'd seen one. Did door-to-door salesmen exist anymore? She remembered them coming by often during her childhood in Pennsylvania. She hadn't been Amish then, and several salesmen had peddled their goods to her parents. They'd had vacuum cleaners, cleaning brushes, and pots and pans, among other things. Even if her stepmother, Glenda, wasn't interested in what they were selling, she always invited them in, offered them a glass of water or a cup of tea, and listened to their spiels. That was Glenda—friendly, kind, and soft-hearted.

Cevilla blinked. She was standing in front of the screen door, but she hadn't opened it. That was happening more often—her mind getting lost in the past. She was still as sharp as a steel needle, so she wasn't worried about losing her faculties. But reliving her youth was comforting. She liked remembering when she was full of energy, without pain, and not dependent on a cane.

She opened the screen door, wondering if it would be wise or safe to invite in the salesman—or sales*people*, since Malachi said two people were here. She read the papers, and although she didn't live with a spirit of fear, a bit of caution was a good thing.

When she saw the man standing at the bottom of the porch steps, she froze. Was that . . . ? It was.

What is he doing here?

-◄◄◄-

Richard Johnson couldn't keep his gaze from the woman in front of him. His mind instantly traveled back to the 1940s, when they'd both been teenagers in a small Arnold City, Pennsylvania, neighborhood. She'd always been so pretty and outgoing. Bunny, she'd been nicknamed by his best friend—and her future fiancé—CJ Manchester. That was nearly seventy years ago, but right now, time stood still. Through his eyes she was the blond-haired, blue-eyed firecracker he remembered.

"Richard Johnson?" She let the screen door bounce closed behind her.

That noise, along with the thumping of her cane, brought him back to the present. He glanced down at his own cane, his constant companion for the last decade. As she made her way to the top of the porch steps, he walked toward her. "Cevilla," he said, his voice raspy from age. He couldn't keep from smiling.

"What are you doing here?" Unlike his, her voice was as strong as ever. But her expression was uncertain.

That made him pause, realizing he'd expected her to be as glad to see him as he was to see her. Then again, he was surprising her out of the blue, an idea now giving him second thoughts. He should have let her know he was coming. Better yet, he should have written to her as soon as he'd found her address, and asked permission to pay her a visit. That would have been the polite thing to do. But he'd uncharacteristically let his emotions overrule his common sense.

"I came to see you," he said, his smile fading a little. He stopped at the bottom of the steps and looked up at her.

"Why?"

Straight to the point. That had been Cevilla's way, ever since he'd known her when they were young, up until she rejoined the Amish when she was eighteen. He hadn't been in contact with her since.

His granddaughter, Meghan, appeared at his side. "I told you this wasn't a good idea."

He turned to her, and another wave of doubt came over him—not about Cevilla, but about letting Meghan accompany him. When he first told her he wanted to track down an old friend, she helped him without too much protest. That changed when he said he wanted to come to Ohio and see Cevilla. Then there was the problem of Meghan behaving like a mother hen since his recent fall, and from the moment they left California she'd been hovering. A part of him wished she would have stayed home. "This is my granddaughter, Meghan," he said, trying to break the ice.

"It's nice to meet you," Meghan said, but her voice was tight.

Cevilla blinked, and her surprised expression disappeared. "Now, where are my manners?" She smiled and gestured to the door. "Come inside, both of you. I hope you like cookies and lemonade."

Meghan glanced at him. His svelte granddaughter was always on a diet of some sort, but he knew that wasn't why she looked thinner than ever.

"Sounds delicious." He'd started for the steps when Meghan's hand slipped around his elbow. "I can climb up three steps on my own," he muttered.

"You just got out of the hospital last week," she shot back, gritting her teeth. "I won't risk you having another fall."

He sighed, mentally fighting between pride and common sense. This time common sense won out, and he let Meghan escort him up the steps. Cevilla held the door open for them, but he noticed she didn't meet his eyes. Maybe Meghan was right. Maybe this had been a mistake.

"We can go into the kitchen," she said, moving in front of them. She glanced over her slightly rounded shoulder. "I'm glad I have enough cookies."

"None for me, please."

Richard glanced at Meghan. She was twenty-five and a brilliant young woman going through a rough spot in her life. That was why he didn't call out her rudeness. "I'll take hers, then."

"Grandfather, your diabetes—"

"I won't go into sugar shock from two cookies." This was getting embarrassing. First, he had to be helped up the steps, and now Cevilla knew he had diabetes. Normally public knowledge of his ailments didn't bother him. He wasn't a spring chicken. More like a winter rooster. And like a rooster, he still had dignity, but Meghan was quickly taking it away.

Cevilla didn't say anything as they entered the kitchen. "I have lemonade. Fresh squeezed, with plenty of . . . sugar." She looked at him for the first time. "I can make you some unsweetened tea instead."

He shook his head. "Lemonade is fine—"

"He'll take the tea."

Richard shot Meghan a hard look. He should have known this was going to happen. Her mother, Sharon, had been beside herself when he'd insisted on making this trip. Only when her daughter insisted on going with him did she finally relent. "It's not like I can stop you," she grumbled. "Knowing you, you'd probably try to *drive* there—by yourself!"

The idea had been tempting, but he wasn't quite up to a long trip, and for the most part he'd given up driving. Not that he wouldn't be up to a trip alone by plane once he completely recovered. He wasn't a cripple, even though his daughter and granddaughter often treated him like he was.

"Tea it is." Cevilla lifted the teakettle from an older model gas stove and walked to the sink. "Make yourself at home," she said as she filled the kettle with water.

Meghan looked at the small wood table. It was simple, like this house. He could see what was running through her mind. As an interior designer, and a very successful one, she looked at décor with a critical eye.

Richard pulled out a chair and sat down. It was solid, like the wood table, and that was enough for him.

Three young boys burst into the kitchen. "We're finished!" the tallest one said.

"I'm ready for cookies." The shortest one with reddish-brown hair went straight to the table.

"Excuse me." Cevilla turned and thumped her cane on the floor.

The three boys immediately turned and faced her.

"Did you wash up outside?"

All three shook their heads.

She pointed to the doorway Richard and Meghan had just walked through with her cane. "Bathroom is to the left. Get all that dirt out from under your fingernails too."

They nodded and raced out of the kitchen as fast as they came in.

"My working crew," Cevilla said as she turned and pulled three teacups out of the cabinet next to the sink. "I suppose you'll want tea, too, Meghan?"

Meghan sat down. "Yes. Please."

"Do you need any help?" He'd missed activity around the house since moving in with Sharon and Meghan. They rarely let him do anything.

"No, thank you. I'm an expert at making tea."

He smiled. This was the confident Cevilla he remembered.

After a few moments of silence, Meghan said, "You have a lovely home."

Cevilla turned around. "You really think so?"

Meghan blinked, her cheeks turning a light pink color. "Ah, yes. I, uh, do."

"Hmm." Cevilla lined up the plain white teacups by the stove. "Seems as though a woman like you would have more sophisticated tastes."

Meghan lifted her chin. "I appreciate simple style as well."

Richard glanced at his granddaughter. Meghan could stand on her own with any man or woman. Much like Cevilla could.

"Like your car?" Cevilla smiled with false sweetness.

Meghan had insisted on renting the most expensive luxury car, something Richard had thought unnecessary. At home she drove the latest model BMW, which cost her quite a bit of money. He thought that was an extravagant expense for a young woman, but he'd made plenty of extravagant purchases in his lifetime. He'd ended up regretting many of them.

"My car suits my needs," Meghan said, folding her hands on the table and meeting Cevilla's gaze head-on. "As I'm sure your humble home suits yours."

Cevilla continued to look at her with an inscrutable expression. He wondered if Meghan had insulted her. That wasn't the impression he'd wanted to make with his visit. *Not even close.*

Then Cevilla laughed, her eyes sparkling. "I like her, Richard," she said, seemingly relaxed for the first time since he and Meghan arrived. "I like her a lot."

-◄◄◄-

Meghan was confused. Then again, this was her normal state of mind when it came to her grandfather lately. He'd fallen two weeks ago and nearly broken his hip. The deep bone bruise he sustained and the bump on his head had kept him in the hospital overnight—and he'd kept her and her mother on their toes after he was released. He was stubborn. Ridiculously so. But she loved him, and she would do anything to keep him safe.

Including making a foolish trip from California to Ohio.

The old woman turned back to the stove the same time the tea-kettle whistled. Meghan was annoyed Cevilla had caught on that she was only making polite small talk about her house. Nothing about the place was special or stylish, which was what she'd expected, but now that she saw how modest this woman's tiny cottage was, she was surprised by its austereness. A trend for "tiny living" had developed the past couple of years, but even those small houses, which could be as confined as four hundred square feet, had been decorated with style. Cevilla's living quarters were . . . dull.

Yet the house was homey too. Bright sunshine filtered through the kitchen window, which was open slightly, bringing in fresh air. The kitchen was set up efficiently for Cevilla's needs. In the modern estate Meghan shared with her mother and grandfather, the kitchen was almost the size of this house. It was decorated beautifully, yet rarely used by the family because they had a cook and a maid. That was why it hadn't dawned on her to offer to help Cevilla, like her grandfather had. She'd never had to help the help. But it would have been polite to offer Cevilla assistance.

"I have black and peppermint teas," Cevilla said, facing them again. Her gaze shot to Meghan, and she smiled. "Which will it be?"

"Peppermint for me," Grandfather said.

"I'll have black," Meghan said.

"No surprise there." Cevilla said that in a loud mumble.

Meghan smiled, something she hadn't done in a long time. She knew she was meant to hear the woman's words, and she could appreciate a good dose of sarcasm. She was starting to like Cevilla too.

The boys ran back into the kitchen. The shortest one went straight to the cookies and grabbed one. The tallest pulled him back and said something in a language Meghan had never heard before. The boy looked up at him with a slight scowl, but he stood back.

"It's all right, Judah." Cevilla pointed at the table. "Go on and get your cookies and lemonade. You can eat outside. But only two cookies apiece, since we have company."

The blond-haired boy with striking blue eyes nodded, and then he left the kitchen with his cookies and a glass of lemonade. The other boys followed suit, and they all went outside through the back door.

"Brothers?" Grandfather asked.

Cevilla shook her head and started toward them with one teacup. "They're related through marriage, though. The oldest and tallest is Judah Yoder, the bishop's son. His sister is married to Malachi's older cousin Adam. He's the blond. He's also the nephew of the other boy, Perry, who happens to be only a year older."

"Wow," Grandfather said. He started to get up to take the tea from Cevilla, but he almost lost his balance.

"I'll get it." Meghan popped up from her chair and took the cup from Cevilla. "You stay put." Grandfather complied with a grumble, but Meghan didn't care if he didn't want her help. The last thing they needed was for him to fall again. She set the tea in front of him and then turned to Cevilla. "I'll get the other two, Mrs. Schlabach."

"It's Ms., and you can dispense with the formality nonsense. Call me Cevilla."

"All right, Cevilla. Please, let me get your tea."

"I really do like her." Cevilla sat down in the chair across from Grandfather.

Meghan almost smiled, but the urge faded quickly. Cevilla was in the minority, especially lately.

Cevilla turned to Grandfather. "If you haven't guessed, I'm surprised to see you here. What brings you to Birch Creek?"

Meghan set the last two teacups on the table as Grandfather replied, "Like I said, I came to see you."

"All the way from California?"

Grandfather raised a bushy gray brow. "How did you know I live in California?"

"I keep up with people back home. Although less than before." A somber look crossed her face. "I have fewer friends to write letters to now."

He nodded, his downcast expression mimicking Cevilla's. "That's true. Some days I feel like I'm the only one left."

"Me too."

Meghan sat down, making sure she didn't make a sound. She wondered if they even realized she was still there. For the first time it dawned on her that her grandfather might be lonely. Yes, he attended church, and he also met with a few men from the senior center to play bridge every other week. But most of the time he was at home . . . and mostly in an empty house, other than the cook and the maid.

Maybe that's why he'd been so insistent on coming here. Or . . . or maybe he'd received news from the doctor he hadn't told them. Maybe something was seriously wrong with him, something possibly fatal—

"Grandfather!" she blurted, her heart squeezing in her chest. "Are you dying?"

— CHAPTER 2 —

Richard nearly dropped his teacup at Meghan's outburst. He set it on the table and turned to her—slowly, since his neck was still a bit stiff after the long plane ride. "Meghan, what's gotten into you?"

"You wanted to come here so badly. And you were in the hospital. And—" She glanced at Cevilla before turning to him again. "And . . ."

"And he's old as dirt, right?"

Richard and Meghan both looked at Cevilla.

"No need to beat around the bush, young lady. Your grandfather and I know exactly how old we are—although a woman doesn't reveal her true age." She smirked, and then she looked at Richard. "Well? Are you dying?"

"No!" His gaze darted from Cevilla to Meghan. "I'm not dying. I had a little fall, that's all."

"It wasn't that little," Meghan said.

"And the reason I came here is . . ." His pulse sped as he met Cevilla's gaze. "I wanted to see an old friend."

His granddaughter slumped in the chair. "Thank God that's all it is."

"I'm not dying, I'm not crippled, and I'm not crazy." They shouldn't be having this conversation in front of Cevilla, but he was tired of Meghan's hovering. "Yes, I'm slower than I used to be. Yes, I have balance problems. And yes, I shouldn't eat carbs and sugar, but the bottom line is I'm still me. And I'm going to live my life the way I want to, so will you leave me alone for five minutes already?"

Meghan flinched. Then she rose from the table. "I see."

Uh-oh. He recognized that look. Pride masking the hurt. She'd been hurt a lot this past month, and now he'd added to her pain. "Meghan—"

"I'm going to get some fresh air." She walked out of the kitchen toward the front door.

Richard sighed. "I handled that badly."

"No one's perfect." Cevilla picked up her tea, took a small sip, and then set down the cup. "I do understand where you're coming from."

"I wish she did." He pushed his cup a few inches with his finger. "Still, I shouldn't have lashed out at her. Meghan's had a rough time of it lately. I didn't need to pile on more."

Cevilla didn't say anything for a long moment. Birds twittered outside, and it struck him how peaceful it was here. He'd noticed that on the drive from the Akron airport. Lush green fields, beautiful oak and maple trees lining the highways and roads, pastures, farmland, and as they came closer to Amish country, buggies and horses. "I can see why you were drawn to this place," he said.

"You can? You've been here only a short while."

"I've lived in LA for fifty years. The contrast is jarring. But in a good way."

She nodded. "I'm curious. How did you find me?"

"You can find anyone nowadays because of the internet."

"That's a computer, right?"

"Sort of. Have you used a computer before?"

"No, but they have a few at the library. I don't have any need for that kind of technology." She frowned, looking a bit disturbed. "I'm on the internet?"

"There's a website similar to the phone book." He went on to explain how she was listed as a related person to Noah Schlabach. With a little more digging, he was able to find her address. "I should have told you I was coming."

"Why didn't you?"

He almost admitted that he was afraid she would tell him no. "Bump on the noggin, remember?" He tapped his head. "Guess it affected me after all."

"Humph. I find that hard to believe."

Since she saw through his fib, he changed the topic. "I didn't want to say this in front of Meghan, but seeing you isn't the only reason I came here." That was the truth.

"Oh?" Her light gray eyebrows lifted.

He was struck by how much she still resembled her younger self. She was a little plumper, a lot grayer, and her formerly smooth skin had as many wrinkles as his did. But the youthful Cevilla was still there—the sparkle in her eyes, the quickness of her wit, the way she always got to the point, sometimes in an annoying way. "I wanted to get Meghan out of LA. She needs some breathing room."

Cevilla nodded. "It's clear she loves you very much."

"Yes. And I love her. I knew I wouldn't be able to convince her to take a vacation, so I insisted on coming to see you." He smiled as he gazed at her face. *Still pretty after all these years.*

"Killing two birds with one stone?"

"I never liked that phrase." He pushed up his glasses.

"Me neither." She drew in a breath. "You're both welcome to stay here. I have only one spare bedroom, but I don't mind sleeping on the couch."

"I appreciate the offer, but Meghan's already reserved hotel rooms for us. I think the hotel is in Barton."

"Must be, since it's the closest town. It also has the only hotel nearby." She paused. "We could use a bed-and-breakfast around here, considering how much Birch Creek has expanded the past few years. We have a few in the area, but they're not real close. They mostly cater to the Holmes County visitors."

"You never thought about starting one?"

She shook her head. "That never interested me. The environment here wasn't conducive to hospitality at the time."

He wondered why, but when she didn't say anything else, he didn't pry. "Sorry. Sometimes I can't shut off my business mind."

"Is that how you made your millions?" She gave him a sly grin. "I know about that too. You've done well for yourself."

"I suppose." He looked her straight in the eye. "Money isn't everything."

"No, it's not. Your faith is." She leveled her gaze. "Tell me, Richard Johnson. What do you put your faith in?"

-<<<<-

Normally Cevilla didn't have a problem getting straight to the point or asking questions no one else did. And usually she didn't feel awkward or guilty about that. She didn't believe in beating around the bush when a direct question or comment sufficed. Yet sometimes she wished she'd been a bit more discreet. This was one of those times.

But the question was out there, and she wasn't about to pull it back. She was genuinely curious. She had known about Richard's business savvy and success. Years ago, the high school in Arnold City was renamed after him when he donated the funds for an additional wing and established a scholarship program. It was in all the news-papers, and her friend Clara, who passed away over a decade ago, had sent her a clipping. She wasn't surprised. Richard had always been kind and generous.

"If you're asking if I go to church, I do."

"I wasn't asking that," she said.

"My faith is important to me." He didn't look away. "The most important thing."

She relaxed a bit, glad to hear it. Not that she would have treated him differently. But it was good to know he had the peace of God. She decided to change the subject. "How long are you staying in Birch Creek?"

"At least a week."

"And what are your plans?"

He adjusted his glasses again. "I'm not sure."

"That's surprising. I figured you'd have your itinerary scheduled to the last detail. You were always so organized."

"I remember being made fun of for that in school."

"Look who's laughing now."

He grew serious. "I don't see it that way. I didn't set out to make a lot of money. That was never my goal. I only wanted to support my wife and daughter and make sure they were comfortable. Then the money started rolling in, and I realized what I could do with it. I made sure they were beyond comfortable."

"And how did that turn out?"

"Not as well as I thought," he mumbled.

Cevilla was a little surprised by his response. Not that she wouldn't expect him to take good care of his family, but providing so well for them, at least materially, didn't always equate to happi-ness. She'd never had a lot of money herself, but she'd seen firsthand what greed could do to a man when the former bishop of Birch Creek hoarded money in the community fund, keeping it from members who needed financial help.

Malachi came inside. "We finished the cookies and lemonade," he said, setting down three empty glasses. "Anything else you need us to do?"

She shook her head. She'd kept them here long enough. "You can go home now, Malachi. Thank you for your hard work."

He nodded, looking pleased by the compliment. "Anytime."

"Did you see Meghan outside?" Richard asked.

The boy frowned. "Who's Meghan?"

"The woman who was with me. She's my granddaughter."

Malachi shook his head. "We were in the backyard, and I didn't see her there. Maybe Judah or Perry did. I'll go ask."

"She might have gone for a walk," Cevilla said after Malachi left.

Richard nodded. "She does that at home. Power walking, though. She always has her watch on her wrist, checking her steps, pulse, and distance." He shook his head. "Amazing what technology can do nowadays. I remember when having a phone in the house meant you were rich. Now everyone's wearing a phone on their wrists."

"You won't see me with one of those. Too fancy." Not to mention very much against the *Ordnung*. She'd never been drawn to technology anyway. The Amish way of life had always suited her.

Malachi poked his head inside the kitchen. "They haven't seen her either, Cevilla."

"Thank you for checking," Richard said.

Malachi nodded, and the back door banged shut behind him.

"I'm sure she's all right," Cevilla said. "She can't get into too much trouble around here."

Richard sighed. "You don't know my granddaughter."

-≪≪≪-

Meghan stopped at the end of the road and looked around. She had no idea where she was. When she left Cevilla's, she planned on only a short walk. The cozy kitchen had suddenly become stifling after her grandfather's admonishment. She'd also been embarrassed, being talked to like she was still a child, especially in front of a stranger. Didn't he understand how much she loved him? That she wanted him to be around for a long time?

Then the tears had flowed, and she walked blindly, wiping them as she continued to worry about her grandfather. He'd always been there for her after her father divorced her mother, when she was only eight. Not only was he her grandfather but he was her father too. She couldn't bear the thought of losing him. His fall had scared her, as had his rapid physical decline over the past year.

Having finally come to her senses, she looked at her surroundings. Nothing seemed familiar. She stood on the side of the road and looked back. Had she taken a turn at some point? She couldn't remember. She'd also left her phone at Cevilla's, and without a way to tell the time, she didn't even know how long she'd been gone.

Meghan took in a deep breath. No need to panic. She couldn't have walked that far. And she'd lost her bearings before. New York, Chicago, London—she hadn't known her way around those cities and she'd managed. *With my GPS.* She didn't have that now. She'd also never been lost in such a rural area. Everything looked the same— grass, trees, a few cows in the nearby pasture. She saw a couple of houses up the road, but even they looked similar to most of the other white homes she'd seen.

She realized she'd have to stop at one of them and ask directions. That was the last thing she wanted to do, but she had no other option.

Reluctantly, she headed toward the houses. She could see the properties were more like compounds, with several different sized buildings on each lot. Some she could identify, like the barns. But others looked like small versions of the main houses. They were set off toward the back or the side, as if multiple families were living on the same lot. She'd never seen that before.

She walked past a large pasture with cows and horses. A huge white barn sat next to it, and a large two-story house stood a little way from the barn. An even larger, matching house was next door. She looked from one to the other, wondering which one she should try.

Did they even have doorbells?

Three boys suddenly darted from behind the largest house. As they chased each other in the front yard, she thought she recognized one of them. "Hello?" she said, hurrying toward them.

The boys stopped. Two of them were identical twins and appeared to be a few years younger than the third one, who she thought might be one of the boys at Cevilla's. All three of them looked at her with curiosity, but they didn't say anything.

"Hello," she repeated, stopping in front of the house but not going into the yard. She wasn't sure what else to say.

"Hi," the familiar-looking one answered. "Why aren't you at Cevilla's?"

She blew out a relieved breath, glad she hadn't been mistaken about his identity. "I went for a walk, and, uh . . ." She cleared her throat. "I got lost."

"How'd you get lost?" one of the twins asked.

Meghan grimaced. "I wasn't paying attention to where I was going."

"*Mamm* always tells us to pay attention," the other twin said.

"I guess she doesn't want us getting lost," his twin brother chimed in.

"I can show you the way back," the older boy said. "You're not too far."

"That's all right, you can just tell me—"

"Mose, you and Mahlon go tell *Mamm* I'm going back to Cevilla's for a minute."

The boys nodded and dashed off.

Mose and Mahlon. Unusual names. She assumed Mose was short for Moses, but the name Mahlon was new to her. "What's your name?" she asked the boy.

"Perry." He stepped over the curb and started walking in the direction she came. She fell in step next to him.

For a few minutes neither one said anything. She'd always felt awkward around children, and she'd never been one for babysitting or volunteering to work with the kids at church. When she went to church. She hadn't been there in weeks. Not since . . .

Desperate to change her thoughts, she said, "It's pretty around here."

Perry nodded. "*Ya*." His voice had a trace of an accent.

"What language do you speak?"

"You mean English?" he looked up at her, the sun glinting off his reddish-brown hair.

"I meant the other language."

"*Dietsch*. Although *Mamm* says I should speak English when I'm around English people. It's rude if I don't."

"English people?"

He stuck his hands in his pockets. "You're not Amish."

She almost laughed. What an absurd idea, her being Amish. "Definitely not."

"Then you're English." They came to an intersection, and he took a right turn.

She followed him. "Is that what you call us?"

"Yes." One rust-colored eyebrow lifted. "Where are you from?"

"LA." At his puzzled look she added, "Los Angeles. It's a city in California."

He nodded. "That's one of the fifty states. Sacramento is the capital."

"Very good."

"My teacher says it's good to know where other states are and their capitals. I got one hundred percent on my quiz."

Meghan smiled. "That's great."

"I like geography." He jumped over a small dark lump on the side of the road. "Watch out for that."

"What is it?" she said, sidestepping it and the smaller clumps that trailed it.

"Horse dung. Don't they have horses in California?"

"They do, but not in LA."

"I don't think I'd like LA."

She paused. "You know what, Perry? Right now, I don't like it either."

— CHAPTER 3 —

C evilla sat in her special chair next to the empty woodstove in the living room. She rarely used the stove in the summer months, except for a rare chilly night. Even unlit, though, she thought it made the room cozy. She glanced at Richard, who was standing, looking out the window and leaning heavily on his cane. She recognized the weariness in his stance. She'd felt it many times.

"Sit down," she said, folding her hands on her lap. Normally she would be crocheting because she liked to keep busy. She just didn't do it when she had company. If Richard was going to keep standing there with his back to her, though, she just might pull out her yarn.

"She's been gone a long time," he said.

"Only thirty minutes or so. Not that long."

He looked at her, frowning. "What if she's lost?"

Cevilla rolled her eyes. "Richard, she's an adult. I'm sure she'll figure out what to do if she is."

But he turned and looked out the window again.

She sighed. She shouldn't be hard on him. True, she'd never had children, or even a husband, of her own. But she would probably feel the same way if her nephew, Noah, was wandering around an unfamiliar place. She'd be concerned if anyone in the Birch Creek community was in trouble. The people in Birch Creek were her family, and in the past several years, even though the community had grown by leaps and bounds, they were all closer than they'd ever been.

None of that would help her friend, though. "Richard," she said, gentling her voice. "There's no need to worry. She's safe here. This isn't Los Angeles."

He turned around, a slight look of relief on his features. "You're right. It isn't." He shuffled to the end of the couch nearest to her and slowly sat down, wincing as he did.

"Does your hip still hurt?" she asked.

"It twinges."

"That looked like more than a twinge."

"Because it's not just my hip that's complaining." He gave her a sad smile. "Old age isn't a picnic, is it?"

"Oh, it has good things about it."

"Such as?"

"Well, for one, you're pretty settled on who you are and what you're about. You no longer experience the confusion and anxiety of youth."

He nodded. "That's true."

"And people respect your opinions." She smiled wryly. "At least they pretend to."

"I'm not so sure about that." He glanced at the window. "Lately Meghan's been . . ."

"Suffocating you?"

"To put it mildly."

Cevilla smoothed the skirt of her gray dress. "She loves you."

"I know. And I love her. I just wish . . . I want her to be happy."

She nodded. It was plain as day that Meghan was troubled about something. She'd seen a dullness to her eyes, and a sharp tension around her mouth, like she was continually sucking on a lemon. Without sugar, of course.

"I thought maybe a few days here in the country would help her . . . relax a bit."

"Too busy? Guess the apple didn't fall far from the tree."

Richard looked down at his lap. "Can't deny that. I worked hard when I was her age. But back then life was still slower. Sunday was the Sabbath, and stores and restaurants weren't open. You didn't have to go to work or have your phone ringing all the time in your pocket. You could visit with family or take a nap or just sit in the quiet and think. None of that exists now."

"It does here." She leaned forward. "Now, I'm not saying we're perfect. Far from it. But we keep a simple and slower pace because that's how we can stay in tune with God."

"I stay in tune with God," Richard said, looking a bit offended.

"But it's harder to do with all that noise and busyness . . . isn't it?"

He blew out a breath. "You're right. And since I've slowed down, I've had more time to spend with the Lord." He frowned. "Meghan's missing that in her life."

"And you think a week here is going to fix it?"

He shook his head. "I'm not that foolish. But it will give her a reprieve, at least."

Cevilla smiled. "You're a good man, Richard."

"Thanks."

His wizened cheeks looked pink, which Cevilla thought was charming—and she didn't dole out compliments she didn't mean.

After a few moments of silence, Richard looked at her. "Did you ever see CJ again?"

She'd known the subject of CJ would come up. It was the main thing she and Richard had in common—their friendship with CJ. Hers had turned romantic, however, and she and CJ had come close to marrying. But she had chosen the Amish faith over that marriage, breaking his heart—and hers, even though she never regretted the decision. "We didn't. But he did write a letter to me, years later."

"I didn't know that. We lost contact after I moved to California. He'd already married . . ." Richard looked sheepish. "Sorry."

"I know he did. And I'm glad he found someone else to love, and who loved him."

"What about you, Cevilla? Your last name is still Schlabach. You never married, then?"

She paused. Normally she answered this question quickly. There was no shame or regret in being single. Not everyone was created to be married, and she had always been content with her single life. Except, oddly enough, over the past months. Maybe that had to do with the numerous courtships and weddings in their community in the past three years. She had put two of them together as a matchmaker. Or maybe she was slowing down more than she liked to admit. Not only could she not work in the yard the way she wanted to, but her hands ached after only a few rows of crochet.

Yet she had a constant companion. Someone who never left her, never allowed her to feel alone. "The Lord is enough," she whispered.

"Pardon?" Richard touched his left ear. "These new hearing aids have been giving me trouble ever since I got them."

She smiled. "No," she said, raising her voice. "I never married. But I'm content with my life. I don't need a husband to make me happy."

His eyes widened. "Okay." He gave her a wry grin. "I heard that well enough, by the way."

She leaned back in her chair. She hadn't meant to speak that loudly. Or to sound like she was trying to convince herself as much as she was trying to convince him. She was content with her life. But the ache was there, underneath the surface. Along with the question, *What if?*

"I'm glad you found happiness, Cevilla. I know that's what CJ would have wanted for you." He paused. "It's what I've always wanted for you too."

Puzzled, she frowned. She'd also wanted happiness for him, and it pleased her that he had found it with his family. But those words, coupled with his genuine tone and the warmth in his eyes, seemed to be saying something more. She just didn't know what that something more was.

The front door opened, and Cevilla pulled her gaze from Richard as Meghan and Perry walked in. Richard turned in his seat. "Where have you been?" he asked, scowling.

Perry pointed at Meghan with his thumb. "She got lost. I had to show her how to get here."

"Which was very nice of you," Meghan said, although she looked a little annoyed at Perry's tattling.

Cevilla hid a smile as she saw the relief on Richard's face. "I think that good deed earns you another cookie, Perry. You'll find a couple left in the kitchen."

The boy's face lit up. "*Danki!*" He disappeared from the living room.

"I'm sure I could have found my way home by myself eventually," Meghan muttered. She spotted her purse on a chair and rummaged in it for her phone. After staring at it for a moment, she looked at her grandfather. "Are you ready to go to the hotel?"

"We just got here, Meghan."

"It's nearly suppertime."

He looked at his watch. "Goodness, time flies."

"Not exactly." Meghan started tapping her foot.

Cevilla grabbed her cane and got up. "I can make some tuna sandwiches for supper, if you'd like to stay. I think I have a few homemade pickles too."

Meghan's nose pinched. "We need to check into our hotel."

Richard gave her a dry look, and then he turned to Cevilla. "Rain check?"

"Of course."

Richard rose from the couch. Meghan was already standing near the front door. While her behavior was off-putting, Cevilla didn't take any offense. Storm clouds were behind this young lady's eyes, and not because she'd lost her way here. Whatever had happened to her, she could see why Richard was concerned.

Lord, help them both, in ways only you can.

"I'd like to stop by tomorrow," Richard said when he reached the front door.

"Grandfather, you need to rest."

"I can rest here with Cevilla as well as I can at some hotel." He looked at Cevilla. "That's if you don't mind me inviting myself here once again."

"You're always welcome. And I don't have any plans for tomorrow, so I'll be here."

Richard smiled, and something stirred inside her. Her hand flew to her chest as Meghan, not bothering to wait for Cevilla, opened the screen door and went outside.

"I promise she's not normally like this," Richard said.

"I'm sure she isn't." She put her hand on his arm. "The Lord will help her through her troubles."

"If she'll let him." He looked at the door. "Right now, I don't think she is." He turned to her. "I had a good time this afternoon. You're great company, like you always were." He smiled. "I'll see you tomorrow."

Again, she felt the flutter in her stomach. "Tomorrow," was all she could say.

After they got in the fancy car, she closed the front door and leaned against it. *I'll see you tomorrow.* She grinned. She was looking forward to it.

-⪡⪡⪡-

"I see you left your manners back in Los Angeles."

Meghan turned onto the highway that led to Barton. Her grandfather had been quiet up until now, and she'd thought he'd fallen asleep. She should have known better. "You're tired," she said, her own voice weary.

"I'm not that tired. And I was having a lovely time visiting Cevilla. If you'll give her a chance, I'm sure you'll find her as charming as I do."

Meghan gave him a side look. He sounded twenty years younger, and she saw a soft smile on his face she hadn't seen in a long time. "I didn't realize you felt that way about her," she said, her tone turning sharp.

"What way?"

"That way. Like you like her. Like you really like her."

"I do. She's an old friend."

"Do you want her to be something more?"

He chuckled. "At my age? I don't think that's possible. Even so, she's not interested."

"How can you be sure?"

Grandfather scoffed. "I'm sure. Besides, I see what you're doing."

"Which is?"

"Changing the subject."

She gripped the steering wheel. She was changing the subject, but she was also curious about Grandfather's feelings. It had never dawned on her that he might feel something for Cevilla. Since Grandmother had died fifteen years ago, he hadn't shown any interest in women. Plenty of them had shown interest in him, though. Some of them had been younger than Meghan, which was unseemly, but it was clear they were after his bank account. She wasn't so sure that the women at the senior center weren't seeing dollar signs as well. That irritated her, because her grandfather was not only still handsome but kind and sweet. Anyone could see that.

"Why were you rude to Cevilla?" Grandfather pressed. "That's not like you."

She let out a sigh, a dash of guilt hitting her. "I'm sorry." And she was. She wasn't rude, especially to people she didn't know. But according to Mother she was acting out of character, and Meghan had to agree with her. "I'll take you over there tomorrow for a visit," she said. "And I'll apologize to your friend."

He nodded. "That's the Meghan I know and love."

They rode the rest of the way in silence, and a few minutes before they arrived at the hotel, she heard light snoring. She smiled. Of course. Grandfather was tired. They'd had a long flight, and then a little more than an hour's drive from the airport. He wasn't used to this much activity. She should have insisted they go straight to the hotel when they landed instead of going to Cevilla's. But he argued with her until she relented. Now she wished she wouldn't have given in so easily.

She pulled in front of the modest hotel. She'd found a lot of bed-and-breakfasts in the area, but most of them were half an hour away or more. Besides, she'd rather stay at a hotel. From what she could tell from pictures on the internet, this one had more amenities than any of the bed-and-breakfast offerings.

"Grandfather?" She nudged him slightly on the shoulder. He

didn't move, and panic ripped through her. What if he'd died on the ride from Cevilla's? Her heart thumping, she nudged him again, this time harder. "Grandfather!"

"What, what?" He jerked awake. "Is the car on fire?"

Meghan breathed out a long sigh of relief. "We're at the hotel."

He blinked and looked at her. "You shook me awake for that?"

Now she felt foolish. She'd overreacted—again. Like she had at Cevilla's. "I'm sorry."

He looked at her, his scowl fading. "It's all right."

The kindness in his eyes brought a lump to her throat. "I need to check us in." She scrambled out the car door and hurried into the lobby before she lost her emotions completely.

An "Under Construction" sign greeted her, along with a bare, plywood floor. Stacks of laminate flooring were against the far wall. Dust was everywhere. She sneezed as she strolled to the front desk.

The clerk, a plump woman who looked to be in her late fifties, gestured to the box of tissues on the counter. "Pardon our dust."

"I didn't see any notice on your website about remodeling the lobby."

The woman sighed and pushed up her red-rimmed glasses. "We're remodeling the whole hotel. And I've sent notices to our webmaster to update the site, but he's ignored our emails."

If there was one thing Meghan couldn't stand, it was incompetence. "You need to get a new webmaster."

The woman leaned forward. "I agree. But since he's the boss's son . . ." She shrugged. "Do you have a reservation?"

Meghan sneezed again.

This time the clerk handed her a tissue. "I really am sorry," she said.

"The entire hotel is being remodeled?"

"Well, not everything. The pool is open." She grinned, but it faded quickly. "The second and third floors haven't been tackled yet. But yesterday we had two large leaks on the third floor, so we had to close half the wing."

"And the second floor?"

She leaned forward again. "It's a bit musty. But fine otherwise."

Meghan huffed. Between the dust, must, and leaks, she couldn't let Grandfather stay here. *She* couldn't stay here. "Is there another hotel near Birch Creek?" Maybe she'd missed one on the internet.

"I'm afraid not. Just some lovely bed-and-breakfasts."

"Any in Barton?"

She shook her head. "We could use one or two, if you asked me. But don't tell my boss I said that."

"Where is your boss?" Meghan had a few words to share with him. This wasn't the way to run an establishment.

"In Aspen."

"Colorado?"

"Yes. He does very well for himself, owning the only hotel around." She started tapping the keys on her keyboard. "I'll look up your reservation."

"I'm canceling it."

The woman peered over her glasses. Then she nodded. "I understand. Name, please?"

After completing the cancellation, she went back to the car. "That took a while," Grandfather said as she got in.

Meghan explained the situation to him.

"I don't mind a bit of dust," he said.

"Your allergies will."

"Pshaw. I don't have allergies." He turned from her and looked out the window.

"Grandfather, you deserve much better accommodations than they have here."

He turned to her. "Because I have money?"

Yes. But she knew that wasn't the answer he wanted to hear. "Because you need to be comfortable."

He didn't say anything for a minute. He just stared at the dashboard in front of him. Then he spoke. "Take me back to Cevilla's, then."

"What?"

"That's the most comfortable I've been in a long time."

Meghan was stunned. "You can't stay with Cevilla!"

"Why not?"

"Because . . . it's unseemly."

He chuckled. "That's an old-fashioned word coming from you."

She pulled out her phone and started searching for another place to stay. She'd take a bed-and-breakfast at this point, even though it would be primitive. Better than dusty and leaky.

Grandfather put his hand over her phone. "I want to stay with Cevilla. If you need to chaperone me, you can sleep on the couch. It's comfortable enough."

She hadn't slept on a couch since her college days, and even then, only once or twice. She thought about her expensive, high-quality mattress at home. Everything else in her life might be falling apart right now, but at least she had her soft bed, where she'd been spending more and more time lately.

"Please, Meghan."

She looked into his gray eyes behind the silver-rimmed glasses. He'd had cataract surgery three years ago, improving his vision, but he still insisted on wearing glasses. He said he felt naked without them. "I've worn them since I was a child, and I'm not about to stop now," he'd said. He could be so stubborn—like he was at this moment.

Did she have the right to refuse his request, though? Couldn't she spend one night on a couch to make him happy? He'd given her so much over the years and asked for so little in return. She put her phone back in her purse. "Are you sure she won't mind?"

"I'm sure." He smiled. "Thank you, Meghan."

She pulled out of the hotel parking lot and headed back to Birch Creek. The whole reason she'd made this trip was for her grandfather, and if he wanted to stay at Cevilla's tonight, she wouldn't refuse him. But tomorrow she would find them a proper place to stay.

-⟨⟨⟨-

Cevilla had just finished her nighttime prayers and was about to climb into bed when she heard a knock on the front door. She frowned. More surprise visitors? Twice in one day was a bit much, so she assumed this had to be someone from the community. A slight stab of panic went through her as she wondered if there was an emergency of some sort. That was the only reason someone would come over unexpectedly at this hour. Everyone knew she always turned in early.

She threw on her housecoat, grabbed her cane, and hurried as fast as she could toward the front door. The sensor lights had flickered on right away. Noah had installed them last year so she wouldn't have to fumble in the dark or carry a flashlight anymore. They were low lights, but bright enough to see. She started to open the door, but then she remembered she'd locked it. She'd lived here more than twenty years without locking her doors, but after the van- dalism at Carolyn Yoder's bakery a few months ago, she heeded her nephew's warning to lock them. She thought it was a shame, and she wasn't afraid of mischievous high school kids. But Noah had been insistent.

She turned the lock and opened the door. The front porch sensor light was already on, illuminating her unexpected guests. Richard stood there, with Meghan right behind him. He was grinning beneath the light, but Meghan looked grumpy. Cevilla glanced down to see she was carrying two suitcases.

"I thought you were going to the hotel." Cevilla tugged her housecoat closer to her, feeling a little self-conscious.

"Change of plans," Richard replied, looking almost giddy.

"We're sorry to impose." Meghan set the suitcases down. "But the hotel is unacceptable."

"They're still renovating?"

Meghan's mouth dropped open. "You knew about that?"

She shrugged. "I wasn't sure. It's been a while since I've been in that area of Barton. But Trevor is always tinkering around with that place. He can afford to, since he has no competition."

"We noticed," Meghan muttered.

Cevilla opened the screen door. "You're welcome to stay here. Although, as you already know, I can't provide five-star accommodations either."

"That's all right by me." Richard shuffled into the living room, and then turned to her. "Thank you, Cevilla."

"We're staying only one night." Meghan picked up the suitcases and went inside. "Got that, Grandfather?"

Richard didn't answer her.

Chuckling, Cevilla shut the door and twisted the lock. Meghan didn't seem to like having her plans altered. But Richard obviously was game to make the best of it. "You can have my bedroom," she told him. "I'll sleep on the couch."

Richard shook his head. "No. I'll sleep on the couch. I insist."

Meghan put the smaller of the suitcases next to the sofa. "I'm sleeping on the couch."

"Meghan, I'm perfectly happy with the couch—"

"Grandfather, you need a good night's sleep. Case closed." She crossed her arms and turned to Cevilla. "I'll be taking the couch."

Cevilla smirked. "This is *my* house, young lady. I will decide the arrangements."

Both Richard and Meghan grew quiet.

"Richard," Cevilla said, turning to him, "you will take my bedroom. Meghan, you'll take the room upstairs. I will sleep here. Any objections?"

"No," they both said at the same time.

"Then I'll show you to your room, Meghan." Cevilla nodded at her and started up the stairs. These two needed to realize who was in charge here.

— CHAPTER 4 —

Meghan's cheeks burned as she followed Cevilla up the illuminated stairs, which the old woman clearly had no trouble navigating. She did move a bit slow, though, and that was fine with Meghan. She needed the time to get over being embarrassed by her and Grandfather's argument.

When they reached the second floor, Cevilla walked to the end of the short hallway and stopped in front of a door on the left. "This room is a lot plainer than what you're used to," she said, opening the door. She went inside and turned on a small lamp on a table by the bed.

Meghan followed, taking in the tidy room. A double bed against one wall had an old but lovely quilt spread over it. A small dresser sat near a door she assumed led to a closet.

"You can put your things in there." Cevilla pointed at the dresser. Then she gestured to the door. "The closet is empty, so if you have anything to hang, you can put it in there. The bathroom is across the hall. You'll find towels and washcloths there, along with soap and shampoo. There's a battery-powered lamp just like the one in here on the vanity. It's easy enough to find. Breakfast is at 5:30 sharp. I don't abide lollygaggers. Any questions?"

"No, ma'am," she said, her tone meek. When Cevilla started to leave, she added, "I do appreciate you letting us stay here."

Cevilla's eyes softened. "You're welcome. I know it's not what you're used to, but the bed is comfortable. You should try to make the best of it, like your grandfather is."

She nodded, her throat inexplicably aching. Then again, her emotions had been all over the place lately. "I know," she whispered. "I'm sorry if I've come across as rude."

Cevilla walked over to her and patted her hand. "Whatever has got you in knots, give it to the Lord. He's more than happy to untangle it for you."

Meghan nodded, unable to speak. Did God even care? She used to think so, but now she had no idea.

"*Gute nacht*," Cevilla said in her unfamiliar language. "I'll make sure the coffee is hot and sugar free when you get up in the morning."

"Thank you."

Cevilla nodded and closed the door.

Meghan sat down on the bed, squeezing back tears. The woman didn't know what pain, failure, and heartache lay just beneath the surface. They were like thorns she couldn't pull out. She wasn't sure if she ever could.

Richard watched Cevilla make her way down the stairs with slow, deliberate movements. He could relate. His knees creaked and groaned when he went down a flight of stairs, and he tried to avoid them as much as possible. He met Cevilla when she reached the bottom. "Everything all right with Meghan?" he said, holding his hand out to her on instinct.

She looked at it with a raised eyebrow. "She'll be fine." She continued to stare at his hand. "I don't need help down one step," she said.

He withdrew his hand. "Sorry. Force of habit."

Cevilla looked up at him and stepped down. "It's a nice habit."

He nodded, glad that she wasn't upset. While she and Meghan were upstairs, he'd had second thoughts about staying here, especially when Cevilla had put a stern end to his argument with his granddaughter. Maybe Cevilla didn't want them there. Maybe she was only being polite. He had just burst into her life after all these years, and Meghan wasn't acting her usual sweet, if a tad high strung, self. But he wanted Cevilla to get to know her, to learn that she was a lovely young woman when her life wasn't falling apart. Showing up on her doorstep tonight probably wasn't the right way to do it. "I'm sorry about our argument, and our imposition."

"Ah, ah, ah." She held up one finger. "That's the last apology I'll hear out of you. I'm glad you're both here." She put down her hand.

That was a relief. But one thing wasn't sitting right with him. "I'll take the couch," he said, his tone insistent.

She rolled her eyes, which made her look youthful, again reminding him of the girl he'd known in Arnold City. "We've settled this already."

"Yes, we have. I'll be sleeping on the couch."

She lifted her chin, her expression becoming stubborn. "No, you won't. And since I'm older—"

"By three months—"

"Like I said, I'm older," she continued with a smile. "I will decide the sleeping arrangements."

He sighed, knowing he had to admit defeat. "I don't suppose I can convince you otherwise?"

"Nope. It's settled. All I need is a quilt and a pillow, and I'm all set. Now, get your suitcase and follow me."

Cevilla was still like her younger self, willing to take charge of a situation. Not because of arrogance, but because of an innate

---

self-confidence. He'd admired that about her back then. He'd been on the shy, quiet side. And when he failed the eye test and was unable to serve in the Korean War, he'd felt like he was letting down his country and his community. She'd talked him through that, and he was able to serve in his own way—writing letters to his friends who were overseas and volunteering at hospitals when they returned.

Not all of them had returned, a fact that had hit their community hard. Shortly after the end of the war, Cevilla left, and that had hit him even harder.

His stomach suddenly growled. He'd forgotten that he and Meghan hadn't eaten supper. She had planned to order in when they got to the hotel.

Cevilla turned around, giving him a scolding look. "Why didn't you tell me you were hungry, Richard? I would have fed both you and Meghan as soon as you walked in the door. I'll go get Meghan and then make you two a bite to eat." She started to move past him, but he touched her arm.

"I already know what she'll say," he said, unable to keep the sadness out of his voice. "She hasn't had much of an appetite lately."

Cevilla nodded. "Then it will be dinner for two."

He liked that idea—and he was glad she felt comfortable enough to just stay in her housecoat. He certainly didn't mind.

They went into the kitchen and Cevilla headed straight for the pantry. "Let's see, I have the makings for sandwiches, of course. Oh, here's some chicken soup Mary Yoder brought over last week." She pulled out a mason jar, and he could see carrots and celery floating in the broth. "I can heat this up with some fresh bread."

"Sounds great." He leaned against his cane. "May I help?"

"I don't know . . ." She shut the door to the pantry and shuffled past him. "Can I trust you with a knife?" She gave him a wink.

"I'll do my best."

"The bread is over there." She pointed at an old-looking wooden box on the counter. "You'll find a knife in the drawer under there and a plate in the cabinet above."

Richard moved to the counter, his own shuffling gait matching Cevilla's. They were quite a pair. He looked at the box—an actual breadbox. He hadn't seen one in years. He pushed up the sliding door and pulled out half a loaf of bread. Behind him he could hear Cevilla placing a pot on the stove.

His heart skipped a beat. He and Nancy used to cook together, especially in the early years of their marriage—before the maids and cooks, before he'd worked long hours that had kept him away from home more than he was there. He touched the crust of the bread. Those were simpler times. He missed them.

"Don't cut the slices too thick," Cevilla said.

Her voice pulled him out of his thoughts, and he chuckled. "Still bossy as ever."

He heard her sniff. "Not bossy. I'm merely giving you guidance."

He looked at her over his shoulder, thankful his neck muscles had loosened. She was stirring the soup. "I never minded bossy."

"Guidance." She lifted one finger before glancing at him over her own shoulder, meeting his gaze. Then she smiled. "All right, bossiness. But with good intentions."

"Of course." He turned to finish slicing the bread, making sure the slices weren't too thin or thick. Then he brought the plate to the table, placing it next to a white, covered butter dish. "What would you like to drink, Cevilla?"

"Tea, of course. I already have the kettle on."

"That suits me just fine. How about I finish stirring that soup while you make the tea?"

She paused, and then nodded.

Richard went to stand beside her and took the spoon from her. Steam rose from the pot, and the soup was already bubbling.

Before long the kettle whistled, and the meal was ready. He filled two soup bowls halfway and carried them one at a time to the table. Cevilla did the same with the teacups.

They settled into their chairs, and Cevilla closed her eyes. Richard realized she was praying and followed suit. When she said, "Amen," he opened his eyes and met her gaze. His heart tripped again. "This is nice," he said, unable to stop smiling.

She nodded, returning his smile. "Yes," she said softly. "It is."

He was about to dip his spoon into the soup when he noticed Cevilla wasn't eating. "Is something wrong?"

She folded her hands under her chin. "I think there's something you're not telling me."

Richard stilled. "I don't know what you're talking about."

"I think you do. You're a man of means, Richard. You could have traveled anywhere in the country. Probably anywhere in the world. Yet you show up here, in this tiny Amish town most people have never heard of. I know Meghan needed to get away"—she tilted her head and met his eyes—"but I can't help thinking there's more to your visit than what you're letting on."

He set down his spoon. He'd thought about how to tell her what he had to say, if the subject ever came up. He just hadn't expected it to come up so soon. "You're right," he said, holding her gaze, his hunger forgotten. "I *am* here for another reason."

"I'm all ears."

A lump formed in his throat, and he had to clear it before he could say what was on his heart. "I came here to see . . ." He cleared his throat again. He hadn't been this nervous since . . . since he'd almost told her the truth about his feelings decades ago. "To see if I still felt the same way. About you."

A puzzled look crossed her face. "I don't understand."

He didn't understand much himself. His marriage to Nancy had been happy, filled with love and mutual respect and admiration. The thought of dating someone again hadn't entered his mind for years, until he fell and ended up in the hospital. What he hadn't told his daughter and granddaughter was that he'd been lucky the bump on his head hadn't killed him. "Folks your age," the doctor had said, "have to be careful. One misstep and . . ."

Richard hadn't needed him to fill in the blank. And while he was in the hospital, he'd thought long and hard about his life. Usually his mind dwelled in the past, but this time he pondered the future. Did he really want to spend the time he had left alone? He had Sharon and Meghan, but they were living their own lives, as they should.

A still, small voice was talking to his heart and soul, reminding him of unfinished business. Reminding him of Cevilla.

"Richard?"

Cevilla's voice pulled him out of his thoughts. How could he tell her how he felt? He hadn't been able to say the words to her when they were young, and he'd lost her to another man. Now he felt like that mute teenager, unable to find the courage to tell the first girl he loved his true feelings.

"What I mean is . . ." He stared at his soup, which he was sure had started to grow cold. "I missed our friendship. We used to be pretty good friends."

"That we were," she said softly, still staring at him.

"And you know what they say." He picked up the spoon and gave her a grin he hoped wasn't as forced as it felt. "Time is long, but life is short. I figured now would be as good a time as any to renew our friendship."

Cevilla didn't say anything, which he knew was unusual for her. After a long silence, she lifted her teacup. "I suppose it is."

-◄◄◄-

Richard picked up his small suitcase and followed Cevilla to her bedroom. The rest of supper had been a quiet affair. They hadn't talked much, and he was grateful he didn't have to explain himself further. The soup was tasty, the bread soft and fresh, and the company perfect. He couldn't remember the last time he'd had such a wonderful meal, despite the simplicity and spontaneity of it, and despite the awkward moments in the beginning.

Cevilla's room was tidy, plain, and simple, which were compliments in Richard's mind.

"Probably a lot less than what you're used to." Cevilla smoothed the top of the well-worn quilt on her single bed before turning to him. "You might be better off at the hotel."

Richard was surprised to see a flicker of uncertainty in Cevilla's eyes. As a teenager, she'd rarely shown that side of herself, only when she was torn between CJ and the Amish. He had listened while she talked about her feelings for CJ, yet how God was drawing her back to her roots. Back to the Amish life she'd loved more than anything. While all that had been hard to listen to, he'd been honored that she'd chosen him to confide in.

He took a step toward her, his cane thumping against the hardwood floor. "Are you all right?"

The uncertainty disappeared with a lift of her chin. "Of course. Why wouldn't I be? You're just spending the night." She chuckled. "And I invited you to do so."

Richard smiled, and he couldn't help but crack a joke. "Sounds a little scandalous, doesn't it?"

Her cheeks turned a lovely shade of pink as she averted her gaze. Another surprise. He grew serious. "If I'm making you uncomfortable, I can go back to the hotel. I don't have a problem with a little dust."

Cevilla looked at him. "You don't have to leave, Richard."

"I don't want to put you out—"

"I want you to stay."

— CHAPTER 5 —

Cevilla bit her bottom lip, and then made herself stop. Really, biting her lip like a silly ingenue! And over something as mundane as an old friend being a houseguest. It made no sense. She'd had houseguests before, but never more than one at a time, and they'd always stayed in the spare room upstairs. No one other than herself had ever slept in her bed.

But the thought of Richard being the first made her feel . . . a little giddy? No, that couldn't be right. Must be the extra dash of pepper she'd added to the soup talking back to her. The older she was, the less tolerance she had for any kind of spice.

But this wasn't the first time she'd felt giddy around Richard. Her heart had been doing tiny backflips during the meal, especially after what he'd said. *If I still felt the same way . . . about you.* The way he'd looked at her and the softness of his words had touched something deep inside her soul. And the way he was looking at her now, with those warm gray eyes of his that had always had trouble with acuity, yet could see things more deeply than anyone she'd ever met . . .

Her heart did another flip. Or maybe she should just cut back on the pepper.

"I invited you here," she said, regaining her senses and resuming her role as a neutral hostess. "And I want you to stay."

"Oh." He tilted his head and looked at her. "I thought you meant . . ." He shook his head. "Never mind."

She turned from him, ignoring the little twirl of emotion in her chest—or indigestion, as the case may be—and fluffed the pillows. "If you need another one of these, I have an extra one in my closet. Also another blanket." She turned to him. "The bathroom is around the corner. Small, but serviceable. Don't worry about lights—my nephew installed these fancy sensor lights all around this house. I told him not to bother, but he insisted. He worries about me, you know." She let out a nervous chuckle. "I don't know why. I've lived on my own for this long just fine." Oh, good gravy, she was rambling. Actually rambling.

"I know." Richard's voice was gravelly from age but still filled with strength. "You're amazing, Cevilla."

For goodness' sake, now her cheeks were heating again. Maybe she was falling ill. But she didn't feel ill. She felt . . . nice.

And foolish. She waved her hand at him. "I get up early," she said, gripping the handle of her cane and making her way to the bedroom door. "If you hear some puttering around in the kitchen, it's only me."

"I rise early too."

Why was he looking at her so intently? She cleared her throat. "Then feel free to join me for tea or coffee."

"I will."

She smiled, her nervousness disappearing. It was nice to have company, especially an old friend. And she had been feeling a bit lonely lately, a bit more steeped in the past than usual. That explained her odd feelings. *Simple as that.* "Sleep well, then."

"You too, Cevilla."

She shut the door behind her and went to the linen closet, where she took a pillow and a lap quilt from the shelves. She carried them to the couch and sat down. She'd had this old sofa for years. It was well worn, but comfortable. It had also been years since she'd slept on it, except for a quick nap every now and then. Usually she fell asleep in her chair.

Cevilla folded her hands in her lap and closed her eyes. She'd said her evening prayers before Richard and Meghan arrived to spend the night, but she felt the need to pray again. She'd been unable to kneel since last year, but she knew God understood. A respectful posture was important, but not more important that the posture of her heart.

She prayed for Richard and for Meghan. Then she sat in silence, as was her habit, and listened. This was the most difficult part of her prayer time, since she normally liked to be the one talking. But she'd learned over the years that opening her ears to God's voice was as necessary as breathing. Sometimes he spoke to her. Sometimes he was silent. Tonight, she didn't hear a thing—and she accepted that.

She arranged her bed for the night, leaned her cane against the coffee table, and laid down. She was tired, and her eyes started to close.

Thump. Thump. Thump.

Cevilla opened her eyes. She was startled, but then she recognized the sound. Meghan was pacing. It wasn't loud, as if she was trying not to make noise, but Cevilla's hearing was sharp. She sighed. The woman really was in some kind of pickle, and Cevilla's heart went out to her. *How can I help her, Lord?*

-◄◄◄-

Meghan paced back and forth in bare feet. The fashionable heels she'd worn all day sat next to the closet, looking out of place in the simple bedroom. She should just lie down and try to get some sleep. She was tired from the flight and worrying about Grandfather. Oddly, he had seemed more energetic than she was. Then again, he'd had a nap in the car.

But she couldn't settle her mind enough to stay still. It was quiet in this house. Too quiet. Although she lived in an upscale neighborhood in LA, she was used to noise, like the hum of the air conditioning system or the computer in her office. In the kitchen, the refrigerator would cycle on and off, and while the dishwasher was top of the line, it wasn't silent. Noise was everywhere in her world. Here it was the complete opposite.

She stopped and stared out the window. It was so dark out there. Now, alone in Cevilla's spare bedroom, she couldn't escape her thoughts. They rang loudly in her head.

She hadn't wanted to go on this trip with Grandfather, but she had to admit it was a good, if slightly frustrating diversion. She wondered what was going on back home. If Conor, her ex-fiancé as of a month ago, had taken his current girlfriend on the Fiji trip Meghan had planned for them before he dumped her. If Tawny, her former work partner as of two weeks ago, was enjoying the profit she made from selling their interior design business out from under her.

If her grandfather, who had issued warnings about them both, was itching to say *I told you so.*

Meghan shook her head. Grandfather would never do that. He was a class act, and always had been. She'd thought she'd found a man like him in Conor—a smart, business-minded, churchgoing man, who was also handsome and kind. She'd thought she'd hit the jackpot.

She heard the phone buzz in her purse. Surprised that it still had a charge, she picked it up. Mother. If she didn't answer it, her mother would blow up her phone until she did. With a sigh, she slid her finger on the screen to make the connection. "Hello?"

"Well, hello to you."

Meghan winced at Mother's sharp tone. "It's kind of late here," she said, glancing outside again. "I was going to call you in the morning."

"It's not even ten o'clock there."

"Oh." It had seemed much later. "Sorry. I should have called you, then."

"Yes, you should of." Mother sniffed. "How is Father?"

"He's fine."

"Is he getting enough rest? Has he eaten well today?"

Meghan froze. She'd been so concerned about the hotel accommodations that she'd forgotten about supper. Her own appetite had been dulled these past weeks, which explained why her clothes hung so loosely, but it was inexcusable for her to forget his. And Grandfather hadn't said a thing. "Uh, yes. He's eating well." *At lunch, at least.*

Mother let out a relieved sigh. "I knew you would take good care of him. When are you coming back?"

As soon as possible. Although, what did she have to go back to? She wasn't engaged anymore. She had no fiancé, along with no wedding. She also had no money from her former business to start a new one—unless she borrowed from Grandfather, and she wasn't about to do that again.

"Meghan? Did you hear me?"

"Ah, yes. Probably in a week." Although what she would do with herself here in the backwoods for a week, she had no idea.

"Humph." Meghan could imagine her mother sipping on her organic pomegranate and beet smoothie she had every night before going to bed. "I thought you'd return tomorrow."

"I think back-to-back flights would be too tiring for Grandfather."

Not to mention that she knew full well he didn't want to leave right away. He was too smitten with Cevilla—and smitten was the exact word to describe how he kept looking at her.

"That's true. I worry about him, that's all."

But you're not worried about me. Meghan gripped the phone. "My cell is dying, so I better put it on the charger." Her mother had no idea they weren't in the hotel she'd booked, a hotel with electricity.

"Very well. Text me your flight information as soon as you make the reservation."

"I will."

"Tell Father I said good night."

Meghan nodded, but then she realized her mother couldn't see the gesture. "I will—"

She'd already disconnected the call.

She put the phone back in her purse. In the morning she'd have to figure out how to charge it—probably in the rental car—but for now she didn't care if it died during the night.

She set her unpacked bag on the floor and sat down on the edge of the bed, tears welling in her eyes. Great, on top of everything else she was going to cry again. Why couldn't she be strong like Mother? She rarely showed her tears, although she had little trouble revealing her temper. But Meghan didn't blame her for being angry. She'd planned the wedding of the season and then had to cancel it. "What will my friends think?" she'd said before unleashing a tirade about how Meghan had screwed up something else in her life.

Meghan looked down at her lap. Mother was right. She was a screwup. She'd lost her love, her business, and now she was losing her faith. Bad things weren't supposed to happen to good people, right? And she was a good person . . . wasn't she?

She laid on top of the quilt and wiped her eyes. None of it

mattered to her anymore. Only her grandfather was important. He hadn't blamed her, hadn't shamed her, hadn't made her feel any more worthless than she already felt.

She needed to be more supportive of him. She also needed to make sure he had something to eat.

She snuck downstairs, and another dim light came on at the bottom of the stairwell. The sensor lights were everywhere, and now that she had experienced how dark it could be, she was glad. She saw Cevilla's small body on the couch, covered with a quilt, her mouth slightly open as she slept. Meghan crept past her and searched for the bedroom. The house was so small she didn't have any trouble finding it.

She lifted her hand to knock. What if Grandfather was asleep? She didn't want to disturb him. Then again, she didn't want him getting up in the middle of the night because he was hungry. The door was open partway, and she peeked inside. Just enough light was coming from the hallway for her to see a lump on the bed, and she could hear light snoring.

"He's fine, Meghan," a whisper sounded in her ear.

She jumped and turned around to see Cevilla standing behind her. She pulled the door closed until it was open just a crack, and then faced her. "We forgot to eat supper," she whispered back. "I don't want him to go hungry."

Cevilla led Meghan back to the living room. "We had some soup earlier, after you went upstairs." She paused. "He said you probably wouldn't want any."

He was right. "Thank you for taking care of him." *For doing what I should be doing.*

"My pleasure."

From the sparkle in the old woman's eyes, Meghan believed her.

"Now, let's feed you."

Meghan shook her head. "I'm really not hungry."

Cevilla peeped over her glasses and gave her a stern look. "And I'm Elizabeth Taylor."

"Who?"

"Never mind. Now come on, into the kitchen with you."

Knowing she better comply, Meghan went into the kitchen with her hostess. Cevilla turned on a gas lamp. A clock on the wall above the kitchen window confirmed it was a little after ten. Meghan felt like two days had passed. "I'm sorry I woke you up," she said.

"I wasn't all the way asleep." She looked at Meghan. "Peanut butter and grape jelly coming right up."

Meghan frowned. She hadn't had peanut butter and jelly since she was a teenager.

"I also have some apple juice."

"I'm not twelve," Meghan blurted as she sat down.

"I'm aware of that." Cevilla shuffled to the pantry, her cane thumping on the floor.

Meghan was about to protest, but suddenly peanut butter and grape jelly and apple juice sounded palatable, which she couldn't say about any other food lately. "May I help?" she asked, feeling contrite for being rude. Continually rude, at that.

"You're just like your grandfather." Cevilla shut the pantry door with her shoulder, a small jar of peanut butter and another small jar that looked like it contained homemade jelly tucked in the crook of one arm. She looked at her. "That's a compliment."

"I know." Meghan watched as the woman made a sandwich and then poured apple juice. When Cevilla started carrying the plate to the table, Meghan popped up and took it from her. She lifted the plastic cup of juice from the counter and walked back to the table. As Cevilla pulled out a chair, Meghan said, "You can go back to bed. I'm fine, really."

"Your idea of fine and my idea of fine are very different, young lady." Cevilla sat down, and then tapped the space in front of Meghan's chair with her cane.

Meghan complied and sat down. She felt like she was being scolded by her grandmother—or NanNan, as she'd called her growing up. NanNan and Cevilla weren't much alike in lifestyle, but the kindness in Cevilla's eyes reminded her of NanNan . . . and brought a lump to her throat.

Cevilla looked at her for a long moment, her head tilted. Silver-rimmed glasses, at least twenty years out of date but still with a timeless quality, sat perched on her nose. Her skin was wrinkled yet had a translucent softness to it. Meghan glanced at the woman's hands. They were even more wrinkled and gnarled, the blue veins almost glowing beneath the yellowish gas light hissing in the corner of the kitchen. Meghan sensed she was in the company of a wise, independent woman who had made it through some tough times and come out better for it.

"You're staring," Cevilla said, raising a thin gray eyebrow.

"Sorry." Meghan looked at her sandwich. She wasn't sure if she could choke it down. Her loss of appetite, the lump in her throat, the tears that were coming unbidden—

"Let's pray." Cevilla reached across the table and slipped her hand into Meghan's. She closed her eyes.

Meghan followed suit, aware of the warmth coming from Cevilla's small hand. For the first time in weeks her mind cleared enough for her to say a few words of silent prayer. *Lord . . . help me.* Cevilla squeezed her hand and she opened her eyes.

"Go on. Eat your sandwich." Cevilla folded her hands on the table.

With a nod, Meghan picked up the sandwich and took a bite. The softness of the bread was heavenly, the peanut butter and jelly comforting. She took a sip of the apple juice. "This is really good."

"It's more like cider than juice," Cevilla explained. "Freshly made by Thomas Bontrager. Perry's father."

Meghan nodded, although she didn't really care who made the apple juice, or cider, or whatever. In silence, she finished both the sandwich and the drink. Cevilla handed her a paper napkin from the wooden holder in the middle of the table.

"Now that you've had some sustenance, let's talk."

She started to shake her head. What was going on in her life wasn't any of this woman's business. But suddenly she found herself answering. "My life . . ." She hung her head. "My life is a mess."

"Whose isn't?"

Meghan's head popped up. "You don't understand—"

"Oh, I understand. I might not know the specifics, but I understand what it's like when things seem to be falling apart."

"Have you ever lost a fiancé?"

Cevilla's gaze held hers. "As a matter of fact, I have."

"That was your own choice, though."

Cevilla chuckled. "You know my story."

"I know a little bit. Grandfather told me you were engaged to one of his friends when you all were young, while the Korean War was going on. He said you broke it off with him and joined the Amish."

"That's the gist of it."

"You broke his heart." Meghan couldn't keep the edge out of her tone.

"Yes," she said softly. "I did. I loved CJ. But I believed God was calling me to be Amish. My only regret is that I hurt him. My heart was broken too."

"And that's your fault." Meghan crossed her arms.

"You can look at it that way."

"What other way is there to look at it?"

Cevilla peered over her glasses. "It wouldn't have been fair to marry CJ when my heart was somewhere else. I could have ignored God's call, stayed English, and married CJ. We would have been happy on some level, I suppose. But CJ deserved someone who loved him completely, without doubts or hesitation. Everyone does." She leaned forward, almost as if she knew about Conor. But Meghan knew Grandfather wouldn't have revealed her secrets.

Tears dripped down Meghan's cheeks. "I'm not so sure I do."

"Oh? I'm sure your grandfather thinks so. And he's a man of impeccable taste." She leaned back. "He's friends with me, you know."

Meghan couldn't help but chuckle as she wiped her tears with her fingers. "I can see why. Although, why did you two lose touch over the years?"

Cevilla glanced out the dark window. "That's a good question," she said softly. Then she turned. "But it's possible we were meant to be reunited only at this point in time for a reason. It's also possible that you were meant to come here for a reason."

Meghan nodded. "To help Grandfather."

"That," she said, pushing her chair back and standing up with the assistance of her cane, "and to help yourself." She yawned as she shuffled to stand beside Meghan. She put her hand on her shoulder. "Remember, child. You are worthy of love. We all are." Then she smiled. "Now, I'm off to bed. You should be too. Those shadows under your eyes aren't going to go away unless you get some good sleep. Just turn that black knob on the lamp to the right before you leave the kitchen."

Meghan watched her go. The lump in her throat was gone, and she felt a tiny flash of lightness in her heart. Did she really want to be with a man who would cheat on her? No.

Then again, was she the only one at fault in their relationship? If she was honest with herself, she'd have to admit a tenseness had developed between her and Conor for several months. She had sensed it but chalked it all up to wedding jitters and refused to discuss anything with him except wedding plans—even though he'd tried to address what was going on between them. That didn't give him license to find another woman, but yes, she was part of the problem with their relationship. She just wasn't the sole problem, like her mother seemed to think.

She went upstairs, sat back down on the edge of the bed, and took her phone out of her purse. After staring at it for a few moments, she turned it on. She still had some power left. She touched the phone icon with her thumb and then checked her recent calls. Conor's name was there, popping up more than five times in the past week. She knew that, of course, just like she knew he'd left a voice mail message each time. She hadn't listened to any of them. She hadn't wanted to hear his voice, to listen to his explanations.

Maybe she should have.

She checked the time. Would he even be home? Or worse, would his new girlfriend answer?

Her eyes closed, and she pressed the phone to her chest. Part of her sleeplessness was because of a lack of closure between the two of them. She knew that, just like she knew she wouldn't be able to move on if they never talked about what happened.

Meghan looked at her phone again. She pressed his number. The phone rang once.

"Meghan?"

Her stomach lurched even as she heard the relief in his voice. "Yes, Conor, it's me."

"Oh, Meghan, I'm so glad to hear from you. When you wouldn't take my calls . . . although I understood. You didn't have to take my calls." He paused. "I'm . . ." His voice was thick. "I'm sorry."

Tears flowed freely now, but they weren't all filled with sorrow this time. "Me too."

— CHAPTER 6 —

Richard sat on the edge of the bed, fully dressed, and stretched out his legs. He did a few leg lifts, simple exercises his physical therapist had given him to strengthen his muscles and hips after the fall. As he went through his regimen, he could hear the birds tweeting outside, see the sunshine streaming through the window, see the gleam of the polished wood trim around Cevilla's closet. Quality work. He recognized it right away. He assumed nothing in this house was slapped together in a hurry, trying to meet a rushed deadline so a check could be collected and the next house built. He'd supervised the construction of his own house, knowing full well that contractors couldn't always be trusted. That probably wasn't a problem Cevilla had ever had to deal with.

His exercises done, he stood, grabbed his cane, and went to the bathroom. A few minutes later he was walking toward the kitchen. A delectable smoky scent reached his nose. He smiled. Cevilla didn't have to go through the trouble of making bacon. However, he was pleased that she had.

When he walked into the kitchen, though, Cevilla wasn't the one at the stove. It was Meghan. Not only was she cooking, but she was fully dressed and wearing a white apron tied around her waist.

"Good morning, Grandfather." She gave him a bright smile, one he hadn't seen in a long time, and then turned over a bacon strip. "I'm making these extra crispy. Just the way you like them."

Richard nodded, dumbfounded. He couldn't remember ever seeing Meghan—or her mother—cook. He hadn't even been aware Meghan knew how, much less how he liked his bacon. He supposed she'd observed how their cook served it to him.

He felt a touch on his arm and looked down into Cevilla's pretty eyes. "Did you put her up to this?"

"Me?" Cevilla scoffed. "Of course not. But I will say this: you *can* lead a horse to water."

But you can't make it drink. His granddaughter and Cevilla must have had a conversation between the time he went to bed and now. He was curious, but he wouldn't pry. It was enough for him to see Meghan smile. The bacon was a bonus.

"Have a seat," Meghan said, pointing in the direction of the table. "You too, Cevilla."

Cevilla started for a seat, but on impulse, Richard grabbed her hand and gave it a squeeze. "Thank you," he whispered.

She nodded, and then looked down at their hands clasped together. Something moved in his heart. It felt so good to hold a woman's hand . . . *this* woman's hand. So much so that he didn't want to let go.

But she made the decision for him. She slipped her hand out of his and went to sit down. He followed her, feeling his heart pounding in his chest. Had he offended her? That was the last thing he wanted to do.

Meghan brought over a platter of bacon and set it down next to a bowl of hardboiled eggs. Again, another one of his favorites. Hardboiled was the only way he liked eggs, never scrambled or fried. He looked up at his granddaughter with tears in his eyes. This was the Meghan he knew, cooking skills aside. Thoughtful. Sweet. Caring. He hoped this meant she was back for good.

She returned to the counter, and then brought two cups of tea and set them down in front of him and Cevilla. She left again and came back with a small white bowl. She placed it in front of him.

"What's this?"

"Sugar," Meghan said.

He glanced up at her. "Really?"

"A tiny bit won't hurt." She smiled, but the smile dimmed quickly. "You've managed your diabetes well all this time. I trust you know how much sugar you can have."

He put his hand over hers. "Thank you, Meghan."

She turned her palm up and squeezed his hand. "Now, you two enjoy breakfast." She took off the apron and hung it on a peg near the cabinets.

"Aren't you going to eat?" he asked.

"I had a couple of eggs a little while ago. I thought I'd take a walk. It's a beautiful morning. And don't worry," she said as she walked out of the kitchen. "I won't get lost."

Richard turned at Cevilla's chuckle. "I really do like her, Richard."

He nodded. "Me too."

—≪≪≪—

Meghan was still out for her walk by the time they finished breakfast. As Cevilla stood and reached to clear the dishes, she noticed Richard was drumming his fingers against the table. "I'm sure she's fine," Cevilla said.

"I know she is." He looked at her and grinned. "Just like I know she's going to be okay."

Cevilla stilled, the flutter in her stomach occurring again, like it had when he was holding her hand. It unnerved her that she hadn't wanted to let go of his hand, so she had pulled away from him, which had brought a new emotion into play—regret. She didn't like this roller coaster of emotions she was on. She hadn't felt this way since . . .

She'd never felt this way. Her love for CJ was the bloom of first love, filled with expectation for a long future together. That's what romantic love had meant to her. But there would be no long future with her and Richard, and that was a fact. More importantly, why had the thought even crossed her mind?

Yet it was crossing her mind again as he smiled at her, spreading warmth and comfort into her heart.

She took their plates to the sink and leaned against it, confused. *Lord, I don't understand this. My time for love has passed, and I've always accepted that. I'm too old for these feelings. It's impractical and illogical and—*

"Cevilla?"

She looked over her shoulder and saw him standing behind her. When she turned around, he moved even closer, the soft look in his eyes intensifying her feelings. "Yes?" Although how she managed to speak, she had no idea, which was shocking for her. She was never at a loss for words.

"I'm glad I came to see you."

"Me too."

-≪≪-

Meghan arranged for them to stay at a bed-and-breakfast, but every morning she took Richard back to Cevilla's house. For several days he'd been a willing participant in Cevilla's guided tour of Birch Creek and Barton, courtesy of what Cevilla called a taxi—someone who lived in the area and drove them around in his car. His granddaughter had spent a lot of time taking long walks, napping on Cevilla's couch, and cooking in the kitchen, which left him and Cevilla time to be together. Time he thoroughly enjoyed.

He'd met several people in the community, including the bishop, Freemont Yoder. His memory wasn't what it used to be so he didn't remember everyone's names, but their friendliness and the beauty of the landscape became etched in his mind and soul. The longer he stayed here, the more at peace he felt. He didn't miss the bustle and superficiality of Los Angeles. It was as if this place, in the span of a few days, had started to feel like home.

But it wasn't home, and the day before he and Meghan were scheduled to return to California, he and Cevilla headed to her nephew Noah's house for an early supper. To his surprise, she'd decided to take a buggy. "I asked Adam Chupp if I could have Judah Yoder come over with my old buggy and Shep, all ready to go," she'd told him earlier that day as they were snacking on homemade date bars, courtesy of his granddaughter. He'd had no idea Meghan could bake too.

Judah had complied, and by late afternoon they were heading to Noah's in a buggy. Meghan had begged off, saying she had some phone calls to make. Richard was glad to see her getting into the swing of things again.

"I'm impressed," he said, as Cevilla steered Shep down the road.

"Don't be too much. I could let go of these reins and he'd get us to Noah's on his own. He's been there enough times."

Richard nodded and looked out the buggy's opening. He breathed in the scent of fresh earth and clear air. "I understand why you moved here," he said.

"Iowa is just as nice," she said, referring to where she'd originally lived after going back to the Amish.

"I meant becoming Amish." He turned to her.

"Don't tell me you're considering it," she said with a small chuckle.

"Would it surprise you if I did?"

She turned to him, her mouth agape. "What?"

"You don't have to worry about that," he said, waving off her surprise. "I have no plans to make a change."

"Oh."

He looked at her, but she was staring straight ahead, her expression unreadable. Was she disappointed? His heart leapt a bit at the thought. He hadn't revealed his true feelings for her this past week, but they were still strong. She, on the other hand, had kept a friendly distance, which disappointed him. But what had he expected? That she'd fall for him after a weeklong reunion?

Richard settled back in the buggy seat. He'd enjoyed his time with Cevilla, even as friends.

They arrived at her nephew's, and she pulled into the driveway. Noah came outside, helped them from the buggy, and immediately led the horse to the barn. Noah was a tall, lanky man with a friendly smile. Richard had already met him and his petite wife, Ivy, at their antique store in Barton. "Why don't you come with me, city slicker?" Noah said to Richard with a grin. "I bet you've never stepped foot in a barn."

"I have," Richard said, pretending to be offended. "I've even fed a horse."

Noah's brow lifted. "Really. You fed a horse."

"Don't give him a hard time, Noah." Cevilla shook her cane at him.

Her nephew held up his hand. "I promise I won't."

"Go on inside, Cevilla," Richard said. "I'd like to take a look at Noah's barn."

She paused, but then nodded and went inside. Richard followed

Noah into the barn and watched him give his horse some grain. Richard was taking in the entire scene. He hadn't specified that his encounter with a horse had been feeding a pony a carrot at a fair he took Meghan to when she was little. He really was a city slicker.

Noah shut the stall door and turned to Richard, his expression serious. "What are your intentions toward my great-aunt?"

Richard was caught off guard. "Intentions?"

"Yes, intentions." Noah met his gaze straight on.

Richard tugged at the collar of his shirt. He hadn't expected to be interrogated tonight. But he also respected Noah for it. "We're friends," he insisted. "When you get to be my age, you don't have many of those left."

Noah's expression softened. "I suppose not. What happens after you leave?"

That question had been on his mind. What *would* happen after he left? Would he and Cevilla stay in contact? Or would they fall away from each other again, this time for good. "I don't know," he answered honestly. "I suppose Cevilla and I will figure something out."

Her nephew nodded. "I'm sorry for prying. Cevilla means a lot to me."

"I understand." *She means a lot to me too.*

-‹‹‹‹-

"What's going on between you and Richard?"

Cevilla looked at her niece. "Humph. Aren't you a nosy posy?"

Ivy smiled. "Of course I am. I learned from the best."

"If you're referring to me," she said, adding a few grape tomatoes to the fresh salad she'd helped Ivy prepare, "I will remind you that I haven't interfered in *yer* and Noah's life since you got married."

"True." Ivy dried her hands on a kitchen towel and walked over to her. "But you did plenty of interfering before we were married."

She couldn't deny that. "Is that the reason you invited us over for supper tonight? For payback? I'll have you know that Richard and I are only friends."

Saying the words surprisingly caused her a bit of pain. She had quickly grown accustomed to his company, and she'd felt younger and more vibrant than she had in years. He was such a gentleman, just as he'd been even at an early age. He was intelligent, able to converse on any subject. But even better were the silent times they spent in each other's company, when they didn't have to say a word. Like earlier today, when she was crocheting in the living room and he was reading a copy of *The Budget* newspaper she'd had in a basket near the couch.

Then he'd put down the paper and looked at her at the same time she looked up from her crochet. His smile had reached her clear to her toes. She would miss that smile . . . She would miss him.

"I didn't mean to upset you." Ivy put her hand on Cevilla's arm.

"Honey, you didn't upset me." Cevilla patted Ivy's hand and smiled.

The men came inside, and after they washed up, they all sat down for supper. Noah and Richard got along wonderfully, not that Cevilla was surprised. The food was delicious, which Richard mentioned more than a few times. "It will be hard to go back to boring eating after this week," he said, adding more gravy to his mashed potatoes.

Cevilla forced a smile but remained quiet. She didn't want to think about him leaving, but he had no reason to stay. Meghan was doing better, and she seemed eager to get back home. Was Richard eager to leave too?

The ride home from Noah and Ivy's was a quiet one. Once there, Richard asked, "Who's going to unharness the horse?"

"I will. I've done it enough times. I can take care of Shep until Judah comes back for him in the morning."

"Can I help? Even though I'm a city slicker? I watched Noah do it, you know."

Cevilla chuckled. "Sure. I think we can get Shep settled between the two of us. Judah brought some grain for him, too, and we'll get him water."

It took a little longer than usual, since Richard still had to be instructed on every detail of unharnessing and putting up a horse. But he was interested in learning, and Shep was soon happily in his stall and ready for sleep.

They walked back to the house together, each of them using their cane, their free hands swinging by their sides. Cevilla's hand brushed against Richard's and she moved away. "Sorry," she said, as they reached the front porch.

"It's quite all right." He turned to her. "Cevilla."

She stopped and looked up at him. There was still daylight left, and she could see that inexplicable spark in his eyes that made her toes curl. "Yes, Richard?"

"This past week with you has made me happier than I've been in a long time. I feel young again."

She understood. She'd had a bit of a bounce in her step this week, too, that hadn't been there before.

He looked at her for a long moment. "You're not saying anything. That's making me nervous."

"I . . . I don't know what to say."

He backed away, a shadow crossing his face before he gave her another smile. This one wasn't as radiant as the others. "I'm sure Meghan is waiting for me inside," he said. "She's ready to get back to LA, and I still have to pack." He looked at her one more time before climbing the porch steps and heading inside the house, the screen door closing behind him.

Cevilla couldn't speak as he disappeared. Of all the times for her to lose her nerve. She should have said something. Told him she was feeling something between them. Asked him to stay and sit on the front porch with her. Adding to her beloved, well-worn hickory rocker, Noah had brought over two brand-new rockers for him and Ivy to sit on when they came to visit. She could picture her and Richard there, enjoying the warm weather, the earthy smell of the summer gardens, the music of the birds, and the occasional clopping of horse's hooves as a buggy drove by.

She shook her head. That was a fantasy. And Cevilla Schlabach didn't indulge in fantasies.

-⟨⟨⟨-

The next morning Cevilla was waiting on the front porch when the screen door opened, and Meghan walked out. Her cheeks were bright pink, and she still had the lovely smile on her face Cevilla had seen at breakfast. Even she'd been surprised by the transformation. Meghan had told her she still had a lot to work out, but she'd made a first step.

"Where's your grandfather?" Cevilla asked as they walked down the porch steps.

"He's in the restroom, which gives me a chance to thank you for everything. As you could tell, I didn't want to be here." She looked around the yard, and then tucked her sleek brown hair behind her ear. "But this has been the best vacation I've ever had. I feel like I'm ready to face my life in LA now. And you've been a big part of that." She hugged her. "You remind me of my grandmother, NanNan." She pulled back. "I'll miss you. If you ever want to come to California, you have a place to stay."

Cevilla nodded. "Thank you, but I can't see me making a trip so far from home."

"Oh," Meghan said as Richard came outside. "But you never know what the future holds."

Cevilla looked at him as he made his way down the steps. He was handsome, charming, as salt of the earth as they came despite being monetarily rich. She had been so in love with CJ that she hadn't noticed Richard except as a friend. A shoulder to cry on. Someone there for her while CJ and others were at war. A beautiful, wonderful man she might have fallen for back then if circumstances had been different.

A man she was falling for right now.

He stopped in front of her. "I guess this is good-bye."

She swallowed the lump in her throat. "I guess it is."

He took her hand and smiled. "It was good to see you, Cevilla." When she failed to reply he let go of her hand and walked away.

Her heart squeezed in her chest as he and Meghan got into their car, their luggage already in the trunk. She didn't understand why, but Richard meant a lot to her too. Somehow an old friend from a lifetime ago had made an impact on her in such a short time. Then again, they both knew very well that life was short, which was why she hurried to the car and tapped on his window.

"Richard?"

He rolled down the window. "Yes?"

"Would it be all right if I wrote to you? Occasionally, of course." She lifted her chin. "I'm fairly busy around here, you know."

His grin was adorable. "You are a busy lady." He reached into a pocket for his wallet, and then handed her a business card. "This one has my personal address on it. I would be pleased to receive a letter from you."

She took the card, trying not to show her joy. "Very well, then. You can expect one."

As Meghan pulled away, Cevilla turned on her heel and strolled back to the porch and into the house. But when she shut the front door behind her, she did a little fist pump.

— CHAPTER 7 —

Dear Richard,

In the week since you've been gone, the garden is all planted, my flower box plants are still blooming, and the front porch has a fresh coat of paint. See, I told you I was busy. Busy supervising, that is. Our little community never lacks helping hands, and although I don't like it, I must acknowledge that getting things done on my own isn't as easy for me as it used to be. But that's our little secret.

I hope Meghan is doing well. I've been praying for you both since you left. I know you have a good life in LA, but we all need prayers, and God doesn't want us to talk to him only during the bad times.

A wedding is coming up in the fall. I'm not surprised—I was rather instrumental in getting these two young people together. The youth of Birch Creek seem to always need a matchmaker. I'd mention the couple's names, but since you didn't get a chance to meet anyone here other than the Bontrager, Chupp, and Yoder boys, Freemont Yoder, and Noah and Ivy, they wouldn't mean anything to you.

Summer in Birch Creek is always a lively time of year. Frolics,
barn raisings, cookouts, vacations . . . it's my favorite season. Maybe—

Cevilla paused. She'd almost invited him back for a visit. It was
one thing to write friendly letters to an old friend, but quite
another to invite him back for a visit. She thought she'd been bold
when she asked permission to write him, which was silly. Boldness
was never a problem for her. Neither was confusion, at least when it
came to the opposite sex. *Until now.*

She erased the word *maybe*, signed her name, and put the letter
in an envelope. After she copied Richard's address from the card he'd
given her—which, of all things, she'd promptly put in the top drawer
of her nightstand next to her bed for safekeeping—she took her cane
and went to the mailbox. As she was raising the flag on the side of the
box, a familiar buggy pulled into her driveway.

"Hi, Cevilla." Ivy leaned over and gave her a wave. "Are you up for
a little company this morning?"

Cevilla smiled. "I'm always up for company. Especially *yers.*"

While Ivy parked the buggy and took care of the horse, Cevilla
made her way back to the house. It was midmorning and too late to
offer Ivy breakfast, but she could at least make some peppermint tea.

Ivy came in the back door without knocking. Cevilla had told her
and Noah to treat her house as their home, and they did. "I brought
two whoopie pies from Carolyn's," she said, placing a plastic-wrapped
Styrofoam plate on the table. "One chocolate and one strawberry."

"Strawberry?" Cevilla took two mugs from a cabinet and placed
them on the counter. "That's a first."

"You know Carolyn. She likes to experiment." Ivy went to the
sink and washed her hands.

A few minutes later they were both seated at the table, sharing tea and the whoopie pies. Cevilla had the random thought that if Meghan were here, she'd be appalled at so much sugar in the morning. Cevilla took a large bite of the strawberry whoopie pie. *You only live once.*

After a few minutes, Ivy spoke. "How are you feeling, *Aenti?*"

Cevilla wiped her mouth with her napkin. "Right as rain."

"Are you sure?"

Cevilla paused in the middle of putting the napkin back on the table. She peered at Ivy. "Why do I get the feeling this isn't just a friendly visit?"

Ivy shrugged, not looking at her. She wiped at a chocolate crumb on her plate. "You know Noah and I love you, and we want to make sure you're all right."

"I see." Although she still sensed there was more to Ivy's visit than she was saying, she couldn't help but smile. This petite young woman who had won the heart of her dear nephew was more like a daughter to her than a niece, one God had provided in her old age. *If God can provide a daughter, why can't he provide a new love?*

"*Aenti?*"

Cevilla blinked and looked at Ivy again. "*Ya?*"

"This is what I mean. You've been distracted lately. Noah and I noticed it after church last Sunday. You barely said three words to Rhoda and Naomi during the meal."

"I don't have to talk all the time."

Ivy gave her a side eye. "Oh really?"

"Sarcasm doesn't suit you."

Ivy sat back in her chair. Cevilla knew her toes just reached the floor.

"Sorry, *Aenti.* And I apologize if I've stepped over a line." She looked at Cevilla and smiled. "You said everything is all right, and I believe you."

Well, didn't that just bring on a wave of guilt? While she didn't relish the thought of talking about Richard, she also couldn't be deceptive to her niece. "Fine. Something is . . . wrong."

Ivy sat straight up. "What is it? Do you need to see a doctor? Do I need to get Noah?"

Cevilla chuckled, remembering how Meghan had been so overprotective of Richard. *It's wonderful to be loved.* Sometimes it felt a little like coddling, but right now she was pleased. "No, there's nothing physically wrong. In fact, I feel better than I have in a long time." Which was true, and she knew it was because of Richard.

Ivy breathed out a sigh of relief. "Thank God." Then she frowned. "What's bothering you, then?"

Her cheeks heating, Cevilla pushed back from the table. "It's really nothing," she said, standing up. She lifted her teacup, even though it was still half full, and went back to the kettle.

"Are you thinking about Richard?"

"A little." Cevilla gave her a pointed look as she sat back down. "Now, don't give me that look again. Richard was and is a friend. I've said that before."

A small smile spread across Ivy's pretty face. "That *friend* has you very distracted. Even after he's gone back home." Her smile widened. "I see."

"Stop that," Cevilla snapped.

"Stop what?"

"Looking like a cat that's licked all the cream from the bowl."

Ivy laughed. "Oh, *Aenti*, how the tables have turned." She leaned forward. "It's okay to have feelings for someone."

"At my age?" She shook her head and stared at her hot tea. "*Nee.* I'm past all that."

"You don't seem to be."

"I should be, though."

"Why? Because you've been single all *yer* life?"

"Because God is enough." That's what she'd said all her adult life, not just to herself, but to others. Whenever anyone asked her why she never married. Whenever she offered advice to young women who struggled with their singleness. Or to anyone who was lonely and felt left out, for that matter. She believed that to her core. God was enough. Which meant she didn't need Richard, or anyone else.

But that wasn't true. She needed community. No man—or woman—was an island. And although God was enough for her and always would be, maybe he had something else in store for her too.

Cevilla pressed her lips together and nodded as she stared down at her hands. Then she said, "Maybe he does."

"What are you talking about, Cevilla?"

She ignored Ivy and picked up Richard's card from where she'd left it on the kitchen table. Not only did it have his address, but it had his phone number. She stood with the help of her cane. "It's time I stopped acting so foolish."

"*Aenti*, what are you doing?"

She held up the card. "I'm going to call my *friend*."

"Um, you know phones aren't to be used for chatting, Cevilla."

"Oh, I'm not going to chat." She grinned, happiness filling her. "I'm going to set things straight."

— CHAPTER 8 —

"You're moping, Grandfather."

Richard peered at Meghan over the edge of his newspaper. "I'm reading," he said. "How is that moping?"

"That paper is old. You read it yesterday."

His eyes focused on the words, which he hadn't been able to do since he opened the paper nearly half an hour ago. Sure enough, he'd read this article yesterday. He folded the paper and set it on the metal and glass table in front of him. He and Meghan were having breakfast on the patio, which not only overlooked an infinity pool but had an exquisite view of the Pacific Ocean. The air was filled with the scents of sea salt, sand, and the cinnamon oatmeal Francois had prepared. Sharon had had her usual black coffee and zipped out of the house before breakfast was served. But Meghan, as she had for the past three mornings, had joined him for breakfast.

She buttered a piece of wheat toast before adding a small spoon-ful of fresh strawberry jam. He had a feeling she had more to say. She was just taking her time.

"It's hard to concentrate with Cevilla on your mind, isn't it?" There it was.

"Humph." He took a sip of his orange juice and looked out at the ocean. Later this morning he would take a swim in the pool, an exercise he'd always enjoyed. Then he would probably meet his friends at the club for a light lunch, return home for a nap, have supper . . . He grimaced. None of that appealed to him, not when he was preoccupied with Ohio Amish country. He felt the draw to go back. Or maybe a woman who lived there was what made him want to drop everything and leave for Ohio.

"Why don't you call her?" Meghan asked.

"That's simply not done."

"Calling a woman?" she scoffed. "I know you've been out of the dating game for a long time, but it's perfectly fine to call a woman you like."

At the word *dating*, his cheeks heated. "I'm not dating anyone."

"You will after you call her."

He turned from the ocean view and regarded his granddaughter. "Since when have you been interested in my social life?"

A hurt look crossed her face. "I'm always interested in what you're doing, Grandfather. I thought you knew that."

He nodded, inwardly sighing. "I do know that." He reached over and patted her hand. "I'm sorry if I've been a little . . ."

"Mopey?"

"If you want to call it that."

Meghan smiled. "Mopey is accurate." Since their return from Cevilla's, she'd gone on two job interviews. She hadn't heard anything back, but that didn't seem to deter her good mood. He trusted his granddaughter to make wise decisions, whether they were professional or personal. She'd learned some lessons, and she'd also proven that she could rebound from serious setbacks.

"I'm proud of you," he said. "You're a strong woman."

"I don't think so, not always anyway. I didn't think I'd come back from everything that happened. Conor dumping me, Tawny selling my business . . ." She touched the edge of the table. "When you dragged me out to Amish country, I was able to get some perspective. I've also been talking to Conor again."

That rang Richard's alarm bells. "May I ask why?"

"It's not what you think. We have a lot to work through. Our relationship wasn't good from the start, on both sides." She sighed. "I know you didn't care for him."

"I didn't care for how he treated you. I think Conor has potential, but he's self-centered."

"That's kind of normal in LA."

"It shouldn't be normal anywhere." He let out a long breath. "I'm not going to pry into your relationship with him, Meghan. I know your mother does plenty of that."

"I haven't told her Conor and I are speaking again. We're not dating, and I don't think we ever will. But we have to work through our past so we can go forward with the future. We hurt each other. He's willing to make amends, and I need to respond in kind." Her gaze grew soft, her eyes teary. "You've taught me well, Grandfather. Thank you for always being there for me."

His own eyes filled with tears. "Thank you for letting me."

She dabbed her eyes with a tissue, and then she pulled a card from the pocket of her suit jacket. "Here," she said, handing it to him. "Consider this a change of subject. I have an interview in an hour, and I don't want to smear my mascara."

He looked at the paper. "What is it?"

"I got the number of that community phone near her house. You know, the one she checked for messages a few times while we were there."

His brow lifted as he took the card. He'd read up a bit on the Amish before going to see Cevilla, and then upon his return he'd devoured several reference books about the culture. They eschewed technology, and they used phones only for emergencies, business owner needs, or to leave important messages, all depending on the district. Never to just . . . talk.

"I can't call her," he said, setting the card down next to his plate of uneaten oatmeal.

"Why on earth not?"

He explained the rules about phones, and while she looked confused, she nodded. "Then I guess you'll have to get on a plane and go see her."

The confidence in her eyes made him chuckle. "Why are you pushing me to contact her again?"

"Because you want to. Because she wants you to."

"I seriously doubt that."

"I don't. I saw the way she looked at you." Meghan batted her eyelashes at him.

That made him laugh out loud. Cevilla had never been the flirtatious type, a quality he'd always liked about her. Among many. "Sweetheart, there's nothing between me and Cevilla other than friendship. And that friendship existed more in the past than it does now. We had a short reunion, and while I'm glad we did, that's all there is to it."

Meghan's face fell. "Are you sure?"

"Positive." He picked up his spoon. "I better tackle this oatmeal before—" The phone in his pocket buzzed. He set down the spoon, and when he took out his phone, he looked at the number on the screen and froze. He might be old, but he was still sharp, and he had seen this number only moments before. He looked at the card next to his plate, and then back to the one on his phone. His palms grew damp. Cevilla.

"Grandfather, aren't you going to answer it?"

He swallowed and nodded. He slid his finger across the screen and put the phone up to his ear. "Hello?"

"Hello, Richard."

-◄◄◄◄-

Meghan could tell by the shocked and excited look on her grandfather's face that Cevilla was on the line. That, and because he kept the volume turned up on his phone, she could hear the woman's strong, familiar voice. Meghan grinned and popped up from her chair. She knew Grandfather and Cevilla had something between them, despite his protests. They were so sweet. And cute. And if she hadn't been so self-absorbed with her own problems, she could have encouraged them more. Then her grandfather wouldn't have spent the past week brooding.

"Hi, Cevilla." His voice was low and shy. *Adorable.* She went to him and took the phone from his hand.

"Hey—"

"Hi, Cevilla," Meghan said.

"Hello, Meghan," Cevilla answered, surprise in her voice. "You sound well."

"I'm very well, thank you. I'm putting you on speaker."

"What—"

Meghan laid the phone on the table and hit the speaker button. "Now we can both hear you." She sat back down and gave Grandfather a smile. He didn't look pleased, and she was definitely crossing a line, but she was going to make sure he didn't do anything to mess this up.

He leaned over and yelled into the phone. "You have to excuse my granddaughter, Cevilla." He lifted his chastising gaze to her. "She can be a bit impulsive."

"Fine with me." Cevilla's voice rang loud and clear now. No surprise. No hesitation. Meghan really liked her.

"I can call you back when we have a little privacy." He gave her another annoyed look.

"You don't have to yell into the phone, Grandfather. Just speak normally. She'll be able to hear you just fine."

"There's nothing wrong with my hearing," Cevilla said.

Meghan balked. "I didn't mean that—"

"And I don't mind who listens in. Let me get to the point, Richard."

Meghan saw her grandfather sit up straight.

"Time is short, and life is shorter," Cevilla continued. "I enjoyed your visit here very much. It's nice to spend time with a gentleman my age. We have a lot in common, and we also have a lot more catching up to do. Consider this your standing invitation to visit me anytime here in Birch Creek."

Richard nodded and didn't say anything.

"Grandfather, she can't see you."

"Oh, that's right." His eyes darted. "Well, uh, Cevilla." He cleared his throat. "I must say, this is unexpected."

Meghan nudged him gently with her toe. "Tell her yes," she said in a loud whisper, knowing that even with his hearing aids he wouldn't be able to hear her.

"Listen to your granddaughter." Cevilla's voice rang through the speaker. "She's a smart one."

Meghan smiled. "Thank you, Cevilla."

Her grandfather looked bewildered. "I, uh . . ." Then his hand went to his throat, straightening an imaginary tie, a habit he couldn't shake after decades of wearing three-piece suits. "I'd be happy to come visit you, Cevilla."

"I'm free next week," she said.

Both Meghan and Richard laughed. "I'll make his reservation right now," Meghan said. Then she stood and picked up the phone. She turned off the speaker and handed it to him. "I'll leave you two alone now."

He nodded, looking up at her with a serene smile on his face. *Thank you*, he mouthed.

She kissed him on the cheek, and then left to finish getting ready for her interview. She sighed as she went up the stairs to her bedroom. Her mother probably wouldn't approve of a relationship between Grandfather and Cevilla because she wouldn't be able to control it. She would never be able to influence Cevilla. But Grandfather wouldn't have to worry about that. Meghan would deal with Mother when the time came. Grandfather and Cevilla deserved their happiness.

— EPILOGUE —

Three months later

Cevilla and Richard stood outside the small house next door to hers. It was almost finished, thanks to Richard's insistence on micromanaging every detail. It was a small house, just enough for two people and made in the Amish style. "I approve," she said, turning to him.

"Is it Amish looking enough?"

She smiled. Richard had decided to move to Birch Creek after his second visit to the community, made shortly after her phone call to him. He'd been back to LA only once, and that was to announce his move in person to Sharon and Meghan. Meghan had been happy for him. Sharon, not so much. But Richard was confident she would come around.

"It's lovely, and very Amish," she said.

"Only from the outside."

Cevilla looked at the house again. Richard was now her neighbor, or at least he would be when the house was completed and his furniture came from California. He'd been staying with Noah and Ivy all this time since it would be improper to stay with her. Over the past three months their relationship had deepened, and she knew he loved her as much as she loved him. But one thing was keeping them from marriage. He wasn't ready to become Amish. His honesty had touched her, and she didn't want him to join her faith unless God was leading him to.

"I'm pleased with it," he said. "It has basic amenities."

"You mean a fancy air conditioner."

"Among other things." He grinned down at her. "Hi, neighbor," he said softly.

"Hi back, neighbor," she said.

He took her hand, and they strolled back to her house. She had made a light lunch for them, placing covered plates on the back patio so they could enjoy the fall weather. After they sat down and said a silent prayer, she felt him take her hand again.

"I love you, Cevilla." His gaze didn't move from hers. "I wish things could be different, and they might be in the future. But I want you to know that I love you very much."

She squeezed his hand, fighting back tears. Only Richard Johnson could bring out her mushy side. "I love you too. And I'm willing to wait as long as you need me to, and as long as God leads."

"He's led me to you," Richard said. "I'm ready for him to do the rest."

"He will," she said, confident. God had brought Richard back into her life after all these years. He was faithful and had filled a void in her she hadn't been aware of until Richard had arrived. Cevilla had always put her trust in God.

And I always will.

— DISCUSSION QUESTIONS —

1. Cevilla had always believed that love had passed her by, until her reunion with Richard. Have you ever thought that you missed out on something, only to have a second chance at it later in your life?

2. Instead of turning to God when she was hurt, Meghan pulled away and questioned his constancy. What advice would you have given to help her?

3. Richard had followed his heart, and God's leading, when it came to Cevilla. Is there a time when you did the same thing?

4. Richard has a big decision to make in the future. If you were faced with the same option to convert to the Amish faith, what would you do? What things would you consider when making your choice?

— ACKNOWLEDGMENTS —

Thank you to the wonderful team at HCCP for their expertise and support, especially my wonderful editors Becky Monds and Jean Bloom. And thank you, dear reader, for joining Cevilla and Richard on their reunion journey. There's more in store for these two in the future.

MENDED HEARTS

-◄◄◄-

Kelly Irvin

To my family, love always.

"Come now, let us settle the matter," says the
LORD. "Though your sins are like scarlet,
 they shall be as white as snow; though they
are red as crimson, they shall be like wool."
                              —Isaiah 1:18 NIV

FEATURED JAMESPORT, MISSOURI, RESIDENTS

Hannah Kauffman and daughter Evelyn Rose (Evie) Kauffman

Laura and Zechariah Stutzman (Hannah's great-grandparents)

Phillip Schwartz (bachelor)

Susie and Declan Yoder, son Thaddeus, and daughter
Mattie (married), and three other siblings

Burke McMillan (widower), owner of Purple Martin Café

Leo and Jennie Graber, owners of Jamesport Combination Store

Ben and Rosalie Stutzman and children
(bishop and Zechariah's grandson)

— CHAPTER 1 —

The aroma of cinnamon rolls wafted through the air, more aromatic than any perfume. Hannah Kauffman grinned to herself as she slid a thick ceramic plate laden with eggs, bacon, toast, and hash browns onto the table in front of an English customer who held up her fork, ready to dive in. The second plate, a Spanish omelet, toast, and a cup of fresh fruit, belonged to the woman seated in the red Naugahyde booth across from her.

Hannah breathed through the ache in her shoulders and elbows. It had been a long morning filled with a steady stream of customers at the Purple Martin Café, Jamesport's most popular Amish restaurant. Staying busy made her happy. Excellent food, nice customers, good tips. Making people smile made the aches and pains worth it.

The stench of mingled perfumes hit her without warning.

She rushed to place two glasses of orange juice and two cups of coffee on the table. The tickle in her nose ballooned faster than she could move.

A gargantuan sneeze broke just as she swiveled away, burying her face in the crook of her arm.

Trying not to sniffle, she turned back to the ladies. "Is there anything else I can get for you?"

The women's delighted smiles faded. "Do you have a cold?" The one wearing a purple dress and purple checked leggings frowned. "Are you sick? If you are you shouldn't—"

"I'm not sick. It's the perfume—"

"Are you blaming my expensive Estée Lauder Bronze Goddess?" The woman with hair dyed the color of cotton candy held up her plate. "You sneezed all over my omelet. Take it back. I want a different waitress."

"I'm so sorry, ma'am." Breathing through her mouth, Hannah accepted the plate. "I really don't have a cold. I promise."

Her baby, Evie, had the sniffles, but Great-Grandma Laura, who'd taken care of hundreds of babies over the years, insisted they were caused by allergies brought on by the gorgeous array of spring flowers blooming in her front yard.

"Take mine as well." Checked Leggings waved her hand over her food with a dismissive air. "I want to talk to your boss."

"I'm right here, ladies." His usual smile on his rugged face, Burke McMillan strode toward them. "How can I help?"

"This girl sneezed all over us."

"I didn't—"

"It's okay, Hannah. Take the food back to the kitchen, please." Burke swiveled toward Hannah and winked. "Have Nicole bring them fresh plates. Tell her I said thank you for helping out."

"I should call the health department." Purple Leggings fingered her cell phone. "Surely you know better than to let employees work sick."

Her querulous voice faded in the distance as Hannah lugged the tray back to the kitchen. How quickly a good day could deteriorate. Just like her daughter's mood. At twenty-one months Evie could be all sunshine and smiles one minute, and dark clouds and squalls the next.

Hannah's gaze caught Claire Plank's. She sat at a table across from Isabel Schrock. The two women, both members of Hannah's

Gmay, stared at her as if she were a cockroach crawling across their eggs. Claire's smile held a combination of pity and condemnation that was all too familiar. Hannah lifted her chin and smiled back with her best I-have-no-idea-what-your-problem-is smile.

"How's Evie?" Claire asked. "She was sniffling at church like she had a cold."

"She's fine. Just allergies."

"Can you ask our waitress to come refill our tea glasses?" Isabel held up her glass. It was still almost full. "And to bring us some more sugar packets."

"Of course."

Claire ducked her head and whispered something to Isabel. Heads bent together, they continued whispering as Hannah worked her way through the tables to the kitchen.

Her punishment might have been six weeks of *bann,* but it continued almost two years later.

Shoving away the thoughts that tumbled around in her head, Hannah caught Nicole Wilson on her way from the serving window, her tray loaded with steaming oatmeal, scrambled eggs, sausage, and cinnamon rolls. Hannah quickly explained the situation. "Sorry to dump on you, but Burke told me—"

"No worries." Nicole flipped her long brown braid onto her back and shifted her tray onto her shoulder. Her pewter eyes were bright with sympathy. "Dump the old tray and put the new order in. I'll sweet talk them so bad they'll leave me a big fat tip."

Nicole was saving her tips for her wedding. She and her fiancé, Tony Perez, wanted to get married as soon as they graduated from high school in another year. Then he planned to join the Navy, and she would start college.

Hannah returned Nicole's smile and pushed through the double doors to the kitchen where she unloaded her tray and asked the cook to put a rush on a new order. She leaned against the wall for a second and breathed. Evie had awakened three—or maybe it was four—times during the night. Congestion and a cough made it hard for her to sleep, which made it impossible for Hannah. Heat sweltered in the kitchen. The morning-shift cook ignored her as she slapped sausages on the grill and made omelets.

The aroma of baking bread mingled with the scent of frying bacon. Hannah's stomach rumbled. Most mornings she had no time for eating her own breakfast. Time spent with Evie was at a premium on days Hannah worked.

What would she do without Great-Grandma Laura to watch her baby? She brushed the thought away. Laura and Great-Grandpa Zechariah didn't judge her like the rest of the world.

The doors swung open and Burke strode through. "Don't sweat it, kid. Accidents happen. I know you didn't mean to sneeze on their eggs."

"I didn't." She straightened, ready to defend herself. "I turned away and covered my face."

Burke shrugged and took a swipe at the salt-and-pepper five-o'clock shadow he never seemed to shave. His hair was cut like the boys' who came back from basic training at Fort Riley, but she didn't know if he'd been in the Army. Burke never talked about himself. "The customer's always right." He snatched a washrag from the sink and began wiping down already immaculate counters.

"I'm sorry I caused a problem."

"You're one of my most dependable, hard-working waitresses." Burke laid the washrag across the faucet and headed for the doors. "By the way, your Regular is out there waiting. Take your break. Have some breakfast. You look peaked this morning. I worry about you."

Every worker received one free meal per shift. That was Burke. A great boss who took care of his employees.

He was also another person who didn't judge. But he was English. Some *Englishers* had different opinions on babies born out of wedlock. What Burke thought remained a mystery. He never brought it up. Instead, he fed Evie homemade applesauce and peanut butter cookies on the rare occasion Hannah brought her to the Purple Martin. He claimed the cookies were good for her because they had protein in them.

Her regular. She had several. But Burke's use of the singular with a capital *r* could mean only one person. Wiping sweat from her forehead with the back of her sleeve, she pushed through the doors and glanced around.

Phillip Schwartz sat three seats from the end of the counter, perusing a menu. Which made Hannah smile. He always ordered the same thing. Two eggs over easy, bacon, hash browns, fried crisp, and two pieces of white bread toasted not too dark, orange juice, and coffee, black. He liked strawberry jam for his toast and ketchup for his eggs.

The last fact always made Hannah's stomach feel squishy. Hot sauce, maybe, like some of the *Englishers*, but ketchup?

Glancing around, she slipped her order pad from her white Purple Martin Café apron pocket, picked up the closest coffee pot, and approached him. "*Gude mariye.*"

"There you are." He smiled. His smile transformed a plain face. He had dimples and long, light eyelashes that framed pale-blue eyes. Thin blond hair hung below the rim of his straw hat. "*Gude mariye.* I was afraid you weren't working today, even though you're scheduled."

He made it a point to know her schedule. Heat warmed Hannah's cheeks. After two years of steady attention from this man, she felt comfortable around him. Almost. She'd given her heart to Thaddeus and look how that ended. She poured Phillip's coffee and returned the pot to its rightful place. Her hand didn't shake. Not much anyway. She tugged her pencil from behind her ear. "The usual?"

She worked to keep her voice nonchalant. *He's just another customer. No one special.*

"*Jah.*" He tossed the menu on the black Formica counter and then patted the stool next to him. "Can you sit? It should be time for your break."

Close. Too close. Too many eyes watching. "I shouldn't. It's not a *gut* idea."

"Do we have to have this discussion every time?" He sighed and shoved his straw hat back, revealing his bangs. His skin was smooth and his chin whiskerless. He was at least twenty-one—a year older than Thaddeus would be now—but he looked younger. Like a teenager. "People don't expect you to remain single the rest of your life. You took your punishment. You repented. You've been forgiven. If you don't court, you can never move on with your life."

Moving on with her life meant trusting someone again. Hard to do after the man Hannah loved left Jamesport for the RV factories in Indiana rather than marry her and be a father to his child. Either she hadn't been worthy of Thaddeus's love or he hadn't been worthy of hers. Either way, she'd committed a terrible sin, and Evie had no father in her life.

A baby punished for her mother's sins.

How would she explain this to Evie when she grew old enough to wonder why other little girls had daddies and she didn't?

That day loomed like a future specter of pain for a daughter who, for now, loved without judgment and without limit.

"Sit." Phillip patted the stool a second time. His huge hands were callused from his work as a carpenter. He had a puffy red scar across his knuckles on one hand. A saw gone wild during his apprentice days? "Or sit two stools down. No one will realize we're together. Or care. I promise."

All the customers at this moment, miraculously, were *Englishers*. Hannah put in his order, then removed an enormous raisin cinnamon roll from the bakery case, laid it on a saucer, and slid onto a stool— one seat down from his, just in case.

He rolled his eyes—which made him look even more like a teenager—and sipped his coffee. "You're a funny girl, Hannah Kauffman."

"I'm not a girl. I'm nineteen and all grown-up. I'm a *mudder*." A mother with responsibilities and no desire to make any more mistakes. "But I'm glad I can entertain you."

His smile widened. "Always. How's Evie's cold?"

"It's not a cold, according to Laura. She says it's allergies." Hannah told him about her own sneeze and the customers. "I lost a tip there."

"You live with Laura and Zechariah. You help with Zechariah in exchange for Laura watching Evie. You shouldn't have many bills to pay."

True, but she liked to pull her own weight. Laura and Zechariah didn't have much. Zechariah's Parkinson's disease meant regular medical bills, big bills. They shouldn't have to pay for her and Evie's food and clothes. Allowing them to live with them was a gift itself. Laura had been her safe harbor since the day Hannah rushed from her parents' home to find her great-grandmother and tell her about her terrible sin before others could.

Laura had done enough for her and Evie. "I don't want to take advantage. They have enough on their plate."

"You're off tomorrow. Come out with me tonight after you put

Evie to bed. Or you can bring her. You know I love Evie." No doubt, he did care for Evie. Sometimes he spent more time trying to make her laugh than he did talking to Hannah. She liked that about Phillip. Among other things. He was kind and considerate. "We'll go for a ride and enjoy the spring weather. The purple martins are returning. Maybe we'll see some."

Like many in their Plain community, Phillip was an avid bird watcher. He sometimes dropped by the house to chat with Zechariah about the older man's favorite topic. He could no longer walk more than a few yards with his walker, so he relied on Phillip's play-by-play of the latest sightings.

And Phillip got his own sightings of Hannah. At least, that's what he told her.

The bell dinged, and Jolene barked, "Order up."

Saved by the bell. Hannah hopped up, trotted around the counter, and picked up Phillip's plate. What would it be like to serve him breakfast every morning? In their own house. Kneading the bread. Making sure ketchup was on the table. The smell of bacon filled her nose. The sound of Evie's sweet giggle when Phillip tickled her as he put her in the wooden high chair Hannah had used as a baby.

Nice. It would be nice.

And maybe people would stop looking at her and Evie with that sour look or, worse, that pitying look. Maybe they would forget as well as forgive.

Another bell dinged, a deeper, more melodic sound. Like wind chimes. It heralded the entrance of a new customer. Hannah glanced at the door. The plate slipped from her hands and crashed to the floor.

No, no, no. It couldn't be.

Thaddeus Yoder stood just inside the door. His gaze held her prisoner. "There you are."

— CHAPTER 2 —

After two years of silence, her child's father stood before her in the Purple Martin Café. Hannah grabbed a tray and squatted behind the counter. Her heart pounded in her ears. Her hands shook. Her stomach heaved. *Don't throw up. Don't throw up.*

She gathered pieces of broken china dripping with egg yolk and dropped them on the tray. Her brain urged her to peek, to make sure her eyes hadn't played a trick on her, but her legs refused to cooperate.

"You're having a bad day, aren't you?" Burke loomed over her, then knelt and began to help her. "Are you sick? You look green around the gills."

"That's Evie's father." Hannah managed a whisper. Her voice didn't shake. Hardly at all. "Please . . . please look to see if he's coming this way."

Burke's gray eyebrows rose and fell. He grabbed the counter and hoisted himself up, then returned to her level. "The tall guy at the door?" He whispered. "He's still standing there like he doesn't know whether he's coming or going."

"Knowing Thaddeus, he's going." A spurt of anger rushed through Hannah. It felt good. Strong. Fierce. "He should go. He doesn't belong here. It's been two years."

"But he's here now."

"What are you two whispering about?" Phillip leaned over the counter and bellowed. His face turned red. "You have company, Hannah. Company you should send away."

"I'm thinking she can decide for herself." Thaddeus's face appeared next to Phillip's. His voice hadn't changed. Deep, slow, and sweet as honey. His eyes found hers. "I came home to see you and my baby."

Hannah catapulted to her feet.

"Your baby?" More than half the seats in the restaurant were filled with customers enjoying their breakfasts. She managed to keep her voice down to a furious whisper. "This is not the time or the place, Thaddeus Yoder. Go. You want to know how the baby is, write me a letter." She pointed at the door. "You still know how to write, don't you?"

In two years, she hadn't received a single letter from him. Not even an inquiry about the baby's birth or health or if it was a boy or a girl. He had shown her he didn't care. Not one iota.

He didn't get to show up now and act like he did.

"Can I know how you are?" His hands gripped the counter. His knuckles turned white. His voice had turned soft and hesitant. So similar to the voice that whispered sweet words of love in her ear eons ago. "You look *gut*."

So did he. The same broad shoulders and mop of curly black hair under his straw hat. The same sapphire eyes. She'd allowed herself to sink against that chest once, to let his long arms wrap her in a hug that went on and on, to feel his full, warm lips on her lips, cheeks, neck, and collarbone.

A shiver raced up her spine and spread across her shoulders. Heat curled around her neck and scorched her cheeks. For those brief moments of sheer pleasure, she had paid and paid. For two years, she'd been the object of whispers and stares. She'd been forced to sink to her knees in confession before her family and friends. She spent six weeks in the *bann*. She gave birth to a child and was raising her without a husband. Members of her district said they forgave her this terrible sin, but they had not forgotten.

Thaddeus had refused to repent or be punished. He fled. As a result, he could have no direct contact with any member of his community.

"Do the Plain folks act differently in Nappanee?" Her voice was low, but steady. "Do they speak of these things in public?"

"*Nee*. I just couldn't wait any longer. Mattie wouldn't tell me anything about the baby. She said it wasn't her place." His gaze, suddenly fierce, went to Phillip. "Do you mind? This is a personal conversation."

"You don't get to have personal conversations with Hannah, not after what you did to her. Or with any member of the *Gmay*." Phillip stood. He was taller and thinner than Thaddeus, but his expression said he was every bit as determined. "You need to leave. The bishop will hear about this."

"Phillip, please." Hannah shook her head at him. "I can handle this."

A mutinous glare on his face, Phillip sat and wrapped his hands around his mug. Hannah faced Thaddeus. "Mattie was right. If you wanted to know about your daughter, you should have admitted your mistake, taken your punishment."

Mattie might be Thaddeus's sister, but she remained a loyal friend to Hannah. One of the few who hadn't abandoned her in her time of need.

"What do you think I'm doing here?" His gaze held hers. The customers, Burke, even Phillip, seemed to disappear into the background. The air crackled with electricity, with all the words not spoken in two years. All the emotion forced down and buried by the weight of their shared experience. "I just want to see my baby before I do it. I went to the *dawdy haus*. Zechariah wouldn't let me in. He said only by-your-leave."

Thaddeus only wanted to see Evie, not Hannah. He'd waited two years. He could wait another fifty.

Would that be fair to Evie? Thaddeus was her father. What if he showed up in his daughter's life only to abandon her again? What kind of damage would that do?

"Just go."

"At least tell me the baby's name."

"Evelyn Rose. For *Mammi*'s mother."

"A girl." His voice broke. His Adam's apple bobbed. He cleared his throat. "I'll wait for you at Zechariah's. They won't let me come in, but that's okay. I'll wait outside for as long as I have to. Whatever it takes to prove to you I've changed."

"You want to prove you've changed? Go to the bishop. Tell him you're ready to repent and make your confession."

He wavered a second longer. "I'm sorry, just so you know." He turned and walked to the door with that same loose-limbed amble that made her notice him when she was a sixteen-year-old attending her first singing. He glanced back at her. "I'll make it up to you. I promise."

He slipped through the door and let it close behind him without a sound.

Burke popped up and lifted the tray filled with the remnants of Phillip's breakfast. Hannah took it from him. He shouldn't be cleaning up her messes. "I'll get the mop."

Hannah turned to Phillip. "You should go. Leo will be wondering what happened to you."

"Don't make the same mistake twice."

"This isn't the place for this conversation."

"*Nee*, it's not." Phillip stood and tossed a few bills on the table. "I've lost my appetite."

"I'll get you a fried egg and bacon on an English muffin to go." Smiling, Burke knocked on the counter. "On the house. It's a long time until lunch."

"*Danki*, but it's not necessary."

Burke disappeared through the kitchen doors. Hannah moved to follow.

"Will I see you tonight?"

The pent-up emotion in Phillip's voice squeezed her heart. Hannah turned back. The misery on his face made her want to look away. He was such a good man. He didn't deserve her mess. The image of another encounter between Thaddeus and Phillip played in her head. She shuddered. "Not tonight. Okay? Give me some time to work this out."

"Whatever you need."

He whirled and strode away. The bell dinged. The door banged this time.

She breathed and pushed through the kitchen doors. Burke stood at the sink, washing his hands.

"I'm sorry for all this drama. It won't happen again. I promise."

Burke dried his hands with meticulous care. His smile reminded her of her father before she'd broken his heart. "I know you think I'm older than the hills, but I actually remember what it feels like to be in love." A strange look, almost like pain, filtered over his face. "It can be the most wonderful and the most horrific feeling in the world."

Burke had a lady friend who visited from Virginia every few months. Occasionally, he turned the restaurant over to its former owner, Ezekiel Miller, and went to Virginia. According to Nicole, he'd been married once, but his wife and daughter both died.

Nicole claimed to know the details, but Hannah cut her off. She refused to gossip. She knew firsthand the damage gossip could do.

Nor should she be discussing matters of love with an English man, even one as nice as her boss. "It's okay. I'm fine."

Burke chuckled. "I can tell by the way you looked out there. Like you didn't know whether to hurl or smack someone with a broom." He hung the towel on its rack and turned back to her. "It may be hard for you to see right now, but God has a plan for you. Scripture promises He takes everything and makes it work for your good. You can count on Him."

She nodded and tugged her order pad from her apron. Time to focus on work. Something she knew how to do. Burke's words echoed ones Laura often spoke. Hannah had given up trying to understand God's plan. One thing was for certain, however. Evie was good. No matter the circumstances of her birth, she was a gift. A joy.

The rest of it was painful and hurtful and a mess. If God planned to make something good of it, she wished He would get on with it. She tried to pray, but how did a woman pray about such a shameful sin?

She couldn't even say the words to herself, let alone to God.

— CHAPTER 3 —

Some things never changed. Thaddeus hopped from his brother-in-law's buggy and stared at his childhood home. Someone—probably his dad and brothers-in-law—had added a fresh coat of white paint, but otherwise the two-story wood-frame house looked the same. Neat as a pin and surrounded by a sea of blooming pink coneflowers; vincas in white and purple; red, orange, and yellow feather flowers; star-patterned petunias in purple and red; verbena in purple and pink; and butter daises, brilliantly yellow.

His mother, whose favorite colors were purple and pink, had out-done herself this year, as she did every year. Some of his best memories were of kneeling in the dirt and helping her weed the flower garden. She sang out the names of the flowers, then quizzed him. Everyone should know the names of flowers, she said, even boys.

His father hadn't agreed, but then Declan Yoder wouldn't know a petunia from a pansy. The vegetable and flower gardens were the only places his mother kept neat and orderly. The house, on the other hand, was always a mess. His dad kept the yard, the barn, every inch of his farm, neat.

The reunion with Hannah was messy too. Just as Thaddeus had imagined. Painfully so. A man couldn't expect any different from a woman he abandoned. A woman in the family way. A woman left to face the censure of her community alone.

How could she ever forgive him? He couldn't forgive himself. How could he make it up to her?

It didn't seem possible.

She looked the same. Better even, if better was possible for such a lovely girl. Motherhood looked good on her. She was a little fuller in the right places. She had her mother's orangey-red hair and a light smattering of freckles on china-doll skin, but it was her eyes that captured him. Summertime blue. Swan Lake blue. Her eyes sparkled when she was about to tease him, which she often did. They were like the sun shining on the water.

He'd known her since childhood, but she first caught his attention—really caught it—at a singing. She was sixteen and brimming with an energy that couldn't be harnessed.

Asking her to let him carry her home in his buggy had been the best thing he'd ever done.

Then he ruined it.

Stop procrastinating. Get this over with. He couldn't stay here. It wouldn't be right, but he had to let his parents know he was back, out of respect. Maybe his dad would have suggestions for where he might get work.

He needed a place to stay and a job. He would confess, repent, take his punishment. Then he could prove himself to Hannah. He would show her he intended to stay and be the man she'd fallen in love with.

He had to move quickly. The words in his sister's letter fueled every step he took.

Come back before it's too late, bruder. Phillip has set his sights on Hannah. I see the way he looks at her when he thinks no one is watching. He eats at the café every day. He looks at her the way you once did. Come back to your family. Come back to Hannah and your baby. Now.

Now. Thaddeus took a deep breath, strode around the house to the back porch, and stomped up the stairs. The windows were open. The sweet, mouthwatering aroma of chocolate cake wafted through open windows. His mother's face appeared in the window over the kitchen sink. Her shriek advertised the moment she saw him.

"Thaddeus!" Her face disappeared.

A second later, the screen door opened, and she shot onto the porch. Arms open wide, she enveloped him in a hug. She smelled of vanilla and coffee.

He gently extricated himself. "Hey, *Mudder.* How are you?"

"*Gut, gut.*" She looked him over. "You're too thin. Didn't Bertie feed you?"

Thaddeus brushed flour from her cheek. She had chocolate stains on her apron and her white *kapp.* Flour caked her hands—and now his shirt. "I ate plenty."

Her second cousin Bertie was a good cook. Not as good as Mother, for sure, but she kept his belly full.

"Come in, come in." She tugged on the screen door with such enthusiasm it banged on the outer wall. "I have chocolate pudding cake and the *kaffi* is hot. I'm making a chicken and vegetable potpie."

Chocolate pudding cake and chicken potpie were his dad's favorites. Thaddeus followed her into the kitchen. Dirty dishes decorated the counter. A basket of unfolded laundry sat on the table. Father was the neat one. They were opposites in every respect. She was short to Father's tall. She exuded affection. Father could be stingy about showing his, although his five children always knew it was there. Thaddeus's throat tightened. Father believed a firm hand and a strong hug, both carefully dispensed, were the recipe for bringing up respectful children. *Breathe. Breathe.* "Sounds *gut*."

"When did you get into town? How did you get here? Are you back to stay? Have you talked to Ben, Cyrus, or Solomon—"

"*Mudder. Mudder*! Stop." Laughing, he held up both hands. "One question at a time. Yesterday. I took the bus to Bethany. I spent the night at the Motel 6 out on the highway and hired a driver to get here. I borrowed a buggy from Mattie, but I won't be staying at her place. I can't."

Just like he couldn't stay here.

"What are you doing here?"

The words were spoken in that deep, disappointed tone that reminded Thaddeus of so many trips to the woodshed. His father stood in the doorway. Dirt and mud caked his boots. His rawhide skin aged by years in the sun was red with anger above a long, ragged gray beard. A familiar look.

"You best move along. Susie, you know better."

"But, Declan—"

"It's okay, *Mudder*." Thaddeus edged toward the back door. "I only wanted to let you know I'm back. It didn't seem right to be in town and not let you know."

"Have you seen Hannah or Evie? She doesn't have much to do with us, but we've been able to keep Evie for an hour or two a few times. We're still her family even if you did—"

"I saw Hannah for a minute at the Purple Martin."

"That's none of our business." Father removed his hat and laid it on the table. "Susie, I'll take a glass of water. A big chunk of fence came down during that thunderstorm last night. It took all morning to fix it."

Thaddeus had been dismissed. He pushed through the screen door and looked back for one last glimpse of his parents. Mother poured water from a plastic pitcher, but her wistful gaze connected with his. It seemed to say, *Don't give up.*

It also said, *I forgive you.*

She was only one of many from whom he needed forgiveness.

He clomped down the steps. This wouldn't be easy. It shouldn't be easy. The entire trip from Indiana those words had pounded in his head. It shouldn't be easy.

What he did was wrong. Now he had to pay the consequences. Only then could he ask for forgiveness and work to be worthy of receiving it.

"Talk to Ben."

His mother's words carried through the open window over the sink.

"I will."

The window slammed shut.

Then the back door closed with a bang.

He was homeless.

— CHAPTER 4 —

The smells of sawdust and wood mixed with varnish smoothed
Phillip's clenched stomach. He breathed in the scent. The shop,
his home away from home, served as a refuge in times like these. Even
though it belonged to Leo Graber, Phillip's boss and friend.

The hodgepodge of tools and materials soothed Phillip. A miter
saw, a band saw, the gas generator used to run the power tools, piles
of wood, finished chairs, half-finished chairs, sculpted pieces of wood
held tight in braces until ready for assembly, cans of varnish, tubes
of glue, stacks of sandpaper, worktables, cabinets, all the tools of
the trade hanging from peg boards on the walls. He could live here.
Sometimes, too tired to drive to the home he shared with his parents,
he slept on a skinny mattress stuck in the corner, under old quilts they
used to cover finished pieces.

He grabbed a piece of sandpaper and went to work on a rocking
chair. Work was the best way to forget the look on Hannah's face that
first second she saw Thaddeus Yoder standing in the Purple Martin.
Before fear and anger shuttered the surprise, the joy, and the longing.

She wouldn't be so fraught with warring emotions if she didn't
still care about Thaddeus.

It had taken two years, but Phillip had made progress. She
would've gone on that ride with him tonight if Thaddeus hadn't

shown up. Gott, *I know I'm supposed to forgive. I've forgiven Hannah for her sin of fornication. For giving herself to another man before me. For having a* bopli *with another man. Thaddeus hasn't repented. He hasn't asked to be forgiven. I don't forgive him.*

What would God make of such a strange prayer? He might reach down and whop Phillip on the backside of the head. What would Ben say? As bishop? And as a friend?

If Thaddeus and Hannah hadn't sinned, Evie wouldn't exist. She was the sweetest little girl on the face of the earth. She had her mother's smile and cheeks, but no one would ever doubt that Thaddeus was her father with their shared black curls and deep-blue eyes.

He would always be reminded of the circumstances of Evie's birth. Always. *I don't care, Gott, I forgive Hannah. She made a mistake. She's paid for it. I wouldn't hold it over her head. I love Evie. She's a gift. I would raise her as my daughter.*

"You're back." Gray plastic bags from the hardware store hanging from both hands, Leo trudged into the shop. His mutt, Beau, trotted in behind him. "How was breakfast?"

Leo's roundabout way of asking if he'd seen Hannah.

"It was fine." Phillip continued sanding the arm of the chair.

"Then why do you look like you just sucked on a gigantic lemon?"

"I do not."

"Do too."

Leo normally went hours without speaking. Naturally, he would pick today to run at the mouth.

"I have a stomachache."

"I ran into Burke McMillan at Clayton's." Leo set the bags on the counter under rows of shelves filled with all manner of supplies.

Beau sat and scratched at his neck, then went to an old blanket laying in the sun. Light poured through the windows that graced one long shop wall. He circled twice then plopped onto the blanket and laid his gray snout on his front paws.

"He said the plopper on the toilet in the men's room at the café broke."

Of course it did. "So?"

"So then he mentioned Hannah had a visitor today."

Burke had a big mouth. *"Jah."*

"You don't want to talk about it, fine."

"Fine."

Leo pulled cans of varnish, stains, and finish from the bags and sorted through them. "I bought some new natural bristle brushes and some tack cloth. I thought you'd appreciate that."

"I asked Hannah to take a ride with me tonight and before she could answer me, Thaddeus walked through the door. After two years. Why now? I don't get it."

Leo stuck a can on the shelf next to a row of stains. He turned to face Phillip. "The question of the day. There are no coincidences. No luck, good or bad."

"Don't say it."

"Say what."

"Gott's plan is unfolding."

"Ask yourself this." Leo tucked a new stack of sandpaper in varying grades under the existing pile. "Why didn't you ask Hannah to take a ride with you before you found out about her transgression with Thaddeus?"

"I didn't get a chance. She only had eyes for him."

"Take it easy on that chair. You'll sand the arms down to a bony point." Leo stuffed the plastic bags in a trash can and eased onto a stool next to the workbench. "When I was about ten, I wanted new ice skates more than anything. It was a tough winter. No money laying around for such a thing. The more Mother said I wouldn't be getting them, the more I wanted them. I imagined myself whirling around on the pond in my new skates. Christmas came and went. No skates."

"Are you saying I'm like a kid who wants what I can't have? Hannah and Evie aren't ice skates."

"I'm saying it's human nature to want what you can't have." Leo folded up the sleeves of his faded blue cotton shirt. "This all started after Hannah's confession."

It started with a simple gesture of opening the door, so she could leave the barn while the district mulled her punishment. Her face had matched the white of her pristine apron against the emerald green of her dress. She was so contrite, so beautiful.

"You made her a cradle before Evie was born."

The icy, frigid winter air was still vivid in his memory from that Christmas Eve two years ago. He delivered the cradle to the *dawdy haus* porch where Hannah served her *bann*. Laura caught him in the act, sending his heart into overdrive under a starry sky. Hannah's great-grandma, bless her sweet heart, had been delivering her own present. She served as Hannah's lifeline in a terrible season.

"Evie is a special gift from *Gott*."

"You talk a lot about Evie." Leo's thick eyebrows rose and fell. "Almost more than you talk about Hannah."

"I like *boplin*. I'm *gut* with *boplin*."

"Even though you're the youngest in your family?"

What was Leo's point? Phillip was the youngest child because his mother couldn't have any more babies after him. "I'm *onkel* to a dozen *kinner*. I have experience." Phillip dropped the sandpaper, picked up a tack cloth and wiped down the rocking chair. "Don't you have work to do?"

"Most people don't get to talk to their bosses like that." Leo offered a good-natured grin. The man needed a haircut. His long curls stuck out from under his straw hat. He had to be in his late thirties, but only a few strands of silver highlighted his long beard. He made a show of looking at the clock on the far wall behind Phillip. "As a matter of fact, I put the finish on the Mitchells' dining room table yesterday while you and Carl delivered the chairs to the Schmidts. I need to sand it down and apply another coat."

"Shall I start on the chairs? They put a rush on that order, didn't they?"

"They did. First do me a favor and carry that box of toys up to the store." He pointed at a large cardboard box filled with hand-carved animals, trucks, and trains. When he wasn't making furniture, Leo spent his time carving toys. "Jennie's been asking for them."

"I didn't see her buggy in front of the store." Leo's wife rarely missed a day at their store. "Is Francis sick?"

"*Nee.* She took a day off to plant her vegetable garden. Francis is at school." Leo began to whistle. Beau raised his head, his mournful eyes landing on his master. "Not you, *hund*. Stay. Christina took her shift at the store."

Christina Weber. Her parents moved to Jamesport the previous year from Haven, Kansas. They had family here. That explained the whistling. Leo always whistled when he was up to something. And since his marriage to Jennie, he always seemed to be up to something. Marriage had changed his entire being. He smiled more. He talked more. Even to *Englishers.* Even to strangers.

Must be nice. "Fine."

"Better get a move on."

Muttering under his breath, Phillip heaved the box from the counter and headed out the door.

"I do not meddle or matchmake." Leo's lazy chuckle floated on the spring air, mocking Phillip. "At least not much."

— CHAPTER 5 —

Business at Leo's store was booming. A load of senior citizens from St. Joseph—according to the sign on the back of their monster charter bus—swarmed around the Combination Store.

Winding his way past gazebos and fort playscapes, Phillip nodded at the bus driver who sat at a picnic table—made by Leo—eating a sandwich and Sun chips. Jennie had planted pink, purple, and white pansies in the flower boxes on the front porch of the building that had once been a barn.

Phillip thanked a silver-haired lady in a purple velour jogging suit and black tennis shoes for holding the door open for him. Inside, he inhaled the scent of wood shavings, scented soaps, and aromatic candles as he slid past two men wearing St. Louis Cardinals caps—twins in their blue jackets and gray slacks. They seemed flummoxed at the price of the quilts hanging on dowels by the door. They couldn't know how many months went into hand-stitching those beautiful creations.

"Hey, Phillip. You brought the toys. *Danki*." Cheeks red, Christina dashed by him, a green-and-purple double wedding ring quilt folded in her arms. "Unload them onto the empty shelves by the children's books, will you?"

The lady following her shushed the man with her. "It will make a perfect wedding gift for Kathleen. She'll love it. Don't be so tight." She settled a mammoth denim bag decorated with appliqued handprints and the words "I love Grammy" onto the scarred wooden counter. "You take credit cards, don't you?"

Christina nodded. She smiled at Phillip. "When you get done, would you mind taking that rocking chair out to the Garcias' van? Mr. Garcia had surgery a few weeks ago on a bulging disc. He'll tell you all about it, if you let him."

"No problem."

George Garcia, a pharmacist who worked in Chillicothe, stood by the door fidgeting with a black brace that covered his middle.

Toys unloaded. The chair in the van. A box of jams from the storage room. The ladder to remove a wall hanging. Five minutes became an hour. Finally, the driver employed a coach's whistle to round up his seniors. They filed out, chatting and showing off their purchases. The doors closed, and the motor fired up. Disc brakes squeaked.

They were gone. Silence reigned. Wiping at her face with a paper towel, Christina flopped into a rocking chair and laughed, a soft melodious sound, like music tinkling. "When they say *Gott* provides, they're not kidding."

Exertion brought out the pink in her cheeks. She was pretty. Looking away, Phillip straightened the peach and strawberry jam jars next to the canned goods including pickles, tomatoes, cherries, green beans, peaches, and more. He picked up the empty box.

"What do you mean?"

"I needed help and you showed up." She fanned her face with the paper towel. "And you stayed. *Danki.*"

"*Gern gschehne.*" Phillip edged toward the storeroom. He should store the box and head back to the shop. "I guess Jennie didn't think you'd have a crowd today."

"It's early. The tourist season doesn't start for a few more weeks, but retired seniors—you never know when they'll show up. The folks who just left attend a community center program, and they have travelogues called 'Trips on a Tank of Gas.'"

"So they came to Jamesport."

"You don't sound too excited."

"I'm glad they came. We can use the business." He tucked the flaps back in the box for something to do with his hands. "There are just so many other places a person could go on a tank of gas."

"I like Jamesport. It's much more interesting than Haven, where I used to live. And prettier than Kansas. It's so flat." Her nut-brown eyes lit up as she said the words. "Haven is tiny and there are only a few shops. I cleaned English houses, but I'd rather do this."

Her free hand fluttered toward the surrounding store with its expanse of goods. They sold all kinds of homemade items and furniture. Hickory rocking chairs, an oak desk, coat racks, dressers, cradles, bed frames, a beautiful pine table and matching set of chairs, all handcrafted by Leo, Phillip, and Carl, Leo's latest apprentice.

Christina talked with her hands. She was a bundle of energy, unlike Hannah, who was so self-contained it was a wonder she didn't combust. She kept her hands tucked in her lap as if afraid they would do something she didn't like.

"Do you want some cold tea?" Christina hopped up from the chair and tossed her homemade fan on the counter next to the oversize, old-fashioned cash register. "I brought a thermos from home. It's fresh sun tea. My *mudder* made it yesterday."

"I should probably go. Leo will wonder where I am."

"He's such a nice man. I love working for him and Jennie."

"He is nice." Aside from the unwanted advice and meddling. "I like working for him too."

Christina pointed to the chair where she'd been sitting. "You made that chair, didn't you?"

"I did."

"It's so beautiful." Her expression wistful, she sighed. "It would be perfect for rocking a *bopli* to sleep at night."

Exactly his thought when he'd sanded and stained the wood. "I hope so. I pray over every piece of furniture I make, hoping it will become part of someone's family. I learned that from Leo."

"Someday I hope to have one as part of my family. Of course, now that I moved here it's not happening anytime soon." Christina's face colored again. She rushed around the counter and began to straighten embroidered tablecloths, knitted sweaters, and crocheted pot holders that covered two nearby tables. "Sorry. I shouldn't be spinning wool instead of working. I'm sure you have better things to do than talk to me."

In their community, many of the men and women Christina's age had already found their special friends. It would be hard to start over. Phillip hadn't been to a singing in a long time. He wasn't tuned in to the grapevine on such things. "People here are friendly. You'll fit right in."

"That's what Jennie says." Christina slipped past him and began to dust the jars of jam. "She says you're a hard worker and you like *boplin*."

So Jennie had been talking to Christina about him. Jennie and Leo were two peas in pod.

"I better get going. Lots of work to do in the shop."

"*Danki* for your help." Her smile was as sweet and simple as his mother's shoofly pie. "And the conversation—it's nice to have someone to talk to when I'm here by myself."

"Anytime."

Now why did he say that?

— C H A P T E R 6 —

The guard previously planted at the Stutzmans's door had moved to sit at a picnic table in the front yard. Thaddeus stifled a groan. If anyone had struck fear into his heart as a boy, it was Zechariah.

With his fierce frown and critical brown eyes, the man knew how to send a gaggle of kids racing away when discovered fishing in his pond without an invitation. He no longer cut such an imposing figure. The Parkinson's disease had ravaged his ability to walk, to talk, and sometimes, to think, but he was still Zechariah.

By the same token, Thaddeus wasn't a child anymore. He had his own child now. One glimpse of her before submitting to his punishment was all he wanted. It would be a memory to cherish while he served his time. He didn't deserve it, but Hannah had a kind, generous heart. From the look on Phillip's face at the Purple Martin earlier, Thaddeus needed to start mending fences now, not two or three or four months from now.

Long days and nights of the *bann* would give Phillip more time to capture that generous heart and make it his own.

Thaddeus won that heart first and then threw it away like trash. What kind of man bailed on a woman he claimed to love? A boy who needed to grow up.

Two years in Nappanee away from family and friends had made him grow up fast. He learned independence. He learned to take responsibility for himself. He learned what the word *lonely* meant. He'd run away from responsibility only to find that he couldn't live without it. Sitting in the service on Sunday mornings watching women across the aisle cuddle babies in their arms had served as an endless reminder of what he'd left behind. The scent of baby on the young woman who served his sandwich after the service was like a memory he couldn't quite place.

Every letter from Mattie reminded him he need only repent and ask for forgiveness and his old life would be his.

He had banked on that knowledge the entire 530 miles from Nappanee to Jamesport.

Right up until he saw Phillip and Hannah sitting on those stools side by side. Sure, there'd been a stool between them—lip service to the *Gmay* elders who would disapprove of them openly courting. But it didn't fool Thaddeus.

He slid from the buggy and stood firm, feet planted just outside Laura's vast array of lantana, vinca, pansies, yellow belles, and marigolds in pinks, purples, reds, whites, and yellows. They were bright against a brilliant sun that hovered near the horizon of the April sky. The great-grandkids must've helped. There was no way the seventy-something great-grandmother with her painful arthritis knelt to plant all these flowers.

Or maybe Hannah planted them. Maybe she found time between working at the restaurant and caring for Evie. The image of her ginger hair shining in the sun, her nose wrinkled in concentration as she dug in the fresh dirt hovered in his mind's eye. She loved to garden with her mother. She'd never tired of listening to him talk about the gardens he would someday design and plant for *Englishers* who didn't have the time or inclination to do it themselves. She'd shared the dream with him before he ruined everything.

Now he had to fix it. Thaddeus took a step forward. "Is she here?"

Zechariah grasped his walker with both gnarled hands. He wore a black jacket even in the warm spring weather. He had to be closing in on eighty. "If you mean Hannah, *jah*, she's here." His jasper eyes bore holes in Thaddeus's forehead. "What do you want with her, *suh*? You know you shouldn't be here."

"I just want to talk for a minute or two." He wrangled his emotions until he had them under control. "To see my *dochder* before I go to the bishop."

"Your *dochder*?" Zechariah snorted. His voice had grown hoarse and his words slurred in the past few years. But his disdain was obvious. "Hannah had a long day at the restaurant. She's tired and Evie has the sniffles. She'll go to bed soon."

"She is my *dochder*."

"And you committed a *Fehla*. You can't come in the house. You need to go see the bishop. See about making a confession."

"I know and I will, but you said I could come back here tonight."

"One, you can't come in my house. Two, I don't believe I said that." Zechariah leaned back on the bench. His left arm jerked, then his right. "I believe I said you can't see Evelyn without Hannah's permission. That little girl doesn't know you from a hole in the ground. You might scare her."

"I wouldn't scare her."

As if to refute his statement, an unhappy wail floated through the screen door. The door opened, and Hannah trudged out. She held a tearful little girl in a pale-blue dress on her hip.

Evie. She had dark, curly hair that had escaped two fat braids hanging to her shoulders. Her skin was fair, except for her cheeks red with exertion. The girl had a healthy set of lungs.

Hannah took two steps. She froze. "Thaddeus."

"I told you I would come." He struggled to keep his voice even. "She looks like me."

"*Gott's* will, I reckon. His design." Both hands on his walker, Zechariah stood. His shoulders were hunched, his knees bowed in. He shuffled toward the ramp that led to the porch. He nodded at Hannah. "If you need me or Laura, call out."

Hannah scurried down the steps. "Let me help you to the door."

"I'm fine."

He teetered off-balance with every step.

Hannah shifted the wriggling girl to her other hip. She put one hand on Zechariah's shoulder. "We can't have you falling again."

Thaddeus held out his arms. "I can hold Evie for you if you need to walk him to the door."

"*Nee.*"

Hannah and Zechariah spoke in unison with equal ferocity.

The slow but steady parade eased up the ramp to the porch and to the door. Hannah opened it and waited while Zechariah entered. She disappeared inside and called for Laura. Then she reappeared and trudged back down the ramp.

"He's worse."

"Much. He'll need a wheelchair soon."

"It must be a lot for Laura. She's no spring chicken either."

"In sickness and in health." Hannah's tone sharpened to a fine, fatal point. She eased onto the picnic table bench and settled Evie on her lap. "But those words mean nothing to you."

"I'm not a monster." The words escaped before Thaddeus could stop them. "She's my *dochder*."

"What does that make me?" Hannah cleared her throat and ducked her head. "Never mind. You might as well sit."

"Since you asked so nicely." He sat. She edged away to the far corner of the pine bench. "How old is she now?"

Hannah's scowl burned the skin from his cheeks. "She's twenty-one months. Her birthday is July nineteenth."

Evie wiggled around on her mother's lap until she faced Thaddeus. Tears streaked her face, and she needed her nose wiped. She smiled a wide smile that featured two lower front teeth and two on the top. His heart did a drum roll. Now she looked like Hannah.

Sweet. Mischievous. Pretty.

"What are you crying about, little one?"

Thaddeus reached to wipe away her tears. Evie drew back. Her lower lip protruded. She stuck her thumb in her mouth and hid her face in Hannah's chest. He withdrew his hand.

"She's shy around strangers." Hannah's tone held no recrimination, but her words sliced through skin and muscle as surely as if she'd stabbed him in the heart with a pitchfork. "She's mostly here at the *dawdy haus* with Laura, although sometimes she plays at the big house with Ruby's grandchildren. We've been living here since she was born. I help *Mammi* and she helps me."

"And she doesn't judge."

"*Nee*, she doesn't. Neither does Zechariah. They saved me." Her expression somber, Hannah stroked Evie's dark curls. "It was hard for *Mudder* and *Daed*. They say they forgive me, but they have a hard time forgetting. They don't want me to be the wrong example for my *schweschders*. I understand that, but it's hard."

A child should have her parents' unconditional love. The rejection must hurt terribly. It was all Thaddeus's fault. He swallowed against the lump in his throat. Finding a new beginning seemed almost impossible—if it weren't for the little girl between them.

"Does she walk?"

"Since she was a year old."

He cleared his throat. "Does she talk yet?"

"She babbles a lot. *Hund* and *kitzn* and *millich* and *kuche*."

Dog, cat, milk, and cookie. "She knows what she likes." Babies had such a sweet, small world. "Not *mudder*?"

"*Nee*." Hannah's cheeks went pink. "I reckon it's because I work so much."

"She knows you're her *mudder*."

"*Jah*, but she likes *Mammi* better."

"I doubt that."

"Why are you trying to make me feel better?"

"If I hadn't left, you'd be at home with her."

"You're right." Anger rippled across her face. Unshed tears shone in her eyes. "You ran away."

"I'm sorry."

"You said that before." Her gaze dropped to Evie. The child's breathing sounded congested, and her thumb popped out. She couldn't suck on it and breathe at the same time. Poor thing. Hannah rubbed her back. "It doesn't help any more now than it did then. You weren't sorry enough to stay."

"I want to explain."

"I'm listening."

"It's hard for me to understand myself." Putting the boiling mess of emotion into words escaped him. Fear. Love. Shame. Disappointment in himself. The knowledge that he'd disappointed his parents, his grandparents, his friends. Weakness. Self-loathing. "I thought you would be better off without me."

"So you ran away and left me to face it alone? You don't get to make that into some kind of lofty course of action."

"I'm not. It was a low, shameful thing to do. I knew it then and I know it now." He shifted on the hard, wooden seat and stared out at the dusk. "I was immature and unworthy of someone like you. There's no excuse. Nothing I can say will make it right. I understand that, but I want to try to make it up to you. I've missed you every single day."

He'd run away from Hannah, but she'd been the first thought in his head when he awoke in the morning and the last when he nodded off to sleep at night. Some nights she visited him in his dreams and he woke up racked with a longing that could not be assuaged.

He dared a quick side glance. Hannah stared straight ahead. Tears trickled down her face. She swiped at them with her free hand. "What are you doing here? Why come back now?"

"Remember when we used to talk about saving our money to open our own nursery?" He stared out at Laura's brilliant array of flowers, the product of being lovingly planted, weeded, watered, and nurtured. "I still want to do that. I was hoping you would too."

"That was a long time ago. We were *kinner* dreaming big dreams. Now I have a *bopli* to think of and you spent the last two years working in a factory."

"I thought working in the factory would be an easy way to earn money to start my own business, but I hated it. Putting together RVs and being inside all day was the worst kind of work." He grasped for words to explain the tedium that dulled his mind during those days. How he'd had to force himself from bed each morning to face yet another day of mindless work. "I realized how much I like working with sun and earth. I came back to find work at a nursery or green-house, get some experience, and work my way up, *Gott* willing."

"So it's about you being happy?"

"It's about doing something pleasing to *Gott* while being with family—my family—and being content with it." Thaddeus studied his dirty work boots. "None of it has meaning, no matter what you're doing, if you're not doing it for the right reasons. I didn't know that before. I know it now."

"Some of us don't have choices." Her voice broke. "Don't you think I long to be outside, grubbing in the dirt, singing songs to my *bopli,* and planting daffodils with the sun on my back and the breeze on my face? Do you think I like waiting tables all day? We do what we have to do."

"I'm sorry. I know it's my fault. I was stupid and idiotic, but I never stopped loving you." The desire to hold Evie mingled with a fierce need to wrap his arms around Hannah. He'd hurt her so much. "I'll make it up to you, I promise. I saved all my money from the RV factory. *Aenti* Bertie refused to take a cent from me. We can have our dream."

"What are you saying exactly?"

"I'm saying I came back here to ask you to marry me."

Marry me.

The world tipped on its side. Hannah's stomach twisted. To hear him talk about dreams that had turned to ashes two years ago ripped open wounds that had only just begun to heal.

For two years he'd been the last thing she thought about before she went to bed and the first image in her head when she awoke.

In her dreams he plucked pink and red roses and arranged them in vases on their kitchen table. His hands were calloused and warm, his face tanned from working in the sun. He was always smiling, always laughing. Those dreams left tears on her face every time she opened her eyes to face another day alone.

She stood and jolted toward the path that led to the house and safety. "Please go."

Thaddeus stood and grabbed her arm. "Please forgive me. I'll make my confession. I'll do my time. Then marry me."

"Don't touch me." The strength of his grip and the warmth of his fingers on her skin threatened her defenses. She swallowed against hot tears and tightened her grip on Evie. "You show up here out of the blue . . . You expect too much." Evie started to wriggle in her arms. "Hush, hush, sweet, *bopli*. You're okay. You're fine. You're just tired like your *mudder*."

"I know. I know it's a lot to ask." His hand dropped. "But I know you. You have a forgiving heart. And you told me that night when . . . when we did what we did . . . that you loved me." His startling blue eyes implored her to forgive him. "It wasn't just what we did. You never would have given yourself to me if you didn't love me. You're not that kind of person. You give all of yourself because you give all your love."

"And knowing that, you walked away." Either he was right, or he thought she was a better person than she really was. Which was it? "You threw away my love and the gift I gave you."

He hung his head. "I had to grow up. To become a better man. To be deserving of you."

"How could I ever trust you again? I work hard every day to forgive you, but trust is a different matter. Besides, there's . . ." She stopped. What was Phillip to her? She couldn't think. Not while standing so close to Thaddeus. Her gaze went to his lips. Those full, soft lips. His firm jaw and the way his hair curled around his ears. The size of his mammoth hands with long sensitive fingers. Hands that turned soft with a touch.

Stop it, stop it, stop it.

"A lot has happened since you left. We didn't sit around waiting for you to return if that's what you're thinking."

"I know. Mattie wrote to me about it." His hand lifted as if to touch her again. She edged away. His hand dropped. "That's why I came back. Before it's too late. I don't expect you to give me an answer now, but I'm asking you to wait. Wait until after the *bann* ends before you make your choice. Don't rush into anything because you feel alone or because you think Evie will be better off."

How dare he ask. He had no right. The searing pain in her heart dissipated, replaced by furious, molten anger. "Don't you dare say you expect me to wait while you are under the *bann*. You don't deserve that."

He deserved her anger. He deserved the *bann*.

"I know I don't . . . I'm only hoping and praying you'll find it in your heart to consider the possibility that I might have changed. That I might be worth waiting for. That the part of me you fell in love with is still in here." He touched his chest. "The part that needed to grow up has."

She hadn't waited for him, but neither had she moved forward. Phillip had tried. He'd tried hard. He had a sunny disposition. He was good with Evie. He loved Evie. Did he love Hannah? Even after two years, she couldn't be sure. Did she love him?

Thanks to Thaddeus, she couldn't trust her feelings for any man.

Thaddeus leaned in so close she could see the tiny scar on the bridge of his nose, the one he got when he and his brother Simon butted heads while playing basketball. For a second it seemed like he was going to kiss her. Surely he didn't think she would allow such a thing. Instead, his lips brushed against Evie's forehead. He touched the baby's cheek. "*Danki* for letting me see her."

Evie giggled. Her chubby hands flailed and reached for Thaddeus. "*Daadi, Daadi.*"

Thaddeus smiled. His smile once eclipsed the entire world. That smile had led her down the path to sin and despair.

"I'm your *daed, bopli.* Zechariah is *daadi.*"

Nee, nee. *Don't let that smile lead you astray. Not again.* "She thinks all men are *daadi.*"

He nodded, but the smile lingered. "She looks like me, but she has her *mudder's* heart."

What did that mean? "We'll see about that."

"I hope so with all my heart."

He turned and walked to his buggy, hopped in, and drove away.

Evie tried to pull away from Hannah. She waved. "Bye-bye. Bye-bye, *daadi.*"

How could a baby know?

— CHAPTER 7 —

Porch swings served as well as rocking chairs. Providing the lull-aby, two blue jays conversed in the oak tree clothed in green buds in the front yard. Hannah gave the swing a push with one foot. Maybe the motion would put Evie to sleep. She sat next to Hannah, drinking milk from a sippy cup. Wide awake.

A breeze rustled the tree branches. The cool evening air caressed Hannah's still warm cheeks. Darkness had settled over the yard, but the birds still chatted in the distance as if trying to settle a long-standing dispute. They were probably gossiping over the heated exchanged they just witnessed between Hannah and Thaddeus. The man thought he could simply return, offer a nonsensical excuse, beg forgiveness, and *oh, by the way, will you marry me?*

Words she'd longed to hear two years ago. Words that hadn't come. Instead he carved a hole in her heart by leaving her. By leaving his unborn child.

Forgiving was one thing. Forgetting was another. Trusting was too much to ask.

Wasn't it?

Exhaustion weighed her down. Evie dropped her sippy cup on the swing, milk drops flying. She clapped and chortled. "Whee, whee!"

"*Jah*, whee, whee, but now is the time to sleep."

If she didn't go down soon, Hannah might drop off to sleep first. "*Mudder.*"

"*Mudder?* Did you say *mudder?*" Hannah scooped up the baby and hugged her tight. "I heard you. You said *mudder.*"

"*Mudder?*" Evie's eyes were wide. She flailed her arms. "*Daadi. Mudder.*"

Soon she would speak in complete sentences, go to school, then to singings, and one day, God willing, to her wedding.

Which brought Hannah back to the bone-aching emotional exchange with Thaddeus. Everything hurt. The words pierced her muscles and sinew. The memories were like boiling water splashed on her heart and soul. She gritted her teeth and settled Evie on her lap. She began to rock and sing Evie's favorite song, "Jesus Loves the Little Children."

Evie sighed and snuggled closer, her chubby hands clutching at Hannah's apron.

Gott? Gott . . .

Stop thinking. Just be. Be still. Rest.

Easier said than done, Gott.

"Is she asleep?"

Hannah started at the sound of Laura's voice. She breathed and glanced down at Evie. Her daughter's eyes were droopy. Her body felt heavy with sleep. "Getting there."

"Scooch over." Speaking softly, Laura plopped onto the swing next to Hannah. She smoothed Evie's rumpled dress with a wrinkled, arthritic hand dotted with age spots. "Zechariah is finally asleep. Poor thing. The jerking around is getting worse."

"Can't they increase his medicine?"

"It's the medicine that causes the jerking."

"I don't understand."

"It helps with some symptoms, like the stiffness, but it has its own side effects. Most medicines do."

"Is it okay to pray for healing?"

"I do, but I also pray for *Gott*'s will to be done."

"Will he die from Parkinson's?"

"The doctors say no. They say he'll die with it." Sadness saturated the words. Laura had lost one husband. To contemplate losing another must be agony. Such strength, such willingness to suffer for love baffled Hannah. Laura had risked everything—twice. "In other words, he might fall and hit his head or die of pneumonia from choking and getting food in his lungs. That's why . . ."

"Why what?"

"Ben wants us to move into his house. The *dawdy haus* here is close to Ruby and Martin's house, but my *dochder* doesn't feel it's close enough." What Laura thought of the idea was obvious in her tone. "They all say I need help. I don't have enough strength anymore to care for him properly. They say he'll fall and I won't be able to stop him or pick him up. They say I'll get hurt in the process."

"You have me to help you."

Laura plucked at her apron. "I know. But Ben worries about his *groossdaadi*. He shouldn't, but he does. Between the two of us, we have what he needs. Loving care. But you're at work during the day, some evenings too."

"That's not the problem." They saw a girl who didn't know how to behave herself, let alone take care of another. "They don't trust me."

"Nobody ever said that."

"They didn't have to. I see it in their looks. I hear it in their whispers."

"That's just your imagination." Laura squeezed Hannah's hand. Her fingers were cold. "You've been forgiven."

"But it hasn't been forgotten. They're not like you. They don't look at me and see the good, only the rotten, nasty parts."

"This isn't about you or me." Laura's tone was tart, but her smile softened its edges. "I don't want to move Zechariah because he's happy here. This little *dawdy haus* is the right size for him to get around. He's home."

"Then don't move him."

"It's not up to me."

Hannah was silent a moment. "I know it's not about me, but if you move, will Evie and I go with you?"

"*Nee.* David and Elijah and Raymond all agree. You would go home to your parents."

Her parents who couldn't look her in the eye. They claimed to have forgiven her, but they didn't want her around her little sisters. It would be a hard transition. Especially for Evie. She spent more time with Laura than she did with Hannah. "Evie loves you and Zechariah. More than me, even."

"I don't know about that, but maybe it's time for her to be with them. I won't always be here for Evie. The more I have to care for Zechariah, the less time I have to watch over her." Sadness clung to the words. "Soon she'll be too heavy for me to pick up. Your sisters can watch her—give her the same blessing of security and love. Besides, my grandchildren need to stop being so stiff-necked with you. Maybe this is *Gott's* plan."

Or maybe it was just meddling from people who were judgmental and hard-hearted. "Men always think they know better, don't they?"

"Which brings us to your unexpected visitor."

Hannah wasn't ready to change the subject. "I don't want to move either."

"You'll do what you have to. Just as you always have."

Laura's no-nonsense approach to life could be irksome, but this time, she was right.

"What was he thinking?" Hannah gave the swing another push. If only its motion could soothe her hurting heart. "Did he really think he could come back and we'd just pick up where we left off? How could he be so thick-headed, so dense, so, so, so—"

"Such a man?"

"Exactly." Hannah couldn't help herself. She giggled at Laura's wry tone and her quick wink. She didn't have to hide her feelings with her great-grandmother. It wouldn't matter if she did. Laura could read her face like a first-grade primer. "I know I'm supposed to forgive. I know my sin was equal—is equal—to his. We were both there. We both made this *bopli*. I thought I forgave him for leaving me in a lurch, but then he showed up here."

"He showed up and had the gall to ask you to really forgive him. To show you forgive him by letting him back into your life."

"I know forgiveness is required, but trusting is even harder. Especially when it comes to Evie."

"You've spent the last two years making amends and living a godly life." Laura removed her silver wire-rimmed glasses and polished them with the corner of her apron. Her green eyes were as sharp at seventy-five as they'd been when Hannah sat on her knee as a child. "You worked hard at making a life for yourself and Evelyn. I'm sure Thaddeus's return feels like a step back."

"It does. Like I stepped back in time."

"Or does it remind you of what you saw in him in the first place?"

Of course not. She wouldn't be taken in again by the humorous glint in his sapphire eyes or the way he smiled as if the two of them shared a joke no one else had heard. She wouldn't be taken in by the strength of his grip or the softness of his kisses. She wouldn't let herself be led about again by her heartstrings. "I was weak and stupid."

"You're a sweet, kind, *gut* girl with a *gut* head on your shoulders. You wouldn't give your heart to just any man. I know you don't want to hear this, but I always liked Thaddeus. More than once after your great-*groossdaadi* died, I went outside to find him mowing the yard or weeding the garden for me. Once he left a bunch of sunflowers in a bucket of water on the porch. You are two of a kind."

Laura had an unerring way of getting to the meat of a situation.

"The Thaddeus I fell in love with never wanted to be a farmer like his *daed*. He liked gardening with his *mudder*. His *daed* didn't appreciate it, but Thaddeus always wanted to grow plants and flowers to make yards beautiful." Her heart hurt remembering the walks they'd taken. He could name all the flowers, shrubs, and trees. He would make sketches of the gardens he dreamed up. "He has his *mudder*'s green thumb, but he never thought his *daed* would understand. Now he says he's going ahead with his plan."

A plan that included her marrying him.

"That he knows what he wants and has a plan to get it speaks to him growing up. I reckon there's something else he wants."

"*Jah.* Tonight he asked me to marry him." The words came out in a whisper, as if giving them voice made the surreal real. The proposal she'd wanted two years ago had finally arrived in a sudden flurry of unexpected words delivered by an unexpected visitor. "I gave him my heart once and he broke it."

"The question is whether he's the only one who can mend it."

"In two years, I never imagined any sort of future with him in it."

"Have you been imagining it with someone else?"

Laura's roundabout way of asking about Phillip. She'd never

commented on Hannah's occasional forays in Phillip's buggy, which had grown more frequent in recent months.

What had started with Phillip's kindness in the midst of the darkest days of Hannah's life had grown into a friendship with the possibility of more over the past two years. Every time he came closer, Hannah managed to edge backward. Phillip made it clear he wanted more and soon. "It's not fair to another man. I didn't save myself for marriage. I have a *bopli*. I'm not what most Plain men dream of when they think of *fraas*."

"Phillip has been patient."

That was an understatement. Any day now, he would throw his hands in the air and give up. "Phillip is a *gut* man."

"Who is *gut* with Evelyn."

He loved Evie. That was obvious in the way he played with her after church and fed her from his plate when invited to Sunday supper. He even left trinkets for her on his late-night visits. "He will make a *gut mann*."

"But do you love him?"

Surely that sweet content feeling—however different from what she had felt for Thaddeus—was love. Every time it swelled, she backed away. "I'm afraid to love anyone."

"I can see why. But look at me and Jennie Graber and Bess Graber and Mary Kay Miller. We were all widows. Our husbands left us. They died. Still, we learned to love a second time. *Gott* gave us second chances and we had the strength to take them. Even Jennie, whose first *mann* was not a *gut* person."

Hannah had attended every one of her great-grandmother's friends' weddings. She'd wondered at their ability to trust love again after losing their first husbands. Death had taken them in various seasons of their lives. Unlike Thaddeus, who simply walked away from the possibility of a future with her and his daughter. "Can I tell you something?"

"You know you can."

"I really want to smack Thaddeus over the head with a cast-iron skillet. Two or three, maybe even four times."

Laura cackled. "There were many times when I wanted to do the same with Eli."

"But he never did something like this to you."

"*Nee.* But we married immediately because we didn't trust ourselves to wait."

Heat toasted Hannah's cheeks. She'd never had a conversation like this with anyone, not even her sisters, not even her own mother. "We should've waited."

"You should've."

"But we didn't and I'm not sorry I have Evie. Does that mean my confession doesn't count for anything? I'm not truly repentant?"

"It means you know that every *bopli* is a gift from *Gott*, regardless of the circumstances."

"I don't know what to do. Evie needs a *daed*."

"I suspect the bishop would say the man who made the *bopli* is the *daed* and always will be. That you made your bed, and now you have to lie in it." Laura returned her glasses to her nose and leaned back in the swing with a sigh. "*Gott's* will be done. That's what the bishop would say."

"What do you say?"

"I say a few wallops with a skillet might knock some sense into a man." She sat up straight and peered into the darkness. "Is that a buggy coming up the road?"

Hannah followed her gaze. Indeed, it was.

Phillip.

— CHAPTER 8 —

Time had never seemed shorter than it did now. Steeling himself against the feeling he was losing a race against the clock, Phillip jumped from his buggy in front of the *dawdy haus* and stomped up the steps to the porch. Laura and Hannah, the latter holding a sleeping Evie on her lap, sat on the porch swing.

Both women had guilty looks on their faces as if he'd caught them pilfering doughnuts from a bakery. He halted, not sure how to proceed. Laura should be inside, asleep or getting ready for bed. Along with Evie. It was far past their bedtimes. Instead, Laura smiled and waved as if they'd just run into each other after Sunday service. He cleared his throat.

"I was just headed inside." Laura stood. "Now that the sun has gone down, it's cooling off. Spring nights are still a bit chilly for this old body. Let me put Evie down for you."

"I'll do it." Hannah started to rise. "You've had a long day."

"It's no problem." Laura scooped up the sleeping baby with the ease of many years of practice. "You deserve a few minutes of free time."

"No need to go inside on my account." *Please go inside.* "I just stopped to say howdy. Is Zechariah still up? The purple martin count is starting to rise."

"He was already snoring when I came outside earlier." Laura pulled the screen door open and looked back. "Don't stay up too late, Hannah. You're tired and dawn comes early."

"*Gut natch.*" Phillip lingered by the steps. When she closed the door, he edged closer to the swing. "If you're too tired I can go."

"I'm not that kind of tired." Her expression more wary than usual, Hannah chewed on her lower lip. Finally, she patted the empty space next to her. "You might as well sit down."

"That doesn't really sound like an invitation." He studied her face. Her fair skin was almost translucent in the dusk. Her nose was red as if she'd been crying. He'd never seen her cry. Not even the day of her confession. "Let me take you for a ride. It'll soothe what ails you."

"I don't think so. Not tonight. It's been a very long day."

He took her hand and tugged. "Come. I promise not to talk about what happened this morning."

As she freed her hand her frown disappeared, replaced by that smile that always crashed through the defenses he tried to maintain. The defenses needed to keep his poor heart from shattering when she said no. Which she surely would. She'd made that clear in the way she leaned away from his intended caresses. The way she sat two feet from him on the buggy seat when they went for a ride, her hands clasped in her lap, knuckles white. She never seemed to relax.

He kept postponing the inevitable by not asking the question, but sooner or later—sooner now that Thaddeus had decided to return—he would have to ask.

They walked to the buggy where he helped her climb in. A few minutes later they were on the road that cut through the Kauffman property to his parents' farm.

Ease into it. Gently. Very gently.

"So what did you do today?" What a stupid question. He held the reins loosely, letting Caramel meander along the gravel road. Not the question he intended—needed—to ask. "Anything interesting happen?"

She sighed. "You promised not to talk about this morning."

So he had. But they needed to clear the air before he could see his way through this morass of emotions. "I was giving you the opportunity to say your piece."

"What piece?"

"That piece where you tell me you can't keep taking rides with me because Evie's *daed* is here and he's her *daed* and I'm not."

Please don't say that. Please.

"Is that what you think I should say?"

If he were in her shoes, he would want what was best for Evie. Was a man who deserted the girl he was courting while she was in the family way good enough to be Evie's father?

The fact remained. He was her father. What about walking in Thaddeus's shoes? Did God expect Phillip to try to understand him? He tugged on the reins and pulled Caramel to the shoulder of the road, next to his father's alfalfa field, and stopped.

"I may not be Evie's *daed*, but I've been here for her since the day she was born. Before, if you count the crib I made."

"I know that."

"I love her." While this was an important piece of his argument, it wasn't the most important one. He took a long breath then let it out. His heart smacked against his ribcage. Blood pulsed in his ears. The world receded. Only her beautiful face remained.

He reached for her hand. "I love *you*."

-◄◄◄-

The buzzing in Hannah's ears made it hard to hear. She shook her head. "What did you say?"

"I said, I love you." Phillip's hand tightened on hers. He leaned closer. "I'm hoping you'll say it back."

Every Plain woman longed to hear those words. Every woman longed to hear them. How many heard them twice in one night—from two different men? Love led to marriage. Surely Phillip meant to ask her to marry him.

Bittersweet pain welled and spread from her head to her toes. For a woman with no choices, she suddenly had too many. Married, she would no longer be the subject of the local gossips. Her past would fade into a yellowed, forgotten page from a book no one read anymore.

Phillip was offering her a way forward, a new, fresh start.

Is that a good reason to marry him?

The voice sounded like Zechariah's. Startled, Hannah glanced around.

Did God sound like an elderly man with a hoarse, slurred voice?

Do you love him?

"I care for you."

"You care for me?" Phillip's tone was a mix of hurt and bewilderment. "So you care for me, but you love Thaddeus?"

"I don't know."

It was an honest answer. Her feelings were a muddle of pain, longing, hurt, uncertainty, fear, and loneliness. Still, it wasn't truly an answer.

The moonlight shone down on Phillip's face. Stars twinkled and small, spritely clouds danced overhead. The aroma of fresh-cut grass and earth filled Hannah's nostrils. And Phillip's woodsy scent.

"You know where I'm going with this, don't you?" The tender eagerness in Phillip's face receded, replaced by indignation. His

Adam's apple bobbed. "You know I'd be a *gut mann* and a *gut daed*. You know that. You have no obligation to Thaddeus. I've been here for the past two years. He hasn't."

"It's not about Thaddeus."

That wasn't exactly true. If he hadn't hurt her, she might be able to trust enough to say yes and marry Phillip. Laura seemed to think if Hannah hadn't loved Thaddeus to start with, she never would have made the mistake she did.

Or had she mistaken physical yearning for true love?

If it wasn't love, why hadn't the ache in her chest receded after all this time?

Phillip dropped her hand and faced the road. His features were etched in stone. "Let me ask you this. What if he hadn't shown up this morning? Would you be able to say it then?"

Not a fair question. Anger welled in Hannah. At Thaddeus. At Phillip. At life. "Let me ask you this. What if he hadn't shown up this morning? Would you be declaring your love this evening?"

Phillip stared into the darkness, his face lost in the shadow of his hat. "I've wanted to tell you for a while. I want to ask you to marry me."

"But you haven't."

"I'm glad I didn't. I know where I stand now."

Phillip was a sure bet. He was sweet and kind and he said he loved her. The question was whether she loved him enough to marry him. Until she answered that question, she couldn't say yes, as much as part of her wanted to fling herself into the security of his arms.

"I don't know where I stand on anything yet. I need more time."

"Maybe this will help you decide."

He swiveled and leaned in. His callused hands cupped her face. His gaze met hers, his intent clear. She closed her eyes. His lips were cool and soft. His breath smelled of spearmint. A shiver started in her belly and raced up her spine. His fingers traveled across her skin to her neck. He felt good.

So good.

She jerked back. "*Nee. Nee.* I'm sorry." She scooted to the far edge of the seat and gripped the side with both hands. "I can't. Please take me home. Please."

"I'm sorry." Hurt mingled with the pain in Phillip's voice. Both hands were in the air as if he had surrendered. "I didn't mean to overstep—"

"You didn't. It's not your fault."

What was she thinking? Letting herself go like that. She had promised herself. She'd promised God she would never do that again. Never give in to those feelings before her wedding night. No matter how much she repented, no matter how much she sought forgiveness, she was still the same wretched, sinful girl she'd been when Evie was conceived.

"Please, please take me home."

Without another word, Phillip turned the buggy around and did as she asked.

The short drive was filled with a million unspoken words. A Plain woman didn't tell a Plain man about kissing another, about letting go and living to regret it every single day or about fear so deep and so strong it threatened to strangle her with every breath she took.

At the house, she jumped down before he could get out. "*Gut natch.*"

"Hannah, please."

"I'm sorry. I'm not who you think I am. I'm not *gut* enough for you. You need to find someone better than me."

"I don't want—"

"*Gut natch.*"

She dashed into the house, shut the door, and leaned against it. Her chest heaved. Her stomach roiled. Her body trembled.

God would forgive her, but would Phillip?

— CHAPTER 9 —

No home. No buggy. No family. Thaddeus dumped his scarred duffel bag on the wood floor and commandeered a stool at the Purple Martin Café. He glanced around. No Hannah. It was just as well. He couldn't face her accusing eyes this morning. He needed coffee to regroup.

Returning to Jamesport was hard. He'd told himself it would be from the moment he made the decision. But the reality of it was so much worse. Nicole offered a brisk hello and handed him a laminated menu. The words blurred. He swiped at his nose and refocused. The thought of food turned his stomach.

"Just a cup of *kaffi*. Black."

"Better add some sugar." The owner beat his server to the coffee pot. He placed a mug in front of Thaddeus and poured the steaming coffee to its brim. "It'll sweeten you up. Even better, have a cinnamon roll. They're fresh from the oven."

The aroma filling the restaurant gave substance to his claim. Thaddeus inhaled. He gritted his teeth against a swell of emotion. His mother made melt-in-your-mouth cinnamon rolls, usually on cold winter days to follow a hearty bowl of venison chili.

"Just *kaffi*, please." He studied the menu, certain his homesickness was written across his face as clear as a postcard from Nappanee. "I'm not hungry."

"I'm Burke McMillan. I took this place over from Ezekiel."

Burke had a military style flattop haircut and piercing blue eyes. His accent suggested somewhere on the East Coast. He extended his hand. Thaddeus introduced himself and shook it. The man had a firm grip.

Hoping Burke would go about his business, Thaddeus stared into his coffee.

"How's it going?" Burke laid an enormous roll slathered in white frosting on a plate and nudged it toward him. "Just a bite or two. Nothing like a hot, homemade cinnamon roll to improve a man's disposition."

"What makes you think mine needs improving?"

"You look like you just lost your best friend."

He had. A long time ago, though. "I'm fine."

"Hannah's not working today."

"That's okay."

"You're giving up?" Burke poured a second cup of coffee and added a liberal dose of milk. "Already?"

"*Nee.* I'm not." He halted. Burke had no business in his business. On the other hand, the man was at the wellspring of information in this small town. News of any sort circulated through the Purple Martin. Thaddeus sipped the hot liquid in front of him. The ice accumulated around his heart and soul refused to melt. "I'm looking for a room to rent."

The height of understatement. Ben's edict rang in his ears. No contact with his family or anyone in the community until the kneeling confession and resulting punishment, which would occur in two days.

Then what? Months of the *bann.* No Plain man would hire him for the duration of his punishment. He had a nest egg, but he still needed to work. For the income and his sanity. Plain men worked. That's what they did. Besides, sitting around thinking about his stupidity and cowardice would drive him crazy.

Sour bile burned the back of his throat. He took a bite of the cinnamon roll to drown the taste.

"As it happens, I have one of those." Burke added a second cinnamon roll to another plate, then strode around the counter. He eased onto the stool next to Thaddeus and grabbed a paper napkin from the dispenser. "I mean I have a spare bedroom in my little domain that's just sitting there. You're welcome to it. It's only four blocks from here. Walking distance."

"That's kind of you, but I don't want to impose."

"You're looking for a room. I've got one. I'm here morning, noon, and night." Burke took a big bite of his roll, chewed, and swallowed. He had frosting on his upper lip. "It's free to the right person."

"Free? I couldn't do that."

"Don't let pride get in your way, son. I make a decent living here at the Purple Martin. A kind man once did me this favor. Now I'm paying it forward."

The man seemed genuine. Mattie had written good things about him, and a free room fit Thaddeus's budget. "Aren't you going to ask why I'm not staying with family or friends?"

"I've been here long enough to learn a little of the Amish ways." Burke wiped his face with a napkin. The frosting on his lip refused to dislodge. "I was here when Hannah made her confession."

"Then you know what I did to her."

"I do."

"So why are you being so nice to me?"

He stared at his roll a moment before answering. "I'm a sinner just like you, son. Just like everyone who walks through that door. I've made my own mistakes. Terrible mistakes." Burke's gaze meandered toward the kitchen window where Nicole was picking up an order. Sadness rippled across his face before falling away. "I would never cast the first stone. You made a mistake—more than one—but God's grace is enormous. For which I'm deeply thankful. He is the God of second chances."

The first inkling of hope trickled through Thaddeus since he'd seen Hannah sitting at this counter with Phillip. "What I did to her was terrible. Horrible. We're taught to forgive. No matter what. But I just don't see how she can forgive this."

"What you did was human."

"A better man never would have abandoned the woman he loved."

"Do you believe God can take anything and use it for your good?"

"What are you? A preacher?"

"I was a Navy chaplain in another life." Burke studied his cup of coffee as if he would find the answer to Thaddeus's questions in the dark creaminess. "Now I cook for a living."

Cooked and dispensed Scripture. "You don't think I'm the scum of the earth for what I did?"

"I think you're doing a pretty good job of punishing yourself."

"How can I make it up to her? How can I make her trust me again?"

"By being a better man."

"You work with her almost every day. You know her. Do you think I still have a chance with her?"

"Give it time." A bell tinkled. Burke glanced over his shoulder. "More customers. I better get my rear in gear and get to work." He stood, dug around in his pocket, and produced a single key on a braided leather keychain. He held it out. "You know where the old Cleary place is?"

"*Jah.*" The Clearys retired to Florida the year before Thaddeus left Jamesport. Their small house and yard had been pristine in its neatness. He took the key. "You're just handing over the key to your house? I'm a stranger."

"Maybe I have my own amends to make. Get yourself settled in. It'll be late before I get home." He waved to Kyle and Mildred Jacobson, then trotted around the counter to stow his mug and the remains of his cinnamon roll next to the coffee pots. "Oh and say hello to Jazz. My dog. Her bark is worse than her bite. She loves company. You can take her for a walk if you want. Fresh sheets are in the hall linen closet. Help yourself to whatever's in the refrigerator."

"I don't understand why you're doing this."

"I told you. I'm paying it forward. I'll tell you the story sometime. Right now, I have to work." Order pad in hand, he paused by the counter. "I imagine you're also looking for a job."

"I am."

"I heard Clayton over at the hardware store is looking for a clerk. Part-time."

It wasn't the nursery job he hoped for, but a man in his position couldn't be choosy. One step at a time. Clayton Bellaire was English. That would work even during the *bann*. As long as the Plain customers avoided him.

"Thank you."

"Don't thank me. I just work here."

From his grin, it was apparent Burke wasn't talking about the Purple Martin.

Thaddeus had a place to lay his head tonight. He had the possibility of a job. God had provided. God and an *Englisher* with an East Coast accent.

— CHAPTER 10 —

In charge. Phillip relished those two words. He unleashed them in his mind, trying to outshout the words Hannah had not said. *Yes, I love you. Yes, I'll marry you.*

More telling than her lack of words was her reaction to his kiss. She'd run away. From him. From his touch. A man didn't need a billboard to understand that message. He jerked open the door to the Combination Store and marched inside.

Leo had left Phillip in charge while he and Jennie went to Branson for a few days of vacation. Just the two of them. Jennie was as flushed and smiling as a newlywed when the driver picked them up the previous day. They were so happy. Phillip wanted that kind of happiness.

A squelching sound emanated from his boots. Phillip glanced down. Water pooled at his feet. The dark-stained puddle stretched from near the front door all the way to the open bathroom door on the far wall. "Christina? Christina!"

"In here!"

Her shout held aggravation.

Phillip stamped to the door and peered inside the unisex bathroom. A crescent wrench in one hand, Christina knelt on the floor next to the bathroom sink. The hem of her lavender dress had turned a darker purple from the water. Her cheeks were rosy, and tendrils of hair escaped from her *kapp*. Grease smudged her upturned nose.

She glanced back at him. "It was like this when I came in this morning. The pipe sprang a leak."

Now the words *in charge* took on a whole new meaning. Phillip might be handier with a saw and sandpaper, but he knew his way around plumbing too.

A little.

"So you thought you'd fix it yourself?" He squatted next to her. "Do you even know how to use that thing?"

"Of course I do. I have five *schweschders* and no *bruders*. I'm the oldest." Her glare did nothing to make her less pretty. The unbidden thought blew by him. An observation, nothing more. "Do you have a Shop-Vac to squeegee up the water?"

"Didn't mean to offend. Leo has a Shop-Vac in the other building." He studied the pipe. The water had slowed to a steady drip. "Is it the gasket or does the nut just need to be tightened? All this plumbing was new when Leo turned the barn into a shop."

"It doesn't look like there's plumber's tape or putty on the pipes." She waved the crescent wrench. "I tightened the nut, but it's still dripping."

"I'll run over to the hardware store and get both. On the way back, I'll pick up the Shop-Vac. You might as well put the "Closed" sign back up and lock the door behind me."

"Leo will be upset."

"Leo approved the work done by his plumber."

"I wouldn't remind him of that." Grinning, Christina straightened, laid the wrench on the sink, and wiped at her face with her sleeve, smudging the grease on her nose.

"You have grease on your nose."

Phillip touched the offending feature with one finger.

Christina's thin eyebrows rose and fell. She smiled. "I must be a mess."

"Not really."

"You're such a sweet talker."

Phillip snorted and laughed.

Christina joined him. Concerns over the leak receded with the sound. They'd take care of it together. She snatched a paper towel from the dispenser and held it out. "Do me a favor?"

"Gladly." He scrubbed with vigor.

"Hey, not so hard." Still laughing, she backed away until her foot smacked into the toolbox sitting in front of the toilet. She teetered. Phillip caught her. "This is one of those days, isn't it?"

"That's what happens when Leo leaves us to our own devices, I reckon."

"He's a *gut* boss, but you're nicer." Her face reddened, and her hands went to her cheeks. "I mean—"

"Hey, no taking it back now."

"My *mudder* says I never think before I speak."

"It's never bad to say something nice about a person."

She picked up the toolbox and edged toward the door. "How is Hannah?"

It seemed everyone in this small community knew about his efforts to court Hannah. "I better go get the supplies."

"I'll start mopping up the water."

Phillip hurried to put space between Christina and himself. He untied the reins from the hitching post and patted Caramel's back. "What just happened in there?" Caramel arched her long neck and pranced. "You don't know either? Then what good are you?"

He climbed in the buggy and set off for the hardware store.

Christina was funny and pretty and open. He found talking to her easy. She carried no baggage.

Shame swept over Phillip. Evie was a little girl, not baggage. From the first time Hannah allowed him to hold her, all blanket and cloth diaper, he'd been held captive by her inquiring gaze and tiny, tiny fingers.

Leo's question from the other day battered him. Had he fallen in love with the mother or the daughter?

Both. He loved both.

But Evie loved him back. Hannah did not. Everything about her reaction two nights ago underscored that fact.

He shoved through the hardware store's double glass doors. The cowbell overhead dinged. The smells of metal, grease, and man stuff greeted him. It reminded him of his dad. He took in a deep breath and the muscles in his shoulders relaxed. Here, he was in his element. He headed for the plumbing aisle, intent on scooping up the items he needed and getting back to the Combination Store. The sooner they fixed the pipe, the sooner they could reopen the store.

He and Christina would take care of it. The thought pleased him. And surprised him. His muscles relaxed some more.

"Is there something I can help you with?"

Phillip turned to confront the owner of that low, rugged voice. Expression indecipherable, Thaddeus approached. He wore a red carpenter's apron with the name "Bellaire Hardware Store" emblazoned in white thread across the chest.

Phillip's shoulder muscles bunched again. His temples began to throb. "It didn't take you long to get a job."

"It's just part-time. Clayton's cutting back on his hours while his wife goes through chemotherapy."

"So you're staying." The words were out of his mouth before he could think about how they would sound. "I mean—"

"I'm staying. I'm making my confession tomorrow."

"You think you'll be able to work here while under the *bann?*"

"Ben says *jah*, as long as I don't wait on Plain customers." Thaddeus crossed his arms over his chest. "So you're on your own here."

On his own. Like Hannah had been for the last two years. Phillip glanced around. No other customers perused the rakes and leaf blowers. No one scrutinized boxes of screws and nails and nuts and bolts. No one needed a hammer this morning.

"What are your intentions with Hannah?"

Thaddeus shuffled his feet and stared at the floor for a second. Then he looked at Phillip head-on. "I know what you've done for Hannah while I was gone. I'm thankful for it. You're a *gut* man." His hands dropped to his sides, his fingers spread wide. "But I'm hoping you'll see it through my eyes. Hannah and I should've married. I'm to blame that we didn't. I want to make things right. I want to marry her and give my daughter my name. I'm asking you to be the better man. To step aside."

Step aside. Give up two years of his life. Retorts like, *It wouldn't be hard to be the better man* begged to be flung at Thaddeus. Phillip bit his tongue. This was about what was best for Hannah and Evie. Sweet Evie. A child growing up without a father. "It's too late for—"

"It's never too late to right a wrong. That's what Ben says. He says Hannah has forgiven me and so will everyone else once I confess and do my penance."

"That doesn't mean Hannah will take you back." Phillip's protest sounded weak even in his own ears. Hannah's face when she saw Thaddeus told a different story. A story of longing and hope that never died. His own doubts were really the only ones up for grabs. "How can she be sure you won't abandon them again?"

How can I be sure you'll take good care of them?

"That's between her and me. But I can't fix things with you between us. She'll at least consider the possibility if you step back."

"Why would I do that?"

"Because you're a *gut* man and you know it's what is best for Hannah and Evie."

"How do you know what's best for them? You haven't been here."

"I know I haven't been here, but I look at you and I know you're not the right man for Hannah." Thaddeus took a step forward, his tone softening. "Even if it wasn't me, it wouldn't be you."

"What do you know about Hannah and me?"

"I know you felt sorry for her. That's not the same as loving her."

Had he and Leo been sharing observations? "You have no idea what you're talking about."

"I know I love Hannah and she loves me."

It was as if he knew about Hannah's hesitation, her abrupt flight after Phillip kissed her. He couldn't know. Only Phillip and Hannah knew. "I shouldn't be talking to you. I have work to do and I need to get some supplies."

Thaddeus backed away. "Sometimes things are right under your nose if you just open your eyes and look."

Phillip thought about Christina. Never truer words were spoken.

— CHAPTER 11 —

K nowing eyes. So many knowing eyes.

Thaddeus ducked his head and focused on the floor where he knelt before the entire *Gmay*. He swallowed. The lump in his throat nearly gagged him. All of his family members, friends he'd known since his mud-pie days, even acquaintances—they all stared. His entire community gathered on long, hard, wooden benches in Ben Stutzman's barn to hear Thaddeus's confession and decide his punishment.

He stared at Zechariah's scuffed, dirty boots. As an elderly man with disabilities he'd earned the right to sit on the front row. His friend Abel, who'd recovered from a recent stroke, sat on one side of him, and Freeman Borntrager, who suffered from some sort of blindness, was on the other. Freeman's cane, carved from hickory, rested at his side. Abel's and Zechariah's walkers kept company in the aisle.

Look up. Look up. Now was the time to face his sin. To face his family, his friends, his community. To face God. He was through running away. He was through making excuses. Instead he would repent and accept his punishment.

He forced his gaze to the women's side. Hannah, with Evie on her lap, sat beside Laura. Evie chortled, and Hannah hushed her.

"*Daadi, daadi, daadi.*" Evie chanted. "Want *daadi*."

She wanted Zechariah.

Hannah's gaze met Thaddeus's. Did he see compassion there? Empathy? She understood better than anyone in the room how this felt.

Was that a slight nod or his imagination? Encouragement? Her glance slid away. She lowered her head and whispered to Evie, who accepted a cookie from Laura and began to sing a tuneless, nonsensical song.

His baby was sitting on her mother's lap waiting for his confession to begin.

Nausea swept over him so acutely he feared he might hurl on those scarred boots in front of him. *Nee. Nee.* He swallowed again and again and inhaled the scent of fresh hay and manure. The simple smells of his life, almost forgotten during those years in the RV factory, saved him.

Ben strode to the front of the room. "We are gathered here today to hear Thaddeus Yoder's confession. Thaddeus confesses the *Fehla* of fornication to the community. He confesses that he did not accept responsibility for his sin or for the child that resulted from this act of fornication." Ben's tone was emotionless, yet crushing, in its neutrality. "Thaddeus chose to leave rather than marry the mother of his child. He abandoned them both. After two years, he has returned with a desire to confess his sins, repent, and accept his punishment."

The silence tore at Thaddeus. Everyone in the barn was aware of the circumstances behind this confession. They knew he was a coward. They knew he abandoned not only Hannah but Evie too.

They had forgiven Hannah and they would forgive him, whether he deserved it or not. Scripture required it. God required it. Even for a cowardly sinner such as himself.

Still, they would always remember him as the man who ran.

"Thaddeus, are you sorry for what you have done?"

Thaddeus raised his head and sought out Hannah. Their gazes collided. "I am so sorry. I seek forgiveness from everyone here and from *Gott*. I seek forgiveness from Hannah and my daughter Evie. I'm willing and ready to take my punishment. To restore myself to their good graces and *Gott*'s."

"Has your heart changed then, Thaddeus?"

"My heart has changed forever."

It had grown, doubled in size, rearranged itself over the last two years. He'd learned what it meant to be totally alone. He learned what love was. He learned how puny his faith was. He learned how much he needed others—how much he loved Hannah. And how wrong he'd been.

"Leave us then."

For a horrible second, his legs wouldn't work. Thaddeus gritted his teeth.

Gott, *please*.

His legs unfolded and he hoisted himself to his feet. Deacon Cyrus Beachy led him to the doors. There, Thaddeus looked back. Hannah swiveled and looked directly into his eyes. This time there was no doubt. She offered a tiny nod.

A small but steady flame ignited in his heart.

Hope.

-≪≪-

Memories, like flashes of lightning, scorched Hannah's mind. That night at Stockton Lake. The kisses. The giving of self completely. The joy followed by abject shame. The hard floor under her knees as she confessed her sins in front of her mother, father, grandparents, great-grandparents, sisters, and brothers. Imagining them imagining her sin. The agony of childbirth. The joy of holding Evie for the first time.

Joy and pain so mingled a person couldn't untangle them in a thousand years.

Laura's hand crept over hers and squeezed. She leaned in. "Do you want me to hold Evie?"

"*Nee.*"

"The worst is over."

"I know."

Much more remained to be endured. Thaddeus's confession brought their sins front and center once again in everyone's mind. The stares and whispers would never die down. They would follow Hannah through the streets in Jamesport and between the tables at the café as she served her friends and neighbors. She'd endured this once before. She would do it again.

"The elders have met. We recommend eight weeks in the *bann*." Ben paced in front of the long benches. He looked far older than he had two years earlier when he became bishop. "All in favor?"

Eight weeks. Two months. Nothing like the two years Thaddeus had spent in Nappanee. It would seem like forever. At least, six weeks had for Hannah. Eight weeks without contact with friends or family. Eight weeks to contemplate his past and his future.

Eight weeks for Hannah to do the same.

Laura elbowed her. She raised her hand with the others.

"It's unanimous then."

Hannah couldn't help herself. She sneaked a glance at Phillip. The look on his face said she didn't have eight weeks.

Phillip wanted his answer now.

-≪≪-

Sin paraded through the barn for all the world to see. Phillip looked away from Hannah. Surely this would remind her of what she suffered at Thaddeus's hands. Surely she would be reminded of his true nature. Yes, he repented now. Yes, he wanted to take his punishment now. But what of those two years he'd been gone, leaving her to face censure alone?

Let her forgive, but never forget.

Was that wrong? Gott, is that prayer wrong?

The barn door opened. Thaddeus entered first, then Cyrus. Thaddeus looked neither left nor right as he passed within a foot of Phillip's seat. His fair skin was mottled red. A pulse worked in his jaw. His Adam's apple bobbed.

A public confession took its toll, as was intended. Still, it hurt to watch, no matter who walked that aisle. To have a person's failings laid bare before the people he loved. It must feel like being skinned alive. Phillip didn't wish it on his worst enemy. And Thaddeus was no enemy.

The thought stole through his defenses, catching him by surprise.

He and Thaddeus cared for the same woman. Thaddeus treated her badly. Led her down a bad path and then abandoned her. Then he recognized his sin and was attempting to rectify the situation. He deserved forgiveness.

Being unable to forgive carried its own weight of sin. Not recognizing his effort and lauding it smacked of arrogance and self-righteousness.

Gott *forgive me.*

Thaddeus reached the front of the room where Ben stood waiting. The bishop faced him. "Your punishment has been set at eight weeks of *bann*. Are you willing to take on the discipline of the church?"

Thaddeus cleared his throat. "I am, more than willing."

"The *bann* will commence immediately. We understand that you are staying with Burke McMillan."

Thaddeus nodded.

"And you have a job."

"*Jah.* At the hardware store."

"You will have no contact with anyone from this district for the next eight weeks. Is that understood?"

"Yes." Thaddeus straightened. His gaze roved over the gathering. "I will be back in eight weeks to join my family and friends in worship."

"Cyrus, Solomon, and I will meet with you before then." Ben nodded toward the door. "Go."

Again escorted by Cyrus, Thaddeus trudged to the door. He looked neither left nor right.

The door closed behind him.

Phillip breathed. He hadn't realized he was holding his breath.

People stood and milled about. The quiet chatter grew louder until it reached a crescendo as they released pent-up emotions.

Suddenly stifled by the warm air and thick smell of hay and manure, Phillip edged toward the door.

Zachariah's walker thumped in front of him. The old man peered at Phillip through thick glasses. "How are you?"

Zechariah's hoarse words were a mess, but Phillip got the gist of them from his kind expression. He held the door for the older man and waited until they were outside to answer.

"Confused."

"Welcome to my world." Zechariah's laugh was more of a croak. "If it weren't for Laura, I wouldn't be able to find my pants in the morning, let alone put them on."

Phillip grasped Zechariah's arm and steadied him. Together,

they trudged across the yard to a row of buggies that wound past the corral and out to the open fields of corn, oats, and alfalfa just beginning to shoot from the warming earth.

"What's confusing you?" Zechariah halted. His breath came in raspy gasps. He leaned into the walker and let his head drop for a few seconds. "The past or the future?"

"Both." How much should Phillip share, given the private nature of his thoughts? Out of respect for Hannah too. "I don't know if one can be separated from the other."

"The most we can do is try to see the world through the other person's eyes." Zechariah tottered a few more steps. Hands out, ready to steady him, Phillip kept time. "Put others before ourselves. Do what's best for another, rather than ourselves."

"Like Evie."

"Your thoughts go to her first."

"As much as I wish her to be my *dochder*, she'll always be the *dochder* of another." And Hannah would always have loved Thaddeus first. And more. That was apparent from the look on her face today. So like the look she gave Thaddeus that day at the Purple Martin. "I can't change the past, and I'm not in control of the future."

"It's *gut* you recognize that." Zechariah stopped. "None of us are, *suh*. Pray for *Gott's* will to be done. Then be willing to accept what happens next."

"How will I know what His will is?"

"I reckon you already do. All that remains is to accept it."

"That's not so easy."

"Look at me, *suh*. If you think this is easy . . ." He let go of the walker long enough to wave his hand at his hunched body. "It's not. Inside, I'm still a young, vigorous man who works hard and goes fishing and birding and hunting. I sing and run around the yard with the *kinner*. This is not me. But here I am in this pokey, achy, stiff-as-a-board, jerky body. Why am I still alive? Because *Gott* wills it. Therefore, I accept it. And besides, I have my *fraa* to thank Him for."

He stopped and gasped for air. Phillip took his arm again. "Should I get Laura?"

"Help me into the buggy first, if you don't mind. Then ask my *fraa* to stop jabbering so we can go."

Phillip did as he was told. Zechariah's chastisement had given him much to think about. So much he might choke on it.

— CHAPTER 12 —

The Sunday morning service should not be considered a break in monotony. Sighing at her own perverse thoughts, Hannah settled back on the hard bench after the kneeling prayer. The days seemed to limp along. Working at the restaurant, helping Laura with supper, putting Evie down for the night, reading to Zechariah until he went to bed, then playing checkers with Laura or having a glass of iced tea on the porch swing. This morning, church and the visiting that would follow.

Something was missing from her life, something she couldn't quite put her finger on. Knowing Thaddeus was in Jamesport, right down the road, irked her. He was back, but not back.

Phillip hadn't shown his face at the *dawdy haus* since Thaddeus's confession. The thought brought only a strange relief. The want in his face, the longing, caused guilt to sneak up and trip her. She wanted to want him like that, but feelings of friendship won out. A person couldn't demand that love show its face. It simply did. Or didn't.

She sighed. *Focus.* God would smite her for thinking about men in the middle of a church service. It was so warm in Cyrus's barn, sweat dripped from under her *kapp* and dampened her neck. Mattie, squeezed in between Laura and Cecily, Hannah's youngest sister, poked her.

"What?" Hannah jolted and glared at her friend. "Why did you do that?"

"Service is over, silly."

"Oh."

They joined the flow of people drifting through the open barn doors. A slight breeze wafted over them. "That feels *gut.*"

"Why were you sighing?"

"Just tired."

"Come on." Mattie was the spitting image of Thaddeus with her dark curls that refused to be corralled by her *kapp* and sapphire eyes. She grinned at Hannah. "Tell the truth. You were thinking about Thaddeus."

"*Nee.*"

"If you lie after a church service, *Gott* will smite you."

Hannah's friend always knew what she was thinking. "Have you talked to him?"

"*Nee. Mudder* would smite me if she caught me anywhere near Burke's house."

They pushed through the crowd and headed toward the kitchen to help bring out sandwiches and cookie trays. Hannah dodged a group of kids headed to the volleyball nets. Folks were already settling at the picnic tables. Conversations punctuated with laughter swelled around her. It was a perfect Sunday afternoon and she still sought contentment.

Forgive me, Gott. *Help me.*

Phillip's deep laugh filtered through the myriad sounds. Biting her lip, she sought him out. He sat at the picnic table near the far corner of Cyrus's house. Christina Weber held a plate of cookies just beyond his grasp.

He reached for a cookie. She pulled the tray higher. He rose from his seat until he towered over the petite blond. She giggled, curtsied, and offered the tray again. He snatched a cookie and then offered it to her. She took it, grinned, and curtsied again.

Phillip looked happy. He never smiled like that on Hannah's front porch. She slowed and then stopped.

"What is it?" Mattie touched her arm. "Oh, that. Didn't you hear? Christina works at the Combination Store now."

"I know."

"She's sweet."

Sweet and a hard worker who always had a kind word for people. According to Laura. Who talked to Jennie. "I know."

Mattie tugged at her. "Come on. The others will wonder why we're not helping. And then *Mudder* will hear about it, which means I'll hear about it."

"Right behind you."

Hannah picked up her pace, but she couldn't tear her gaze from Phillip's face. He deserved to be happy. He deserved to be carefree. He would never have that with her. His eyes connected with hers. His smile became diffident. She nodded.

He nodded.

Time passed quickly in the kitchen. The women stayed busy making more sandwiches and carrying out cookies and pitchers of tea and lemonade. Jonelle, Hannah's sister who was a year younger, watched Evie while Hannah worked. Something inside her relaxed for the first time in months. Something had been decided. She didn't know exactly what, but *Gott's* plan was moving around her.

Finally, the feeding and the cleaning were done. She scooped up a napping Evie and headed for Zechariah's buggy. Knowing him, he'd be ready for a nap too.

"Hey."

She turned to see Phillip a few yards away at his own buggy. He glanced around and then strode toward her.

"Hey."

"We should talk." He stopped within arm's length. "I'm sorry it's been so long. I needed to think."

"I'm the one who's sorry. Did you find your answer?"

He smoothed his fingers over Evie's rosy cheek. "She's so peaceful when she sleeps."

"I can't do it."

"I know. It's okay." His smile was genuine. "I've been thinking and praying, and I know what to do now. I have to bow out. I have to let you find your own way. I can't take care of Evie. I can't be your savior. That's *Gott's* job. I have to make my own way."

Hannah nodded. "You were laughing with Christina."

"She's nice."

"And simple. Uncomplicated."

"She doesn't flinch when I get too close." His hands curled around his suspenders. "I do care for you, you know."

"But you care for Evie more. She loves you too." She kissed her baby's damp forehead. Evie cooed in her sleep and snuggled closer. "Would you like to hold her for a minute?"

"*Nee*, you'll wake her."

"We can still be friends. You can be her *Onkel* Phillip."

"I'm not sure Thaddeus would like that idea."

"What makes you think Thaddeus will have a say?"

"I see it in your eyes every time you look at him. I see it in his face when he looks at you. Some bonds only strengthen with time and missteps. The mistakes cement two people together, instead of tearing them apart."

"How did you get so smart?"

"I listen when old men like Zechariah talk."

"He is a wise man."

Voices sounded. Her parents were headed toward them. "I hope you find happiness, Hannah Kauffman."

"You also."

He slipped away. With him went the possibility of a different ending.

A different life.

"It's you and me, *bopli*." She held Evie to her chest and drank in the scent of milk, oatmeal, and diaper cream. "You and me. We can do this."

You, me, and your father?

A question that badgered her morning, noon, and night. Seeing Thaddeus those few times had made her miss his presence all over again. It made her dream the dreams. Dream their dream. To sow, grow, weed, and reap.

Not just flowers.

The thought didn't scare her the way it once had. She came from a long line of strong, faithful, God-fearing women.

Gott, thy will be done. For me and for Evie. If that means being alone, so be it. I know You have a plan. I'm waiting for it to unfold.

— CHAPTER 13 —

Asleep or awake? Hannah started and opened her eyes. Darkness still prevailed. Had she dreamed the *thump, thump* or had something fallen? Maybe it was thunder. A storm had blown in around bedtime.

In the three weeks since Thaddeus's kneeling confession and Phillip's exit from her life, she hadn't been sleeping well. Her mind wouldn't stop trying to fit the pieces together. With her job, Evie, and helping with Zechariah, she was exhausted, but sleep still didn't come easily. No matter how much she prayed for patience and discernment for God's plan, she couldn't keep thoughts of Thaddeus at bay. They slipped up on her unbidden at the most inopportune moments. She would walk past the hardware store so she could peek inside and caught herself more than once on the verge of asking Burke how his roommate was doing.

No contact meant no contact.

Now that she was forbidden from seeing him, the desire for a glimpse dogged her. Just a glimpse. Was it human nature or feelings that couldn't be cast out by a simple *bann*? She could do this on her own. She could ignore the stares and whispers. She could raise Evie.

Yet her thoughts kept turning to Thaddeus and his proposal.

The life she wanted with him was now within her grasp. All she had to do was step out onto the high wire, balance herself, and take one step at a time until she found him in the middle.

She wouldn't fall into his arms this time. She would hold out her hand and take his.

Forever and ever.

"Hannah! Hannah, wake up. I need you."

Laura's anxiety-stricken scream pierced the darkness. Hannah threw back the covers and flew down the hall to the bedroom Laura shared with Zechariah.

In the dark, she stubbed her toe on their half-open door, stumbled, and caught herself. She danced around on one foot. "What is it? What's wrong?"

"He fell."

A terrible moan floated in the dark.

Zechariah.

Hannah's eyes adjusted. Laura knelt on the floor next to Zechariah's prone body. A lamp lay next to him, the glass globe shattered.

He writhed and moaned again. Laura pushed him back. "Lie still. You're hurt, my love."

She glanced up at Hannah. "Get the other lamp. I need some light to see him better. I think he hit his head on the side table."

Hannah scurried across the room and fumbled with matches to light the second lamp. She knelt across from her great-grandmother. Laura and Zechariah both looked so different in the middle of the night. Neither wore their glasses. Laura's silver hair hung loose and reached below her waist. Zechariah's bald head was smooth and white from years under a hat.

He muttered something unintelligible and struggled to sit up. "My head. What happened to my head?"

Laura smoothed her hand over his head and examined his face.

"There's a big egg on his temple and a cut. He's bleeding. I need to get my bag. Help me get him into bed."

Laura grabbed one arm and Hannah the other. They attempted to hoist Zechariah from the hardwood floor. He groaned. "*Ach, ach! Nee, ach!*"

"Something's wrong. Put him down." Laura's voice filled with fear. "Easy, gently."

They eased him back to the floor. "Where does it hurt, my love?" Laura ran her hands down Zechariah's arms and his legs. He shrieked in pain when she touched his left leg. "I think he's broken his hip."

Hannah jumped to her feet. "I'll run to the phone shack and call 911."

"I'll get my bag. I need to stop the bleeding on his head." Laura grabbed a quilt from the bed and laid it over Zechariah, gently tucking it around him. "You make the call and then run to the house and tell Martin and Ruby."

The minutes passed in a strange, surreal mixture of fast forward and slow motion. Every breath hurt as Hannah inhaled the humid night air. Raindrops splashed her face, cooling her warm skin. Rocks and twigs bit into the soles of her bare feet. Mud squelched between her toes on the path to the phone shack, the sensations telling her this was really happening.

Squashing her panic, she reached for the calm necessary to punch in the numbers and say the English words, to answer the 911 operator's questions.

How badly was Zechariah hurt? Would someone be mad that she hadn't hidden her hair under a *kapp*? Should she help Laura dress before the ambulance arrived? Thoughts rushed through her mind as she ran to the main house.

Would Zechariah die and Laura become a widow once again?

Gott, no. I know it's Your will and not ours, but please don't let him die.

She pounded on Martin's door. The seconds dragged and then he was there, nodding and on his way to tell Ruby.

Hannah sped back to the *dawdy haus*, raced up the stairs, and hurried down the hallway. In the bedroom, she knelt next to Laura and wrapped one arm around her great-grandmother.

Laura had twisted her hair in a bun and covered it with her *kapp*. She wore the same dress she'd worn the previous day. Her whispered prayers filled the air. Hannah leaned in and closed her eyes. Hours seemed to drag by. *Gott, let them hurry. Please let them hurry.*

"Martin is calling a driver to take us to the hospital behind the ambulance, and Ruby is getting dressed and getting the *kinner* up."

"I'm going in the ambulance with him."

"We'll be right behind you."

"His *kinner* were right. I should've moved him to the house." Tears gleamed on Laura's cheeks. Her entire body trembled. "This is all my fault."

"*Nee.* You've taken care of him like no one else could." Hannah wrapped her other arm around Laura and tightened her hug. "He'll be fine. They'll fix him up at the hospital and he'll be home in no time."

"*Gott's* will be done."

"Do you truly believe that? Even if it means going through losing a *mann* again?"

"I want him to live more than anything I've ever wanted." Laura touched his forehead and adjusted the quilt. "But *Gott's* will is *Gott's* will, and in death, he'll suffer no more. My wanting him to stay is selfish. In death, he receives the ultimate healing. I want that for him."

"I'm so sorry"

"Don't be. I could've avoided all this." Laura wiped at her face with a nightgown sleeve. "But I would've missed all these evenings sitting in the swing with him. Or eating ice cream with him. Or taking him to Swan Lake."

Sirens sounded in the distance. Finally. Laura eased from Hannah's grasp and stood. "You should stay here with Evie. There's nothing you can do at the hospital."

"*Nee.*" Hannah stood too. "I'll get dressed and get her ready. I'll be right there with you."

At the door she paused and looked back. Laura once again crouched by Zechariah, murmuring prayers. "Is it worth it?"

Laura looked up. Her face seemed ancient in the flickering lamplight. The lines and grooves ran deep. "Absolutely. Don't ever let fear stand in the way of love. Take a chance. The years slip away, the chances for love and happiness with them. Don't let that happen to you. Love is a home where your heart can live forever."

Home. Hannah let her imagination have full rein.

Thaddeus. Dark, strong, stormy, a tornado in July.

He had been her home since the day of that first singing when he took her hand and helped her into his buggy.

— CHAPTER 14 —

Chicken fried steak. Fried chicken. They were almost the same dish, but not quite.

Hannah hefted the tray of rejected food and trudged through the kitchen door. Burke followed, hot on her heels. Her shoulders ached, and her head pounded. This entire shift had been a disaster. She brought customers iced tea when they asked for Coke. She gave another customer two tens for change instead of two fives. She was too tired to concentrate.

Two days of sitting in the hospital, waiting for Zechariah to turn a corner, had taken their toll. The surgery to fix his broken hip had been difficult, but successful. A week had passed. The doctors said he wasn't out of the woods yet, but they were "cautiously optimistic." Doctors talked like that.

Laura hadn't left his side, but she had instructed Ruby to prepare a place for them in the big house. Hannah had moved back home. Little Evie was now in the hands of her sister Jonelle. Both seemed happy with the arrangement.

She turned and nearly ran into Burke. "Oops. Sorry, boss."

"That's the third order you've mixed up tonight." His expression a mixture of concern and well-deserved irritation, Burke took the plate of chicken fried steak from Hannah and set it on the kitchen counter. "You might as well go. You're exhausted. This business with Zechariah has taken its toll on everyone. Go home."

"He's better." She needed to work. She'd missed too many shifts already. "I'm fine, really I am."

"You're not fine. You're worn out, and your heart is somewhere else."

"I'm sorry. I truly am. Zechariah, the move, everything has piled up." Hannah clasped the tray against her chest like a shield. "It won't happen again. I promise."

"You're right. It won't. Not tonight." Burke held out his hand. "Give me your apron and your order pad. The supper crowd is light. I can fill in for you. You'll get credit for the whole shift. Go home."

Home wasn't home. As much as her parents tried to pretend nothing had changed, everything had. Hannah was too old and too worn around the edges to live at home like her sisters.

Laura's words whirled in her head. She wouldn't be home until she found her heart. Watching Laura with Zechariah had told her everything she needed to know. Life was short. Chances at love were fleeting. It took guts to love. It might hurt, but not being with the person she loved hurt more.

"I have someplace else I need to go."

A grin stole across Burke's face. "You've decided then."

"I have. I need to finish what I started. I had the right idea, I just took a bad shortcut."

"Take him a meal. I have it on good authority that he likes my stuffed pork chops with mashed potatoes and gravy. Be sure to take a slice of banana cream pie too. Use the Styrofoam to-go boxes."

"The thing is, I'm not supposed to go anywhere near him. I don't want to mess this up again."

"You're just dropping off a meal at my house. Put the paper sack on the doorstep. If you want, put a note in it. Knock and run away. You don't even have to speak. You'll feel better and so will he. He's been moping around the house like a poor old hound dog somebody kicked to the curb."

She could do that. Show her feelings without taking another shortcut. Just like Laura brought her a gift on Christmas Eve during her *bann*. It was no more wrong than Phillip's cradle that arrived at her doorstep that same evening. Phillip had chosen a new path and rightly so. Her feelings for Thaddeus told her so.

"Better go now before it gets too late."

"Are you sure?"

"The look on your face tells me all I need to know." Burke smiled. "You're afraid, but you can't stop yourself from wanting to go. It's driving you crazy. You know you could be hurt again, but still, you want to go."

"Why do we do things we know are bad for us?"

"You don't know this is bad for you."

"It was the first time."

"Are you the same person you were two years ago?"

Hannah backed away from the swinging doors, making room for Nicole, who, looking harried, squeezed by with a bowl of creamed corn in her hand.

"*Nee.*"

"Then accept the possibility that Thaddeus used that time to grow up too."

"If you two are done gossiping, we kind of have some hungry folks out there waiting to be fed." Nicole ducked between Burke and Hannah as she headed back out the door. "The natives are restless, boss."

"Right behind you," Burke called after her, but his gaze remained on Hannah. "What he did was wrong, no doubt about it, but what he wants to do now is right."

"How can I be sure?"

"You can't."

"That's not very comforting."

"It's not meant to be. Life is a series of forks in the road." Burke pulled a Styrofoam container from a stack under the stainless-steel counter. He moved to the stove where he began to heap food into it. "Don't just stand there. Take one road or the other."

"He's been living in your house. Do you think he's changed?"

"I didn't know him before." Burke slid the Styrofoam boxes into a paper bag. "But we've had some good conversations. Some good discussions. He's repentant and working hard to be a better man. I know you pretty well. You're smart. You'll figure it out."

"That's what Laura says."

"Laura is a wise woman."

Fifteen minutes later, Hannah stood on the front porch of Burke's small, A-frame, one-story house. The muscles in her legs shook. Her face felt damp despite the early May breeze. Curtains in an open window next to the door fluttered in that breeze. She raised her free hand to knock, then let it drop. Somewhere inside, a dog barked. Not a menacing snarl, but a joyful yippy welcome. Jazz wouldn't serve as a guard dog.

Thaddeus's woebegone face during his confession loomed in her mind's eye. He had repented. Just as she had. He was forgiven, just as she was. The tremble in his voice still plucked at her heart strings. Every time she looked at Evie's face, she saw Thaddeus.

The man she'd loved since she was sixteen. The man she never stopped loving even when he broke her heart. He'd come back to her and he deserved to be forgiven. With forgiveness came a new beginning. Old hurts were healed. New possibilities were born.

She set the bag in front of the door, knocked, whirled, and stumbled down the stairs.

"Don't go." Thaddeus's words floated through the open window. "Stay."

"I can't." She halted without turning. "We can't talk."

"We won't look at each other."

"I can't talk to you."

"Then just listen. I have so much to say to you."

Memories of the *bann* in Laura's house filled Hannah's mind. Even with his job at the hardware store, Thaddeus would be starved for companionship. For conversation.

"I'll turn off the porch light."

His voice's husky timbre sent a jolt through her. Slowly, she turned and trudged back up the steps. "I brought you supper. You need to eat it before it gets cold. I have to go."

She was saying one thing but doing another. She didn't want to go.

"*Danki.* Turn your back and I'll grab it. Will you stay for a few minutes and keep me company while I eat it? We won't talk ... much."

She did as he asked. The door creaked when it opened. A second later it thumped closed.

Rustling sounds emanated from the open window once again. "Stuffed pork chops. My favorite."

She leaned against the door and stared at the starlit night. *What are you doing, Hannah?*

I'm standing at the fork in the road, trying to catch my breath.

"How's Evie?"

"She got another tooth yesterday. She's been in a foul mood, but now she's better."

"She's moody like her mother."

"I'm not moody." Hannah slid down to sit, back against the door, on the porch floor. She wrapped her arms around her knees. "I was the easy one to get along with."

Or Thaddeus could always coax her from her moods by tickling her until she shrieked with laughter. Or by bringing her flowers he picked from his mother's front yard. Or by telling her one of his grandpa's silly jokes.

"Do you remember when we snuck out of the house and went to Stockton Lake and I fell in the water and you laughed so hard you snorted?"

The first time he kissed her. "A person doesn't forget something like that."

Did he know how safe she felt in his arms, how happy she'd been, how certain she would be his wife and he would be her husband? Did he remember how they'd snuggled together, his clothes sopping wet and dripping all over her? They'd kissed and kissed until her face hurt and her bones melted and floated into the shimmering lake in front of them.

"I've never felt about anyone the way I feel about you." He cleared his throat. "What we did, we did because we loved each other. Everyone thinks we committed a lustful act. And we did. But those feelings came from love. What we did was wrong, but not the feelings."

"That doesn't change anything."

"I'm trying to say that I believe every part of us was in love. We loved. We love. There's no separating any part of it. We should've waited. I should've been stronger. I never should have led you down that road. For that, I'm sorry. But I will never be sorry for loving you."

Blood beat like a drum in Hannah's head. She couldn't think. Swirling, vast emotion tugged her deeper and deeper until she had no breath.

"Hannah, are you there?"

"I dream about us all the time." She dreamed they were husband and wife with flowers growing as far as the eye could see and children and the life she once thought they would have. "Then I wake up and I'm mad at you all over again."

For what they'd lost.

Every time she was sure she'd forgiven him, she would overhear a snide comment at The Book Apothecary or catch a knowing look from a group of women at Sweet Notions, reminding her what they'd done and what he'd done. It was as if the wound was new again, the bandage needed changing, and she had to rip it off and start over.

"If you could find it in your heart to truly forgive me, we could start over again. At the beginning. When I finish the *bann*, we could go for a ride—"

"Can we just sit and be quiet?"

"We can do that."

She leaned her head against the door and stared out at the dusk. A warm breeze—the precursor to a Missouri summer—washed over her. Leaves rustled in the trees. She inhaled and exhaled. It smelled like summer. Cardinals and blue jays argued over the best real estate in Burke's two oak trees.

The fork in the road reared up to meet her.

"I love you." She whispered the words. "I will always love you."

"*Gut*. Because I will always love you."

His words were filled with barely tethered emotion.

She closed her eyes and let a future full of endless possibilities envelop her.

"Will you marry me?"

Longing for his touch welled up in Hannah. The hugs and kisses would wait. The sheer enormity of her love—their love—would bind them together far beyond any physical touch. The time for hugs and kisses would come soon enough, sweeter for the wait. She drew her knees closer and tightened her arms around them. "*Jah*, I will."

Love needed no more words.

Feelings floated on the star-kissed breeze. They intermingled. The air became electric. There wasn't a cloud in the sky, yet lightning crackled and sparked against the velvety richness of night.

"When?"

Hannah laughed. She scrambled to her feet and blew a kiss through the open window. "As soon as possible. I'll be waiting for you."

Thaddeus's kisses floated on the air around her as she skipped down the steps and into a future filled with many more days and nights of love and laughter.

Seven weeks later

The stares no longer held contempt or pity. Only delight. Hannah strolled through the throng of family members and friends wishing her and Thaddeus a long and happy life together.

She couldn't stop smiling. Under the circumstances a small wedding had been Ben's decree, but his smile had softened the implied criticism. The past was behind them. They'd been forgiven and now they would live the life everyone had hoped and prayed for.

The small crowd parted and slipped from the barn. Laura waited, her hands wrapped around the handles of Zechariah's wheelchair. He had both arms around Evie, who crowed with delight at every person who passed by. Zechariah looked wizened, a frail ghost of his former self, but his smile radiated as brightly as the sun overhead.

"Congratulations, my girl." One arm flailed while the other remained firmly anchored around Evie's waist. "Thaddeus, Godspeed."

Hannah ran ahead. She wrapped him in a hug. His skinny body was all pointy bones. "I'm so glad you could be here."

"I ain't going nowhere, girl. Not yet anyhow."

"He's too ornery." Laura joined in on the hug. "The doctor says he'll beat us all by ten years. Get over here, Thaddeus, I want to hug your neck."

Thaddeus obliged. "*Danki* for everything. Both of you."

"We didn't do nothing." Zechariah snorted. "You best take *gut* care of her now. And this *bopli*."

"*Daed, daed!*" Evie flung both chunky arms in the air. "Take me!"

"She called me *daed*." Thaddeus's smile widened. He took her into his arms. "She knows me."

They'd spent every possible moment together over the past three weeks since his release from the *bann*. Evie had taken to following him around the house like a little puppy, sitting on his lap, and begging him to sing to her.

"Take her in the house with you." Laura patted his arm. "Have a seat at the *eck*. I'll come get her as soon as I say hi to everyone."

Only a few people had come from out of town. Ben had made it clear that weddings under these circumstances were to be low-key, forgiveness or not.

Nothing could mar Hannah's happiness. Life would not be easy. Scripture contained no words that said it would be. But she and Thaddeus had overcome their sin and made it right through repentance and penitence. Their slates were clean.

She squeezed Thaddeus's free hand as they neared her parents' house. He squeezed back and grinned.

"Now?" He glanced around. That mischievous glint was back in his eyes. "Now can I kiss you?"

She followed his gaze. People were everywhere. Friends, family, visitors.

They were married after all.

"Quick." His grip tightened. He tugged her up the porch stairs. "Thaddeus!"

Inside the front door, he pulled her along the hallway and into the bedroom that had once belonged to her. "Little one, let's play hide and seek. You hide your eyes." He freed his hand and slipped it over Evie's eyes. He leaned into Hannah's space. "Come here, *fraa*."

"I'm right here, *mann*."

Hannah wrapped her arms around the two most important people in the world as she kissed him back.

The kiss was sweet, long, and filled with promise.

Their lips parted. He straightened. "The first of many, many kisses."

"Promise?"

"Promise."

And then he made good on that promise.

1. The Amish follow biblical Scripture that says sex is intended to be enjoyed within the confines of marriage. Premarital sex is a sin. Today's culture says otherwise. How do you deal with the pressures to conform to the world? What do you say to those who call this attitude old-fashioned and out of step with the modern world?

2. How do you feel about Thaddeus's family shunning him when he refuses to repent and face punishment for his sin? Do you find the eight-week *bann* after his confession harsh or not harsh enough for what he did to Hannah?

3. Phillip recognizes that he has sinned by not forgiving Thaddeus and he asks God to forgive him. Have you ever been in a situation where you were called to forgive, but found it impossible to do so? How did you resolve the situation?

4. Hannah feels as if her family and friends have forgiven her, but they haven't forgotten what she's done. People often say they may forgive, but they'll never forget. Is that a scripturally sound attitude? Why or why not? Have you experienced similar situations? How did it make you feel?

5. Hannah chooses to forgive Thaddeus and forge a new life with him and their daughter. Do you think she did the right thing? Put yourself in Hannah's shoes. Could you do the same?

6. Do you think Hannah should've chosen Phillip? Why or why not?

Enjoy these Amish collections for every season!

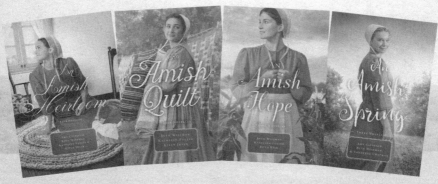

AVAILABLE IN PRINT AND E-BOOK

AMY CLIPSTON

Photo by Dan Davis Photography

AMY CLIPSTON is the award-winning and bestselling author of the Kauffman Amish Bakery, Hearts of Lancaster Grand Hotel, Amish Heirloom, and Amish Homestead series. She has sold more than one million books. Her novels have hit multiple bestseller lists including CBD, CBA, and ECPA. Amy holds a degree in communication from Virginia Wesleyan University and works full-time for the City of Charlotte, NC. Amy lives in North Carolina with her husband, two sons, and three spoiled rotten cats.

Visit her online at AmyClipston.com
Facebook: AmyClipstonBooks
Twitter: @AmyClipston
Instagram: @amy_clipston

BETH WISEMAN

Photo by Emilie Hendryx

Bestselling and award-winning author Beth Wiseman has sold over two million books. She is the recipient of the coveted Holt Medallion, a two-time Carol Award winner, and has won the Inspirational Readers Choice Award three times. Her books have been on various bestseller lists, including CBD, CBA, ECPA, and *Publishers Weekly*. Beth and her husband are empty nesters enjoying country life in south central Texas.

Visit her online at BethWiseman.com
Facebook: AuthorBethWiseman
Twitter: @BethWiseman
Instagram: @bethwisemanauthor

Kathleen Fuller

With over a million copies sold, Kathleen Fuller is the author of several bestselling novels, including the Hearts of Middlefield novels, the Middlefield Family novels, the Amish of Birch Creek series, and the Amish Letters series as well as a middle-grade Amish series, the Mysteries of Middlefield.

Visit her online at KathleenFuller.com
Instagram: kfstoryteller
Facebook: WriterKathleenFuller
Twitter: @TheKatJam

379

KELLY IRVIN

Photo by Tim Irvin

Kelly Irvin is the bestselling author of the Every Amish Season and Amish of Bee County series. *The Beekeeper's Son* received a starred review from *Publishers Weekly*, who called it a "beautifully woven masterpiece." The two-time Carol Award finalist is a former newspaper reporter and retired public relations professional. Kelly lives in Texas with her husband, photographer Tim Irvin. They have two children, two grandchildren, and two cats. In her spare time, she likes to read books by her favorite authors.

Visit her online at KellyIrvin.com
Instagram: kelly_irvin
Facebook: Kelly.Irvin.Author
Twitter: @Kelly_S_Irvin